ZURALIA DREAMING

ZURALIA DREAMING

ALFRED TELLA

WILDSIDE PRESS

To the memory of Howard Phillips Lovecraft
From one Providence born to another

Published by Wildside Press LLC.
www.wildsidebooks.com

PROLOGUE

Beneath the fetal heartbeat, hidden within a fledgling soul, flickered a mote of rubric light, and the light was as a torch to kindle the soul's heart. Lo, the soul flared up, illuminating the universe within: its spreading warmth touched the slumbering seed nestled in its shadow and was as nourishment, and the seed split asunder. The life force within shuddered and took wing. Fast it flew, emanating ever outward, transgressing the barriers of its inner world. Beyond the earthly sphere it sped, beyond sun's light, into the ether, breaching the very walls of dimensional space, into the boundless reaches of the higher planes.

A New England shopkeeper muttered to himself as he hunched over a wooden bench mixing colored powders in a shallow dish. He stirred the shimmering particles with a glass rod, then divided them into small even piles. Each pile he gently pushed onto a yellowed sheet of parchment, which he used to guide the mix into small pear-shaped bottles. The last bottle filled, he held it up to watch its rainbow hues sparkle in the light. An odd feeling overcame him; his hand trembled and the bottle slipped from his grasp and shattered on the floor. A sudden lightness, as though a stirring inner breeze, passed through his body. The air seemed to be alive, to unfold and close about him. Then all was still. He scratched the mole on his chin, which always seemed to itch at perplexing moments. Realization struck like a bolt; his face ignited; he hurried to a nearby bookshelf and pulled out a worn leather-bound volume. Impatiently he flipped page to page, and when he found the passage he was seeking, his lips puckered in a low whistle.

On a distant plane, midst swirling spheres of nightmare dream, a dark enchantress, queen of countless worlds, stood upon the ramparts of her palace surveying the teeming heavens of her domain. Most of what she saw pleased her. But not all. A gaping emptiness in the glittering canopy brought a frown to her brow. Suddenly her breath caught, and she shuddered as though struck by an invisible wave. The emanation passed on, the outer darkness rippling in its wake. The sorceress clutched at her neck and fear filled her eyes, for she had read a message in the fleeting current. Gradually her eyes narrowed; the hint of a smile pushed at the edges of her lips, and she thrust out her arms in a gesture of embrace toward a dark empty space in her firmament.

On yet a higher plane, beneath four miniature suns and triple moons, three lords of dream sat within a great chamber upon whose curved walls swirled the images of countless spheres. The three conversed with much animation, and at length they touched hands and nodded as though in agreement. One of them pointed a forefinger at the great wall map. In the small empty spot on the map where he pointed, a small green dot appeared, and the three nodded once again in apparent approval. As they rose to leave the chamber, the air about them suddenly crackled and bent. They momentarily froze as though grazed by an invisible force, then instinctively grasped one another's hands as if to share the sensation. When the disturbance had passed, the three embraced each other knowingly and tears of joy filled their eyes.

Deep beneath the land's crust on an island world in a dimension adjacent to Earth's, an ancient primal entity bestirred itself. A fleeting emanation from afar touched its mind, and in empathetic reverence it offered homage. Its psychic tribute radiated through its miles of length, rippling the surface of the land to the sea, and the children playing in the shallows wondered at the outgoing wavelets that gently broke upon their breasts.

Not long after, on the morn of the summer solstice, a child of Earth was born.

CHAPTER 1

THE SHOP OF HECUTICAR

Jonathan Spenser pulled up his jacket collar and buried his hands in his trouser pockets as he waited for the traffic light to change. He shifted from foot to foot and squinted through the drizzling rain at the dark haze that blanketed the city skyline. A raindrop spattered against his glasses, exploding the red glare of the traffic light into myriad glistening fragments. The chill spray stung his cheek. He cursed to himself. The city streets were nearly empty and it annoyed him that an unthinking technology had brought his life to an abrupt halt. Yet it did not occur to him to cross against the signal, accustomed as he was to living by the rules and requirements of an ordered life. He felt like a fool venturing out in such foul weather, but rainy days were not uncommon in New England in the fall and, after all, his mission was pressing.

He glanced at the young couple across the street who were also waiting for the light to change. They kissed and a pain jabbed at his heart. He envied the young man and despised his own timidity toward women. The young man put an arm around the girl, brushing his hand across her breast. The girl didn't seem to notice, or pretended not to.

The crude athletic boyfriend type, he thought. They always seem to win out. Oh well, sooner or later he'd get lucky. He hoped.

A passing bicyclist splashed water on the young man's trousers, which gave Jonathan some small satisfaction.

The light changed. As he hurried across the street the young lady smiled at him, which buoyed his mood considerably.

He hoped he would reach the public library before closing time. He dreaded the thought of having to suffer through a long weekend alone without anything new to read. Maybe the library would have a new novel by Friendship, one of his favorite authors. He would rather have hunted for a book in a used book store to add it to his small collection of fantasy and adventure stories, but his meager salary as a laboratory assistant rarely permitted such luxury. No matter: he was no stranger to privation. His upbringing as the son of a Midwestern dirt farmer and later as a student living off the stipend of a state scholarship had taught him to 'live lean and make do,' as his mother used to say. And now, here he was, two years out of college, still without any savings and living in a small rented room. But he had a respectable job and was self-supporting, and if his parents were still alive he was sure they would be proud of him.

True, his job at the lab was mostly routine and less than inspiring, but it gave him a degree of independence. Most of his workday he spent by himself peering at slides under a microscope and taking notes for the senior scientists. When his workload was light, he could take more time examining each slide; he could let his imagination run free as he sifted through the infinite universe of the small, searching out the mysteries that he was sure lurked just beyond the power of his lens, ever wondering what microcosmic worlds swirled in the limitless space just beyond his gaze.

A diligent worker, he knew that if he performed his job well, in a few years he would be promoted to the position of lab associate and be permitted to do some research of his own. He looked forward to that. And even if he hadn't really considered whether he could endure spending a lifetime within the confines of a small laboratory, at least it gave him a secure feeling to be able to predict his future with some degree of assurance.

His job also had the virtue of limiting his contact with his fellow man. Human interaction had always made him slightly uncomfortable. He preferred the inner life, the world of mind and imagination. It was also safer that way. He had learned it wasn't advisable to get mixed up in conversations that took unexpected turns and evoked unpredictable reactions in others. When on occasion he had been drawn into discussions with his colleagues at the lab, he inevitably seemed to say the wrong thing, despite his best intentions. And he knew that could be dangerous in a job where everyone was his senior and had the power of life and death over him—or at least over his economic survival, which was much the same thing. So he kept a quiet demeanor and tried not to run afoul of his superiors.

Even though he didn't indulge in idle chat, sometimes he couldn't help overhearing his colleagues conversing, often to his great annoyance. Scientists to the core, no matter what the topic, be it the weather, movies, literature, or art, they would cold-bloodedly analyze and dissect it, completely blind to any beauty or romance in the subject, as though they were coroners debating the fine points of an autopsy. They saw the universe only as an antiseptic reality, leaving no room for the imagination to paint in the unknown dimensions with speculation, dreams, and fancies. It began to worry him that perhaps he didn't possess the requirements to be good scientist.

Twilight was approaching. The library would be closing soon. He didn't know his way around the city very well but decided to try a short cut and so turned down a narrow cobblestone street. A sign on a lamp post said "Thayer." The street was lined with austere shingled houses, and when a flock of starlings flew by in the direction he was going, he felt sure he was heading the right way. He remembered the great numbers of the small gray birds that perched each night on the stone ledges of the library building, and guessed they were heading for their roost. Sometimes, when leaving the library, he would stop to listen to their raucous chatter and admire their iridescent plumage. He also admired their gregariousness, crowding together as they did, like one big happy family.

After walking a dozen blocks he found himself at a dead end. Annoyed, he was about to retrace his steps when he noticed a short way up the block an inconspicuous alley which seemed to lead in the general direction of the library. He decided to follow it.

The alley was lined with the backs of tall houses, huddled so close together that they formed a wall stretching into the dimness. The dark towering dormers, overhanging gables, and steeply sloping roofs of the storied dwellings told him that he must be in an old section of the city. The looming giants seemed to appraise him disapprovingly, and as if in empathy the heavens complained and released a torrential downpour. He quickened his pace, nearly slipping on the wet pavement, and was relieved when the row of houses yielded to commercial buildings and the promise of sanctuary. Not far ahead he spotted the entryway of a small corner shop. Jogging the last few steps, he took grateful refuge beneath its protective cover.

He waited impatiently for the rain to slow. His clothes were soaked through and he was shivering. A street light a block away blinked on and he knew that by now the library would be closed. He sighed, and his misery reminded him that he really needed to get a watch, when he could afford one. But he also knew that if he had the money, he would spend it on books instead.

His eyes wandered idly about and came to rest on the display in the shop window next to him. Lined up in evenly spaced rows like so many toy soldiers were hundreds of small bottles, uniform in size but varying in shape, each filled with colorful liquids, powders, or crystals. In the reflected street light the effect was mesmerizing. He peered deeper into the store, wondering what kind of business it was, but it was too dark inside to see anything. There was a small faded sign above the door that was all but unreadable, but he could make out one word, POSOLOGY, which puzzled him even more.

Suddenly a light flicked on somewhere at the back of the shop, and he stepped back from the window. He could hear the sound of footsteps approaching from within. A lock clicked and the shop door creaked partly open.

The snow-white head of an old man peered out. He was bent and wrinkled and wrapped in a drab bedrobe, though his dark twinkling eyes were alive and penetrating. He pursed his lips, his rosy features dimpling with curiosity as he surveyed the stranger on his doorstep.

Mmm. What stray has nature brought me? Not a bad looking young man. Has a sad but intelligent face, a lithe sturdy figure—a little gangly perhaps—and unruly hair that needs to be introduced to a comb. Tall with deep questioning eyes, broad brow, strong straight nose, all tolerably put together. And big feet that could use new shoes. Plain but decent clothes. Mmm. There's curiosity and consideration in his face—probably the type that watches insects on pavements and moves them out of harms way. Looks promising.

The old man sniffed the air and looked up at the sky, revealing a large brown mole under his chin.

"Rain, rain, rain! Bah! And it looks like there's more to come." His voice was firm but not unfriendly and scarcely betrayed his age. "Boy, you're soaking wet. You'll catch a death. No, I guess you won't—that's a dumb saying. Well, you'll catch a cold anyway—as if colds could run. Heh, heh. You'd better come in and dry off. Come along, come along, I don't bite."

Jonathan hesitated a moment, but felt assured by the old man's kindly face and friendly manner. "Thank you, sir." He followed the old man into the shop.

"This way. I have an apartment in back. Small but comfortable."

As Jonathan walked through the dimly lit shop he could make out the outlines of bottles, vials, and tins lined up on the ceiling-high shelves, which cast a faint multicolored glow over the room. A subtle odor of sweetness tinged with mustiness hung in the air.

"Here we are. Come into my parlor," said the old man. "Oh, I hope that doesn't make me sound like a spider, because I'm not." He chuckled. "And I know you're not a fly.

"Now, sit yourself down on that stool by the fireplace while I get us some tea. But not too close—hickory wood burns hot. Oh, by the way, my name is Hecuticar—Hecuticar Lemselecus. And you are...?"

"Jonathan Spenser. Thank you for your hospitality."

The old man waved the thank you away and disappeared into an adjoining room. Jonathan looked about: the place was rather plainly decorated with only a few basic furnishings. But to his delight the walls were lined with high wooden bookcases, each one crammed with books. He could barely resist the temptation to examine the books, but restrained himself lest he be thought rude.

The old man reappeared carrying two steaming mugs on a tray, one of which he handed to his guest. He then eased himself into a rocking chair near the fireplace with an audible grunt of relief.

"Ah, nothing like a comfortable chair and hot tea on a stormy night, eh my young friend?"

"Yes."

"Yes, indeed. Now tell me, what brings you out in such weather?"

"I was headed for the public library and got lost—I haven't lived in the city very long."

"Library? You're way off course, my boy. But it's a noble destination. You're a book lover, then?"

"Yes, sir. I read a lot."

"Good! Good! So do I, as you can see. On these shelves are some of my dearest friends. Been with me many a year, many a year." The old man fell silent, a distant expression in his eyes as he sipped his tea and nodded to himself.

Jonathan took advantage of the pause to ask a question.

"May I look at your books?"

"Well, of course, of course. Help yourself. And handle them if you like. Books like to be handled, just like people."

Jonathan quickly went to the nearest shelf. His eyes fairly leapt from book to book. Though fascinated by the dusty tomes on astronomy, alchemy, orientalia, and mythology, he skipped over them until he came to a shelf of rare first editions by the masters of the fantastic—Aberitt, Kinlot, Friendship, Lews, Diggs. His hand trembled slightly as he reached for a gilt decorated volume of Asgram's classic, *The Silent World*. Gently he opened the cover and his breath caught at the inscription penned therein: "To Hecuticar Lemselecus, Dream Sender—A vision and a debt for all time. Your grateful pupil, Larkin Asgram." Openmouthed, he turned toward his host, who was most amused at his guest's bewilderment.

"Ah, I see you are a connoisseur of the supernatural. You've chosen an inspired book. Have you read it?"

"No..."

"Well, take it then. A loan. Return it when you've finished."

"Oh no, I couldn't. It's a first edition—a presentation copy. It's very rare and valuable."

"I insist. Take it." The old man waved the refusal away with a flourish. "I can tell by the way you handle books that you love them and can be trusted."

Jonathan could hardly believe his good fortune. "Thank you. Thank you very much. The inscription—it's to you. You knew Asgram?"

"Oh dear me, yes. We spent many an hour together in this very room talking about—well, what didn't we talk about?"

"It says he was your pupil. And he calls you Dream Sender."

"Flattery. Just flattery. Pay no heed. But enough of books for now. Tell me something about yourself, young man."

Jonathan disliked talking about himself, nor was he very good at answering broad open-ended questions. His words stumbled over one another as he spoke about his background and his job. But the old man seemed genuinely interested, and nearly an hour later he realized he had told practically all there was to tell about himself. It occurred to him how utterly boring his life had been, and he felt embarrassed. Falling silent, he resumed sipping his tea, which by now was cold.

A pensive look fell over the old man's face. Jonathan could hear the sound of the rain on the roof diminish to a gentle patter, then die out. He rose from his chair.

"My clothes are nearly dry now, and since the rain has let up it's probably a good time to make a dash for home. My thanks for the tea and the book. I promise to return it next weekend. Do you have something I can carry it in, in case it starts raining again?"

The old man smiled and nodded, then retreated into the next room and emerged with an umbrella and a waterproof bag.

"Here you are, my young scientist, this should do it. You can return the umbrella with the book. Now, to get back to the center of town just follow Dexter Street for six blocks and turn right. But be careful—the cobblestones are wet and slippery."

The old man patted Jonathan on the shoulder and ushered him out a side entrance. The sky was dark and starless and the temperature had dropped. Jonathan turned to wave good-bye to his host, but he was gone.

As he made his way home he realized he had forgotten to ask the old man about his shop and its many strange bottles and tins. No matter, he would ask next week. He tightly clutched the treasure under his arm and could hardly wait to get back to his room to begin reading.

Lying abed that night he read until nearly dawn before drifting off into an uneasy sleep. Most of the weekend he also spent reading, and became so engrossed that he missed some of his meals. By late Sunday he finished the book, and would have finished sooner except that he reread many favorite passages. Finally, weary but exultant, he put the weighty volume aside and set his alarm clock for early wakeup so he wouldn't be late for work the next morning.

During the week he thought of little else but his next visit to the old man's shop, more particularly his library. His work fell behind as a result, and he had to stay late at the lab Thursday and Friday nights to complete his assignments. But he didn't mind since it made the time go faster.

On Saturday morning, after a hasty breakfast, he made his way with a light heart to the old man's shop. But to his surprise and disappointment he found the door locked and the interior of the store dark. He knocked several times and was about to leave when he heard the door lock click. The door swung open and the old man's smiling face peeked out at him.

"Good morning, sir," Jonathan fairly chirruped, "I've come to return your book and umbrella."

"Good! Good!" said the shopkeeper with much animation. "Come in, come in. Chilly today. But at least there's no rain. Hmm, good thing there's no farmer around to hear me say that."

Jonathan grinned and followed the old man to his apartment where he was offered the same stool by the fire. A hot mug of tea soon appeared, this time accompanied by a plate of chocolate cookies. Neither spoke as they sipped and ate. Jonathan thought the cookies delicious, though he didn't say so for fear he might be offered more than he could eat.

The old man smacked his lips and put down his cup.

"Well, young man, tell me, did you enjoy the book?"

Jonathan's face brightened. "Oh, very much—more than I can say."

"Good. You can put Mr. Asgram back in his niche. Books like to come home, just like people. Of course they like to be read even more, even if it means a little traveling."

Jonathan returned the book to its shelf, gently pushing it into place.

"Quite a magician with words, Asgram, don't you think?" asked the old man, his casual tone belying the curiosity in his eyes.

"Oh, yes!" Jonathan beamed. "Especially his descriptions of dream worlds—so mysterious and yet so realistic—and beautiful."

"Yes, very true. He had marvelous dreams and described them with great precision. He was a gifted lyricist."

"Do you mean his stories were actually his own dreams?"

"Quite so, most of them. Though a few were the stuff of imagination."

Jonathan looked amazed. "Oh! How wonderful," he blurted, "to have such dreams."

The old man nodded in agreement. "We all dream, but some of us have, well, special dreams. Have you ever had that kind of dream?"

"No, sir. Actually, I've never dreamed at all. At least not that I can remember."

The old man's eyebrows rose and a look of incredulity spread over his face.

"What? What's that? You say you haven't dreamed? Ever?"

"No."

"Oh, dear me, dear me. What a terrible thing. Everyone deserves to dream. Why, dreams are whole worlds waiting to be explored. They're a great gift. They help make life bearable—except nightmare dreams of course. My boy, you've been cheated. Cheated!"

The shopkeeper began to mutter to himself and looked off into space, an absorbed expression in his eyes.

Jonathan, somewhat perplexed, remained silent, waiting for his host to emerge from his reverie.

"Oh!" the old man said quite suddenly. "I'm afraid we have an unexpected visitor, a friend of mine who simply won't be ignored."

Jonathan watched in surprised amusement as a small brown whitefooted mouse scampered up the old man's chair and climbed onto his open hand. The old man smiled.

"Ah, good day to you, Lemanuel. It's good to see you. Now, now, don't tickle. You know I hate that. Mmm, I see you left the missus at home this time. But I guess I know the purpose of the visit anyway—you want some chocolate cookie. You've got a discerning nose. Why is it you never show up when I have vanilla cookies? Yes, I know, you've got a thing for chocolate, eh? Very well, here you are—take a big piece and then off with you. I've got another visitor today and he was here first."

The mouse got up on its hind legs and accepted the treat from its benefactor's fingers, turning the tidbit about with its tiny paws until it was positioned just so, then carefully placed it in its mouth. Its prize well secured, the little creature turned and stared a moment at the stranger sitting by the fireplace. Its dark eyes seemed to take on a reddish glow from the firelight. Suddenly it came to life and scampered down the chair and disappeared beneath a bookcase.

"I like your little friend," Jonathan said. "A tenant, I gather."

The old man wore a somber expression and said nothing.

"Uh, is there something wrong, sir?"

"Oh! No. Please excuse me. I sometimes get distracted. Old age, I guess." The old man brushed his hand across his face as though to wipe away any seriousness that might be showing. "Well, that was Lemanuel. He and the rest of his clan live in the basement. The little fellow and I have been friends a long time—I knew his parents. He's a mischief maker, though. If I don't have a tidbit for him when he shows up, he's apt to knock over some of the bottles in the shop. Mmm. Bribery, or more likely mouse terrorism." The old man wrinkled his brow. "Maybe Lemanuel knocks the bottles over in protest, because he thinks I'm a male chauvinist. Maybe he's a she and I should be calling her Lemanuella."

They both laughed.

"Sir, about your shop. You have so many interesting and colorful containers. I was wondering what it is you sell. I saw the word Posology on your sign."

"Oh, that has to do with doses, measuring out things. But I'm afraid I don't sell very much any more. I'm an old school chemist of sorts—old remedies for odd ailments—but these days there's not much call for my products. But maybe I can interest you in one of them. You were saying before Lemanuel's rude interruption that you don't dream. Well, I just might have a remedy for that—that is, if you want to dream. It's something everyone should do, you know."

"Oh yes, I would! But can you really do that? Make me dream?"

The old man smiled impishly. "I think so. Just a moment and I'll see what I can find."

Jonathan watched the old man disappear into the dimness of his shop and return a moment later holding a small bottle of bright red pills.

"Here you are, young master. Dream pills. No charge. Take one before bed. They're guaranteed to work or your money back." The old man chuckled.

"Thank you," was all Jonathan could think to say. He was skeptical and wondered if his host might be playing a joke on him. But he kept his doubts to himself lest he give offense.

The old man, looking pleased with himself, gestured toward the bookshelves.

"Well, now that your dream problem is taken care of, why don't you pick out another book to take home. Then I'll have the pleasure of your company again when you return it."

Jonathan fairly leapt off his chair and made for the fiction shelf. Without hesitation he withdrew a large leather-bound volume intricately stamped in gold. He savored it a moment, then carefully opened the cover.

"Another good choice, my boy. Friendship's *Beyond Time's Shadow*. Splendid book."

"S…sir, it has the author's personal bookplate," stammered Jonathan.

"Yes, it was Friendship's own copy. He gave it to me just before he… disappeared."

Jonathan's heart skipped a beat. "You knew him, then?"

"Oh, yes, we were good friends. A kind and thoughtful gentleman, although he had some strange habits. He hated sleeping and did all his writing at night. Liked to wander about in old cemeteries. Would you like to hear about the time he showed up at my door at three in the morning carrying a coffin? Empty, of course."

"Oh yes, please!"

Jonathan listened, enthralled, to the old man's story. Others followed and he became oblivious to the passing hours. It wasn't until his host yawned that he noticed the waning sunlight had dimmed the room.

"Forgive me, I've taken up too much of your time," he said, rising from his chair. "I really enjoyed your stories, but I should be going now."

"I confess I'm a little tired myself. These old bones aren't what they used to be. But come back next week and tell me what you think of Friendship's book. And, more important, you can tell me about your dreams."

Jonathan made his way home with a happy heart. He stopped at a convenience store to buy a sandwich and a soft drink so he wouldn't have to fix supper. That way he would have more time for reading.

Back at the shop, Hecuticar Lemselecus muttered to himself as he rummaged among his bookshelves.

"Mouse sign. Lemanuel's eyes turned red when he looked at him. But he says he doesn't dream. That doesn't fit. Makes no sense. Where's that cursed book? Ah, here it is."

From a low shelf the old man withdrew a large brown volume, its covers frayed and unlettered. He blew the dust from it and hefted it as he carried it to a nearby table.

"Pthagius, my friend, you're overweight. Always thought you were too wordy."

Setting the book down, he ran his fingers across the top corners of the pages until he felt the bent corner he was looking for. The book's spine made a crackly complaint as he gently opened the pages, as though he were unfolding the wings of a delicate bird.

"Here we are, the chapter on Dreamers and Creators. Let's see. Ah, yes—Animal Sign. Hawks...wolves...reptiles... Mice! Mmm. Yes, I know that, the eyes of mice turn red in the presence of... No, that's not exactly right, Pthagius old friend, the mouse has to be looking directly at the subject for it to happen. But that's not what I'm looking for. Tell me something I don't know. Ah, yes. Interesting. The ability to dream can be suppressed by the unconscious to protect the dreamer. This can happen when the unconscious mind senses the latent power of the dream potential, sees it as a source of disturbance, even danger, and sets up a block against it. This is most likely to occur when the nondreamer has been reared in a socially repressed environment, especially if he has a sensitive nature. Makes sense. And from what I know about the boy the description seems to fit."

The old man closed the book and scratched his mole as he continued to converse with himself.

"Well, it seems we have a special case here. Under the circumstances I can't be sure the power of suggestion that I used on the boy will work. If he were just some ordinary lad, the pills would work. No matter that they're placebos. But if the suggestion I implanted has to overcome a powerful unconscious resistance, it could fail. Unless he's a strong believer, or wants to dream very badly. Hmm. He seemed the nervous type, probably a perfectionist. Maybe I should have given him the purple pills."

It wasn't until well after midnight that Jonathan put his reading aside. Images of the author's creations swirled about in his mind—fantastic creatures and brave heroes that dwelt in magical dream worlds of dread and splendor. He envied the writer's talent and his wonderful dreams. If only he could dream like that.

He remembered the old man's pills and retrieved them from his trousers pocket. Should he take one? Why not.

CHAPTER 2

ZURALIA

The swirling yellow brightness hurt his eyes, and he raised his hand to block out the glare. As his vision cleared, Jonathan looked about and saw that he was standing alone on the summit of a grassy hill beneath radiant twin suns swirling in an ocean-blue sky. In the distance, nestled within the sky's cup, a sparkling city spread forth its wings in terraced arcs bounded by snowcapped mountains, their white breasts melting into gleaming cliffs splashed by the waters of a crescent sea. Masted ships with billowing sails traversed the blue harbor escorted by flocks of birds, their cries wafting up the grassy slopes on currents of the breeze. Rows of ivied houses marched down to the sea in chiseled tiers edged with white stone roads and green pathways broken here and there by quaint parks and gardens. Within the city's heart, beyond its broad promenades, spiraled cloisters and tree-lined squares, rose majestic structures of noble design, their corbeled domes and slender spires shining golden bright beneath the heaven's arch.

The city seemed to beckon him, and he walked down the grassy slopes, across broad meadows, through lush groves with fruit-laden trees that swayed before him as though in welcome, past thatched cottages set among fragrant arbors, over arched footbridges beneath which ran rippling streams whispering of the sea, their voices mingling with the sweet trills of birds in the brush, invisible save for a sudden flash of scarlet wings.

He walked beneath the towering granite arch at the city's edge, and the people he passed on the road nodded to him and smiled serenely. They were of many races and clad in gaily colored clothes of elegant simplicity. He trod down long marble stairs that wound from terrace to terrace, each level lined with splendid statues of bronze or carven stone, of stern-visaged gods of the sea, naked nymph-like maidens astride serpents gliding among the waves, and fearsome hydra-headed creatures of the deep. Their hollowed eyes seemed to watch him, as though in appraisal of the stranger among them.

He passed through streets of brightly painted dwellings, where a pretty girl threw him a kiss from a window and laughed, and by tall windowless warehouses with muralled walls, and great docks where tall sailing ships yielded up their cargo.

Within the city he stopped to admire the ornate temples and museums, the massive stadium, the sweeping colonnades and majestic buildings of state. At a small park set amidst the imposing structures, he watched the ritual display of opal peacocks perched on alabaster benches and hanging flower baskets, their feathers shimmering iridescent in the sunlight.

He did not notice the dark shadow cast from above momentarily touch the ground and flit across the manicured lawn, and he wondered why the peacocks, as one, ceased their bright spectacle and looked upward in alarm. His eyes followed theirs, but he saw only a fleeting hint of shade that might be a trick of the double suns. The sky was clear and cloudless once more, and the peacocks resumed their florid display.

A young mother with her prettily dressed child in tow walked by. He smiled as the little girl shook her long red-ribboned braid to and fro and laughed. She reached up and grasped him by the hand and lead him to an open kiosk at the park's edge, then ran back to her mother. The walls of the kiosk were covered with colorful posters and announcements of coming events—concerts, sporting competitions, craft shows, and citizen meetings. One particular poster, illustrated with handsome sailing ships, caught his eye. It said: *For adventure, sail with us to the Outer Isles.*

Further on he passed a marketplace where vendors lined the roadway selling ripe fruits and honeyed sweets, bolts of cloth of many hues trimmed in silver and gold, carven bowls and urns of wood and bronze, and sparkling jewels in the shape of strange birds and beasts. He stopped at a street of shops, all neatly arrayed in a row, which, from their displays, told him they catered to the sea trade. The store fronts were painted in shades of brown, blue, or gray and edged in white, save for one painted a bright crimson red, which drew his attention. A script-lettered sign above the shop entrance said: *Map Maker.*

The shop window reflected the twin suns' light, and he had to shade his eyes to see the large nautical map it displayed. The map seemed to cover a vast area of land and sea. But it showed no continents or large land masses, only islands. Curious, he entered the shop, the tinkling of a door chime announcing him.

A man standing behind the counter was speaking to a customer, a ship's officer by his dress. A map was spread out on the counter before them.

"I hope this is drawn to your satisfaction, Captain. We followed your instructions as best we could. As you know, we have no other maps of the area, so if there are any errors we will be glad to make the necessary corrections."

The captain—tall, clean-shaven, with chiseled features that bespoke strong character—examined the map carefully.

"Well drawn and essentially correct," he said in a deep baritone voice. "Except for one detail, here, at the tip of this inlet. It needs to be rounded a bit, like so. Fix that up and you'll have it."

"Very good, Captain. I'll have that change made tomorrow. Oh, please excuse me one moment. I have another customer."

The shopkeeper frowned at the blank-faced young man, betraying a slight annoyance at having to interrupt his business.

"Can I help you?" he said in a crusty tone.

"I…I'm not sure. Can you tell me the name of this place, this city? And show it to me on a map?"

The shopkeeper, a portly man, sucked in his stomach and pouted.

"Are you making a joke? If so, I really don't have time for that. You can see I'm with a customer."

"No, sir. I just want to know where I am."

The captain, overhearing, interjected himself into the conversation.

"Perhaps I can help you, young man. Do you mean you want to know what island you're on?"

"An island? Yes, sir. What island is it?"

"This is the island of Zuralia, sometimes called Celadon Isle because of its beautiful waters."

The name Zuralia struck at Jonathan's brain like a hammer blow. Zuralia! Zuralia! It spun around in his head, repeating itself like an echo, as though it were calling to him. His vision blurred and the walls of the shop began to whirl round and round. He felt dizzy; the world about him began to break apart and fade from view. He felt himself falling.

Sweating and gasping for breath, Jonathan bolted upright, his bed sheet clutched in his hand. Looking about wide-eyed, he saw that he was in his own bed. The word Zuralia came to his lips as if of its own volition, and he whispered it to himself over and over. He had dreamed! The old man's pill had worked. He had dreamed of an island called Zuralia. As he repeated the name to himself, a long-buried memory suddenly shot into his brain. He remembered—this wasn't his first dream. Once before, long ago, he had dreamed. And it had been the very same dream then as now!

The revelation delighted and amazed him. Imagine, he had dreamed not once, but twice. It gave him much to think about; he decided not to take another dream pill until he spoke with the old shopkeeper first.

On Saturday morning he jogged all the way to the old man's shop, where he was greeted warmly and ushered to the same seat by the fireplace. A hot mug of tea and a plate of cookies appeared in short order.

"Vanilla flavor this time," said the old man, "so I don't think we'll be seeing a certain chocolate-loving mouse today. Well, you're looking bright and shiny. What is it they say? Full of vim and vinegar. Find the Friendship book exciting, did you?"

Jonathan smiled to himself at his host's habit of mixing aphorisms.

"I enjoyed the book very much. But something else happened— something wonderful! I have to tell you. The pills you gave me worked. I had a dream!"

The old man clapped his hands together. "Ah! A dream. Well, I'm glad. It's about time. You certainly had one coming. I hope it was a pleasant dream."

"Oh, yes! A wonderful dream. And I remember every detail. Oh, I would love to go back."

"Really? Would you like to tell me about it?"

As Jonathan's words came tumbling forth, the old man's eyes grew brighter and deep furrows crept up his brow.

"Well, my boy, that was a fascinating dream indeed. You say the island, Zuralia, seemed for a moment to be calling to you. Hmm. And you now remember having had the same dream before. When was that?"

"Let's see. It was during my first year in high school. I was home sick with a fever."

"Illness, you say." The old man shifted in his chair and muttered to himself. "Mmm. That could be important. Illness not only affects the body but can have an unpredictable effect on the unconscious."

"Sir?"

"And you say that you would like to visit your dream world again?"

"Oh, yes! Very much."

"Why? Now think carefully before answering."

"Because it was so beautiful and exciting. And it was mine, my personal dream, a thing of my own creation. And because, as crazy as it sounds, I have this strange feeling that Zuralia wants me to go back."

The old man fell silent and took to scratching the mole beneath his chin. When he spoke again, his voice was uncharacteristically sober.

"My boy, I think it's time I explained something to you. In fact I believe it may be necessary. The reason will become clear to you. Can you keep a secret?"

"Yes, sir."

"Good. Now listen. The old man you see before you has a rather peculiar occupation, one seldom used during these times of reality and reason. I'm a dream sender, and as such I know a little something about dreams."

Jonathan smiled. "I know. It was your pill that sent me to Zuralia."

"No. You were responsible for your own dream. You dreamed because you wanted to. The pill was the rationalization your mind needed to overcome a deep-seated resistance buried in your unconscious. Your dream was quite normal. When you dreamed, as when most people dream, your unconscious spirit-self was simply transported into your dream world. What I mean by dream sending is that I can send the real self—body as well as spirit—into the world of dream. Zip! Just like that. You disappear from this world and reappear in your dream world. That's what happened to dear Phillip Friendship. He wanted passionately to live in the world of his dreams. So, when the time was right, I sent him there."

Jonathan stared blankly at his host, too stunned to speak. The old man continued.

"Now, for you to understand what I'm about to tell you, you'll need to know something about dream worlds and their origins. Dream worlds actually exist. They exist in other planes or dimensions, which are just as real as our earthly plane. How many such planes there are, I don't know—many I expect. A single plane is its own universe and can contain many dream worlds, and natural worlds as well, and it's possible to move from one plane to another.

"Where do these dream worlds come from? They are created, by very special beings called dream creators. A dream world can be created by the unconscious mind while the creator is having a sleeping dream. But that's unusual and a risky proposition to boot. Most dream worlds are created through waking dreams, where the creator's conscious mind has control and direction over its creation.

"Creators are rare creatures, at least here on Earth. But every once in a while someone comes along, like Friendship, who has the power to bring life to his dreams. He learned the creation technique on his own— my knowledge is too scanty to have been of much help there. By sheer determination he learned to shape and control his power, an ability that was also dependent on his maturity, self-discipline, and life knowledge. Where the creation power comes from is a mystery. But its possessor can bring a dream world into being by the exercise of sheer will. In the blink of an eye the world springs alive somewhere on a dream plane, as full blown and developed as the dream itself. The dream world can be primitive or advanced, familiar or alien, bounded only by the limits of imagination.

"Fortunately, the world creating power is limited in one important way, to just that—worlds, worlds of planetary magnitude. Larger entities, like dimensions, are out of scope. Of course a creation can be smaller, like an island or continent, for example. Still, as the expression goes, that's bigger than a bride box.

"A dream world can have amazing depth and complexity. It can spring into being with an evolved population, a developed culture, advanced technology, and a full-blown history, a history alive in the minds of its people. Once created, the world continues to evolve on its own. It cannot be erased even by its creator, although he can influence its growth, but only as a normal dream-world inhabitant. Is all this a bit too complicated for you, my boy?"

Jonathan half nodded, then shook his head from side to side. "I want to know more. Please go on."

"Mmm. Well, dream worlds needn't all be safe or beautiful like your Zuralia appears to be. They can be ugly and dangerous. Imagine the kind of monstrous worlds that might conceivably be, and probably have been, created by the mind of a demented creator. But it's reasonable to expect that most creations are not fundamentally different from the home world of their creators, though they would probably be cleaned up and idealized a bit and modified in interesting ways. An earthly creator, with a conditioned or so-called civilized mind, would tend to create a world with characteristics that are familiar to him. And since created worlds for some reason tend to materialize on a neighboring plane—for earth that would be the second dimension—an earthly visitor to that dimension would probably find it palatable, or at least recognizable.

"Now as for yourself, Jonathan, I believe it's possible that you may be a dream world creator. Zuralia may be real, and you may be its creator. What do you say to that?"

Jonathan sat erect. "Me? That can't be! Create Zuralia? I've...I've only dreamed twice."

"That doesn't disqualify you. Besides, there may have been other dreams you don't remember. The number doesn't matter. Once could have been enough. There are strong clues in your case. You didn't dream for many years, then you suddenly have an old dream again. And you felt your dream world beckoning—the child-creation reaching out to its father. You've also given off a powerful sign. When my little friend, Lemanuel, looked at you, his eyes turned red.

"It's possible that your first dream of Zuralia years ago may have brought about its creation. True, you didn't then, and you still don't, have conscious creation skills. But your illness at the time could have weakened the protective barrier erected by your unconscious mind so that your dammed-up psychic powers were released into your dream. And zing! It happened. If so, your island world has existed, and has been evolving, these many years. And it may now be beckoning to you, its creator, for some reason—maybe because, like any offspring, it instinctively is seeking its creator; or maybe it's gotten into trouble and needs your help—who knows?"

Jonathan's heart pounded as the old man's revelations raced through his brain.

"If you're right and I am Zuralia's creator, and if it is in trouble, then I want to do something. Couldn't I help by going there again in my dreams?"

"I'm afraid a dream visit wouldn't work. You'd have little conscious influence over yourself or your surroundings. You wouldn't be able to control your dream; you'd simply have to go where it took you. No, to do anything you'd have to go there in person—your physical self. But, of course, that's out of the question. It could be dangerous, especially for one who is untrained. You should stick to the life you know, right here. But what you can do is try to learn some creation skills, maybe practice mental exercises to strengthen your conscious mind...."

"But if I wanted to go to Zuralia, could you send me?"

"Think what you're saying, boy. You'd disappear from this world in body and spirit. You'd be naked in another dimension, prey to anything and anyone. No, it's definitely not a good idea."

"But Zuralia's not dangerous—it's beautiful. You sent Friendship to his dream world. Why won't you send me to Zuralia?"

"That was different. He was experienced and had explored many worlds in dreams before actually setting out on his own. He learned how to control his creative powers. And not least, he was older and wiser, and certainly less impulsive than you."

The shopkeeper smiled nostalgically as he recollected his friend of old. His voice softened. "He was a lovable eccentric, that man, and not a whit less determined than you."

"But suppose it's a matter of life and death," blurted Jonathan in frustration. "There are people who live there. If I did create Zuralia, then I'm responsible. My life isn't important here, but maybe it can be worth something there. And if it turns out there's nothing wrong, at least it would be a wonderful vacation."

The old man, both moved and amused by Jonathan's words, renewed scratching his mole. "Well, young master, where did this boldness come from all of a sudden, I wonder?"

Jonathan's face reddened; he realized he hardly sounded like himself. The old man made a patting gesture in the air.

"Oh, I know how you feel, my boy. All my life I thought of doing the same thing—going off to dreamland in search of adventure. But here I am. Leaving this comfortable mother earth of ours and disappearing into the unknown is a bigger step than you think. Yes, I have a pill that will transport you to your dream world. But it's a decision that requires considerable thought. There are complications you haven't begun to think about. Without thorough preparation, you'd be bound to get into trouble."

"But even if I did get into trouble, couldn't I just return to this world again?"

"Well, yes, theoretically. I have a pill for that too."

"Then why couldn't I go for a short visit, to get my feet wet so to speak?"

The old man chuckled. "Such a trip would be shorter than you think. Time is compressed on dream planes compared to our time—just like in sleeping dreams. In a dream that lasts only seconds, we can dream of events that span hours, days, or years. So you could leave this plane after breakfast, get a one-week tan on your island of Zuralia, and be back in time for dinner the same day. Unless, of course, something happened to you while you're away, like being killed. That, I'm afraid, is a permanent condition even in the higher dimensions. And if you were injured it would stay with you when you returned home. So you see, it's not as simple as you might think.

"But I'll admit there are some points in your favor. Your impetuousness aside, there could be a genuine need for your presence on Zuralia. And there's another reason I haven't mentioned. The different dimensions are not independent of one another—the fate of one can affect the fate of another. So it might be useful to at least check out this otherworldly summons of yours, if it be one, for the possible good of all. If Zuralia is in danger, it could mean trouble for the whole second plane— and potentially our earthly plane and the higher planes as well."

Jonathan jumped to his feet. "Then time could be important. Maybe we shouldn't delay."

The old man waved Jonathan back into his seat and stared pensively out into space.

"You could be right. But we're building supposition upon supposition. Let's both think about it for a week. Nothing like sober reflection and restful sleep to clear the cobwebs. I'll give you a pill that will temporarily prevent you from dreaming. It'll be safer that way. Then if you still feel the same in a week, then maybe—I say, maybe—we'll go ahead.

You'll also have to think about making arrangements at your place of work and where you live so that no one will ask questions, just in case you're away for more than a couple of days."

Jonathan grinned. "Unless, of course, I decided to stay on Zuralia. Then I'd be a missing person, like Friendship."

"Harrumph!" The old man shook his finger. "Young man, you'll get no sending pill from me without a promise to return. So don't go getting ahead of yourself."

A dreamy look came into Jonathan's eyes. "I wonder, is it possible that I could actually meet him on another plane? Friendship, I mean?"

The old man's voice mellowed. "Oh yes, it's possible. Even though he was a bit of a recluse, he also liked to travel. So he might be any-where. I'm sure he would be delighted to meet you—you two have a lot in common. Mmm. Now you've got me getting ahead of myself. You've got a way about you, boy, I'll say that."

Jonathan savored the compliment and the possibility of meeting one of his heroes.

The old man yawned. "Well, I think we've—what's the expression?—touched a few goal posts. But we'll go over it again next week, just to be sure, and kick a few more bases besides. Then there are questions like what clothes to wear and what can be used for exchange in that world of yours. But enough for today."

At the door Jonathan turned and clasped the old man's hand warmly. His voice cracked. "I…I can't thank you enough."

He jogged all the way home, his heart light in his breast. He had forgotten about borrowing another book.

At the lab the next week he was restless and moody. On one occasion he talked back to an ill-mannered supervisor, which was unlike himself. Fortunately, he had already gotten permission to begin his vacation at the end of the week. He told the landlady at his rooming house that he might be away for a while. At night he had trouble sleeping and relived in his mind every detail of his visit to Zuralia. He wondered if he would ever see the kindly sea captain again.

When Saturday finally arrived he was travel-ready in the hope that this would be the big day—if he could convince the old shopkeeper. He dressed in light sports clothes, which he thought would be best suited to the warm climate of Zurlia, and packed a small traveling bag with only the bare essentials. He had nothing valuable to take for trading; he would just have to live by his wits.

When he arrived at the shop, the old man was waiting at the entrance. Jonathan flushed when he saw his friend's eyebrows rise upon spying his traveling bag.

He tried not to reveal his nervousness as he took his seat by the fireplace. A hot mug of tea soon appeared, only this time without cookies. The old man's somber expression was ominous.

"Well, young man, I can see you've made up your mind and don't want to wait."

"No, I mean yes, sir."

"Well, you should really wait a little longer. But I suppose there's no talking you out of it."

"No, sir."

"You've made the necessary arrangements where you work and live?"

"Yes, sir."

"You're not really ready, you know, but I can't in good conscience hold you back. Your cause is a noble one, and you're deserving if anyone is. But more important, a few nights ago I received a powerful dream suggestion in your favor. I suspect it was interdimensional, but I don't really know its source. That's what pushed me over the hill, er, line. So I guess you win. But let's go over a few things first."

An hour later the old man took a deep breath and put on a forced smile. "Well, we've covered the essentials and might as well get started. Remember, if you experience any difficulty at all on that island of yours, immediately take the return pill and come on home. Keep your eyes open and your mouth shut, except to eat and ask questions. And stay alert to any opportunity to learn about how to use your dream-creation powers. That's important. The local library might be a good source of information.

"Now, come over here and sit in this easy chair and get comfortable. When you return again to this plane it will be this same chair you'll return to. I won't use it meanwhile, but I can't promise about Lemanuel. Now place your bag on your lap. Relax. Good."

The old man reached into his shirt pocket and withdrew a small silver case etched with glyph-like symbols. Lifting the lid, he picked out two oblong pills, one pale yellow, the other bright green, and handed them to Jonathan.

"The yellow is for sending, the green for returning. The return pill is only good for traveling from one plane to the immediately adjacent one. It can't be used to leap dimensions. But since you'll be returning from the second plane back to the first, that won't be a problem. Put the green pill in your pocket and keep it safe. Do it now. Good. The other pill I want you to swallow whole with a bit of tea. Not yet! Look at the clock on the table there. It's forty seconds before the hour. Exactly on the hour take the pill. It will take a minute or so to take effect. You'll get drowsy and you might feel a little dizzy. That'll be the worst of it. Then you'll be off.

"Are you ready, then?"

Jonathan felt like his insides were floating up to his throat. He stiffened his leg muscles for fear they might start shaking.

"I'm ready."

He watched the second hand creep slowly up the face of the clock, as though it were struggling against invisible chains. When finally it pointed straight up, he popped the pill into his mouth and swallowed it whole, forgetting the tea.

The old man's voice was soothing.

"Now rest your head back and close your eyes. Relax…relax."

The words seemed to be coming from far away, rising and falling, stretching themselves as though caught in a phantom wind. Tired…he felt so tired.

Hecuticar Lemselecus stared at the empty chair before him and nodded to himself. He couldn't help feeling a little envious of his young friend. He sat down on the stool by the fireplace, an absentminded look in his eyes. A small mouse suddenly appeared, which crawled up his leg and nestled in the warm cup of his hand.

"Ah, it's you Lemanuel. Looking for a little extra warmth on a cold day, eh? I believe you were right about the boy. And now he's gone. To his real home perhaps. Well, a soul needs to find its season. I hope I did right by sending him. He wanted to go so badly. What's more, someone else wanted him to go. The dream suggestion I got was unmistakable. I wonder whose it was—I couldn't tell. A friend, I hope.

"Don't tickle, Lemanuel, you know I hate that. Or down you'll go. Oh, you want to be scratched on the head? I think I can manage that. Mmm. All in all, it's been a satisfying day. Such days don't come along very often. It's good to be usefully employed. Would you believe, Lemanuel, that in this world of ours there are people who get to use their skills every day? Lucky devils. And I expect you're one of them."

CHAPTER 3

THE GOD OF ZWEG

Jonathan's eyes blinked open. The swirling fragments of color that met his vision slowly began to come together. A cool breeze touched his face and helped to clear the cobwebs from his brain. He looked about and saw that he was lying on the same grassy hill where he had first arrived in his dream. Blazing twin orbs swirled in the sky above, and spread out below him sparkled the fair city of Zuralia.

He had arrived! His heart pulsed with joy. But suddenly doubts and questions began to assail him. Maybe he wasn't really here. Maybe it was only another dream or a hallucination. Maybe the shopkeeper had hypnotized or drugged him and he was still sitting in the chair in the old man's apartment. He felt a sinking feeling in the pit of his stomach. No, it must be real—his traveling bag was on the grass beside him. He shook off his doubts and felt ashamed for distrusting his old friend.

A pain jabbed at his back. Reaching into the grass beneath him, he pulled out a sharp stone and tossed it aside. Rising to his feet, he pondered what he should do. He didn't exactly know, but somehow he wasn't worried. Why not continue where his dream had left off, he decided. He would go back to the map maker's shop.

Bag in hand, he made his way down the same sloping paths as in his dream, only now he paused to drink in the clean sweet air, feel the cool offshore breeze against his body, and savor the beauty of his surroundings. Passersby smiled or nodded to him, and he returned their greetings. They gave no sign of viewing him as a stranger or as someone different from them, which gave him some confidence.

As he passed through the city, he took mental notes on its layout and the location of buildings. It struck him that there were no vehicles on the streets, save for an occasional bicycle, and he guessed that since the city wasn't very large they weren't needed, or perhaps wanted. Nor, for that matter, were there many people walking about, suggesting that the island was not heavily populated.

He stopped at a kiosk to read its postings. Mostly they were notices of cultural and athletic events, as he remembered from his dream. One announcement was an invitation to join in a two-day hiking trip across the island, which gave him some idea of Zuralia's size. A list of forthcoming science lectures also caught his eye, particularly one titled *On Hypothesizing Multiple Planes*. Apparently the fact of alternative dimensions was not yet known here, but still only a theory.

From a nearby trash bin, he withdrew a page of discarded newspaper. From its feel he could tell it was made from synthetic material rather than wood pulp. Its heading bore the date *Tenth Day of the Second Quarter of the Year of the Double Suns*, and showed a pictogramic calendar that indicated an annual cycle of ten months of forty days each, with each day divided into equal periods of light and darkness.

The page contained a notice of a forthcoming election for members of the city council; on its verso was a cartoon of a large balloon labeled *Taxes*, showing a group of citizens blowing air into one end of the balloon and another group letting air out at the other end. Not everything was harmonious on Zuralia, he concluded.

Continuing on, he passed by a broad, tree-lined thoroughfare and noticed at its terminus a magnificent multi-columned edifice, its marbled portico announcing in bold letters: *Municipal Library*. He remembered the old shopkeeper's suggestion—as if he needed prompting to visit a library—and marked its location in his memory.

Upon arriving at the map maker's shop he peered through the window, and to his delight he saw that the sea captain he had spoken with in his dream was there. The captain was conversing with the proprietor, and although he couldn't hear their words, he saw the captain hand over a gold coin and receive a cylindrical case in return, which he guessed must contain a map. He wondered if it might be the same map the captain had been perusing in his dream. If his dream and his present reality were connected, then perhaps the captain might remember him. But it hardly seemed likely. How could a person who had been dreamed remember the dreamer?

The captain emerged from the shop and noticed the young man by the window looking at him intently.

"Good day to you, young sir," he said. His deep voice resonated musically. "Become a little more familiar with our fair island since we last met?"

"Good day, Captain," replied Jonathan, pleased, and also surprised, that the captain remembered him. "I'm afraid I still don't know my way around very well. I'm still exploring. But maybe you can help me with some information, if you would."

"Be glad to, if I can." The captain approached and clapped his hand on Jonathan's shoulder. "Well, what do you want to know?"

"I'm a stranger here, and I need to find a job and a place to live, at least temporarily. I want to learn more about Zuralia and the surrounding islands, but first I have to solve the problem of survival."

"An aspiring scholar, eh? Well, I'd be the last one to criticize the search for knowledge. As for a job, there's always something for a good man to do in Zuralia. Why not consider working down by the docks? Walk along with me and we'll talk about it. I'm headed that way now."

"Thank you." Jonathan fell in beside the captain as they headed downhill toward the sea.

"My name's Othin, captain of the trading ship, Pelagin. And how are you called, lad?"

"Jonathan Spenser."

"Jonathan Spenser." The captain repeated the name slowly, as though assessing every syllable. "That's a seaworthy name if I've ever heard one. And where do you hail from, Jon lad?"

"Oh…uh…from up north."

The captain chuckled. "As you like. We sailors are private folk and know how to mind our own business. I just thought if you were familiar with some of the outlying islands, I might be able to use you on my ship. I mean, if you were so inclined."

Jonathan perked up. "Oh, I would like that just fine. I haven't traveled very much. But I'd like to see the neighboring islands, and explore more of Zuralia."

"Well, in my experience those who want to go to sea are either running from something or looking for something. I hope you're a seeker and not a runner."

"Yes, sir. Definitely a seeker."

"Good. Do you have any skills, lad?"

"My education is in biology and chemistry, and I've had some laboratory experience. But I'm looking for a change from that."

"Well, your experience wouldn't be much good aboard ship. But the important thing is—do you love the sea?"

"Oh yes, it's always fascinated me."

"Good! Because it's love of the sea more than anything that makes a good sailor. Have you had lunch yet?"

"No, sir."

"Then why not join me aboard ship? I've got one of the best cooks on land or sea. And if I were a betting man—and I am—I'd wager you don't have a coin in your pocket to weigh you down."

Jonathan half smiled, more embarrassed than amused. "My thanks, Captain. I'll be pleased to have lunch with you."

"Good. And don't go worrying about a lack of coin on Zuralia—nobody goes hungry here. This is a noble island with a good heart.

"You say you want to know more about her—Zuralia. Well, I can sum it up for you in a few words. The island's rich, beautiful, independent, and chock full of knowledge, and her people are healthy, happy, and long-lived. You may have noticed the wealth of beauty possessed by some of the fair sex yourself." The captain laughed at his own joke, but when he saw his companion's intent expression, he cleared his throat and continued in a more serious vein.

"Zuralians are generous by nature, but follow a live-and-let-live philosophy, demand high standards, and bridge no nonsense. They respect individualism, follow democratic rule, believe in education and the arts, and will protect anything that grows in, crawls on, or flies above Zuralian soil. For the most part they follow the rule of reason, though, I'm glad to say, with some exceptions.

"Strategically, Zuralia is located at the heart of the greater island world, and her affluence owes mainly to an ideal location for sea trading. The surrounding islands, which vary considerably in size, are at different levels of economic and social development, ranging from primitive to highly advanced. Some of the islands are still unexplored. But Zuralia, despite her small size, is the sweetheart of them all, at least in this captain's opinion. If I ever give up my sea legs, this is where I'll plant them."

Jonathan listened in fascination, and doubt began to nibble at him once again. Zuralia had a long history, one that far preceded the time he had first dreamt of the island. Despite what the old shopkeeper had told him, he found it hard to accept that an island could be created with a fictitious history implanted in the minds of its people. More than that, he questioned that he, or any mere mortal, could create the infinite complexity of a whole world. But perhaps it was no different than a parent creating the wonderful complexity that was its own child. Perhaps the mystery of creation simply had to be accepted on faith. Why must he always be the scientist? The skeptic? Ever questioning? He wanted to believe.

"Yup, there's no better place to drop anchor than Zuralia," said the captain with a flick of his head for emphasis. "It's peaceful, not a serious care in the world, and the climate's unbeatable. But, I also have to say, that for someone who craves adventure, like myself, it can sometimes get a little boring. That's one reason I'm a seaman—that way you get the best of both worlds." The captain cast a sideways glance at Jonathan. "And traveling the oceans is not a bad life for the curious, either."

The smell of fish in the air and the squawking of sea birds announced that the docks were near. As the pair rounded the corner of a wharf, the captain's face brightened.

"There she is, lad—the Pelagin. Prettiest yawl that ever sailed. And she's all mine, earned and paid for."

Jonathan's eyes glided over the tall stately ship gently bobbing in the water at dockside. He thought it handsome indeed, with its sleek wooden hull sporting a shiny coat of white and gold, spotless oaken decks, polished brass railings, high double masts that seemed to kiss the sky, and a quartet of furled snow-white sails that seemed like great captive gulls eager to be released.

The captain watched Jonathan's face as he looked over the vessel and was pleased at the young man's admiring expression.

"And there to guide me across the waters is my very favorite lady," said the skipper, nodding toward the bow.

Jonathan gazed wide-eyed at the imposing figurehead of a voluptuous mermaid rising out of the prow. Finely carven, her long ropelike tresses encircled a face to shame a goddess and fell languidly over proud naked breasts. Jonathan's obvious appreciation caused the captain to break out in a broad smile.

A dark shadow cast from above suddenly glided across the ship, and Jonathan and the captain jerked their heads upward as one. Against the glaring twin discs high overhead they saw the outlines of two giant birds with pointed bat-like wings. Slowly the great creatures circled, marring an otherwise unblemished canopy of blue.

"What are they?" asked Jonathan, his voice a near whisper.

"Zytox!" growled the captain. "Devil birds! This is the second time I've seen them over Zuralia. The first time was only a few weeks ago. They're fearsome creatures, flesh eaters. In groups they'll attack anything. I've seen a few in the far north isles. Wonder what they're doing around here?"

Slowly the giant birds drifted from view. The captain shook his fist at the sky, shrugged, and put on a cheery voice.

"Well, let's not let two scrawny birds spoil our lunch. Come on, lad, let's go aboard and see what's in the cook's pot."

After a hearty meal of fresh-baked bread and hot stew in the captain's cabin, the skipper gave Jonathan a tour of the ship. Afterwards they lolled about on deck watching trading ships sail in and out of the harbor. The captain puffed contentedly on an old pipe and was moved to tell a few of his favorite stories about the strange islands he had visited and the incredible creatures of the deep he had encountered. The excitement of seagoing life could not help but stir his young guest's blood, which was perhaps the captain's intention.

"I thing you'll like a sailor's life, lad," said the captain. "I know you don't have the experience, but you've got that wayfarer's look about you. I'll give you the job of captain's apprentice. The pay's not much and you'll have to tackle whatever tasks I give you. But you'll get to ride the waves on the best ship afloat and visit many a fascinating island to boot. And you already know the vittles are good. Now what do you say to that?"

Jonathan, all smiles, replied without hesitation. "Captain, I'm happy to join your crew."

"Good! I should have mentioned, we sail in three days time on a trading tour of the northern islands. So you'll have until then to look around Zuralia at your leisure. Meanwhile, you can bunk and eat on board. There's a small cabin next to mine—you can use that for the time being."

For the next two days Jonathan explored the island on foot and by bicycle, an old two-wheeler the captain was kind enough to lend him. That suited him, not that he had any choice, since smoke-emitting machines were not allowed on the island, nor indeed were any devices that posed a threat to the pure quality of the air or water. Electrical power for lighting and other purposes, he learned, was supplied by a water conversion process that was nonpolluting.

In the city, he visited museums, art galleries, and great halls, and was in awe of their treasures. His search at the municipal library for information on the subject of dream world creation proved unavailing, though he was impressed with the library's vast collection of books, many of which he wished he had more time to study. It intrigued him that in some areas Zuralian knowledge was ahead of Earth knowledge, but in others it was far behind.

He especially enjoyed the Zuralian countryside: its green rolling hills dotted with quaint farms and orchards, its great forests that ran down to the sea, its white chiseled cliffs that stood tall like grand cathedrals, and the abundance of nature's creatures, some of which were new to him. On a knoll overlooking a lake, he shared his lunch with a gentle fawn-like animal with tasseled ears, and his heart swelled to think he might have been responsible for such beauty.

Too soon the day came for the Pelagin to weigh anchor. The crewmen began arriving, and the captain introduced him to Balu, the chief mate, a muscular seven foot giant with a smile a yard wide, who patted him atop the head in friendly welcome. He had little doubt that the chief mate's orders to the crew would be promptly obeyed. He was next introduced to Tabber, the night helmsman, who was a sober quiescent soul, thin and pale with a shaven head and the gift of night vision. The helmsman bowed low to the young apprentice, a gentlemanly gesture which Jonathan appreciated, though it made him blush. He learned later from the captain that Tabber had once been a priest of mysterious Klell Island but had been defrocked for using logic in a religious debate.

Next he met Zyl, the navigator, who was of yet a different sort: a yellow-skinned dwarf with perennially blinking bloodshot eyes, a parrot-like beak, and a furtive expression which he kept hidden under a black hood. A recent addition to the crew, the captain had hired him when his regular navigator had mysteriously disappeared. Nevertheless, the little man drew praise for his uncanny ability to navigate difficult waters. When introduced to the new apprentice, Zyl said nothing, which elicited a grunt of displeasure from Balu.

The captain then took Jonathan to the galley and introduced him to Nynt, the cook, a nearsighted fidgety little man with a red beard and bald pate. Nynt mumbled something incomprehensible by way of greeting, then took to complaining about the condition of his wood-stove and the problem of buying good quality foodstuffs.

The captain and Jonathan returned to the main deck.

"You can meet the rest of the crew in the course of your work, lad," said the captain. "Any questions?"

"Yes, sir. I noticed that we're not carrying much cargo."

"That's true—just some blankets, knives, and body ornaments, which we'll trade to the natives of Zweg, our first stop. What they give us we'll trade for other goods at our next port, and so on, from island to island. You'll see how it works soon enough. Now it's time to get under way."

The captain took the wheel and gave the order to cast off the lines. Slowly the Pelagin drifted seaward on the outgoing tide aided by a line of polers dockside. When the ship was clear, the skipper gave the order to unfurl the mainsails. The great white sheets billowed out and snapped taught, and the Pelagin obediently responded to her masters of wind and rudder, gliding effortlessly through the waves, eager to meet the challenge of the sea.

Breathing deeply of the salt air and spray, Jonathan followed the line of the crescent bay with his eye until it merged into the open sea. Looking back at the receding city, he felt a sudden lump in his throat. The flickering sunlight played magically over the tall spires and domes, as though it were a heavenly instrument or a ballet of lights being performed on some godly stage. As the city shrunk yet further, it took on the semblance of a great bird, its outstretched wings pinioned to the land, captured in the embrace of looming mountain kings, their white crowns half hidden in shadow. He felt a twinge of conscience, as if he were somehow abandoning his charge. But that's silly, he told himself. To occupy his mind and assuage his conscience he joined a seaman coiling rope, who was glad to have the company.

His days at sea were happy ones. The captain kept him busy, mostly performing menial tasks, and from time to time shared his knowledge of the outlying islands, which he liked to call Zuralia's bratty neighbors. But when Jonathan asked about the Pelagin's first port of call, the island of Zweg, the captain only laughed, saying it was a merry-go-round and loony bin all wrapped into one.

It was from Balu, a native of Zweg, that he learned more about the island. The Zwegians, it seemed, were a primitive race ruled by a hereditary tribal chief, Zwez, though the real power on the island lay in the hands of a small group of priests who were the guardians of the omnipotent two-headed god, Mkhat. All Zwegians feared and bowed low before the great wooden idol of Mkhat. Though two-headed, Mkhat only wore one head at a time, since the heads were bitter enemies. His one head was black and the other white, while his body was red from neck to toe. When Mkhat wore his smiling black head, peace and contentment prevailed on Zweg. But when he wore his angry white head, savagery and cannibalism were the order of the day.

The priests of Zweg, as Balu explained, were divided into two competing factions—the guardians of the black head and the guardians of the white. Each faction strove to place its head on the trunk of the idol and keep it there as long as possible. The guardians of the reigning head kept constant vigil lest the competing faction sneak up on the idol and switch heads. All manner of strategy and trickery were used in this never-ending contest of rotating heads. As a consequence, trading with the Zwegians was sometimes difficult. The young apprentice could readily believe that.

On the Pelegin's fifth day out to sea Jonathan was treated to a rare sight. The captain called him to the starboard rail and pointed to two huge half-submerged objects moving slowly through the water about a hundred yards away.

"Wolf sharks," said the captain. "Nasty creatures, those. Leviathans of the deep, a hectometer in length. They have teeth the height of a man and a voracious appetite to match. They've been known to attack ships and leave only splinters. Fortunately for us they don't seem to be hungry. But I'll feel better when we're out of deep waters, which should be some time tonight. By tomorrow morning, if the wind holds, we'll reach Zweg."

Next day Jonathan was up at first light and found Balu at the bow rail searching the horizon for sign of the island. As the great orange eyes of the twin suns blinked over the horizon, Balu gave out a cry.

"There! See, Jon. Zweg! My home."

"Yes, I see it!" Jonathan kept his eyes glued to the small spot of land as it gradually grew larger. He wondered: might it hold any clues to the mystery of his dream-world summons? From what Balu had told him, he doubted it.

It wasn't until late afternoon that the Pelagin swung about offshore and dropped anchor in a small sandy bay. Jonathan saw that the island was lush and tropical, its jungle foliage rising up like a wall just above the beach line, impenetrable to the eye. The captain ordered a crewman to climb to the crow's-nest and report.

From aloft the crewman scanned the perimeter with a glass.

"Captain!" he yelled. "The birds' nests are empty! They have settled offshore!"

"Hell's fire and be damned," shouted the captain. "The blasted idol has its white head on. We can't go ashore. We'll have to wait for a switch."

"Excuse me, Captain. But how can you tell? About the heads, I mean?" asked Jonathan.

"The Goona birds tell us. They're big ugly creatures that nest in the top of trees. When the idol has its white head on, the Zwegians will kill everything in sight, including the Goona birds. That's when the birds leave the island and wait it out on the rocks offshore. When the heads are switched and everything's calm again, the birds seem to know and return to their nests. Right now, they're hiding out offshore, so we know what that means. There's no telling how long we'll have to wait. Blast that mangy two-headed god!"

"Why don't we just slip ashore tonight and switch the heads ourselves?" asked Jonathan, innocently.

The captain guffawed. "Aren't you the brave one, lad? And just how do you propose we accomplish that?" He winked at Balu, who was listening nearby and grinning from ear to ear.

"Well," replied Jonathan, "Balu is a native Zwegian. He probably knows how to sneak in without being spotted."

"That's true, I do," interjected Balu. "But the priests of the white head will be guarding the idol. It won't be possible to get near it."

"Maybe we can create a diversion of some kind to get them away from the idol," offered Jonathan.

There was a long silence.

"That might be possible," said Balu. "But there's another problem. We don't know where the black head is. The priests of the black head have it hidden somewhere. We'd need it to be able to make the switch."

The captain, now interested, pushed into the conversation. "But the priests of the black head want their head back up just as much as we do. If we can make contact with them secretly, maybe we can work out a plan together. We have the element of surprise on our side, since I don't think the Zwegians know we're arrived at the island yet."

Balu grunted in agreement. "A good idea. I have a cousin on the island, Isko, who's a priest of the black head. When it's dark I can sneak ashore and try to contact him. What do you think, Captain?"

"I say let's try it. But at any sign of danger, you hightail it back to the ship. Is that understood?"

Balu's grin broadened. "Yes, Captain."

"And as for you, lad." The captain tried to look stern, then smiled. "Good thinking."

In two hours it was dark, although, as Jonathan had noticed, it never got quite as dark on the island plane as on Earth. Even though the island world had no moon or stars that he could see, the reflection of the twin suns, even after they set, cast a dim ghostly light over the night sky.

Balu, wearing a leather loincloth and holding a short-bladed knife in his mouth, saluted to the watching captain and crew before slipping silently into the water. Thereafter time dragged slowly, as it does for those who wait.

Once on shore, Balu followed a well-hidden animal trail he knew through the dense brush, which, after many twists and turns, took him to a small clearing just outside the southern edge of the Zweg village. There he crouched behind a tree, placed a strip of leaf between his lips and made a cricket-like noise. He repeated the sound several times.

A lone figure slipped quietly out of a nearby hut and ducked into the foliage. A few moments later Balu felt a tapping on his shoulder and leapt up in alarm, knife in hand.

"Isko!" Balu grunted. Though he had been taken by surprise, he still had the sense to keep his voice down. "Did you have to do that?"

The robed figure chuckled. "Greetings, cousin Balu. You never were very good at looking after yourself in the jungle."

Balu grimaced. "Never mind that. I have something important to talk to you about. I've just arrived from Zuralia...."

"I can see that, cousin."

"Curse you, Isko! just listen, will you? I need your help."

An hour later Balu pulled himself up the aft rope ladder of the Pelagin and plopped down on deck, panting. The captain and the crew quickly surrounded him.

"Balu, are you all right?" asked the skipper.

"I'm fine. Just out of wind. It's hard to stay in running condition on a ship, you know."

Balu regained his breath and told what had transpired.

"The priests of the black head will join with us, and gladly. It's been more than three months since Mkhat has worn his black head, so they're anxious. Isko has a plan. Tonight, at the hour when the sky glow is weakest, six of us will go ashore. We will meet six of the priests of the black head in a clearing that I know. They will have the head with them. The priests will lead us along a hidden jungle path they know to the central village clearing where the idol is. By then everyone will be asleep, except the guards around the idol—six, Isko says. He and the other priests will hide in the trees behind the idol while our group, from the other end of the clearing, draws the guards away from the idol. Isko says that while the guards are attacking us, his group will rush in and switch heads."

"Hmm. Not a bad plan," said the captain. "Except that we're taking all the chances. We'll have to run like the blazes. I don't have to tell you what will happen if the guards catch up with us. Your cousin and his friends had better make the switch fast. Tell me, Balu, if worse comes to worse and we should kill one of the Zwegians, will that ruin our chances of trading here? I don't want to risk that."

"Oh no, Captain," Balu replied. "If—I mean—once the black head is put back on the idol, all will be forgiven."

"I hope you're right. Now, how about our escape route?"

"I know a path that will take us back to the beach quickly," replied Balu. "Anyway, as soon as Isko and the other priests put the black head on Mkhat, all fighting will stop."

The captain humphed. "But who's going to give that news to the guards who'll be tearing after us through the bush with dinner forks in one hand and spears in the other?"

At the appointed hour a skiff was lowered over the side and six men got aboard: the captain, Balu, Jonathan, Zyl, and two burly deck hands, Kik and Yos. The captain had a short club tucked in his belt, while the others carried knives. Jonathan refused a weapon, but the captain insisted so he chose a short-bladed knife like Balu's. Zyl carried two serpentine blades of his own, one strapped to each arm.

The captain looked hard at Jonathan and sniffed. "I'm probably out of my mind letting you come on this screwball expedition. Now you stick to me like deck varnish, you hear?"

"Yes, Captain."

The ship's party arrived safely at the meeting site where they joined up with the six robed priests of the black head. Two of the priests carried a large straw basket, which Jonathan guessed held Mkhat's good head. The combined group then quietly made their way through the jungle to the edge of the main village clearing, which was lit by a small fire at its center. There the group split up, the six priests circling around to one end of the clearing and the six seamen to the other.

Through the trees Jonathan could see the red potbellied figure of Mkhat, its terrible white head glowering with disapproval upon the world. It had wild protruding eyes, a long swollen tongue, and sharp savage teeth, and was altogether intimidating. More threatening, however, were the twelve guards protecting the idol, each clutching evil-looking spears with long jagged points at one end and knobby clubs at the other.

The captain cussed under his breath. "That fool Isko said there would be six guards. Does he count by twos, like heads?"

When everyone was in position, the captain gave a hand signal and, as one, the six seamen emerged from their hiding and walked boldly into the clearing. The guards surrounding the idol quickly spotted them and let out whoops and shouts of warning. Ten of the guards rushed toward the intruders with raised spears, emitting warlike yells. Two remained behind to protect the idol.

"It's working," cried the captain. "But two are sticking with the idol. Balu, I hope your cousin and his pals can handle them."

Balu looked glum. "The priests of the black head are a peaceful lot, Captain, inexperienced in combat. But I hope so, too."

"You hope so?" sputtered the captain in exasperation. "You're the one who set this up! The devil help us—the guards are halfway here. Why don't those dizzy priests make their move?"

Balu shrugged. "They're probably waiting for the guards to chase us into the jungle just to be safe. Taking off the old head and putting on the new one isn't easy and can't be done quickly, so it would be better if the guards were completely out of sight first."

"*Now* you tell me that? Nobody seems to care if we're live bait or dead bait. Whoops! The guards are getting close. Let's go, boys. Balu, you know the jungle paths. Get us out of here. Fast!"

Balu darted into the bush, the crewmen close behind. Jonathan was exhilarated by the chase and easily kept pace. Zyl ran beside him, and Jonathan was impressed that the little man, with his short stubby legs, could run so fast. A Zwegian spear whizzed by and thudded into the ground a few yards in front of them. Zyl let out a hoot of delight and, grabbing the still quivering spear shaft in both hands, he vaulted himself forward through the air. Jonathan gasped at the bold catapulting maneuver and watched in admiration as the little man hit the ground running and barreled out of sight ahead of him. He could hear Zyl's high-pitched cackle through the brush, which he used as a guide to keep on the path. He was panting and his legs ached, and he vowed that if he lived to see the morrow, he would begin regular exercising.

Suddenly something grabbed at his ankle and he was flat on his face. A hideous scream assailed him from above, and he whipped the knife from his belt and swung it blindly in a wide arc as he flipped his body over. The scream became a maniacal laughter, which all but froze his blood, and his gaze locked onto two coal-black eyes staring at him. A red-bearded monkey was peering down and seemed to be laughing at him from a tree branch. And as for his ankle, it had simply gotten caught in a vine. He felt ridiculous, yet his hand shook as he pulled his leg free. He quickly took to the path again.

In seconds he heard a crashing through the brush, unmistakably the sound of someone running, only it was coming towards him rather than from behind. His heart leapt—he must have gone in the wrong direction after he fell. He stopped short and turned, only to feel two arms clamp down on his shoulders from behind.

"Jon, why aren't you keeping up? Come on, boy, this is no time for dawdling." The captain's voice betrayed a mix of annoyance and worry.

Jonathan sucked in a breath of relief.

"Sorry, Captain. I guess I'm a little out of shape."

Balu knew a short cut, and soon all the crewmen were aboard the skiff and in deep water, well ahead of their pursuers. By the time the guards arrived at the beach, the seamen were halfway back to the ship. All laughed heartily at the antics of the furious guards as they jumped up and down and threw their spears into the sea.

Early the next morning the captain sent a crewman aloft to spy out the tree-nests of the Goona birds. He held his breath awaiting the verdict.

"They're back! They're back!" yelled the crewman from the crow's-nest.

The captain, all smiles, raised his arms to the heavens.

"Yes! By Titan's tits, we're going to trade today!"

Chapter 4

THE SKIRLA HUNT

The ship's fog horn broke the morning calm, announcing to the people of Zweg that the men of the Pelagin were coming ashore to commence trading.

Jonathan helped load the trade goods into rowboats and noticed there were construction materials going ashore—wire mesh, nails, hand tools, and various hardware—marked "not for trade." He gave the captain a questioning look, but received only a smirk by way of reply.

A group of Zwegians were gathered on the beach to greet the traders as they came ashore. The seamen were roundly cheered and showered with flowers and blessings. Jonathan was hugged and draped with a garland by a bear-sized but kindly-faced man, whom he recognized as one of the bloodthirsty guards who had chased him only hours before. Out of the stew pot into what? he wondered.

The Zwegians helped the seamen unload the boats, then formed a human caravan to cart the goods through the jungle to their village. As they trekked through the bush, they sang a merry song in an old tribal tongue, its rhythm matching their pace. Balu, who knew the trail and walked at the head of the column, the captain and Jonathan following, wore an ear-to-ear grin and tittered to himself. Seeing the captain's puzzled look, he explained.

"It's the song my brothers are singing, Captain. It tells the story of how the fish of the sea came ashore to worship the great god, Mkhat. As proof of their devotion and in their desire to please the divine one, the fish offered their lives up for his dinner by jumping into his mouth."

Jonathan laughed, though the captain only emitted a surly grunt.

"Captain," asked Jonathan, "I've been wondering. What are the Zwegian goods we'll be trading for?"

"Skirlas, lad. In exchange for soft goods, the Zwegians allow us to trap skirlas—Zwegian swamp rats."

"Uh, did you say rats, sir?"

"Aye. The rats will be our trading goods at our next port."

The skipper enjoyed his young friend's dismayed look.

"But who would want rats? And why?"

The captain chuckled. "You'll see soon enough when we reach our next port."

Jonathan squelched his annoyance. "Yes, sir. Then the tools and wire we're carrying must be…"

"To make traps and holding cages for the little monsters."

Jonathan's brow knit. "Captain, if the skirlas are valuable for trading, why not breed them yourself and avoid having to deal with the Zwegians?"

"A reasonable question. But we can't. Only the male skirlas come up out of the ground and can be caught. The females stay in their burrows beneath the swamp where the males bring them food from the surface. They live mostly off the cane stalks that grow wild in the swamps. Which is, by the way, a task you'll be helping with—to cut the stalks and cart them to the ship. We'll need it to feed the critters aboard ship."

"But aren't there rats on other islands? Why do we especially need Zwegian rats?"

"That's true, many islands have rats. But not skirlas—these little devils are one of a kind and can only be found here on Zweg. For trading, there isn't any substitute."

"What makes the skirlas so special?"

The captain took a deep breath, and Jonathan could see the skipper was running out of patience.

"For three reasons—their fur, their size, and their liking for fat. They'd rather eat fat than cane stalks, if they could get it. But that's enough questions for now. You're wearing me out. It'll all become clear soon enough."

From the corner of his eye the captain saw Jonathan's frustrated expression and smiled to himself. He loved to tease, and his new helper was so eminently teasable.

Joyous hoots filled the air as the caravan entered the village. Hundreds of Zwegians came running from their huts and crowded around the visitors in happy greeting. The tribal chief, Zwez, a rotund little man wearing a toothless smile and bright red robe, stepped forward and embraced the captain as though he were a long lost son. With much waving of arms, the chief loudly proclaimed the ship's coming to be nothing less than a blessing bestowed upon the people by the generous and all-powerful black-headed god, Mkhat. Indeed, no Zwegian seemed to remember the events of the previous night, as though Mkhat's black head had been reigning forever. But the captain knew better, and his eyes searched the jungle edge for any sign of the rebel priests of the white head.

The chief suddenly fell silent as a tall statuesque figure of somber demeanor, draped in a half black, half white robe, entered the clearing. His face was hidden beneath a hood, but his very presence cast an immediate pall over the proceedings.

"It's Imsalu," whispered the captain to Jonathan, "the tribal shaman and the chief's adviser—kind of a supernatural interpreter, priest, and seer all rolled into one. He's very powerful and feared by all, even the chief."

The priestly figure halted at a distance. The air grew tense and the silence utter. Jonathan could feel his own heart pumping. Finally the shaman's hood tilted slightly in a nod, a motion which elicited a deep sigh of relief from the chief and a cheer from the crowd. The shaman's blessing had been given. Jonathan glanced at the captain and Balu for confirmation, and when he looked back the shaman was gone. The captain made little of the drama, saying that the shaman really had little choice but to approve the seamen's presence—that is, as long as the black head of Mkhat was reigning.

If the shaman was indeed a seer, thought Jonathan, then perhaps he could shed some light on the mystery of his dream world summons. He hoped there would be an opportunity to speak with the priest alone.

Zwez, the chief, visibly relieved at the priest's departure, resumed his vocal celebration of the great god, Mkhat. Soon, however, the audience began to grow restless and the chief was obliged to bring his peroration to a close. As was the custom, the captain then presented the chief with gifts: a handsome bone-handled knife, matches and candles, a bolt of red cloth, and sundry household gadgetry, all of which pleased the chief immensely. It was now the chief's task to distribute the trade goods among his people, and they crowded around in anxious anticipation.

The captain clapped Jonathan on the back. "Now we can get to work."

The captain gave Balu orders to have the men carry the building equipment to the far end of the main clearing and begin constructing the traps and cages. Jonathan lent a hand, and as he worked he learned more about the skirlas from his shipmates.

First the men gathered fallen tree branches—the Zwegians objected to cutting healthy ones when the black head was dominant—and trimmed and nailed them together to form boxes measuring about three foot square. The frames were then covered with wire mesh, and a one-way door was fastened on the front of each that pushed in but not out. A shallow tray was placed inside each trap to hold the bait—lumps of fat that would be provided by the Zwegians.

When the traps were completed, the men began constructing the larger holding cages. Within each cage an enclosed shelter was built to house the captured rats. One of the seamen, Kik, explained that the skirlas were shy and unaccustomed to sunlight, and the enclosed shelters were necessary to simulate the darkness and privacy of their underground dwellings. With that knowledge, Jonathan went from cage to cage, hammer at the ready, to be sure that the walls of the enclosures fit tightly together and no light shone through.

The captain especially kept a sharp eye on every phase of the construction, and if the smallest detail wasn't right, he would see that it was corrected.

The apprentice cast an admiring eye at the captain for his apparent humanitarian concern toward the rats. Unfortunately, the skipper read Jonathan's look, and his face reddened. Clearing his throat, he reminded his men in a slightly huffy voice that building the shelters right was purely a matter of economics since any environmental upset to the skirlas would cause their fur to lose its texture and ruin their trading value. Jonathan knew better and suppressed a grin, not wanting to embarrass the captain further. He was sure the men knew better too.

When the building work was completed, a group of young Zwegian volunteers helped the crewmen carry the traps and cages inland to the skirla hunting grounds. The jungle was dense and humid and the trails narrow and overgrown, which made the going slow.

Jonathan, following behind Balu and the captain, more than once stumbled over vines, his eyes cast upwards rather than on the path. He was awed by the lush majesty of the jungle and fascinated by the sounds of unseen creatures in the canopy overhead. He marveled at the giant rough-barked trees that spiraled upward on tangled leg-like roots, their trunks covered with hairy moss and exotic flowering creepers, and the massive broad-leafed plants, like great umbrellas, mottled with patches of sunlight that peeked through the ceiling of green. When bird song filled the air, the Zwegians imitated it in perfect counterpoint, their sonorous melody overlaid by the occasional raucous cry of an unseen parrot or the hoot of a Goona bird.

In little more than an hour's time the party arrived at the swamp, a vast low-lying area dotted with weedy tufts and saw-toothed rushes, and smelling of decay. Jonathan saw that on the edges of the swamp grew dense stands of wild cane stalks, the main diet of the skirlas. Pockmarking the banks just above the water line were numerous round foot-wide holes—the entrances to the skirlas' underground burrows.

The captain divided the company into two working teams. Jonathan, Balu, and Tabber joined the group cutting and gathering the stalks, while the captain, Zyl, and the remaining crewmen busied themselves setting the traps.

Jonathan's shirt was soaked with sweat and his muscles complained at the hard work of harvesting the stalks. But he endured it gladly, happy to be part of a team performing a useful task. How strange, he thought, that back on Earth he had been shy of others and preferred to work alone, while here it was quite the opposite.

As he heaved yet another bundle of stalks onto the growing pile, he felt a call of nature and looked around for a place to make reply. In the nearby forest he spotted a growth of tall ferns which he thought would do nicely.

Having satisfied his need, he was about to return to his labors when an unusual odor assailed him. It was subtle and sweet and strangely enticing. He looked around for its source—doubtless it was a flower of some kind—but there were no blooming plants in sight. Curious, he walked a little further into the jungle, and as he did so the fragrance became stronger. He inhaled deeply of its perfume. How utterly delightful, he thought. Surely there would be no harm in hunting for it just a little longer.

The fragrance was elusive, and he followed it here, then there, in a zigzag pattern through the brush. Finally, coming upon a small hollow, he stopped. There before him was the arboreal owner of the intoxicating perfume: a giant flowering plant, the height of a tall man and lovely to behold. He gazed transfixed upon the titan bloom, so unlike anything he had ever seen or imagined, and he wondered if it might be an apparition.

Sinuously it rose out of the dark jungle soil on a spiral emerald-green stem affluent with slender upward-bending leaves, shiny and smooth, all pointing to a magnificent solitary yellow blossom. He breathed deeply of its scent. How heavenly. His thoughts began to swim; his head seemed to empty itself, then refill with swirling colors. The shining yellow face and finger-like petals ever beckoned to him, commanding his attention. How could he not yield to such enticing beauty? How could such loveliness and the pleasure it promised be refused?

He stepped closer to the open bloom. How light and carefree he felt. He laughed. Nothing in the world seemed to matter except the wonderful flower. Oh, how he longed to embrace it, to rest his head upon its soft leafy bosom.

Overcome with joy, he closed his eyes and the sweet fragrance seemed to enter his very being, lulling his mind as it searched and sifted among long-forgotten memories. Scenes from his past flashed through his brain like pictures in a dream.

He was a child in grade school in winter, clapping erasers in the school yard as punishment for wearing old and dirty shoes to class, which were all his poor parents could afford. Before dismissing him the teacher rubbed his freezing hands and placed them between her soft breasts to warm them. How good it felt and how much he adored her.

It was the time of his high school prom. He couldn't get a date and his mother embarrassed him by asking a neighbor's daughter who was older than him. And when the girl danced with him, she pressed her breasts tightly against him and, later, when they were alone, took off her clothes and undressed him and revealed to him the sweet mysteries of love.

The beautiful flower knew all, for was it not the mistress of love? Yes, it would give him back all the sweet moments of his childhood, and promised yet more glorious pleasures within its soft embrace.

Balu unloaded an armful of stalks and looked around to see how Jonathan was faring. Not seeing him, he asked one the Zwegian workers, who pointed toward the clump of ferns where he thought he saw the young man heading a while earlier.

But Jonathan was not there. Balu muttered a host of ungodly curses as he searched through the jungle for his friend. Fortunately he was a skilled tracker and soon found the spoor. An all too familiar fragrance reached him, and his expression changed from one of worry to fear. Hastily he tore two small pieces of cloth from the leg of his trousers and stuffed them into his nostrils. Resuming the search, from time to time loosening one of the bits of cloth to be sure he was on the right track, he soon came upon the hollow and his lost shipmate.

The sight that greeted his eyes confirmed his worst fears. Jonathan was locked in the embrace of a giant flowering plant, his head resting on its broad yellow blossom, a look of blissful stupor on his face.

Balu sprang forward. Grasping the plant's long clinging leaves, he tore them from his friend's body, one by one, his hands burning from the acid-like liquid they exuded. Sharp needle-like spikes shot out from the main stem into his arms, and a gas ejected from the flower head all but blinded him. Slowly, exerting all his great strength, he pulled his friend free of the growth. Then lifting the limp body in his arms, he carried it a safe distance and set it gently down against the trunk of a tree.

As fresh air filled his lungs, Jonathan gradually came to. He blinked and saw he was looking up into his friend Balu's face. In a flash he remembered what had happened. He blushed and his expression turned sheepish.

"Are you all right, Jon?" asked Balu.

"Yes. I'm fine now. Thank you for saving me. Are you hurt?"

"No, just a few pricks. I'm fine."

"I feel pretty stupid."

"Don't. Many brave men have been tempted by the evil Eeroz plant and have died in its embrace."

"Died? How? What kind of plant is it, Balu?"

"It's a love plant. Some call it the Deadly Lady. It probes men's weaknesses, seduces their minds, and lures them to their death. If you're suicidal, there's no better way to go."

"Strange that something so beautiful kills people."

"No, not people, only men. Somehow it doesn't affect women. The women of the village pluck its petals for perfume and walk away unharmed. But if you were to look among the flower's roots, you would find the bones of many men."

As they made their way back to the swamp area, Jonathan asked Balu a favor.

"Please don't tell the captain or the men about what happened. It's so embarrassing."

"Very well, I won't. If anyone asks where we were I'll say we went to investigate a suspicious noise in the bush, but it turned out to be a false alarm—just a pair of cooing love birds."

They both laughed.

By late afternoon the traps had been set and baited and the stalks gathered and tied into bundles. The traps would be left overnight, since the skirlas were nocturnal creatures, emerging only after dark. On the trek back to the village, everyone carried a bundle of stalks on their back. The crewmen sang bawdy songs of the sea and the Zwegians sang native ditties to the entertainment of all.

Upon arriving at the main village clearing Jonathan saw that his hosts had set out a generous outdoor spread for the weary mariners. It was his first gourmet picnic, which he enjoyed immensely, bravely tasting of dishes he didn't have the courage to ask about. That night he shared a hut with Tabber and slept as sound as a rock.

In the morning, after a bath in a nearby spring and a breakfast of fruits and coconut milk, he joined the assembled retinue returning to the swamps. The captain was unusually reticent and wore a tense expectant expression.

Upon arriving at the hunting site, to the delight of all, they found that every trap contained one or more skirlas. Hopping from trap to trap, Jonathan was intrigued with the strange looking creatures. Each measured the span of two open hands and was covered with bristly golden-brown fur. Their round stubby faces and sad dark eyes gave them a cherubic look, although when they opened their mouths their sharp chisel-like teeth gave quite a different impression. The captain came along as Jonathan was peering into one of the traps, his mood now quite cheery.

"What do you think of our trade goods, lad?" he asked.

"They're certainly odd looking—but kind of cute. And they seem friendly enough."

"Oh, they're quite docile. Some Zwegians keep them as pets. Unfortunately, the little beggars don't live long. Their natural life span is only a few years. Which is why we periodically return to Zweg, to replenish the supply for our buyers."

Jonathan stuck his forefinger through the mesh and stroked the head one of the creatures.

"They feel like brushes!"

"And it's important they continue to feel that way," offered the captain. "Otherwise our voyage would be for naught."

Jonathan was about to regale the captain with questions again, but didn't get beyond "why" before the skipper cut him off.

"Jon, I can see that you like the little devils. How would you like the assignment of caring for them, starting right now? It's a big responsibility since the skirlas are important to us, and to others as well."

Jonathan brightened and came to rapt attention. "Oh, I'd like that very much, sir." Then his voice became hesitant. "But I need to know one thing first. After we trade the skirlas, they won't be hurt or killed, will they?"

The captain let out a hearty guffaw. "No, lad, that's one thing I can promise you. The little beasties will think they're in paradise."

That remark only made Jonathan all the more curious, but before he could probe further, Balu approached.

"Good news, Captain," reported the chief mate. "Our total catch numbers eighty-one skirlas—a one-day record."

"Aha! Good news indeed," exclaimed the captain. "If we continue to be this lucky it'll take us only three days to trap the two hundred we need. Then we're off, and Mkhat's dancing heads be damned."

"Captain," asked Jonathan, "what will be our next..."

"Celeucia, lad. Our next port will be the great Isle of Celeucia. Now you best get busy looking to the welfare of your new charges. They need to be transferred to cages and taken back to the village. Handle them gently. When you pick them up, use both hands. And see that the men don't jostle them too much on the way back."

Once back at the village, Jonathan picked out a shady spot on the periphery of the central clearing to stack the skirla holding cages. The spot was quiet and out of the bustle of traffic, and the overhanging palms would shield the little animals from direct sunlight. Declining an offer of help from Tabber, he personally carried each skirla to a holding cage, distributing them evenly to avoid overcrowding. A few of them were nervous or agitated, and he petted and talked to them softly in an effort to calm them. No sooner did he place them in a cage than they scurried into the darkness of the shelter within.

For their food, at Balu's direction, he put three lengths of cane stalk in each cage, then filled their water containers. A Zwegian boy, anxious to assist, brought him a bucket of beach sand for litter, and Jonathan let him sprinkle some in each cage to the youngster's delight.

At day's end Jonathan felt quite pleased with himself and at dinner indulged in a cup of Zwegian fruit liquor. No voice rose louder than his as the sailors sat around an open fire singing songs of the sea. Balu accompanied them on the Zote, a native guitar, which to the lightheaded apprentice was like the harp of an angel.

Jonathan blinked up at the great idol, Mkhat, looming silently over the fest, its sunken eyes unmoving, an enigmatic smile upon its face. He thought this would be a terrible time for Mkhat to change heads, though he felt somewhat reassured upon counting a complement of fifteen guards surrounding the rotund deity. He wondered about the village shaman, Imsalu, and where he might be. Perhaps he should seek him out: he had many questions. No, he decided. He was tired and his wits were slightly blunted. This wasn't the best time for something so important.

The next two days went swiftly, and before the twin suns met the horizon on the second day, Jonathan counted two hundred and ten healthy skirlas in the holding cages.

"Excellent job, Jon lad," chirruped the captain as he patted his skirla keeper on the back. "Not a ratty looking critter in the crowd. Tomorrow we'll load the cages on board and, weather willing, the morning after we'll set sail. But tomorrow night, I'm afraid, we'll have to endure chief Zwez's usual going-away party. The food and drink are fine. It's Zwez's infernal after-dinner speeches that are hard to swallow. A word to the wise, lad—make that an order—stay away from the chief's special brand of firewater or you'll be wearing a head the size of Mkhat's for days."

Next morning Jonathan was up early to check the skirla cages to be sure the carrying poles were securely tied on with strong vines. The captain and Balu then organized the men into a caravan, two to a cage, for the trek through the jungle to the sea. Along the trail Jonathan scurried up and down the line, keeping a sharp eye on his little charges, ignoring the playful razzing from his shipmates. As he trotted to and fro, Kik would yell, "Watch out, here comes mother rat," which evoked merry laughter. But his watchfulness was not wasted: when one of the native bearers tripped on a root and fell, he made a flying leap just in time to catch a toppling skirla cage before it crashed to the ground. After that the men ceased their teasing.

Soon enough the column and its precious burden arrived safely at the beach. The carrying poles were dismantled, and Balu joined Jonathan in seeing that the cages were carefully loaded aboard rowboats for their short journey to the ship. Once the transfer was completed, the cages were stacked on deck amidships beneath a protective canopy Jonathan had rigged up from an old piece of sail.

He talked quietly and soothingly to the skirlas as he scrubbed and scraped each of the cages and replenished them with fresh food and water. The furry creatures tickled his fingers with their soft damp noses as he eased them from one spot to another in order to clean every nook and cranny. He couldn't help liking them, though he tried not to think of them as pets. "You're nothing but trade goods," he whispered affectionately to a fat rabbit-faced skirla who nuzzled his hand. He was opposed to uprooting wildlife from their native habitat, and he hoped the captain wasn't joking when he said the rats were going to a better place.

By the time his work was done it was nearly time for chief Zwez's farewell party. The captain called to him to join the rest of the crew, who were gathering on the main deck. When all hands were assembled, the captain summoned up his most intimidating expression and proceeded to deliver a stern lecture on the virtues of temperance, threatening dire punishment to any crewman who failed to return to the ship by midnight on his own two feet. The men only offered blank faces by way of reply, and upon being dismissed they dashed en mass to the deck ladders, piled boisterously into rowboats, and headed hell-bent for shore.

Jonathan got into a boat with Balu, Tabber, and three deck hands, and as they rowed shoreward, he overheard two of the men snickering and whispering something about Zwegian virgins. Balu, spying his young friend's curious expression, put on his trademark grin and explained that on the occasion of a chief's party it was the Zwegian custom to relax certain social formalities, including the usual restraints on the young women of the tribe. Jonathan's eyes brightened, though still were questioning.

"Well," continued Balu in a quieter more serious voice, "let me put it this way. Tonight the single ladies of the tribe will be allowed to express their appreciation to their seafaring guests—us—in sundry special and delightful ways."

As Jonathan's expression metamorphosed into a smile of enlightenment, Balu's grin reappeared wider than ever and they both laughed. The crewmen joined in. Even Tabber wore a happy smile, a phenomenon rarely witnessed by any of the crew.

The village was brightly lit with torches, and it seemed to Jonathan that the whole island population had turned out for the celebration. Chief Zwez invited the captain and his men to sit by him, whereupon, without further ado, a lively entertainment of music and dancing commenced as scantily clad maidens paraded out heaping platters of exotic foods for all to enjoy.

As he munched on a succulent fruit the Zwegians called Sarkut, which tasted like a mixture of pineapple and muskmelon, Jonathan noticed that Nynt the cook, sitting nearby, was fretting and grumbling, apparently about the food. As offerings were passed, the little man stubbornly refused to partake of any dish, muttering something about not eating any cooking but his own and complaining that the crewmen never exhibited such pleasure when eating at the ship's table. Jonathan worried that the cook might say or do something rash and spoil the party. But when a jug of native brew was proffered, Nynt had a sudden change of heart and soon got into the spirit of things.

At a sign from the chief a group of village maidens clad in colorful frocks and bedecked with garlands performed an erotic dance, during which they cast coquettish glances at their cheering guests. Balu, seated next to Jonathan, whispered to his young friend that it was an ancient Zwegian fertility dance being performed specially for the occasion. A particularly comely young maid danced over to where Jonathan was sitting and cast an enticing smile at him, and he resolved to approach her after the dance. But an unexpected distraction changed his plans.

At the perimeter of the village clearing he spotted the lone figure of Imsalu the Shaman hovering in the shadows. No one else seemed to notice the priest. This was the chance he had hoped for.

Quietly withdrawing from the festivities, he made his way around the edge of the clearing. At a far corner, in the dim shadow of an outlying hut, he suddenly came face to face with the berobed figure of the shaman. The priest peered into his eyes as though to read his thoughts, then bowed solemnly and gestured for him to enter the hut. He complied without question, and the shaman followed behind.

The hut was dimly lit by a flickering oil lamp on a low reed table and smelled of fish. The only other furnishings were a trunk in the corner and a woven floor mat. But it was the walls of the hut that drew Jonathan's attention: they were hung with hundreds of miniature wooden carvings of the god, Mkhat. Each statue was an exact likeness of the original except that all the heads were half white and half black, vertically divided in the same pattern as the shaman's robe.

Imsalu seated himself cross-legged on the floor and gestured for Jonathan to sit across from him. The shaman's face was half hidden by shadow and thus unrevealing of its sentiment. The priest spoke, his voice somber and monotonic.

"Welcome, O keeper of the skirlas. I have sensed your desire to speak with me and have consented only because of your great accomplishment."

Jonathan looked surprised. "My accomplishment?"

"Was it not you who was responsible for defeating the white head of Mkhat and raising up the black in its place?"

"Well, I only had an idea."

"You are modest. A becoming quality, though sometimes out of place. But I see that your heart is troubled, and you have questions of me. Ask."

Jonathan hesitated, not quite prepared for the shaman's sophistication and directness. "I...I had a strange dream, and I wonder if you might be able to interpret it for me."

"Ask."

"Yes. Well, in my dream I felt I was being mysteriously beckoned by something or someone, and in answer to the call I traveled to another world. But in the new world the caller still eluded me. That's kind of a quick summary, and I'm curious to know what it means."

"Did you sense danger when you felt the call?" asked the shaman.

"Yes, I think I did."

The priest was silent for a moment. "Your dream is of great significance, that much I am sure. It portends something important. But I am unable tell you its meaning. For that you must consult a dream reader."

"A dream reader?"

"Yes, one with the power to fathom the hidden meaning in dreams. Few possess such power, but I have heard of a reader who dwells on one of the islands to the north. Seek him there."

"I thank you for that information, O Imsalu. But is there nothing more you can tell me?"

"No—unless the spirit of the great god, Mkhat, knows something. Would you like me to ask him?"

"Uh...sure."

"Very well. But you must not move or speak while I summon him."

Imsalu reached into the shadows behind him and brought forth a small wooden box from which he took a bit of charcoal and a dried leaf. With the charcoal he made two vertical stripes on his brow and cheeks; the leaf he placed on his tongue. He then closed his eyes and began swaying slowly from side to side. Gradually his breathing became labored and his body began to twitch spasmodically.

The shaman's face lifted upward out of the shadows, revealing a transformed visage of indeterminate age. Its deathly pallor and remoteness brought beads of perspiration to Jonathan's brow. The priest emitted a low moan, as though in pain, and suddenly a look of utter horror appeared on his face. His breathing ceased as though sucked from his body, and he became rigid as a statue.

"Imsalu, are you all right?" cried Jonathan in alarm.

The shaman's body trembled and sucked in air in a rush. His eyes snapped wide open and his hands jerked upwards, clutching at his face like claws, raking his flesh in bloody furrows. Then he emitted a bone-chilling scream, leapt up, and ran from the hut screeching like a madman.

Jonathan, momentarily frozen with fear, jumped up and dashed outside. He could hear Imsalu's screams somewhere in the distance. But he could not make out the priest's demented ravings, his cries of "She! She! The Destroyer! Greater than Mkhat!"

Time to retreat, Jonathan decided. Heart aflutter, he made his way through the trees around the edge of the village clearing with the intention of finding the captain and telling him what had happened. That's when he bumped smack into the skipper.

"Captain! I was just coming to find you. It's the..."

"Never mind that now, lad." The captain was breathing hard and his tone was urgent. "We're in big trouble. Mkhat is wearing his white head again. The switch was made during the festivities. The word's out and our lives won't be worth two barnacles unless we get back to the ship before we're caught. Every native on the island is now a cannibal after our hides. Except Balu, of course. The crew scattered so we're on our own. So let's go. Stay close to me."

Ducking low and keeping to the dense foliage, Jonathan followed the captain around the perimeter of the village. Through the trees they could see Zwegian warriors running every which way and yelling, spears aloft.

"Jon," whispered the captain. "Look for the same path we took when we hightailed it to the beach a few nights ago. It's around here some-where."

A spear thudded into a tree inches from the captain's head.

"We've been spotted, lad!" cried the skipper. "We'll have to risk it and cut across the clearing. Let's go!"

The captain, Jonathan at his heels, tore through the brush into the open. Not fifty yards in front of them stood the squat figure of Mkhat surrounded by a dozen priestly guards of the white head. Luckily, the guards were all looking the other way, and the fleeing twosome quickly saw why. Huddled in a knot at the opposite end of the clearing were a dozen priests of the black head shaking their fists in the air, making every effort to work themselves into a frenzy and gather enough courage to rush upon their white-robed enemies.

One of the black-robed priests picked up a stone and flung it at the guards, but the throw was wide of the mark. As the stone rolled harmlessly past the idol, one of the white-robed priests turned to retrieve it, and in doing so spotted the two fugitives running through the clearing. The priest let out an infuriated cry of alarm, and the heads of his cohorts swung about as one. Jonathan gulped, even as the captain reached down and scooped up the stone the black-robed priest had thrown. The skipper hurled it mightily into the air. Upward it rose in a gracefully rising arc. To Jonathan it seemed to move in slow motion, almost hovering midair at its zenith. But soon enough it reached its destination, square in the center of Mkhat's glowering white head.

Down toppled the idol's head amidst the anguished cries of the guards, even as a chorus of cheers erupted from the watching priests of the black head. Near panic ensued. Mkhat's fallen white head rolled down the clearing towards the enemy, its guardians in frantic pursuit from one direction and the insurgents from the other. Jonathan saw that foremost among the scurrying champions of the black head was Isko, clutching Mkhat's smiling black head tightly in his arms.

"Now's our chance!" yelled the captain. "The beheading has got everybody on the run. There's the path. Come on, lad, run for it!"

As the captain and Jonathan raced through the jungle towards the beach, they saw Balu and some of the crewmen running in the same direction. They joined up at the beach where two of the Pelagin's rowboats were in the water waiting for them. The men aboard hailed their shipmates as the captain made a quick head count. To his relief all hands had made it back safely, which he deemed a near miracle since not a few of the men were thoroughly besotted.

"Quickly, everybody into the boats," ordered the captain. "They'll be on us any minute."

"Maybe not," said Jonathan. "Maybe Isko and his friends managed to put the black head back on Mkhat."

"I don't think so, lad. Look there."

The captain pointed toward the horizon. Against the dim night sky Jonathan saw a flock of birds heading out to sea.

"It's the Goona birds. I guess you're right, Captain. Maybe we should just steal Mkhat's white head and give it a permanent burial at sea."

"Won't do any good," chimed in Balu. "The priests have lots of spares."

By the time the boats reached the Pelagin a large contingent of Zwegians had gathered on the shore shouting and capering.

"Why don't they swim after us?" asked Jonathan.

"Oh, they won't do that," Balu explained. "When Mkhat wears his white head, the people are afraid of the water. But when he wears his black head, they swim like fish."

Jonathan and the captain laughed, though Balu didn't see what was funny.

"Sir, will we be returning to Zweg again?" Jonathan asked.

"Certainly, when more skirlas are needed. Without the skirlas a very old civilization would soon die out. But you'll learn more about that at our next port."

The men gathered together on deck and merrily exchanged stories about their narrow escape, though Tabber, the ex-priest, shook his head in utter disgust at the blatant exaggerations. But when the crewmen bemoaned the brevity of the Zwegian feast and its lost delights, Tabber nodded in agreement, and indeed, he seemed more vexed than the others.

Jonathan told the men about the captain's good aim with a rock, which drew a resounding chorus of cheers.

"Where did you learn to throw like that, Captain, and on the run?" asked Balu.

"A lucky toss," the captain replied. "But as a youngster I wasn't bad at bopping top hats at fifty paces."

Tabber raised his hand and sniffed at the air.

"Captain, there's an offshore wind coming up."

The captain pondered a moment. "It's getting dark, but Baal's balls, let's go with it anyway. The sooner we're away from this devil-cursed island the better. Tabber, we'll need your night vision to guide us. To your stations, men!"

Later, as he lay alone in his bunk, rocked by the swelling tide, Jonathan reflected on the events of the day, especially the strange behavior of Imsalu. He wondered what the priest had seen in his trance that had so terrified him. But his visit had not been fruitless—he had learned about dream readers. And the ship was heading north where the shaman said one might be found. He wondered, too, if he should tell the captain about himself and his dream journey. He trusted his friend and would like to have someone to confide in. But he remembered the old dream sender's warning to keep his own counsel. He sighed, feeling very much alone.

Chapter 5

CELEUCIA

In the days that followed, Jonathan spent nearly all his waking hours looking after the skirlas. Their habits became familiar to him, and he indulged their preferences in every little way. Though his shipmates took to teasing him again for his motherly attentiveness, his affection for the animals was catching, and he pretended not to notice whenever a crewman stole up to a cage and quietly popped in a tidbit.

It was on the third morning out of Zweg, while he was cleaning the skirla cages, that he noticed something odd. It was the habit of the skirlas to stay inside their enclosed shelters during the day to avoid the sunlight, and to venture out only at night to eat and drink. But today Jonathan saw that in one of the cages the rats were outside their shelter huddled in a corner. He counted seven quivering noses in the big furball they formed, and since the cage housed eight skirlas, he knew that one must be in the shelter. Thinking that the eighth rat might be sick or dead and the others were avoiding it, he reached into the cage and lifted the hinged roof of the shelter to look inside. His jaw dropped at the scene that met his eyes.

There, crouched within the shelter, was indeed the eighth skirla, and half hidden beneath its fur were two tiny newborn babies, naked and pink. The mother skirla looked up at her keeper with large doleful eyes, then protectingly nudged the babies closer to her, prompting one of the little ones to let out a plaintive squeak.

Jonathan stared blankly at the new family, but when he saw the mother rat blinking uncomfortably at the intruding sunlight, he quickly lowered the shelter lid. He then transferred the seven homeless males—doubtlessly evicted by the mother skirla—to an empty cage and wondered which one of them might be the father. But none seemed to betray any sign of paternal nervousness or anxiety.

Bursting with excitement, he scrambled off to tell the captain of the happy event.

"What?" The captain's eyes widened and his mouth became a circle. "You wouldn't be playing a joke on me, would you, Jon lad?"

"No, sir. I swear."

"Well let's go have a look."

Jonathan held the shelter lid open, positioning himself so that his body blocked out the suns' glare, as the captain gaped in amazement at the mother skirla and her babies. An audience quickly assembled, and oohs and ahs tumbled out of the mouths of the roughest of the crewmen.

"Gentlemen," said the captain in a voice tinged with solemnity and awe, "we are looking upon a sight never before beheld by mortal man—a female skirla."

There was a moment of reverent silence during which one of the babies squeaked. Jonathan beamed as though he himself were the proud father.

"It talked!" exclaimed the captain. "I mean squeaked. But skirlas are mute. They can't make any sound—that's an established fact. Unless… unless the females can, and one of the babies is a female."

"Or," added Jonathan, "maybe they only make noises when they're born, but lose their voices when they get older."

The captain frowned at having his hypothesis muddied.

The babies began to suckle and one of them gave its mother a firm poke, which elicited a squeaky maternal complaint.

"Hah!" cried the captain. "The females do talk—I mean, have voices. By the good graces of the twenty gods of Llagin, we may have *two* females on our hands. Men, a fortune is ours!"

A cheer rose up. Jonathan, worried that the ruckus would disturb the skirla family, not to mention his other charges, closed the shelter lid and waved off the crewmen, addressing them in a firm tone.

"They need quiet and privacy, not a commotion. The peep show is over."

"Back to your duties, men," ordered the captain, smiling at his skirla keeper's commanding voice. "We can rely on Jon, here, to look after our treasure for us. In three days we'll reach port. And a golden day it'll be for us. And a historic one for Celeucia."

A question gnawed at Jonathan. "Captain Othin, I think it's about time you told me what's going to happen to the skirlas."

The captain's eyebrows rose, not only because of his helper's demanding tone, but also because none of his men ever called him by his surname.

"Well, if you put it that way I guess I'll have to. Come on, let's go to my cabin. I was going to fill you in anyway when we reached port."

In his cabin the captain unrolled a large map and showed Jonathan the location of the island of Celeucia.

"There she is, one of the great isles—ten times the size of Zuralia. It's a country that's rich in nature's bounties and supports an affluent society where all material wants are provided for. Before you can understand about the skirlas, you need to know a few things about the people.

"The Celeucians are an ancient race and have a highly developed culture. They're happy and carefree and live an unrestrained, almost libertarian, lifestyle, which makes it a popular port with the crew. The people have a nominal ruler, called the Tsarl. The present Tsarl is a kindly old fellow, Orl by name, a widower who inherited the throne from his former wife, the Tsarla, Myn. Orl is popular among the people mainly because of his active disinterest in ruling, which nobody wants or needs anyway.

"The number two man is the Temprate. He's supposed to oversee the problem of abundance—sees to it that the absence of want doesn't corrupt the people—that they don't overindulge themselves. Now don't smirk, Jon, unless you've had the pleasure of wrestling with that problem yourself."

They both laughed.

"Anyway, the Temprate goes around preaching social moderation and the evils of excess, which everybody pretty much ignores. The present holder of that mighty office, as I recall, is one, Droxt, a humorless stick of a man whom we would both do well to avoid."

"Captain, the skirlas."

"Be patient, lad, I'm getting to that. The skirlas are needed by the Celeucians for the Hhor—short for Hhorelembus. The Hhor is as ancient as Celeucia itself, and is the primal life source of the island. Hhor is a creature, a sentient living being, that is one of the marvels of the island world. It is a highly intelligent, beneficent, powerful being beloved by all the people. Indeed, the Hhor is the working source of all energy on the island and makes possible the leisurely and artistic life style the Celeucians enjoy.

"The Hhor is a creature as large as the island of Celeucia itself. It lives in a stationary state deep beneath the soil and has tenticle-like appendages that extend to every part of the island. In certain places on the island its great arms break the surface and can be seen and touched. It is by touch that the Hhor mentally communicates with the Celeucians. The central system of the Hhor's body, which extends throughout its miles of appendages, is hollow, and it is through these hollow passages that the Hhor breathes. But the Hhor has a problem. Possibly because of it's great age, these passages have been gradually clogging up with a fatty excretion from its body, which must be cleared away. Otherwise the Hhor will die and the Celeucian civilization with it.

"That's where the skirlas come in. They live inside the Hhor where they scrape away and consume the excess fat. Don't look so shocked and disgusted. Believe me, the rats never had it so good. You know they thrive on fat, and they're just the right size to fit into the Hhor's passages. As they pass through the Hhor's body channels, their bristly fur scrapes against the passage walls, keeping them open and clean. In the process they get enough fat to live like kings—more like gourmets—for life. The Hhor's interior is dark, just like the skirla's natural environment, and it generously caters to its tenants every whim, including producing water for them and even absorbing their waste. The Hhor's body contains many cavities where the skirlas can rest, play, and do whatever skirlas do. Jon, your little friends will lead a happy life, I promise you."

The captain could see that Jonathan's skepticism was waning.

"There's been only one drawback," the captain went on. "The little fellows have had to live as bachelors, without any female companionship. But sex isn't everything, right?"

The captain saw that his attempt at humor failed miserably. Indeed, Jonathan's half-convinced expression retrogressed noticeably.

"But don't worry, Jon. That's no longer a problem because now we have a female, maybe two. The little beasties can go at it. They'll multiply like rats! Soon there will be plenty of females and sex all over the place."

At that, Jonathan's facade cracked into a smile. Encouraged, the captain became animated.

"Before you know it the critters will be setting up house and raising families just like back on Zweg. Why there's even proof they like their new home. The Celeucians will tell you that whenever one of the fur balls living within the Hhor happens on one of the open-ended appendages, even at night, it turns right around and heads straight back to the larder. Like I said, the Hhor knows who its little doctors are and takes good care of them."

Jonathan nodded. He believed his friend and uttered a sigh of relief.

"Well, lad, that's the long and short of it. I would guess there are three hundred or so skirlas now living in the Hhor, and the ones we'll add will guarantee it a healthy life for a while. And as the females multiply and the skirla population becomes self-sustaining, I expect we won't have to make any more deliveries. The men won't like that, but my guess is that the payment for the female will more than make up for it. Hmm. I hope the Hhor is a pro-natalist."

The captain chuckled at his own joke, though Jonathan looked a little concerned.

"Jon, since it was you who discovered the mother skirla, and she being so special, I think it's only right that you should name her. So, what should we call her?"

"I think you've already named her, sir. You called her our good fortune. So we'll name her Fortuna."

"Fortuna it is, then."

Next morning Jonathan was up in time to see the double suns peer over the horizon and spill their yellow over the dark waters. He looked in on the mother skirla and her babies and was pleased to see them doing well. He gently rubbed the mother rat behind the ears, but the message in her toothy look was only too clear, and he quickly withdrew his hand. Motherly protectiveness, he decided.

At that moment Nynt, the cook, happened by, wearing his usual scowl, and peered into the skirla nursery.

"They'd make a tasty morsel for the stew, they would," he blathered. "Though the little ones would barely make a mouthful."

Jonathan glared at the little cook, who felt quite safe in spouting his heresy before the young keeper. But unfortunately for Nynt, two less scrupulous crewmen standing nearby overheard his remark. They were on him in a flash. Nynt howled at the top of his lungs under the thrashing, which Jonathan saw was being only lightly administered. Thanks to the cook's small size he managed to squirm between his antagonist's legs and beat a hasty retreat back to the galley. Jonathan never particularly liked Nynt, but now his dislike was unequivocal.

The time passed all too quickly for the busy keeper of the rats, and so he was taken quite by surprise when one morning he heard a cry ring out from the crows-nest: "Land ho! Off the leeward bow!" He ran to the rail and searched the horizon until, between the rolling waves, he spotted a tiny green dot: the island of Celeucia. He tingled with excitement, the wind burning his cheeks, as the distant green dot gradually grew larger.

The breadth of the sea soon receded, and the land rose up large before him: an emerald-green jewel studded with pearly beaches set in a sparkling blue broach of sky and water. His eyes ran along the meandering shoreline dotted with tall palms that swayed and bowed to the land in graceful curtsies, traversed the white shimmering stretches of wave-kissed sand, leapt up to the undulant hills beyond, which were stacked one upon the other like rows of humpbacked green giants, and higher, up to a broad sun-limned plateau scored with cascading waterfalls.

As the Pelagin rounded the tip of a crescent bay, the ancient terraced city came into view. Jonathan's heart swelled as he gazed upon the glistening white capital, its great marble buildings sweeping upward from the sea like a toy fairyland. Rows of sculpted columns lined the broad boulevards, stone stairways, and tessellated thoroughfares, all overlooked by botanical parks and gleaming palisades; and midmost, upon a broad promontory, a circular multi-tiered coliseum cast its giant shadow to the foot of the glimmering sea. Yet further, upon the northern cliff side apart from the city, loomed an ivory-white palace trimmed in alabaster and gilt, its resplendent double-tuliped domes a radiant challenge to the twin suns overhead, which Jonathan guessed could only be the house of the Tsarl.

As the ship pulled into dock, a cheering throng of Celeucians crowded around and threw flowers and streamers. Jonathan saw that the people were vibrant and handsome to look upon. All wore brightly colored toga-like costumes, which hung to just below their knees, and fabric sandals upon their feet. A small procession parted the crowd and made its way to the dock.

The ship made fast, the captain ordered the gangplank lowered and asked Jonathan to accompany him dockside to greet the approaching dignitaries. From the captain's earlier descriptions, Jonathan had no trouble recognizing the two officials leading the train: Orl, the Tsarl, and Droxt, the Temprate.

The Tsarl, all smiles, warmly embraced the captain, at least as much as his pudgy middle would permit. The wispy Temprate, however, simply bowed without a word or smile.

The captain introduced Jonathan as the official keeper of the skirlas, which clearly impressed the Celeucians, and they welcomed him with great dignity. When the introductions were completed, the captain gave the order for the skirla cages to be unloaded, which set off much excited conversation among the assembled group. The crew carried the cages to the dock amidst the applause of the citizenry, and it was hardly a surprise to Jonathan when he saw that one particular cage had been left on board.

The old Tsarl, all aflutter, bustled from one cage to another, whispering and cooing into each one, even though the furry occupants were huddled in their shelters hidden from view. The skirlas were then turned over to the Celeucians, and Jonathan watched with some misgivings as a cadre of trained skirla handlers, called Zheks, transferred the cages onto carts for transportation to temporary holding quarters.

The ebullient Tsarl issued an invitation to the captain and his men to attend the traditional dinner honoring the arrival of the skirlas to be held at the palace that evening. The captain, on behalf of himself and his crew, graciously accepted, whereupon the Tsarl and his entourage took their leave. The assembly of Celeucian citizens also dispersed, save for a handful of lovely young ladies who lingered at dockside waiting for the captain to dismiss the crew. The captain teased his men by delaying a few minutes before announcing liberty, enjoying their impatient expressions and foot-shuffling. When finally he granted leave, the crewmen made a mad dash, and pairings occurred with such rapidity that the dock was all but emptied within minutes.

"Well, Jon," said the captain with a wink, "I don't think we'll be seeing many of the men at the Tsarl's dinner tonight. But I'll expect to see you there. It'll be a night to remember, I promise you."

A lone woman walked onto the dock, tall and buxom with long brown tresses and hooded eyes. Jonathan noticed her immediately. She possessed a proud stature and mature beauty that bespoke dignity and inner assurance, which he found intriguing. She smiled in his direction. Gathering up his courage, he was about to excuse himself from the captain to try his luck, when the captain's voice rang out: "Ahoy, Lora! I'll be right with you."

"She's an old friend, Jon," the captain explained. "We met on my last voyage. So if you'll excuse me now, I'll be off. You won't have any trouble finding female company on the island, so have a merry time. I'll meet you back on board just before sundown and we'll go to the palace together."

Envy nibbled at the young apprentice as he watched the skipper slip his arm around the lady's waist and buss her smartly on the lips before they disappeared around the corner of the dock. He sighed and decided he would walk around the city awhile and be glad for any adventure that fate might care to offer. But then, remembering the mother skirla and her young ones still on board, he thought he had better check on them first before wandering off.

"Well, Fortuna," he said, as he peered into the mother's shelter, "stuffing the twins again, I see. They're growing fast, and starting to sprout hairs too. In fact I'd say your babies look big enough now to be picked up. If I'm very careful, do you promise not to bite me? I know that male skirlas don't bite, and you don't want the men to have anything on a clever lady like you, do you? Well, here goes. Ah, that's it. Now easy, little ones, I won't hurt you. Well I'll be! Fortuna, I do believe you've got two daughters here. Wait till the skipper hears about this."

After a little cuddling and fondling, Jonathan replaced the babies and decided he had better clean the cage, change the water, and restock the food container before leaving. Since Nynt the cook wasn't aboard, he went to the ship's galley and stole a bit of fat as a treat for the mother skira. By the time his self-appointed tasks were completed it was too late to take a sight-seeing trip, so he remained aboard and read one of the captain's books instead. He chose a book on island geography in the hope he might discover something that would help illuminate his dream quest.

Later, when the captain returned, looking unusually bright and chipper, Jonathan told him about the skirlas.

"Two female babies? Incredible! Wait till we spring that on the Celeucians. Oh, it's going to be fun."

Jonathan was concerned that he didn't have fine enough clothes to wear to the dinner that evening, but the captain said not to worry, that informality was the order of the day on Celeucia, no matter the occasion.

Later, as they made their way to the Tsarl's palace, the captain led Jonathan to an open arch by the roadway, which served as an entranceway to the city's public transportation system.

"Come on, Jon, it's a lot easier getting around this way. It's a moving walkway. Just step in and hop on. That's it. Now off we go."

Jonathan was amazed at the ingenuity of the conveyance, which, the captain explained, ran all through the city and was especially convenient because of the many hills.

"Just another one of Hhor's toys, lad. Whatever requires energy, the Hhor takes care of. Nice little creature to have around. Did I say little?"

As the walkway took them through the city from terrace to terrace, Jonathan was able to get a closer look at the stately buildings, the finely sculpted statuary, and the beautifully landscaped parks, all of which reminded him of Zuralia, although the Celeucian style in art and architecture was decidedly older, freer and more eclectic. The thought of Zuralia plucked at his heartstrings, and he felt a little guilty for having abandoned his dream isle so soon after his arrival.

Many citizens along the way recognized the captain and waved to him, and a few who had attended the welcoming ceremony at the dock remembered Jonathan and extended their greetings to him also. At intervals the moving walkways crossed one another, and the seamen had only to step from one to another to keep in the right direction.

Upon arriving at the Tsarl's palace, despite its great splendor, Jonathan noticed there were no sentries or fancily dressed guards stationed about, nor, for that matter, was there anyone at the entrance to greet the incoming guests. If he had had any doubts about what the captain had told him, he was now convinced of the Celeucian's social informality.

As they passed into the palace's main hall, Jonathan's breath caught at the magnificence of the great room. The floors were of polished pink marble inset with turquoise and aquamarine, and upheld towering rose-tinted walls of sparkling porphyry embedded with red beryls, upon whose heights rested a vaulted mosaic dome of green jade trimmed with obsidian lace work and dotted with oval stained-glass windows. From the ceiling's center hung a great chandelier, its innumerable tiers spreading out like the veined wings of a giant crystalline bird, supporting row upon row of flickering snow-white candles, their reflection casting a dream-like glow over the vast chamber. Larger than life statuary lined the walls, of past Tsarls and Tsarlas, Jonathan guessed, and at the center of the hall was a long table of variegated stone inset with jewels upon which was spread a sumptuous feast to please the most jaded eye and palate.

The captain tugged at Jonathan's sleeve and led him to Orl, the Tsarl, who was conversing with some of his guests.

"Ah, Welcome, Captain. Welcome, Jonathan," gushed the Orl. "Let me introduce you to some of my guests. We were just talking about the Hhor, whom I know will benefit greatly from the valiant Zwegian squirrels you brought us today."

Jonathan looked at the captain in surprise, and when he got a sharp elbow jab in the ribs he immediately comprehended the aesthetics of the situation. Squirrels it was.

The old king was loquacious, and Jonathan listened with great interest to his tales about the Hhor. The more he heard, the more he hoped he would have the opportunity to see this marvelous being.

A tinkle of bells sounded and the Tsarl asked the assembled guests to be seated. The captain was given a seat of honor at the right hand of the Tsarl, while Jonathan chose a less conspicuous chair further down the table. Without further ado, they all proceeded to dig in and help themselves to the various culinary offerings.

A young lady sat down in the chair to Jonathan's left, and when he turned to look at her he was so thunderstruck by her beauty that he bit his finger along with the plum he was eating. His lips parted in a silent ouch, and his face reddened to the color of the plum when he saw that the young lady had noticed his gaucherie, though she turned her head away, politely pretending she hadn't.

"Uh…good evening," he said, immediately hating the awkward, slightly wavering sound of his voice. His lips felt dry as a desert and he had to lick them.

"Good evening," she replied, only half turning her head towards him. Her voice was merry and mellifluous and sent tingling sensations down his spine.

"Who is this lout?" she thought to herself. *"Probably one of the Temprate's quirky followers."*

Jonathan nervously cleared his throat, hating himself even more at the crude rasping noise he made.

"Uh, I'm Jon—Jonathan Spenser. I'm with the captain…." His hand made a jerky motion toward the head of the table where the captain was seated. He had forgotten that he still held the half-eaten plum in his hand, and his gesture caused it to slip from his grasp and bounce unceremoniously down the table. It came to a stop in front of an elderly woman three seats away. As fate would have it, and to his great relief, the woman was looking the other way. He would have liked to sneak over and snatch up the offending object, but didn't dare.

He was sure the young lady had witnessed his latest faux pas, and could feel the heat of humiliation rising up out of his collar.

"If this land has gods," he wondered in his misery, *"why do they hate me so much?"*

"Ugh! What a boor," thought the young lady. But she nevertheless smiled politely.

"How do you do," she replied. "I'm called Llanya. You're with the Pelagin, then?"

"The cabin boy, no doubt," she thought.

"Yes, I'm the captain's helper...er, apprentice."

"I see. You're learning to be a captain, then?"

Jonathan squirmed in his chair and thought he detected a facetious note in her voice.

"This girl is toying with me."

"Uh, not exactly," he replied. "This is only my first voyage. But the captain's taught me a lot already. He's a great skipper."

Her face brightened, and its beauty stabbed at him.

"A fine man, indeed, the captain. My father thinks highly of him."

"Your father?"

"The Tsarl."

Jonathan gulped.

"Not only my father, but all Celeucia honors the captain. If it weren't for him the Hhor would surely die, and I would lose a dear friend."

Jonathan looked bewildered. "Friend? But how...I mean, does he—it—the Hhor speak with you?"

She giggled. "You can call the Hhor either he or she, but the Hhor doesn't really have a sex. I don't like to use the word it—much too impersonal." This time when she smiled, her eyes joined her lips, and Jonathan felt a Cupid's arrow drive into his heart.

"To me the Hhor is a he," she continued. "At least that's the sense I get when I touch him. He doesn't speak, but he does communicate by thoughts and feelings."

"I would like to see this wonderful creature...."

"He's not a creature!" she interrupted, sharply. "He's an intelligent loving being."

"What an oafish thing to say," she thought.

"I'm...I'm sorry. I meant being."

"Drat! I messed up again."

Her tone moderated. "Anyone can see the Hhor by just going to one of the touching stations on the island."

Their conversation was interrupted by a tinkling of bells, and the Tsarl rose to speak. There was a shifting of chairs as all turned toward the head of the table. Llanya was sitting nearer to the speaker than Jonathan, so she was directly in his line of vision. This afforded him an opportunity to study her more closely without being noticed.

His heart seemed to meet in his eyes to consume her every feature: her smooth silken tresses, the color of spun gold, angel hair that fell upon slender gently-sloping shoulders and teased the rise of her firm round breasts; the perfect symmetry of her oval face, which could have only been designed by a god, its high-set brows of the moon's bow embracing sparkling emerald-green eyes that harbored mysteries beyond imagining and the power to lure the most resolute soul into their fathomless depths; her rounded cheeks and slightly upturned nose, miniature gems that lent so much to her character; her full wine-red lips, slightly parted as though on the verge of pouting, so sensual and inviting, like succulent fruit to tempt the famished, their smile a burst of radiant sunlight to shame the sibling suns and melt the most steadfast of hearts. There was a proud dignity in her every feature, and beneath her outward beauty he sensed a rich inner spirit.

Llanya, gifted with the sensitivity of all Celeucians, felt her neighbor's eyes upon her.

"What a churl," she thought. *"I'll be glad when the dinner's over."*

Jonathan was snapped out of his reverie by the sound of his own name. The captain was speaking now, telling the assembled Celeucians about the Zwegian skirla hunt and its dangers, boldly exaggerating at every opportunity, and giving much of the credit for the success of the mission to his chief skirla keeper.

All eyes turned toward Jonathan and he was given a hearty round of applause, which pleased him mostly because Llanya turned towards him with a look of surprise on her face, and perhaps even a hint of interest.

"I want to share with you now a discovery my young skirla keeper made," continued the captain as he nodded to a crewman waiting at the back of the hall. At the signal the crewman, Yos, carried a skirla cage forward and set it down before the captain.

"What have we here, Captain?" asked the Tsarl. "Another fine skirla, perhaps, to administer to our venerable Hhor?"

"No not one skirla, but three. And they're quite different from the others."

"Different?" asked the Tsarl. A buzzing undercurrent of conversation set up around the room.

"Behold!" pronounced the captain as he reached into the cage and gently lifted the roof of the skirla shelter within, and not without a touch of the dramatic.

"Three females," he said, "a mother and two babies."

A stunned silence fell over the hall. Jonathan could feel the electricity in the air. Then the old Tsarl rose from his chair, wobbling on his feet, his face white as a sheet and frozen in a look of utter disbelief. Slowly, in uneven steps, he walked over to the skirla cage and looked in. The silence in the room seemed to thicken tangibly.

"It's true!" the Tsarl shouted, throwing up his hands. "By all the glory and majesty of Hhorelembus, it's true!"

A deafening cheer rang out as the Celeucians jumped to their feet and scrambled to get a look at the incredible miracle in their midst.

Llanya turned and stared at Jonathan with wide wondering eyes, moist with the suggestion of tears. She started to say something, her lips moved, but she couldn't find the words. Her hand reached over and grasped his, and he read the joy and gratitude in her eyes. Rising from her chair, she led him by the hand out a side door to a secluded balcony overlooking the city. Without saying a word she turned toward him, put her arms around his neck, and kissed him softly on the lips.

"That's my small way of saying thank you for what you have done for my people, and for my beloved Hhor." She stepped back, a light blush on her cheeks.

Jonathan waited for his heart to slow to a sprint. His wits mustered, he spoke in what he hoped was a coherent voice.

"Thank you for your…expression of appreciation," he said, "which I would like to return." With that he swept her into his arms and repaid her fully and in kind.

When their bodies parted, their eyes met and held one another in warm embrace, prisoners of the moment. The impassioned voice of the Tsarl drifted onto the balcony from within and broke the spell.

"Let's listen a moment," said Llanya, softly.

"Fellow Celeucians," exclaimed the Tsarl. "This is a historic day. And in honor of Captain Othin, Jonathan, and their shipmates I hereby declare this to be the Year of the Pelagin."

The announcement was greeted with hearty applause.

"I further declare that tomorrow will be a national holiday to be called Mater's Day in celebration of our little mother here, so aptly named Fortuna by her heroic keeper."

More applause. Llanya smiled and clasped Jonathan's hand.

"Moreover," continued the Tsarl, "from this day henceforth I declare the gallant men of the Pelagin, one and all, to be honorary citizens of Celeucia with all the rights and benefits attached thereto."

The applause was interspersed with cheers.

"And lastly—and I hope not least, Captain—the usual payment for the Pelegin's treasured cargo will be multiplied a hundred fold."

As the final applause died away, Llanya squeezed Jonathan's hand, her eyes all asparkle.

"Oh Jonathan, how wonderful! You're a citizen of Celeucia now."

"Call me Jon, please."

"Very well, Jon." Her voice fairly caressed his name and sent an instant ache to his heart.

"Your father said I'm entitled to all the benefits of citizenship. But I'm not sure I know what they are. I'll need to be instructed."

Llanya laughed, a gay trill that sent warm shivers through his body. "Well, perhaps I can help," she said, coyly.

The sound of scraping chairs and receding footsteps reached the balcony, announcing the end of the festivities. The terrace doors opened and the captain strutted onto the balcony, his pleasure at his night's work only too evident.

"Ah, there you are, Jon lad. Taking advantage of your new citizen's rights, I see. Llanya, a delight to see you again. You're even more beautiful than the last time I saw you."

Llanya blushed and curtsied by way of thanks. "Captain, Jon, if you will both excuse me now, I must go. I hear my father calling my name. I'm sure we'll meet again soon. All Celeucia owes you a great debt. Good night."

Llanya departed and the captain read a look of regret mixed with annoyance on his friend's face.

"Sorry, Jon, I didn't mean to interrupt your private party, but we've been invited to stay at the palace, and the majordomo is all apuff waiting to show us our rooms. So come along now. I'm tired and need some shuteye, and I dare say you need some too."

Jonathan was overwhelmed at the opulence of his suite. After a brief tour of his rooms he happily flopped down on his oversized bed whose softness all but swallowed him. His stomach growled in hungry complaint—he had hardly touched a bite at dinner—but he paid it no heed as his thoughts turned to the princess, Llanya. His pulse quickened as he recalled her radiant beauty, her warm embrace and ever-so-soft lips, and not least, her wit and grace. Was she beyond his reach? he wondered. Perhaps not. After all, the people here considered him a hero, and she did seem to like him despite his stupid behavior at dinner. And they were under the same roof.

Then he caught himself, remembering the reason for his visit to the second plane, and his promises to the old dream sender. He dug deeper into his bed and pulled a pillow over his head.

CHAPTER 6

HHOR

When he awoke the next morning, Jonathan found a breakfast tray waiting beside his bed and his clothes washed and set out for him. There were also several choices of colorful local garb to choose from, but he preferred his own. He helped himself to some fresh fruit, berry muffins, and milk, and after a sudsy bath in his own private pool, he dressed and went looking for the captain. He didn't have to look far. From the balcony of the adjoining suite he heard a familiar baritone voice humming a sailor's tune. It was a connecting balcony, and he joined the skipper who was admiring the panoramic view of the countryside.

"Morning, sir. Lovely day."

"Ahoy there, Jon. Indeed it is. Have a good sleep?"

"I didn't know they made such soft beds."

"Ah, everything is soft around here."

The captain leaned over the balcony. "I see there's a crowd gathering already. See there, by the palace gate."

"Yes, I see. Everyone seems to be in a gay mood. Does that mean we're in for another celebration?"

"You might say. Today's the day for the big parade. It's called the Procession of Liberation. It's the day the skirlas are released, and it's a tradition for the Tsarl and his people to march together to the release site. It's always done with a lot of fanfare and folderol. This time there'll be a bigger crowd than usual because of the female skirlas."

"I wonder if Llanya will be going?" asked Jon, half to himself.

The captain smirked. "Oh, she'll be there, without a doubt. The way she feels about the Hhor, she wouldn't miss it for the world. And in case you've forgotten, we're the newest heroes in town so we'll be expected to join in. It's the price of glory, lad. But I think you'll find it interesting."

"Sounds like fun, and since Llanya will be there…"

"Now hold on, Jon. I think it's time I gave you a bit of advice about the ladies of this fair isle. And I'm not talking about anyone in particular, mind you. They're real friendly—I should say warm and open—so their actions can easily be misinterpreted by outsiders. There's a kind of culture gap. What I mean is, it might be a mistake to take them too seriously, especially sailors like us, here today and gone tomorrow."

Jonathan was puzzled and annoyed, but before he could launch a question, a uniformed Zhek appeared at the balcony entrance.

"Good day, honored citizens of Celeucia," he said. "I am here to escort you to the palace courtyard. The procession will be starting shortly."

"Let's go, lad," said the captain. "I hope you put on your walking legs. It's going to be a long haul."

Upon arriving at the courtyard the Zhek showed them to a position at the front of a long line of skirla cages. Jonathan saw that the cages were made of gold inset with precious stones. Each cage rested upon a poled litter manned by Zheks front and back. The sides of the cages were shielded by a shaded glass that protected the skirlas from the sun yet also allowed onlookers to see within. He counted forty-one cages in all, forty holding five skirlas each, plus the lead cage, just behind him, which held the mother skirla and her young.

He knelt and peered into the mother's shelter and was glad to see that the family was doing well. The babies had grown noticeably bigger and were crawling about, curiously sniffing out the mysteries of their new environment.

A gaily outfitted band carrying strange-looking musical instruments took their place in line. Shortly thereafter the Tsarl and his daughter appeared, accompanied by an entourage of officials, and joined the captain and Jonathan at the head of the formation. Jonathan was delighted to see Llanya again, though he was disappointed that her assigned position was not next to his. But her wave and warm smile did wonders for his spirits.

After greeting the captain and the skirla keeper, the Tsarl gave the signal for the parade to get under way. The band struck up a merry tune—"the March of the Squirrels," whispered the captain to Jonathan, struggling to swallow a grin—and the procession moved forward at a sprightly pace. The crowds lining the roadway waved and threw flowers at the passing cages, and all craned their necks trying to get a look at the mother skirla and her babies. The captain and Jonathan were roundly cheered, though the Tsarl, marching just in front of them, generously acknowledged the huzzahs in their stead.

The procession made its way out of the city and into the countryside, and eventually turned down a quaint tree-lined road. Jonathan enjoyed the hike—the countryside was lovely—though he was not displeased when the road came to a dead end and the parade to a halt. A large assembled crowd was waiting, gathered around a grassy knoll by the roadside. The crowd parted as the Tsarl and his entourage came forth followed by a line of Zheks carrying the skirla cages.

The Zheks carefully set down the cages on the grass, one behind the other in a long row, such that the front cage rested against the side of the knoll. Each cage was then locked firmly to its neighbor with golden clamps, with the exception of the cage holding the female skirlas, which was placed to one side with a special guard. The Zheks then raised the individual cage dividers so that all the cages in the row were open to one another.

Llanya came over to Jonathan and, to his delight, took him by the hand and escorted him to a position beside the lead cage.

"Here is one of the many mouths of Hhor," she explained, pointing to a fleshy hole in the side of the knoll. "The skirlas will be released into it."

"Why, it looks just like an opening to their burrows on Zweg," said Jonathan.

A hushed silence fell over the crowd as the Tsarl signaled to the head royal skirla handler, whereupon the Zhek slowly raised the front of the foremost cage, which was set flush against the knoll facing the Hhor's open vent. The skirlas immediately became active, scampering about and sniffing the air with nervous excitement.

"They smell the fat," explained Llanya. "Now watch."

The skirlas in the foremost cage, following the lead of their noses, crept up to the fleshy opening and stopped to peer inside. After a long interval of cautious sniffing, apparently satisfied, they scurried into the hole one by one, disappearing from sight. The skirlas in the other cages, taking the cue, scurried forward and quickly followed the leaders, and in minutes not a single skirla was left. The crowd broke into spontaneous applause and the assembled officials of state extended their hearty congratulations to the Tsarl and to one another and gleefully shook everyone's arm, as was the Celeucian custom on such special occasions.

The Tsarl raised his hand and again a hushed silence fell over the crowd. The cage containing the mother skirla and her babies was brought forth and placed before the opening. The Tsarl, tense and nervous, took a deep breath and nodded to the head Zhek. The cage front was slowly lifted. A minute passed by and no movement could be seen within the cage. The tension mounted. Llanya squeezed Jonathan's hand tightly. Then a twitching nose appeared at the door of the mother skirla's enclosure.

"Come on, Fortuna," muttered Jonathan beneath his breath. "Show them what you're made of."

The mother skirla cautiously sniffed the air. Then she darted to the front of the opening in the knoll and stopped to sniff the air again, raising and lowering her head in a suspicious manner. Suddenly, without warning, she dashed inside the hole. Jonathan gasped.

"Oh, no! She forgot her babies," he cried.

"I don't think so," said Llanya. "She's probably just gone ahead to investigate, to be sure there's no danger, and maybe to find a cavity where she can nest with the babies."

The next three minutes stretched to an eternity for everyone assembled. Suddenly the mother skirla reappeared, and an audible sigh of relief arose from the onwatchers. Without hesitating she dashed back into the cage and a second later emerged carrying one of her babies in her mouth. All business now, into the vent she disappeared, and in a minute she returned, relieved of her burden. Back she scurried into the cage, grabbed up her second babe, and dashed back into the opening. Cheers rang out as the Tsarl mopped at his perspiring brow with a lace handkerchief.

"Not so much as a glance good-bye," mused Jonathan, his voice both sad and glad.

"I'm sure she'll be happy," said Llanya. "After all, she's going to be the founder of a great dynasty. Lucky girl, don't you think?"

Jonathan shuffled his feet. "Uh, yes, I suppose so."

Following a short "Mater's Day" speech by the Tsarl, the proceedings were concluded and the crowd began to disperse.

"Jon, would you like to meet the Hhor now?" asked Llanya. "I'll take you."

"Now?"

"Why not?"

"Well, yes then." He wondered why he had been such a dolt to question the opportunity.

"Good. There's a touching station not far from here. It's a lovely day and it will be a pleasant walk."

"First let me tell the captain...."

"Oh, I doubt he'll miss you, considering that he's leaving with a friend," twittered Llanya. Jonathan saw that she was right and recognized the captain's companion as the attractive lady who had met him at the dock.

Lanya took Jonathan by the hand and led him across country, through flowering meadows alive with butterflies and over hills that gently rose and fell like the sea. More than once he had the urge to take her in his arms and kiss her, but wasn't sure she would be receptive and, not knowing local customs, was afraid he might offend her.

"Tell me about the touching station," he asked.

"It's where one of the great arms of Hhor breaches the surface," she replied with enthusiasm. "There his greatness can actually be felt."

"What is it that you feel when you touch him?"

A distant look came into her eyes. "I feel his deep love and friendship, completely selfless and all-giving. But, of course, the Hhor and I have a special relationship. It's not the same for everyone. Hhor senses the individuality in each person, and his emanations are different in each case, though they're always personal."

Jonthan looked puzzled. "Does the Hhor recognize the touch of someone who has touched him before?"

"Oh, yes. He remembers each and every person. No Celeucian is a stranger to him, except on their first visit."

As they rounded the top of a hill overlooking a small valley, Llanya stopped and pointed.

"There, the touching station."

Jonathan saw in the valley's cup a long low rectangular wall about two hundred meters in length and fifty wide surrounded by a broad stone platform. A few people were standing on the platform leaning over the wall.

Llanya anxiously increased her step, pulling Jonathan along with her. Upon reaching the station, she ushered him down a descending escalator and onto one end of the platform. The atmosphere was subdued and austere.

"Let's go to the middle," she said. "You can see more from there. The other people are leaving so we'll have privacy."

She led him up to the waist-high wall and watched his face to note his reaction.

Jonathan gaped in amazement as he looked upon the great Hhorelembus, or rather a portion of one of the Hhor's tentacles. It was monstrous. Gray and reticulated, it rose out the soil in a long arc, like the bent finger of a colossal god poised to strike life into the world. Its flesh was moist and shiny, and from time to time it quivered, revealing a multi-layered membrane flecked with red and blue veins.

Jonathan met Llanya's gaze, and she smiled at the wonder in his eyes. Without speaking, she reached out and placed her open hand on the Hhor's great appendage. Her eyes fluttered and closed, her lips parted slightly, and a joyous, almost dreamy, look came over her face. Her lips moved slightly as though she might speak, though she made no sound.

Jonathan saw the Hhor's flesh pulsate beneath her hand, and his heart jumped as she threw her head back in a gesture of ecstatic abandon, a gesture so personal and intimate that it both embarrassed and unnerved him.

After a few moments Llanya opened her eyes and withdrew her hand. The ground rumbled slightly.

"Look!" she cried, pointing to a grassy area just beyond the platform.

Jonathan watched in disbelief as a patch of soil nearby puckered and opened, and a dozen flowers sprang forth, growing instantly to maturity, their dainty yellow blossoms unfolding like fairy arms reaching for the sunlight.

Llanya's face glowed with happiness.

"A special gift of friendship from Hhor," she explained. "He does it only for me, when we touch each other deeply. And now it's your turn."

Jonathan hesitated, intimidated by the Hhor's impressive display of power, not to mention the obvious personal nature of the experience. But he didn't want Llanya to think him a coward.

"Touch him there, Jon, on that mottled patch. He's very sensitive there."

Bracing himself, Jon reached out and lightly placed his hand on the now quiescent appendage. It felt cool to the touch and slightly leathery, like the arm of a pet turtle he once had. For a moment nothing happened. Then he felt a slight tingling sensation in his fingers which quickly spread up his arm and into his body. The moist flesh beneath his hand became warm and began to quiver, and he was instinctively repulsed. He only prevented himself from pulling away by an act of sheer will.

Another stranger sensation assailed him, like a whispered thought clothed in feeling that seemed to be searching through secret places in his mind and heart. It was invasive, yet also soothing and reassuring, without a trace of fear or threat, so he willingly, if reluctantly, yielded to its probings. Something deep within him seemed to understand and respond by unlocking itself and melding with the warm alien current. His body—no, it was more than that—perhaps his soul—seemed to lighten; his mind quickened and expanded as all the primordial guilt and inhibitions of mankind seemed to slowly peel away, releasing his innermost self that it might soar into the boundless universe within. Oh, how naked he felt, his essence exposed, bereft of all secrets, and yet so warmly clothed by the all-caring being who embraced him, its emanations flowing through him, enwrapping him in a protective layer of understanding, acceptance, love, and friendship.

Time seemed no longer to have meaning; the external world had been banished. He seemed to be swimming in a boundless silence. Suddenly, out of the silence a distant voice came to him. It seemed to be calling to him and gradually getting closer.

"Jon! Jon! Are you all right?"

It was Llanya's voice. His mind returned to his body, though he still felt a bit giddy. He smiled at her reassuringly and withdrew his hand from the Hhor.

"I'm…I'm fine. That was quite an experience." He took a deep breath.

"Oh, Jon, I was worried. Your contact with Hhor was long for a beginner. And you had a strange look on your face. Did you feel…"

Lhanya's question was interrupted by a shaking of the ground around them. Suddenly the grassy meadow beyond the station shuddered and, lo, the land for as far as they could see spewed forth a blanket of flowers of many hues, thousands upon thousands, a bright carpet to delight the eye and gladden the heart.

In a moment all was quiet again. Llanya turned toward Jonathan, her eyes wide with amazement. Instinctively, she grasped him by the hands as if to siphon off any of the remaining magic energy he possessed, but then felt quite foolish. She didn't have to ask, she knew what had happened, that Hhor had discovered in him something unique and wonderful. She couldn't help feeling a little jealous: the Hhor had never reacted so powerfully toward her, or indeed, anyone else. But she was also glad for her new friend, whom she now looked upon in an entirely new light. She believed with all her heart in the Hhor, and in his judgment. And the Hhor had spoken, profoundly and without reservation. How, then, could she not love this stranger who called himself Jonathan Spenser?

Llanya gently squeezed Jon's hand, caressing it with her thumb, and the warmth that was returned passed into her and melted the thin shield that guarded her heart. Long they stood motionless, gazing into one another's eyes, and in that magical moment their heart's love sprang forth as full-blossomed as the flowers of Hhor. Love's mystery had whispered its secret, and their hearts became as one heart, their souls as one soul, each to each, for theirs was a newborn love that would not be denied, as much a part of them now as the song to the birds, the fragrance to the flowers, the warmth to the suns.

Unspeaking, they walked among the flowers and through the sunlit hills, and in a lonely glen they kissed, and their bodies became as one, joyously and completely, cementing the bond their hearts had made, their passionate embrace joining with their soaring spirits in a pledge of eternal troth.

Later, as they made their way back through the hills, their arms encircling one another, their hearts full to overflowing, signs of civilization appeared, returning to them thoughts of the mundane world. Jonathan wondered if he should tell Llanya of his earthly origins and the riddle of his presence on the dream plane.

They came to a grove of swaying palms and stopped within their shade. There, sitting hand in hand, he told her his story, from first to last. She listened in silence, though her expression bespoke her wonderment, and when he finished she smiled and hugged him.

"It seems you have a destiny to fulfill, my love." Her voice was light-hearted yet trembled slightly. "The Hhor sensed something special in you. He understood. I will not be one to stand in your way or become... an inconvenience."

Jonathan clasped her to him. "Don't say that. I will never leave Celeucia without you. But will you...will you come with me?"

"Oh, yes! Yes! I was afraid you wouldn't ask." Her face brightened with joy and the hint of a tear peeked out of the corner of her eye.

"Oh, Llanya, I'm so glad. But I don't know what the future may hold. There could be danger."

"Oh, poo! That doesn't matter, just as long as we're together. Your secret will be our secret. Now kiss me, Jon."

He enthusiastically obliged, and for the moment their happiness dismissed all else; time and the world did not exist, for their love was a universe beyond all things.

Resuming their journey back to the palace, a question crept into Jonathan's mind.

"Should we considered ourselves engaged, Llanya?" he asked somewhat timidly.

"Engaged? What is engaged?"

"It's an Earth custom. It's when two people agree to be married and tell their family and friends."

"Married? What's that?"

"Uh, another Earth custom. It's a ceremony performed by a priest or an official of the state where the man and woman promise to love, honor, and...be faithful to one another. After marriage they live together."

"Oh, I understand. On Celeucia we don't become engaged, but we have a custom similar to your marriage. We call it pair-bonding. It's very simple. When a person wants to pair-bond with another, he or she simply asks the other person. If there's agreement, they live together and have children if they like. There's no ceremony, just a pledge between the two, though it's considered courteous to inform one's parents first."

"That's all there is to it?"

"Yes."

"So if I wanted to pair-bond with you and you were agreeable, I would have to speak with the Tsarl first?"

She beamed. "Oh, Jonathan! I accept! We will both speak to my father."

Jonathan gasped. It seems he had proposed. "But what if your father disapproves?"

"He won't. I'm of age. When one becomes of age, parents never interfere with pair-bondings. That's considered bad manners. As I said, informing one's parents is simply a courtesy."

"I thought that maybe because I was a stranger and a foreigner, your father might object."

"But you're a citizen now and a hero to all Celeucians. I'm sure my father will be delighted." Her voice became teasing. "But perhaps you're having second thoughts."

Jonathan leapt up, gathered her in his arms and swung her around in circles.

"Second thoughts? Not a chance. We'll speak to your father."

"His birthday is in a few days. That will be a good time. It will be a wonderful gift for him."

"I'll also need to speak with the captain," said Jon. "But just as a courtesy." He grinned.

"Don't forget to tell him the Pelagin will be getting another crewman—I mean crew-woman."

"Shipmate. Yes, that too."

Upon arriving at the palace grounds they found a lonely bench beneath a flowering arch in the garden where they could be alone.

Unseen, on a balcony above, Droxt the Temprate looked down upon the happy lovers kissing, his eyes burning with jealousy and rage. Long he had coveted the fair Llanya, though he had not spoken of his desire. He had been waiting for the right moment to declare himself. And now, before his very eyes, he saw his plan of conquest crumbling. He knew he must act quickly if he was to have any chance of success.

Retreating to his chambers, the Temprate paced to and fro like a caged beast, talking to himself the while.

"How dare she display such moral laxness, and with an outlander no less. Education. She needs education. She must learn self-discipline and temperance. Her passion should be saved for one worthy of her, one of high office, like me. I could make her a Tempretta, second in importance only to myself. She doesn't know what she's losing. It's that boy, that foreigner. Him and his cursed rodents. He's turned her head. He's evil and should be destroyed. But how? I don't possess a weapon—none are permitted on Celeucia. The boy's the type who would probably fight for her anyway. Unless he could be killed secretly, from a distance. But maybe there's an easier way, through her. I'll talk with her, convince her of her duty to her people and show her the error of her ways. Maybe if she's told what she might yet become, perhaps she will come to her senses."

Llanya touched her fingers to Jonathan's lips, explaining that she must go. It was agreed that they would meet again in the garden at sunset.

She hummed a happy tune as she made her way to her rooms in the west wing of the palace. As she turned the corner of a corridor she was confronted by the lean figure of Droxt the Temprate.

"Ah, Llanya my dear. A good day to you." His voice was cheerful, and being unaccustomed to that temper, it cracked slightly. "Ahem. If you have a moment I've been meaning to speak to you about a matter of some importance. Please, let's step into this alcove and I'll explain."

Llanya complied and they sat on a stone bench before a large stained glass window that bathed them in a rainbow of colors.

"As you know, Llanya, I've spoken with you at various times over the past year about the philosophy and practice of temperance and, I must say, you have been an apt pupil. Therefore I have decided to invite you to join me and my followers in our blessed crusade to save our people from the evils of excess that have infiltrated the very bowels of society. Although it is rare for a neophyte to be so honored, I plan to appoint you to the rank of Assistant Temprate, and as such you will serve at my right hand. Well now, my dear, what do you say to that?"

The Temprate gave Llanya a friendly pat on the arm, though the touch of her flesh was as a hurricane wind inflaming the passion within him.

"You are most generous, Temprate," she replied. "And I sincerely thank you for the honor. But I regret I cannot accept. I have made other plans for my life. I'm sure you will find another who is better suited to the task. Now if you will please excuse me, I must be going."

The Temprate watched Llanya's graceful departure through slitted eyes. A cold fury swept over him. His teeth ground together as he pondered his next action. Gradually his scowl melted into a furtive smile and he shuffled off down the corridor.

Jonathan found the captain sprawled on a couch idly smoking a byl, a Celeucian pipe. The captain smiled and winked.

"Nothing like a sweet woman followed by a sweet pipe, a combination hard to beat, lad."

"Captain, that's pretty foul smelling stuff."

"To each his own." The skipper took a long puff. "Mmm, I saw you were keeping charming company at the release site. Be careful now, boy, that's the Tsarl's daughter you're playing with. He's the treasurer around here, you know."

Jonathan's face flushed with anger.

"I wasn't playing!" he blurted. "We're going to be married—I mean, pair-bonded."

The captain jumped up, dropping his pipe to the floor.

"You're what?" The captain's face froze in a look of incredulity.

"You heard correctly—pair-bonded. Llanya and me."

"What...? Why...? How...?" the captain stammered.

"If you calm yourself I'll tell you." Jonathan's voice softened. "We... we fell in love, that's all. It happens, you know. So we decided to pair-bond."

"Just like that? Bingo?"

"Yes."

"And when did this momentous decision take place?"

"This afternoon."

The captain sighed. "This afternoon."

"But we haven't told the Tsarl yet, so you mustn't tell anyone. We're going to tell him on his birthday, in a few days."

"And I suppose you're going to live on Celeucia happily ever after?"

"Yes, I mean no. Happy, yes. Celeucia, no. She's coming with me—with us—on our voyage. With your permission."

The captain clapped his hand to his brow and flopped back down on the couch, muttering something about having a bad dream.

"Well at least you're asking me about *something*. I can tell there's no talking you out of this, and knowing you I suppose you won't leave her behind."

"No."

The captain picked up his pipe, wiped it on his sleeve, and began puffing again. He blew three perfect smoke rings toward the ceiling. When he spoke, his voice was calmer.

"It's really not a good idea, you know. But considering who she is, and who her father is, and the rich reward we'll be hauling out of here, I suppose it's possible. I should say, likely. The Tsarl will probably approve of the alliance since he will want to please his loving daughter. Which puts me square in the middle, thank you."

The captain cast a withering glance at his friend, a look normally sufficient to shrink the stoutest of crewman, but Jonathan stood firm and refused to blink.

Seeing that his glower had failed, the captain's expression melted into a look of sly amusement not untinged with warmth.

"Well, then, I guess she'll be coming along with us. So there's nothing else for me to do except congratulate you."

The skipper's best smile returned full force, and he reached over and grasped his young friend's hand. "Good luck to you, Jon lad. Quite a coup, quite a coup."

"Thank you," said Jonathan, taking a deep breath, his relief only too apparent. "Your approval means a lot to me, and I promise she'll be no trouble on board."

The captain coughed. "No trouble. Mmm. Well, that remains to be seen." He blew another perfect smoke ring. "Anyway, right now I'm hungry. What say we call for some room service and get a bite to eat?"

The eyes of the twin suns, weary from a long day's vigil, drooped over the edge of the land, hovering a moment to take a last look at their fading realm before dipping below the horizon. Though lost from view, the sunken orbs yet cast a pale reflection upon the sky, and spread an orange glow over the garden pool where sat two lovers whispering in fond embrace. Attracted by the moving shadows on the surface of the pool, a golden fish rose up to nibble at the shadows' edge, sending shimmering circles over the water, a gay silent ballet bereft of eyes to behold its grandeur.

The same skylight cast its dim glow upon two shadowy figures crouched in a secluded corner of the dock that housed the Pelagin. The one was dressed in the white garb of a Celeucian and the other in a hooded cloak. The figure in white held out his hand, his fingers unfolding to reveal a gleaming jewel, which the other quickly snatched up and hid beneath his cloak. The hooded figure spoke, his voice a low growl.

"For such a gem, name your desire. A rifle? A pistol?"

"No," replied the other. "The weapon must be silent. A crossbow. Get me a crossbow and arrows."

"Very well. But you must destroy it after it has served its purpose. No one must know it came from the Pelagin."

"Agreed. Nor must its ship's absence be discovered."

"It won't, I'll see to that."

"Good. Now hurry. I cannot linger here."

The one becloaked crept along the wharf, keeping to the shadows, then darted up the gangplank of the Pelagin and disappeared. In a few minutes he emerged carrying a package tied in plain wrappings. Cautiously he looking about, then hurriedly retraced his steps. As he handed the package to its purchaser, his face twisted in a sinister grin.

"Aim well, Celeucian. Death serves many masters."

The figure in white tucked the package beneath his robe and quietly slipped away, too much in a hurry to ponder the meaning of the cloaked one's words.

Next morning Jonathan was up and about early, as usual, though he lingered longer in front of the mirror fussing over his appearance than was his habit. The captain's voice hailed to him from the adjoining suite and he went to answer its call.

"Come over here to the table, lad, I want to show you something." His eyes shone and his tone was jubilant.

Resting on the table was a wooden casket the size of a bread loaf intricately carven with Celeucian motifs. The captain whistled a few bars of music to effect a note of drama, then quickly flipped open the casket lid.

"Da-dum! Feast your eyes on that, me shipmate. A treasure to corrupt a king—diamonds, rubies, pearls, sapphires, bloodstones—enough to bring cheers to every hearty aboard the Pelagin. It's part payment for the skirlas, with a humungous bonus thrown in for the females. Well, don't just stand there gaping, boy, say something."

"It seems a goodly price, indeed."

"Goodly price? Goodly price? Why, with your share alone you'll be able to buy a fine house on Zuralia for you and your lady, and keep her in a style she's not accustomed to."

They both laughed, though Jonathan less heartily.

"Captain, did you say the treasure was only part payment?"

"Yup. The rest is the usual stuff—you'll see later. But these jewels, ah! The least of them is enough to turn the head of the prettiest wench in any port. Well, almost any port. The Tsarl presented me with the casket last night while you were out, no doubt playing lovey-dovey with your lady. You should have been there at the unveiling, though—a grand moment indeed."

"Have the men seen the treasure yet?"

"No, except Balu. I'll wait until we're under way before showing them. And no one will get their share until the end of the voyage. Otherwise we might be missing a few hands along the way. And when the men do collect, I'm afraid with so much in their pockets it's going to be hard to pull them together for the next voyage. But fortunately, most of them are spendthrifts.

"Which brings me around to another matter. We can't linger on Celeucia much longer, so the day after the Tsarl's birthday we'll set sail. I'll get the word out to the men, and there's a few loose ends I have to tend to before we go."

That afternoon Lanya took Jonathan for a walk in a wooded forest not far from the palace. As they traipsed along hand in hand through the tall trees, Llanya, ever curious, plied her lover with questions about his past life, and especially about earthly customs. She listened intently and sometimes laughed merrily at what he told her. Political and dating customs she thought particularly silly and wondered if Earth might be the creation of some playful god, an idea that also set Jonathan to wondering.

She, in her turn, spoke about life on Celeucia, which to him was idyllic, but which she often thought lacked excitement and adventure, the very things she hoped to find in her travels aboard the Pelagin.

Coming upon a dense thicket, Llanya playfully pushed Jonathan into a bush and ran off into the trees to hide, calling out to him to come and find her if he could. If he found her quickly, she cried, there would be a reward. He thought the game a little childish, but was attracted by the incentive.

Darting from tree to tree he searched the immediate area, but to no avail. What he needed was a strategy, he decided, so he began to walk in gradual ever widening circles, systematically covering the surrounding territory.

Nearby, hidden in the shadows of a stony outcropping, a lone figure watched the young man searching through the wood. Droxt the Temprate licked his thin lips, his fingers tightening on the crossbow he held in his hands. Soon the unwary seeker would be in range of his bow shot. His hand trembled, though not from nervousness or fear, but in anticipation of the sweet reward a well-aimed bolt would bring him. Closer came his quarry. He propped the crossbow on a rock to steady his aim. Hate bubbled up in him like hot lava as he slowly pressed upon the trigger.

But the crossbow moved and spoiled his aim. He attempted to steady the weapon, but the very rocks themselves seemed to be moving. Suddenly the ground around him shook violently and heavy stones came tumbling down upon him. Cut and bleeding, the Temprate lost his footing and fell to the forest floor. No sooner did he strike the ground than it trembled and split asunder, opening into a crevasse into which the dazed Temprate toppled head first. The ground then became quiet.

Lying on his back, shaking in terror, the Temprate looked up at the sheer walls of the crevasse. He was trapped, imprisoned by a freak event of nature. Fortunately, except for some cuts and bruises, he didn't seem to be badly hurt. As he reached down to push himself to his feet, his hand came in contact with a damp fleshy surface that quivered at the touch. Horrified, he leapt up and pressed his body tight against the wall. His heart beat wildly in his throat as he forced himself to look down at the floor of the crevasse. And lo, an only too familiar sight met his twitching disbelieving eyes: the great arm of the Hhor.

Though the Temprate had observed parts of the fleshy appendage many times—an inescapable requirement of his office—never before had he come into physical contact with it. Always he had managed to avoid its touch for fear that the creature would fathom his true nature. But now touch it he must, for its glistening tentacle comprised nearly the entire floor of the fissure.

Its quivering became agitated, a throbbing palpitation. The Temprate stood on his toes, pressing hard against the unyielding wall. He suddenly realized that the monster knew he was going to kill the outlander and had intervened to stop him. And now it was going to exact retribution. The terror that gripped his heart tightened like a vice, and in mindless desperation he leapt up, again and again, clawing at his prison walls, finally falling down exhausted, his body now in the full embrace of his tormentor.

The quivering floor of flesh sent electric tremors though his frail body, as though hot fingers were probing every fiber of his being. He knew the Hhor had found him out, had sensed his true nature. He was naked before its power. Suddenly there was a low rumbling sound and the ground tremors resumed. The walls of the crevasse began to move. To his utter horror, he saw they were closing in upon themselves. He would be crushed alive like an insect.

As the inevitability of his fate settled in his brain—that he was about to be ignominiously crushed, flesh and bone, and buried alive in this horrible chasm—he began to weep and babble unintelligibly. The crunching walls pressed ever closer upon him, stretching his mind to the brink of madness. He shuddered and whispered a single coherent word: forgive.

In that instant the walls ceased to close, and a soothing emanation flowed into his body as balm to a wound. His fear fell away as though washed by divine thought, and the strange sensation that now filled him spoke a silent message to his heart, the timeless message of beneficent love.

He understood. The Hhor had forgiven him. Tears poured from his eyes and he gave heartfelt thanks to his generous benefactor, vowing then and there to change his ways and selflessly serve his fellow man to the end of his days. The great arm throbbed and the walls of the chasm fell away, enabling the yet trembling but newly born Temprate to crawl back to the forest floor.

Jonathan, unaware of the drama that had taken place not far away, continued his search for Llanya. As he crept upon a small coppice—an ideal hiding place, he thought—two hands clapped themselves over his eyes from behind.

"Surprise!" cried Llanya. "What a terrible seeker you are. It took you much too long. So I decided to stalk you instead."

"I'm glad you did. And for that you deserve a reward." With that, he pulled her to him and kissed her thoroughly, and not to be outdone she gave him better.

Later, as they strolled back hand in hand, Llanya asked: "Jon, during our game, I felt the ground tremble. Did you feel it too?"

"Yes, but it was only slight and didn't last long. I thought that maybe ground tremors weren't unusual on Celeucia. They're not uncommon in many places on my planet. But maybe it was just the Hhor stretching."

"Oh, Jon! What a poetic thought."

The days that followed passed all too quickly for the happy lovers, and soon the day of the Tsarl's birth anniversary was upon them. For the celebration the Tsarl hosted a small private dinner, to which he invited a few close friends, and at which the captain and Jonathan were the guests of honor. Following a sumptuous dinner and the subsequent departure of the guests, the Tsarl retreated to his chambers thinking to do some reading before retiring. But there came a knock on his door and Llanya entered, asking if she and Jonathan could speak with him.

"Well of course, child. Come in, both of you. Sit down. I was about to do some reading, but I tell you, Jonathan, it's not as enjoyable as when my daughter reads to me. She has her mother's voice and can make the driest prose sound like music. What father was ever more blessed?"

Jonathan shifted about nervously in his chair, only too aware that Llanya was the apple of her father's eye, an apple he might not want plucked from the tree.

"Now what is it you young ones want to speak to me about?" asked the Tsarl.

Llanya looked toward Jonathan, waiting for him to speak, though he had assumed that Llanya would be the one to speak first. But, now, with all eyes upon him, he had no choice. His throat felt tight, and his mind grappled with the right words to say. But when he opened his mouth, only a muted half-croak escaped his lips. An awkward silence ensued during which he could feel a deathlike numbness creeping up his body as an enormous weight pressed down upon him from above.

The Tsarl looked puzzled. Llanya sighed.

"Father, I will speak for us both."

At those words Jonathan felt life and breath return to his body, though a normal heartbeat still seemed a thing beyond hope.

"Jonathan and I have decided to be pair-bonded," she said, matter of factly.

Jonathan waited for her to say more, but she didn't. The brief silence that followed seemed to him an eternity.

"Wonderful!" gushed the Tsarl. "I couldn't be more pleased. My boy, my daughter could not have made a better choice. My congratulations to you both."

Jonathan felt the knots inside him loosening and his body parts returning to their normal places.

"Th...thank you, sir," he sputtered. Llanya beamed.

"We want to pair-bond right away, father, since the Pelagin sets sail in two days. Of course, I'll be going with Jon. It will be our pair-bonding trip—what Jon calls a honeymoon."

The Tsarl looked disappointed. "I would rather you and Jonathan remained here, child. But if you want to go, sobeit. I know Jonathan and the captain will look after you. But you must promise to return before too long, even if only for a visit."

"Oh, of course we will." She ran to hug her father.

"Good. Jonathan, are you allowing any observers at the pledge-taking?"

"Uh…"

"We want to make our pledge privately," interjected Llanya.

The Tsarl nodded. "As you wish. I understand completely. Your mother and I did the same. My blessings on you both."

Later, as the two lovers sat together by the pool in the garden, Llanya wrinkled her brow and a mischievous twinkle came into her eye.

"Well, bond-mate-to-be," she said in mock disappointment, "you were most eloquent speaking to my father this evening."

Jonathan flushed. "Oh, Llanya, I'm sorry. I was nervous. My tongue got twisted and…"

Llanya laughed merrily. "I was only teasing. You see, it wasn't really so bad, was it?"

"Uh, no. Not very." He held out his hands and the lovers kissed.

"Jon, let's make our formal pledge right now. I don't want to wait a moment longer. Then we'll be what you called married."

Jonathan gulped and turned slightly pale. "Now? Here? Just like that? I…I don't want to rush you."

"Why not now? A Celeucian bonding is only one sentence long, you know. Unlike your earthly customs, it doesn't require official sanction, witnesses, or anything else. Just the two of us."

Jonathan felt the blood draining from his body. He took a deep breath and couldn't tell if he was smiling or not.

"Very well."

Llanya, her face angelic, took her betrothed's hands in hers and looked softly into his eyes.

"First I'll say the words, then you."

He nodded, his courage suddenly renewed, warmed by his beloved's touch and the radiating waves of her love. She spoke, her voice like a whispered song calling to his heart.

"I, Llanya, do declare my love for thee, Jonathan, and herewith pledge myself as your bond-mate with all my heart and soul."

Jonathan gulped a mouthful of air and swallowed. It was his turn now. He worried that his voice might crack, but when he saw the love in Llanya's eyes, his words were clear and steady.

"I, Jonathan, do declare my love for thee, Llanya, and herewith pledge myself as your bond-mate with all my heart and soul."

Llanya dreamily closed her eyes to savor the moment, and when she opened them, they sparkled and fairly danced.

"Now, my dearest," she said, her voice suddenly brighter, "we belong to one another, officially. And here's a Celeucian custom that's the same as yours." With that she clasped him to her, raised her lips to his and kissed him warmly. Then she grinned. "And now my bed is yours, also officially. Hark, I think I hear it calling to us even now, commanding our presence. Come, my love. We mustn't be rude."

Jonathan smiled and hardly needed persuading.

The next morning the Tsarl summoned the two happy bond-mates and presented them with a gift.

"My dear children, I want you to have this. It's a small piece of skin from the body of our beloved Hhor, sloughed off many years ago. It's very rare and special, and may prove useful. It has powers, not all of which I understand myself. It can warn of danger. It is also said to have certain communication powers. But if nothing else it will remind you of Celeucia, which will always be a home to you both. Divide it between you that it may succor you both."

Jonathan and Llanya accepted the gift with thanks. It was the size of a large coin and felt smooth to the touch, like leather only firmer. Jonathan made a mental note to examine it more carefully later.

News of the bonding spread quickly, and among the notes of congratulations the newlyweds received was one from the Temprate, Droxt. Both Llanya and Jonathan were touched by its outpouring of sincerity and warmth in wishing them a long and happy life together, and Llanya wondered if she had perhaps misjudged the Temprate in the past.

That afternoon Llanya took Jonathan on a walking trip to see some of the natural wonders of the island. She showed him the famous Celeucian upward-flowing waterfall, enshrouded in triple rainbows, and the singing desert spouts—whirlpools of sand that whistled eerie melodies as they spiraled up out of the ground. He was especially fascinated by the magnificent giant blue ice flowers that grew upon a remote cliff side, immune to the tropical climate, though when he touched one of the delicate blue petals it quickly melted away.

As they stood alone upon a grassy palisade looking out over the sea, the breeze whipping at their hair, Jonathan again felt the strange summons that had drawn him to the dream plane. Now that he was pair-bonded, he thought perhaps it would be wise to ignore the call, which might hold danger for his beloved. Yet he knew that he could not, and that Llanya would not wish him to.

"Jon, what place will we be sailing to next?" asked Llanya.

"The captain called it Klell, an island to the north."

"I have heard of it. Oh, Jon, it's going to be so exciting. I can hardly wait."

CHAPTER 7

THE WALL OF KLELL

Llanya found life at sea to be everything she had hoped. When she wasn't in the arms of her bond-mate, she was on deck communing with the gods of the deep, her tresses a golden banner in the wind. Awed by the immensity of the ocean, its great power and fickle ways, she would stand at the bow gazing out over the rolling foam-flecked hillocks, listening to the faint whisperings of sea and air, intimations of the vast unknown hidden beneath the waves and beyond the limitless horizon. Her heart thrilled when the Pelagin heeled over or dipped into the valley of a swell, when the whipping sails billowed full out, straining and creaking to be free of their tethers, and when, of a sudden, the wind changed its mood, releasing its mighty grip on ship and sea, its quiet breath brushing the blue-green carpet with shiny rippled kisses.

Too, she liked to watch the playful antics of the dolphins as they leapt and dived beside the ship, and to hold out bits of bread for the sea gulls to snatch from her hand. And if a hungry beak nipped her finger, she would cry out in mock fright which quickly became a laugh of delight.

At first some members of the crew were disgruntled at having a female aboard, but Llanya's outgoing ways, her spontaneity and infectious laughter and, not least, her unblemished beauty, soon won them over. Perhaps there might have been more objection had not the crew still been basking in the warm afterglow of their Celeucian holiday and its bounteous rewards. There was also the anticipation of an unusual and generous payment at their next port of call to add to their good spirits.

Without the skirlas to look after, Jonathan begged the captain to let him try his hand aloft. The captain agreed, albeit reluctantly, instructing Balu to keep a sharp eye on the novice sailor. Llanya, however, had every confidence in her bond-mate and encouraged his desire. Indeed, she envied his opportunity and wished she might join him in his climb to the sky. Nor was her confidence misplaced, for it wasn't long before Jonathan had mastered the art of furling, trimming, and securing the sheets, demonstrating to all that he was a born seaman.

He enjoyed the feeling of freedom at the top of the rolling masts as though he were at the top of and one with the world, the ocean's breast heaving beneath him, the great expanse of blueness sparkling in the brightness of the twin suns. From his perch between sea and sky he would wave to his bond-mate below, wishing he had wings that he might swoop down and carry her aloft in his arms, that they might behold together the wondrous ocean world as only sailors and birds may witness.

As yet, he knew not fully the fickle moods of the mother ocean, of her cold indifference and her treachery. These were lessons he had yet to learn.

On a night when the blackness lay heavy on the waters, with only Tabber the night helmsman on deck, his eyes fixed upon the dark unfolding sea before him, a cloaked figure rose out of the shadows of an open hatch. The figure crouched, waiting until the stillness was broken by a wave slapping against the hull, then darted to the mainmast and, nimbly as a spider, climbed the rigging to the topmost spar.

In the dimness of that starless moonless world there was no reflection from the unsheathed talon at its work, no sound to hear, to draw the helmsman's eye aloft. The figure worked quickly, camouflaged against the night. It's task complete, the dark shape slipped down the mast to the deck and disappeared into the open hatch from which it came.

The early morning's light was greeted by a cry of alarm from the crow's-nest.

"Wolf sharks off the port bow!"

All hands scrambled to the rail to see the giant dorsal fins of three wolf sharks swimming parallel to the Pelagin less than a kilometer away. Llanya, never having seen such creatures before, was aghast at their monstrous size and read the fear in the faces of the men. She held tightly to her bond-mate's arm.

"Hop to, mates!" rang out the captain's voice. "They're getting closer. I think we'll be able to outrun them—we're with the wind. All sheets full out."

Jonathan squeezed Llanya's hand, then ran to the mainmast and began the ascent to his duty station. A nimble climber, he quickly reached the topmost spar, and as he was about to unfurl one end of the mainsail, the ship suddenly heeled. Thrown off balance, he grabbed at a tie line to catch himself, but the rope snapped under his weight and he pitched headlong into the sea.

Llanya's scream was swallowed up by the wind, but the captain saw what had happened and quickly spun the wheel, turning the Pelagin leeward.

Feeling himself falling, Jonathan held his breath and straightened his body to cut the water cleanly. He was a good swimmer, and as he hit, he arched his back and quickly shot to the surface. The shock of the cold water numbed his body, and though he could barely feel his arms and legs, they still followed his orders.

Treading water, the waves battering his face, he looked about to find his direction and saw the Pelagin at a distance straining to come about. The pocket of a swell swallowed him and he momentarily lost sight of the ship. As he rose up again he saw that the ship had turned and was coming his way. The flutter in the forward sheets told him the captain was sailing as close to the wind as he dared, but a strong tidal drift was working against the ship. There would be time for only one pass to pick him up. He could help by swimming toward the ship.

Keeping his face down to gain speed, his benumbed arms churned the choppy surface, but no matter how hard he swam it seemed like he was standing still. He swallowed water and his coughing forced him to tread water. Through burning eyes he thought for a moment he saw a mermaid rising up out of the deep, only to see that it was the figurehead of the Pelagin bobbing in the waves. A lady to strive toward, he told himself as he dropped his head into the water and plunged forward once more.

Whether only seconds or minutes had passed, he wasn't sure, but when he looked up again, spewing water and gasping for breath, he saw the ship was much closer. But the ocean drift was forcing the ship on a sideward path that would take it beyond his reach. There was only one chance. If a long line were thrown overboard, he might be able to swim to it in time.

His arms were turning slower now and he didn't know if his legs were still moving at all. He rose and fell as though in slow motion. The sea seemed to take pleasure in toying with him like a bit of flotsam, ever trying to pull him back, to thwart his progress. A white froth slapped at his face and he looked up. But his burning eyes wouldn't focus: all was a dark blur. He heard a strained creaking noise somewhere to his right, a sound well known to sailors. Then suddenly he felt himself engulfed in a turbulence which he knew must be the ship's wake. Flailing about blindly, he beat at the frothy brine with his hands, feeling for a line. Something scraped against his side. Grabbing at it, his hands closed on a knotted rope and he was jerked forward through the churning maelstrom.

He could feel himself being hauled in. Suddenly a shock wave beneath the water struck his body, then another, as though it were a rippled warning of something huge traveling toward him deep below the surface. The wolf sharks! A stab of fear brought bile to his mouth. Frantically, he began to pull himself hand over hand along the trailing line. With each pull he counted…seven, eight…fourteen, fifteen… His head began to spin and vague distorted pictures flashed through his mind. The rope—it was slipping. He wasn't able to hold on any longer. As he gently fell back, something roughly grabbed his arms and lifted him bodily out of the water. The world was a pandemonium of noise and light spinning wildly on its axis. From somewhere in the distance he heard the captain's voice: "Full with the wind!"

Slowly his eyes regained focus, and high above he could make out a lone seagull riding the currents of the wind against a clear blue sky. A wave of nausea struck him. His body jerked and he spewed up what seemed like half the ocean. Leaning back, exhausted, he saw that he was on the aft deck, a blanket draped around his shoulders. Llanya was beside him, a frightened look on her face, vigorously rubbing life into his hands. He gave her a wan smile only to receive a smothering hug in return.

"Oh, Jon! I thought I'd lost you."

"I wouldn't do that to you." His throat was hoarse and it hurt to talk. "But the sharks. What about the sharks?"

Balu, standing by looking like a worried father, replied: "It was close, but we're outrunning them. We'll soon be out of danger. What we need to do now is get you below and in your bunk. I'll get some balm for those rope burns on your hands."

The captain came below decks to the cabin Jonathan and Llanya now shared.

"You gave us a nasty scare, lad. But you've got your color back, I'm glad to see."

"Thanks for turning about for me, Captain. I know you risked the ship doing that."

"No thanks called for, so let's hear no more about it. You owe your life to yourself. You showed courage and good sense. But tell me, what happened aloft? Lose your balance?"

"No sir, the tie line snapped. I checked the lines only yesterday, but I guess I didn't do a very good job."

"The important thing is that you're alive. But there'll be no climbing the ropes for a while, not with those burns on your hands. You can do some map reading instead. And maybe devote a little attention to some of your new responsibilities," he added with a wink.

After the captain departed, Llanya said in a mock serious tone: "I think the captain's suggestion was an excellent one, I mean about you devoting more attention to your new responsibilities. What do you think?"

Jonathan grinned. "I think so, too."

On deck the captain hailed Balu and whispered something in the first mate's ear. Balu nodded and returned to his duties. Later, at twilight, when the crew were at chow below decks, Balu climbed the mainmast and replaced the broken tie line that had caused Jonathan's fall. The piece of old line he tucked inside his shirt. Later he went to the captain's cabin as he had been instructed.

"Here it is, Captain, as you requested. There's no question—the line was cut. All the other lines are intact."

The captain closely examined the piece of rope. His eyes narrowed and his tone became deadly serious.

"It was cut with something razor sharp, but not quite all the way through, so when a man's weight was put on it, it would break. It seems we have an assassin aboard, Balu. Since the mischief was done only at Jon's duty station, there's no question but that he was the target."

"But why?" asked Balu, straining to contain his anger. "Why would anyone want to harm young Jon?"

"I don't know. Nor does the lad know, I'll wager. We'll just have to keep a sharp eye out from now on. No one's to know about this. No sense frightening the young ones or letting the culprit know we're on to him."

Next morning Jonathan was up and about, though not quite as early as usual, and ready to assume new duties. His hands were not badly burned, but the captain insisted that he rest up a bit longer after his ordeal and put him on temporary deck leave. Knowing better than to argue with the skipper, he and Llanya took the opportunity to query Tabber, a native Klellian, about the mysterious island of priests that would be their next port.

The helmsman, an ex-priest himself and reticent by nature, at first gave only brief reply to their questions, but their persistence coupled with Tabber's natural politeness eventually elicited the desired information.

Klell, Tabber explained, was an ancient isle, not much larger than Zuralia, populated by ascetic priests called Imshis. The priests lived a private life, and outsiders were generally not allowed on the island except for the occasional trading vessel and a handful of guest workers needed for physical labor. The island was ruled by a head priest, the High Catex—catex meaning custodian of knowledge—who was thousands of years old, very wise, and a recluse seldom seen by his followers. The priests, all males, were vegetarians and celibates; women were not allowed on the island.

Llanya huffed and puffed at that, strongly protesting such scandalous sex discrimination to an utterly dismayed Tabber. Jonathan intervened to calm her, and it was only with difficulty that he was able to coax the gentle Tabber to continue.

The Klellian priests, it seemed, possessed a remarkable secret which they guarded very closely—the secret of long life. Though outsiders had long lusted for the secret, none had ever succeeded in stealing it. Even the boldest seekers dared not invade the island, in part because of its dangerous reef barriers, but mostly because they feared the priests, certain of whom possessed, or were thought to possess, fearsome psychic powers capable of emptying human minds at a glance. Thus, the priests had kept their secret safe for centuries. Although they did reward certain outsiders with an extension of life for valuable services rendered, but in a way that protected their secret knowledge.

Thus, by possessing the power of longevity, only rarely did a priest die. When death did occur, it was usually by accident, at which time a male child was imported from a neighboring island to be trained as a replacement. The population of priests was thus maintained at a constant five thousand—the divine equilibrium quantity as defined by the High Catex.

The High Catex was also known as the All Father, for he was in fact the actual blood father of all the priests of Klell. From ancient times his sperm had been stored in protective capsules, and when the occasion required, a capsule was delivered to a pre-selected maiden on a neighboring island who was granted three years of extra life in payment for birthing a child for the priests. If the child happened to be female, additional attempts were made until a male was born. No boon of longevity was granted for producing female offspring, so as not to create the wrong incentive.

Thus, explained Tabber, as a consequence of their singular paternal origin, all the priestly brothers looked remarkably alike, namely like him: pale, prematurely bald, large-nosed and gaunt to a man, features which, on Klell, were widely admired.

The daily lives of the priests, and indeed their very reason for being, centered around one sole purpose—to contemplate and care for the sacred High Wall of Klell. The great wall cut across the full width of the island from sea to sea, the priests living on only the southern half. Older than the High Catex himself, the wall had originally been built by the Daduks, the ancient ancestors of the Klellians. It was believed that the Daduks had built the wall as a protective barrier against some unnamed monstrous creature that lived on the island, though over the centuries the mysterious threat had been all but forgotten, and the wall took on an entirely new meaning to the evolving society of priests. It eventually became a thing to be worshiped in and of itself, a sacred Imshi symbol, an object of slavish reverence attended to with obsessive duty and un-wavering devotion.

The priests of Klell, Tabber explained, being contemplative by nature and physically frail by inheritance, are incapable of manual labor. They therefore have to hire outside workers to constantly mend and strengthen the ancient wall. For their labors the workers are paid in years of life. For each year spent working on the wall, a worker earns two additional years of life.

When Jonathan asked what trade goods the Pelagin was carrying to Klell, the helmsman surprised him by saying he would do better to ask his bond-mate. Llanya, taken aback, declared she had no knowledge of the ship's cargo. Tabber would say nothing more. Perplexed, the couple sought out the captain and posed the question to him.

"It's bags of Celeucian powder to be used for cement," replied the captain. "The powder's part payment for delivery of the skirlas."

"Powder?" asked Jonathan, confused. "For cement?"

"Yup. It has miraculous binding power. The Klellians use it in making brick and mortar for their wall. Llanya, I'm surprised you didn't know about the powder, considering its source."

Llanya looked puzzled. Then her face brightened.

"Oh, I think I know now. It's from the Hhor. It's that fine white powder that accumulates on the ground around his openings."

"Correct. A waste deposit of some sort, but a valuable trade good for us. You'll learn more about it when we reach Klell."

At suns rise two days hence there came a familiar cry from the crow's-nest: "Land ho! Dead ahead!"

Jonathan and Llanya dashed to the rail.

"Look Jon, there! See? The island of Klell! It's the first land I've ever seen outside of Celeucia. Oh, it's so exciting."

Jonathan nodded. "Let's hope it won't be too exciting."

Nearer to land the captain relinquished the wheel. It would require the special talents of Tabber and Zyl to navigate the submerged reefs surrounding the island. Steadfast and true, working together they guided the Pelagin through the treacherous barrier, safely into the calm waters of a tree-lined cove. Jonathan watched as the main sheets were trimmed, wishing he could be at his post aloft. The captain resumed the wheel and guided the craft to a narrow dock where waiting hands—hired work-ers—tied the lines fore and aft.

Four somber-looking priests, all Tabber look-a-likes down to their bald pates, thin frames, stiff manner, and mincing walk, were waiting on the dock. The captain disembarked alone to seek permission for the crew and cargo to come ashore. Klellian rules and regulations required that certain ritualistic identification and clearance procedures be followed, even though the captain and his ship were well know to the Imshis. The crew lined up against the ship's rail to watch the dockside proceedings, Jonathan and Llanya among them.

Jonathan saw that the each of the Imshi priests wore a robe of a different color. Tabber was standing next to him and he tugged at the helmsman's arm for an explanation.

"Robe color denotes rank—blue for Poonwat or third level, green for Bhukar or fourth level, yellow for Mysopt or fifth level, and brown for Silku or sixth level."

"What about first and second rank?" asked Llanya.

"The High Catex is the only first level official, and to maintain the appropriate differential in status among ranks, there is no second level." Tabber added somewhat wistfully: "There was once a Vice Catex, but the position withered away for want of any meaningful duties." Jonathan chuckled, though why he did so escaped both Tabber and Llanya.

The clearance procedures completed, the senior member of the Imshi welcoming party, the Poonwat, surveyed the ship and noticed the presence of a woman standing at the rail. His eyes widened to saucers and he became visibly alarmed. Indeed, so nonplused was he that he skipped the traditional welcoming speech, though to no one's regret, and instead began to regale the captain, reciting chapter and verse of the particular priestly law forbidding the presence of females on the island.

The captain looked up at the sky, straining to remain calm, then replied that if the lady couldn't come ashore, neither would the Celeucian powder come ashore. Moreover, since the lady was the daughter of the Tsarl of Celeucia, who was the supplier of the precious powder, any insult to her would surely preclude any future deliveries. At that the Poonwat's face turned the color of a Bhukar's robe and he humbly begged the captain's pardon, assuring him that in such special circumstances the lady would be a welcome visitor indeed.

The priests watched anxiously as crewmen carried the precious bags of powder ashore. The Poonwat carefully counted each bag as they were placed in a secure storage shed near the dock, to be later carried by hired Klellian litter bearers to the great wall.

The crew, having visited Klell before, had no desire to spend more time on the island than was necessary, knowing it to be totally devoid of entertainment or, indeed, any diversion agreeable to non-abstaining mortals. Upon petition, the captain agreed to let the crewmen remain temporarily aboard ship to enjoy some libations and card games, except for Tabber, Jonathan, and Llanya who joined him ashore. The captain informed his men that he would send for them when the time came to collect payment for the Celeucian cargo.

Thereupon the priests formed in single file according to rank and proceeded to escort their guests down a forest path towards the Klellian village. The Poonwat's stiff walk and occasional twitch gave evidence of his nervousness in the company of a woman, though the other priests seemed meekly curious, casting sidewise glances from time to time in Llanya's direction.

Jonathan was about to ask Tabber the location of the famous wall when Llanya grasped his arm.

"Jon! There, above the trees!"

Jon looked up and saw towering over the distant tree line a great mass of brick and stone rising into the heavens—the legendary High Wall of Klell. It's imposing magnificence all but took his breath away. With each step it seemed to grow higher, as if to consume the horizon. How could so massive a structure be man-made? he wondered. Indeed, its very existence seemed alien and unholy and struck fear into the heart. But when he looked at Llanya and saw her thrilled expression, he felt ashamed at his own timidity.

The path turned parallel with the wall, blocking out the suns' light. Walking now within the wall's sacred shadow, the priests touched their brows and uttered muted prayers of thanksgiving. Tabber explained their actions, and Jonathan asked in a whisper who it was they were thanking. The ex-priest declared that he didn't know and wasn't sure the Imshis knew either, adding that it would be unwise for an Imshi to ask such a question, especially if one wanted to remain a priest.

Further on they passed a great mud pit where hired workers were making bricks for the great wall. Tabber pointed out one man he remembered, who had been working in the pits for over a century and had outlived his friends and family and still had many earned years as yet unused. Jonathan thought this was carrying the virtue of saving to an extreme if not absurd length, and he wondered if all the extra years of life the worker had earned would ever be of use to him.

Llanya seemed to read her bond-mate's mind. Her eyes twinkled.

"Maybe he'll find a new young wife. And when she's gone, then another, and another. He has the time."

Tabber half smiled, though Jonathan decided it would be the better part of valor not to reply.

Soon the party reached the village. It was simple and pristine in appearance, which Jonathan thought well suited a community of monks. Tabber pointed out the sights. At one end of the village neat rows of one-story stone buildings served as dormitories where the priests ate and slept. The buildings were strictly segregated, the doors of each structure painted the appropriate color denoting the rank of the priestly occupants. Standing alone at the opposite end of the village in a broad clearing was a stone temple, circular in shape and triple-tiered, topped by a rectangular pinnacle in the shape of a wall. The structure, Tabber explained, was the Temple of Everness, where rituals and devotions were held, and which housed the sacred person of the High Catex.

The captain, who had been conversing with the Poonwat, came over and put his arms around Jonathan's and Llanya's shoulders.

"The man in blue tells me we're to help ourselves to rooms in that empty building at the end of the first row. Dinner will be brought to our quarters at twilight, which should be in a half hour or so. The food's not much here, but we'll survive it all right. Tomorrow morning is payoff time, when we collect our earnings. In the afternoon, if you like, we can take a closer look at the wall."

Jonathan and Llanya enthusiastically agreed, anxious to visit the fabled edifice. Their eyes turned toward the great wall and they didn't think to ask what the priestly payoff might be.

As the foursome walked toward their quarters, Jonathan asked Tabber if there would be an opportunity to meet the High Catex. Tabber stopped dead in his tracks and looked at his young friend in utter astonishment. The captain, overhearing, replied for the tongue-tied helmsman.

"There's slim chance of that, lad. Hardly anybody gets to see the old boy. To outsiders he's the big mystery of mysteries. In fact I sometimes wonder if he might be only a rumor."

Next morning the captain sent a message by way of a Silku summoning the men on the Pelagin to attend a special ritual in the seamen's honor at the Temple of Everness. The men responded with unusual promptness, and within the hour all hands were assembled, spick-and-span, in the temple courtyard.

At the appointed time for the ceremony a gong sounded and the temple doors swung slowly open. A Poonwat appeared, the same one who had met them at the ship, and ushered the group into a large domed hall. The hall was empty except for a single row of wooden benches encircling its perimeter. Jonathan and Llanya, hands clasped, followed behind the captain, their footsteps echoing on the stone floor like falling pebbles on glass. The Poonwat gestured for everyone to be seated, then disappeared behind a white-curtained door at the far end of the hall.

A quiet shiver ran up Jonathan's back. The atmosphere within the temple was laden with solemnity and premonition such that no one dared speak or even whisper. The brooding stillness descended over the waiting congregation like a living creature. The leaping shadows cast by flickering torch lights on the chamber walls seemed in reckless defiance of divine will. Llanya tightened her grip on Jonathan's hand.

A tinkle of chimes broke the silence and the curtained door opened. The Poonwat emerged followed by a single line of barefoot priests, Bhukars by the green color of their frocks, each carrying a round wooden tray upon which rested a small tulip-shaped glass. Each glass contained an emerald-colored liquid which sparkled in the torch light as though it imprisoned a thousand fireflies. Slowly, in measured half-steps, the Bhukars marched in a circle, circumambulating the great hall, until they reached a position directly in front of the seated visitors. At a hand signal from the Poonwat the procession halted and, as one, the Bhukars turned so that each faced an individual guest. A reverent period of silence followed, interrupted at intervals by the distant tinkling of chimes and the whispered response of a sacred but indistinguishable word by the priests.

Jonathan stared into the emerald-green liquid that danced before his eyes, and fantastic images seemed to leap out at him from its fathomless depths—spiraling planets and exploding suns in a whirling galaxy of blinding color, all the myriad worlds he had looked for in the vast universe beneath his laboratory microscope. Invisible hands seemed to reach out to him from within the reeling panorama, as though in welcome; but the miniature universe suddenly darkened and a pulsing amorphous shape descended upon it, enveloping and consuming it, until only the darkness remained. A bolt of fear shot through him, and he forced himself to look aside to break the spell. Llanya squeezed his hand, and as he looked into her radiant face, his courage flowed backed into him in a torrent.

The Bhukars began a low hum and held out their trays, whereupon the proffered glasses were eagerly accepted by the crewmen. Most of them quickly downed the liquid in a single gulp. Jonathan and Llanya, glasses in hand, watched the captain next to them and saw the look of relish in his eyes. He smiled and winked, and they followed his example and slowly drained their glasses. The taste was pleasantly sweet.

The empty glasses were returned to the trays, and the priestly procession departed as they came. The Poonwat, however, remained behind to escort the visitors out of the temple, and once they were back in the courtyard, the great temple doors creaked to a close.

The crewmen, in a merry mood, made their way back to the ship laughing and capering. Tabber remained behind with the captain and the wondering bond-mates. Llanya and Jonathan surrounded the captain to ply him with questions.

"Oh, that was so thrilling," gushed Llanya. "But I can't imagine what it was all about. Please tell us, Captain."

"Yes, and tell us what we drank," added Jonathan.

The captain labored to look nonchalant. "Oh, we just collected payment in exchange for our trade goods, that's all. The ritualistic rigmarole was just the Klellian way of paying off." The skipper then broke into a grin. "That lovely green stuff we drank was nothing less than the infamous Klellian Elixir of Life. With that one swallow we pushed back old man time by fully five years. Llanya, my sweet, you're going to stay young a little longer than you thought."

Llanya squealed with delight, though Jonathan could only gape in amazement.

"But our mortality is as frail as ever," added the captain. "So it's no excuse for carelessness."

Just then four brown-robed Silku priests came rushing up the road, arms flailing and wearing panicked expressions. They ran to the temple and pounded on the door, and an annoyed Poonwat soon emerged. The Silkus whispered something in his ear and a grim pallor fell over the Poonwat's face.

"Very unpriestly behavior," said the captain. "They never carry on that way. Something big must have happened. Let's find out."

The Poonwat bounded down the temple stairs and headed helter-skelter down the road, followed by the four Silkus scampering along with hiked robes as though pursued by demons. As the priests rushed past, the captain stopped one of them and asked what had happened.

"The wall!" sputtered the Silku. "A black stone has fallen from the top of the sacred wall." With that the priest took off down the road in pursuit of his colleagues.

The captain turned to Tabber. "What's so special about a black stone?"

"Very special, Captain. Only the topmost row of stones in the wall are black, placed there by the ancient Daduks themselves. They are very sacred and are believed to impart magical powers to the wall. According to myth, the protective power of the wall depends on the unbroken chain of black stones. It is said that the great spirit of the wall will not smile upon his followers with a missing tooth."

"Well, then, all they have to do is replace the black stone," offered the captain.

"That cannot easily be done," replied Tabber. "The top of the wall reaches to the clouds. None of the workers are able to climb that high."

"Well, what was done in the past when a black stone fell from the wall?"

"This is the first time a black stone has fallen."

The captain shrugged. "I guess that accounts for the panic, then."

Jonathan was fascinated. "Captain, we planned to visit the wall today anyway. Let's go now and see what's happening."

"Oh yes, let's do!" chimed in Llanya.

The captain smiled. "Very well, off we go, then."

Upon arriving at the great wall Jonathan was even more impressed with its immensity than he had been from a distance. Looking up from its base of massive hand-chipped stones, he was unable to see its summit, only an endless white expanse stretching into the dim reaches of the sky.

Crowds of priests milled about muttering prayers, some moaning in despair like helpless children. He spotted the Poonwat from the temple kneeling at the wall, surrounded by a group of green-robed priests. Upon approaching, he saw the object of the Poonwat's attention: a black rectangular stone, slightly larger than an ordinary brick, lying in the dirt. The surface of the stone was smooth and, except for some scratches and a bit of old flaking mortar along one of its edges, it did not appear to be seriously damaged. The scratch marks, however, looked fresh and were slightly curved, as though the stone had been raked by something sharp.

Jonathan pondered the stone, then looked up toward the summit of the wall. The corners of his lips curled in the beginnings of a smile. Turning to the kneeling Poonwat, he said calmly:

"Excuse me, I don't mean to interrupt. But if the High Catex will agree to grant me a private audience, I will replace the black stone on the wall."

The Poonwat fainted dead away.

CHAPTER 8

THE ZYTOX

The captain couldn't stop laughing. The four of them—Jonathan, Llan-ya, the captain, and Tabber—were heading back to the village following their visit to the wall. Jonathan simply repeated what he had said to the Poonwat and the captain broke out in uncontrollable laughter.

Jonathan was annoyed at his friend's reaction, and as the exhibition of body-doubling hilarity continued unabated, it became downright embarrassing. A passing group of mournful Silkus stopped to watch the strange goings-on. They had never witnessed a demonstration of human jollity before and it puzzled them. Such merriment was wholly alien to their training and life style.

The captain, aware of his audience, heroically tried to contain himself by sucking in the mirthful outpouring, but the effort was strangling, and the resulting pent-up glee was released in an explosion of bellows and guffaws. With flushed face grimacing in torture, eyes blinded with tears, and clutching at his midsection, he sucked in air in a sudden gasp, then let out a wild whoop followed by a series of half-choked snorts punctuated by labored moans. Straightening up with great effort to snatch another breath as might a drowning man, he forced down a chuckle and stared red-faced and wide-eyed at Jonathan, biting his lips to suppress another round of laughter. But his young friend's expression of perplexed innocence was more than he could take, and he exploded once more in a deafening roar and staggered about in circles, until finally, in an orgy of agonized yelps and wrenching coughs, his body rebelled and choked him into silence.

The Silkus, gaping at the extraordinary display, whispered among themselves, speculating as to its meaning, finally deciding that it must be one of two things: a mariner's ritual of empathetic understanding to demonstrate their sympathy with the priests' sorry plight over the fallen stone, or a heartfelt soul-searing prayer offering to the spirit of the wall to come to their aid in this, their greatest hour of need. Either way it was a worthy and generous gesture on the part of the leader of the seafarers, and one in which the priests felt they could in good conscience participate and possibly benefit therefrom. Their inhibitions thus duly rationalized and dispelled, they allowed the contagion of the captain's mirth to infect them. Giggling at first, they soon worked themselves up to an outpouring of merry cackles, and finally into a frenzy of inharmonious laughter that rivaled the best of the captain's offerings.

Though the captain had ceased his demonstration, the priests, wholly caught up in this new and opulent form of prayer, continued to bray on until, as fate would have it, a Poonwat happened by. The Poonwat could only stare in astonishment at the incredible exhibition. One of the Silkus spotted the Poonwat through tear-streaked eyes, and his joyous bawl suddenly rose in pitch to a shriek. The alarm instantly silenced the other Silkus, who stared openmouthed at the glowering Poonwat. The Poonwat raised his arm and pointed toward the village, and at that, without stay or delay, the Silkus took to their heels and disappeared down the road, the Poonwat following after them at a brisk pace, muttering something about the presence of faulty genes which doubtlessly came from their mothers' side.

But, alas, now a new wave of mirth swept over the captain, inspired by the ridiculous sight of the merry, then terrified, Silkus and their nonplused superior bouncing down the road. At this point Jonathan and Llanya could no longer contain themselves and also burst into laughter. Tabber, sober as always, patiently waited for this latest silliness to exhaust itself.

Resuming their walk, the captain spoke in a somewhat forced monotone lest he involuntarily release a snicker.

"Tell me, Jon, just how were you planning to get to the top of the wall to replace the fallen brick?"

The reply was matter-of-fact: "In a hot-air balloon."

The captain stopped short, bringing the procession to a halt again. His eyebrows rose.

"A hot-air balloon? Hmm. Not a bad idea. But where are you going to find one, pray tell?"

"I'll build one. There's extra sailcloth in ship's storage, some of it lightweight. It could be sown together to make the air bag. There are plenty of reeds on the island to make a passenger basket, and extra rope on board...."

"And how about a burner to heat the air in the balloon?" interjected the captain. "Where do you expect to find one of those?"

"I've been thinking about that, and I believe it can be done without a burner. The balloon can be inflated over a ground fire and then tied off. When it's buoyant enough it should rise in a fairly straight line to the top of the wall—the offshore breeze blows against the wall so the balloon won't drift in the opposite direction. Stone or sand ballast can be used to control the rate of ascent, and a handheld pole will keep the balloon from scraping against the wall. When the top of the wall is reached, a hook over the top row of stones can be used to hold the balloon fast while the repair is made. Replacing the black stone shouldn't take long, and as the air in the balloon begins to cool, the balloon will gradually descend."

There was a long silence. Jonathan watched the captain's face intently as the skipper pondered the matter, and so did not see the worried look in Llanya's eyes.

"Well, it may be possible," mused the captain. "But it will take two fools in that basket to get the job done. The priests would be quite impressed, and we need all the good will we can get around here. Besides, if the wall doesn't get fixed, it could affect the demand for the powder we bring in. Mmm. It's worth a try. And since I wouldn't trust anyone else to go with you, lad, I guess it will have to be me. But, tell me, why in Davy's dipper would you be willing to risk your skin just to speak with that old sperm bank, the Catex, anyway?"

Jonathan made no reply except to thank his friend for his willingness to go aloft with him. The captain could tell by his young apprentice's expression that it was a private matter and so didn't press him.

"Very well, it's your own business. Anyway, it's all theoretical at this point. The boss man may not agree to the deal. And if he doesn't agree by tomorrow morning, we'll be having our lunch aboard the Pelagin at sea. We can't hang around waiting for someone who doesn't know the meaning of time. Are we agreed on that, Jon?"

Jonathan sighed. "Agreed, sir."

The captain grinned. "I'd have given a Celeucian pearl—a small one—to have seen the look on that Poonwat's face when you offered the deal."

Llanya remained silent, offended that her bond-mate had not asked her feelings about the venture. But she understood his reasons and would not have stood in his way. She guessed he knew that.

Jonathan awoke later than usual the next morning after a fitful night and found Llanya unloading a breakfast tray of fruit, milk, and meal cakes, which had been left at their door.

"Jon, there's a note here with your name on it."

"Read it for me, please, will you?" he asked, stifling a yawn.

"It says your offer has been found acceptable by the Honorable High Catex and that you should commence upon the project forthwith."

Jonathan perked up. "Oh, good! I'll inform the captain and we'll get started at once. There's lots of work to be done."

"Hold on," exclaimed Llanya in a firm tone. "First you'll eat your breakfast, and then maybe it'll occur to you to ask your bond-mate if she's willing to let you go on such a madcap adventure."

"Uh, I'm sorry. Is she willing?"

"Not yet. She'll have to be asked in a much nicer way than that."

Jonathan smiled slyly. "Well, a poor bond-mate can only do his best." And with that he tackled her, and her squealing lack of protest and subsequent caresses he interpreted, not incorrectly, as willing acquiescence.

Upon hearing the news, the captain assembled the crew to ask their help in the construction of the balloon, convincing them that it was in their interest to maintain good relations with the priests considering the uniqueness of what the the Imshis had to offer. They set to work.

Jonathan made a rough sketch of the type of craft he had in mind, and with his background in science he was able to work out most of the technical details. What he couldn't figure out he made a good guess at. Llanya and two of the more nimble-fingered deck hands cut and sewed the fabric for the air bag. Other crewmen cut the lengths of rope needed to encircle the balloon and fasten to the gondola. Tabber located a ready-made reed basket the priests used for their laundry, which was large and strong enough to hold two people. Eyeing it nostalgically, he was sure that it was the very same basket he had been obliged to weave as punishment many years earlier when, as a novitiate, he had had the temerity to ask a superior what island his mother was from.

By day's end the completed sections of the balloon were ready to be transported to the wall. Llanya tacked a neatly printed sign she had made to the side of the basket. It read: High Wall Climber. But after further consideration she changed her mind and put up another she liked better, which said: Jonathan's Chariot.

A column was formed to cart the components of the balloon to the wall, and as it wended its way through the countryside, crowds of priestly onlookers assembled to gawk and whisper, many following along in the caravan's wake. It was twilight by the time the entourage reached the launching site by the wall. There the sections of the balloon were laid out in a neat row, ready to be assembled the next morning. An ample supply of kindling wood was already stacked nearby, gathered by the Imshi's hired workers, a task seen to by the temple Poonwat. The captain also arranged for a few of the priests' hired hands to keep watch on the equipment through the night, despite the Poonwat's assurances that no guard was necessary.

On the way back to the village Jonathan asked Tabber to tell him more about the wall and learned that some of its older stones were engraved with mysterious Dadukian symbols that for centuries had been the object of serious study by Mysopts. Unfortunately, very little was known about the stones near the top of the wall. Attempts had been made to observe the upper regions of the wall with a powerful glass, but the haze that perennially hung about the summit made that impossible. It seemed reasonable to conclude, however, that the wall tapered to the thickness of a single stone at its summit, at least judging from the fallen black stone. Jonathan asked how the priests knew the black stone was from the top of the wall, and Tabber replied that it was so written on an ancient Dadukian tablet kept by the High Catex.

That evening, weary from his day's labor, Jonathan dozed off in Llanya's arms, disappointing her amorous aspirations, and slept soundly till daybreak. After a hasty but hearty breakfast the two of them joined the captain and crewmen in the temple courtyard, whereupon the company set out for the launching site. Upon arrival they saw that thousands of priests had already gathered, waiting to observe what for them was to be a momentous event in Imshi history. Jonathan tried not to let the crowd unnerve him, and set immediately to work checking each section of the balloon to be sure everything was in order.

The captain assigned various tasks to his men, and assembly of the balloon began. Meanwhile, a team of immigrant laborers drove wooden stakes into the ground to hold the tie lines, and dug a shallow pit and lined it with kindling. Tabber produced two long but lightweight wooden poles, one with which to push against the wall, and the other with a metal hook at one end, calibrated to the width of the fallen stone, for grasping the top of the wall. The temple Poonwat stood by nervously, clutching the sacred black stone in one hand and a bucket in the other, the bucket containing a silver trowel, Celeucian cement mix, and a bottle of water.

In an hour's time the balloon was fully assembled. Several crewmen propped up the air bag over the heating pit with poles, and the captain gave the signal for the kindling to be ignited. Slowly the bag began to fill amidst the buzzing of the gathered multitude. Llanya held tightly to her bond-mate's arm as they watched the strange-looking vessel come to life.

Jonathan's heart seemed to swell along with the balloon. It was only as the air bag jerked into shape like a creature newly born that the boldness, and the foolishness, of the venture suddenly impressed itself upon him. He tried to push out the negative thoughts that crowded into his mind. After all, the captain would be with him, and even if there was trouble, it wouldn't be anything the two of them couldn't handle together. Besides, Llanya believed in him, and that was enough.

As the balloon rose up to its full height, a clerical chorus of oohs and ahs rose up with it. Shiny-white and majestic, like some plaything of the gods, it swayed gently to and fro, tugging at its lines as though impatient to get on with its task. To the temple Poonwat it was nothing less than the great white eye of the wall-spirit himself looking down upon his people. He secretly envied the outlanders their noble task, though he would as soon have been demoted to the rank of a lowly Silku than step into that basket.

The fire was doused and the air bag tied off. It was time to get aboard. Jonathan hugged his bond-mate, stopping short of a kiss before so many pious onlookers, though Llanya bussed him squarely on the lips anyway.

"Come on, lad," said the captain. "You get aboard first—it's your brainchild."

Jonathan stepped into the basket and the captain hopped in beside him. Tabber handed them the poles, and the Poonwat with shaking hands gave them the black stone and the bucket.

"Ready, Jon?" asked the captain.

"Yes, sir."

"Release the lines," the captain called out.

A sudden hush fell over the crowd of priests as all eyes fastened on the instrument of their deliverance, waiting for it to begin its ascent into the heavens. But nothing happened. The balloon failed to rise.

"The devil's droppings!" cursed the captain. "We're too heavy for the blasted thing. We'll have to add more cloth and make the bag bigger."

"No, I'll go alone," insisted Jonathan. "We've used up all the extra sail. It's now or never."

"No you won't!" asserted the captain, his voice flaring up.

Jonathan grabbed the captain by the arm and looked straight into his eyes, and the captain saw how deadly serious he was. It was a side of his young friend he had not seen before. Jonathan held the captain's defiant gaze, and finally the captain sighed and lowered his eyes.

"Very well, Jon. If you must, you must. But promise me you won't take any crazy risks."

"I promise."

The captain stepped out of the basket and immediately the balloon slowly began to rise. Suddenly, from out of the crowd dashed the diminutive figure of Zyl the navigator. Zyl ran helter-skelter for the balloon, and barely in time he leapt into the air, caught the side of the rising basket, and scrambled inside with Jonathan's help. With only the slight addition of the little man's weight, the balloon continued on its upward course. A cheer rang out among the crewmen, though it was swallowed up in the swell of a thousand priestly sighs of relief.

"Welcome aboard," said Jonathan. "I don't know why you're here, but I'm glad to have the company."

Zyl only grunted as he peered about glumly through bloodshot eyes.

"Oh-oh! No time for friendly chitchat now," Jonathan cried as he grabbed a pole. "Here comes the wall."

The air bag grazed the wall then bobbed gently away in response to Jonathan's prod with the pole. Zyl was ready with the other pole in case the balloon rotated and headed inward again. Jonathan was relieved that they were rising in a fairly straight line, as he had calculated, though they were moving a little faster than he had expected, helped along by a slight updraft.

As the balloon rose higher, the Imshi village came into view, which to Jonathan looked like a poster painting in its perfect symmetry. Yet higher, he could make out the cove where the Pelagin was at anchor, looking much like a child's toy glued to a shiny glass mirror. Gradually the island shrunk and the mirror grew larger until all he could see was a blurred mass of green floating on a sparkling sheet of sun-drenched sea. Wisps of cloud began to appear, though as yet there was no sign of the top of the wall.

Higher up, the wall began to change its complexion. The individual stones were smaller and darker now. Some bore strange glyphic inscriptions while others were engraved with images of the twin suns, and yet others with fearsome serpents and catlike creatures with bared claws and protruding tusks. Zyl muttered a sailor's curse under his breath to ward off evil spirits.

A sudden gust of wind blew the balloon momentarily out from the wall. Zyl pointed upward, and Jonathan saw through an opening in the clouds what the keen-eyed navigator had already spotted: the top of the wall.

"Zyl, it's coming up on us pretty fast. Let's see if we can slow ourselves down by scraping the poles against the stones."

The tactic worked, though in the thinner air the exertion made breathing hard, and as the clouds became denser, seeing also became more difficult. Crosswinds arose and threatened to blow the balloon sideways, but the drift was largely checked by the pair's deft maneuvering of the poles.

"We're almost there," cried Jonathan. "Get ready with the hook."

A horizontal black line eerily descended upon them from out of the clouds—the wall's topmost row of bricks. As the top of the air bag rose above the edge of the wall it was struck by a crosscurrent of wind and the turbulence knocked the basket hard against the wall. Jonathan's pole broke under the impact, and with the loss of resistance the balloon began to rise faster. Zyl desperately grabbed for the top of the wall with his pole-hook. It caught, clamping firmly onto the topmost row of stones, its serrated bottom edge biting hard into the slight recess between the rows.

Zyl strained to hold the balloon in place. Jonathan dropped his piece of broken pole and grabbed onto the pole-hook to help hold it securely.

"I think we're stable for the moment," he grunted, "but the wind above the wall is gusty so we'd better hurry. Zyl, can you hold the pole by yourself for a few seconds while I try to tie the pole handle to the basket?"

Zyl nodded, panting heavily, and Jonathan released his grip. In a few moments the base of the pole-hook was roped securely to the basket, and Zyl was now able to hold it in place by himself with considerably less effort.

Jonathan's eye sped along the top row of stones in both directions, seeking out a gap in the continuous line of black.

"Damn, I don't see it. Zyl, I think we drifted westward a little, so it's probably to our right. I'm going to try to grab onto the top of the wall and pull the balloon along sideways. As the balloon moves, release a little pressure on the hook and slide it along the wall as we go. But be sure to keep it over the top row of stones in case I lose my grip." Zyl wrinkled up his brow, spat, and nodded.

Sucking in his breath, Jonathan leaned out over the basket as far as he could, stretching to reach the top of the wall. His eyes kept wanting to look down, but he forced them to remain glued to the black fringe of stone. He couldn't quite make the reach. Zyl began to pull on the pole-hook, and the basket inched closer to the wall. The tips of Jonathan's fingers touched the stones and then locked over them. At the moment of contact, he felt a sudden warm sensation in his side, and he remembered that he carried the bit of the Hhor's skin in his pocket. He could only guess that the skin was responding to the contact with another great power like itself. But there was no time to ponder that now.

Gripping the row of stones with both hands, he pulled himself sideways, and as he had hoped, the balloon moved with him. Zyl slid the hook further along the wall, and ever so slowly the strange vessel crept sidewise through the sky, to any passing bird as ungainly and monstrous a sight as might be conjured in the worst avian nightmare.

Whether minutes or an hour had passed, Jonathan couldn't tell. His hands were numb and every muscle in his body ached. They had crept a good distance along the top of the wall but still could see no sign of the break. Several times a gust of wind threatened to tear them from their fragile mooring, but with Jonathan's tight grip on the wall coupled with Zyl's valiant efforts, they were able to hold fast.

Zyl rarely spoke and hadn't said a word since he had boarded the balloon, so Jonathan was surprised when he heard his shipmate suddenly cry out: "Look!"

Jonathan followed Zyl's eyes and saw further along the wall the long looked-for gap in the endless row of stones. He was too exhausted to feel elation, but the weight he had been carrying in his chest lightened and felt like a heart once again.

Soon enough they reached the fateful spot. Wasting no time, Zyl held the craft steady as best he could while Jonathan mixed the cement. But the Celeucian powder was highly absorbent, and there wasn't enough water in the bottle to soften it to the proper texture. Turning away from Zyl, Jonathan did the only thing he could under the circumstances to produce the needed liquid. He wondered what the priests would say if they knew, and smiled to himself.

With the Poonwat's silver trowel he cleaned the wall cavity of old mortar and also bits of a bony substance that looked like they might have come from a horn or a bird's claw. That puzzled him, but in the exigency of the moment he didn't dwell on the matter. Next he laid a neat lining of cement along the sides and bottom of the gap. Then, carefully picking up the black stone, he gently set it into place in the wall, tamping it with the handle of the trowel to make it flush with its neighbors. Finally, he scraped off the excess cement with a flourish, as might a conductor concluding a symphony, thereby signaling the task finished and done.

"Now the wall-spirit has all his teeth back," he quipped. "See, he's smiling."

Zyl's nose twitched and he almost grinned.

"All we have to do now is wait for the air in the balloon to cool a little and down we'll go," said Jonathan. "There's hardly any lift left as it is, so it shouldn't take long. In fact we should be able to force the balloon down a few meters now with the pole-hook. That way at least the air bag will be out of the overhead crosswind, which will make the waiting easier. Let's try it."

Suddenly an ear-piercing screech cut through the air, followed by a high whistling sound as though the very sky were being rent. Jonathan's and Zyl's heads jerked upward simultaneously, and they saw a gigantic flying creature hurtling down out of the clouds coming straight at them. In their shock and terror, neither moved, their bodies frozen, their eyes riveted on the creature's outstretched claws cutting through the sky like a phalanx of thrown spears. The creature folded back its great black wings to gain speed, its crystal-white eyes fixed unblinking upon its target.

Down it swept upon the hovering balloon, blotting out the heavens, and in the instant before it struck, Zyl threw himself in front of Jonathan, taking the full brunt of the impact. There was only a brief thud and a terrible crunching sound as the outstretched talons pierced the dwarf's chest. Rising up in a smooth arc, the giant bird glided into the clouds, the broken body of Zyl dangling limply from its claws.

The force of the impact knocked Jonathan to the floor of the basket. Striking his head against the metal bucket, he lost consciousness. With no one now to hold the balloon fast, it drifted slowly upward over the wall.

Jonathan's senses returned to him sluggishly at first, then slammed into place with an awful certainty. A surge of horror overwhelmed him, and he leaned over the basket to puke. Zyl was dead! The little man, someone he hardly knew, had offered up his life to save his. Why?

The image of the flying creature leapt into his brain, and he instinctively ducked down, scanning the heavens with his eyes. There was no sign of it now. But he remembered having seen a bird like it before, hovering over the dock in Zuralia. The captain had called it a Zytox.

He suddenly realized the balloon was descending and peered over the edge of the basket only to see the ground coming rapidly toward him. A hissing sound reached his ears, and looking up he saw that the air bag had a tear in it, doubtless caused by a swipe of the bird's claws. But he didn't think the descent was so rapid as to be dangerous. He huddled in a ball on the floor of the basket waiting for the impact.

The basket struck hard against the ground, tipping on its side and forcefully expelling its contents. Catapulted down a grassy slope, Jonathan rolled head over heels into a brier bush. For a moment he lay still, grateful to no longer be in motion. Then, bruised and scratched, he crawled out of the thorns, feeling thoroughly miserable again. Looking about, he saw that the balloon had landed on a hilly grassland not far from the wall. But the place had a wild look about it that was strangely ominous. Looking up at the twin suns and back at the wall, it suddenly dawned on him: he was on the wrong side of the wall!

He guessed what must have happened. Plopping down on the grass, he wondered what he should do next. Since there was no way under or around the wall, he would have to go over it. Again.

Pulling himself to his feet, he examined the tear in the air bag. Fortunately, it wasn't very big, but he would need a heavy needle and some thread to mend it.

Biting the edge of his shirt, he loosened the weave in the fabric and unraveled several lengths of thread, which he then braided into a single heavy strand. For the needle he revisited the brier bush and broke off a long thorn, notching its blunt end with the trowel from the basket, to which he tied the strand of thread. The instrument was crude but worthy, and he made the necessary repair in short order.

Next he would need some wood for a fire to heat the air bag. There were no trees nearby, but at the northern edge of the grassland he could see a wooded area. He borrowed some rope from the basket, which he would need to tie the wood. Since he didn't have a saw or hatchet, he hoped there would be enough fallen limbs to meet his need.

As he trekked through the tall meadow grass, he kept a wary eye on the heavens, but except for a few clouds the sky was clear and birdless. Indeed, there seemed to be no sign of animal life in the area, though wild berry bushes grew in abundance. He nibbled on some plump red berries as he walked along to appease his complaining stomach and found them quite tasty.

Passing by a stony outcropping at the base of a hill, he heard a sudden rustling noise coming from somewhere nearby. Freezing in his tracks, he listened and waited. The rustling sounded again, as though something were creeping through the tall grass. It seemed to be coming from behind him. Whirling about, he caught a flash of movement in a bush. Then nothing. He waited again. Then, out of the corner of his eye, he saw a small furry tail disappearing behind the outcropping of stones. Tiptoeing to the spot, he peered around the rocks only to find himself looking into the mouth of a cave in the side of the hill. Whatever small creature he had seen must have run into the opening, he guessed. As he peered deeper into the chamber he could make out a dim green glow coming from somewhere within. It provoked his curiosity. Ever the scientist, he decided to take a moment to investigate.

He hadn't gone very far when to his amazement the cave opened up into an enormous cavern, its walls bathed in a luminous green light emitted from the very rock itself. The pale viridian glow lent the great hall a mystical otherworldly aura, and for a moment it seemed to him that he had stumbled upon a magical fairy kingdom. His fascination was interrupted by a dripping sound coming from somewhere not far away, which reminded him that he was thirsty. Following the sound to the center of the cavern, he came upon a clear rocky pool fed by dripping stalactites from above. The water, though it reflected the green of the surrounding cavern, looked eminently drinkable.

As he sucked in the sweet liquid, he heard a lapping noise beside him. Turning, he saw the furry owner of the elusive tail he had espied earlier. It was a tiny kit, fluffy gray with yellow stripes and a tufted wisp of tail upraised like a miniature pennant. He smiled: if he had seen such a cute animal in a pet store window, he would have been hard put not to take it home. As it drank, it kept its dark round eyes glued to its oversized neighbor, though it showed no sign of fear.

"Hello, little one," said Jonathan. The sound of his voice reverberated throughout the chamber in a chorus of echoes. The kit blinked at him and twitched its ears, and as the echoes faded into silence he could hear it purring. He held out his hand to the small creature. It sniffed his fingers with interest, then, seemingly satisfied, licked them with its sandpaper tongue. Jonathan gently picked up the kit, which only amplified its purring, and he saw it was a male.

"I think you'd make a lovely pet for my Llanya, little fellow—that is, if I make it back." This time he kept his voice to a whisper so as not to set off another round of echoes. "Would you like to come along with me? Purr if you're agreeable and don't purr if you're not. Well then, the verdict is unanimous."

Jonathan tucked the kit in his pocket with only its little head exposed to the world, then made his way back to the entrance of the cave. Just inside the entrance he spotted a pile of old bones, which looked like the skeletal remains of a giant catlike creature.

"I hope that's not one of your family," offered Jonathan, "or else my bond-mate will be in for a big surprise."

Continuing on to the wooded area, he found to his relief there were plenty of fallen branches lying among the trees. By tying some limbs together he was able to make a land raft big enough to haul all the wood he needed in one trip.

As he gathered the wood, he came upon a strange object hanging in the trees. He thought it fascinating, but couldn't imagine what it was. Several times the height of a man and extending to his left and right farther than the eye could see, it looked like a gigantic white paper-like cylinder trailing through the forest. Semitransparent and crinkly to the touch, its entire surface was beautifully marked in an intricate diamond pattern, which he could only liken to the skin of a snake.

Dropping the load of wood he was carrying, the realization struck him like a shot. What he was looking at *was* the sloughed-off skin of an enormous serpent, and considering its sheen and intact condition, it probably hadn't been shed very long ago.

The kit in his pocket mewed.

"You're right, little fellow, it's time to go. We have enough wood, and I don't think we want to wait around to meet the owner of this tree decoration."

Jonathan piled the branches onto the makeshift raft, then hastily rigged up a rope harness. Fortunately the grass was thick and pliable, cushioning the weight of the sledge, and he was able to make the trek back to the balloon in good time.

Working quickly, it wasn't long before the balloon was in position and the wood was ready to be ignited. But the matches he thought he had in his pocket weren't there. He would have to find a substitute. Then he remembered the bottle of water the Poonwat had given him to mix the cement. He could use the glass to magnify the rays of the sun. But the bottle wasn't in the basket, and he guessed it had been thrown free upon landing. Searching about in the grass, he soon found it, unbroken. Holding it up to a bit of dried grass, he concentrated the suns' rays on the tinder, but the twin suns were waning and their weakened rays were broken by clouds. It wasn't working and time was running out. He knew that if he didn't launch the balloon before dark, there would be no other chance that day: only in the late afternoon did the Klellian winds blow northward, and he would need their help to keep close to the wall.

Searching again through his pockets, he came upon the bit of Hhor's skin. It was warm to the touch and he pulled it out. The kit mewed at the removal of its private heater.

"Hhor, my friend," he said as he looked at the unpresuming piece of hide, "can you warm up a little more and maybe light a fire?"

No sooner had he spoken than the piece of skin became hot in his hand, and he tossed it to the edge of the kindling. In seconds the wood burst into flames. He quickly retrieved the skin, relieved to see that it was undamaged. Now cool to the touch, he replaced it in his pocket, though not without offering silent thanks.

It was nearly twilight before the air bag was full and pulling on the tie lines. Jonathan doused the fire, tied off the bag, and got aboard. Throwing off the lines, he let out a cheer as the balloon began to drift slowly upward. He was much too excited to hear the dull crashing and scraping sounds in the distance, sounds of falling trees and the tearing of the land's crust.

"Jonathan's Chariot rides again!" he yelled, and the kit ducked into his pocket in apparent disgust.

Rising above the hills, the frail craft was soon caught in the grip of the north wind which steered it unerringly toward the wall. Jonathan stood ready with the salvaged pole-hook to guide his ascent. On reaching the wall the balloon caught a strong updraft and was swept rapidly upward. Despite the speed the ride was smooth, and the young navigator had little difficulty keeping the craft in position without it striking the wall.

Had he not been so intent upon his task and taken a moment to look down one last time, he would have seen the trees in the wood toppling over like matchsticks and the long glistening body of a giant serpent sliding through the grass toward his launching site. Then perhaps the true reason for the great wall would have occurred to him; perhaps he would have understood the great fear in the hearts of the ancient Dadukians as they set upon their monumental task of construction.

Wisps of cloud began to appear and Jonathan knew the top of the wall was fast approaching. He scraped the base of the pole-hook against the wall to slow his rate of ascent, but he was rising too rapidly and the maneuver had little effect. If his speed wasn't reduced he knew he would be unable to grab onto the topmost stones with the pole-hook. He had to slow the balloon down, and the only way he could think of was to release some air from the bag.

With the end of the pole-hook he reached up and poked a small hole low in the air bag. He could hear the hissing, like a bucket of snakes, as the warm air escaped. The balloon slowed a little, but still not enough. He opened the hole a little more and the craft slowed to a manageable speed. And none too soon, for the top of the wall suddenly loomed into view.

As the horizontal black line of stones rose up before him, he swept the pole-hook downward as a falcon upon its prey. The hook caught and held fast; then freeing one hand, he tied the pole handle to the basket.

Now came the difficult part: to transfer the basket to the other side of the wall with him in it.

Straining to hold the pole-hook fast with one hand, he took the kit out of his pocket with his other hand and placed it on the floor of the basket lest he accidentally injure it in his maneuvering. He then kicked a hole through the upper left side of the basket and pushed his leg through it, hooking himself firmly onto the wicker frame. The lift in the balloon was still too strong for the trick he had in mind, so he had no choice but to wait until more air escaped. Then, taking a deep breath, he reached out and grabbed onto the top of the wall with his left hand and released the pole-hook with his right, letting it fall into the basket. Grasping the wall now with both hands, he slowly pulled the upper half of his body out onto the stones, turning gradually sideways as he did so. Stopping a moment to catch his breath, he gathered all his strength and pulled up his leg that was hooked to the basket, slowly dragging it and the basket up and over the wall. In so doing, he was aided, as he had counted on, by the buoyancy of the balloon. Still holding onto the wall, he then un-hooked his leg from the wicker frame and stood once again on the floor of the basket. The maneuver had succeeded. And thankfully, he had not dislodged any of the black bricks in the process.

The balloon's buoyancy continued to weaken, and just as he was about to reattach the pole-hook to the wall, without warning the craft began to descend. He had to prevent it from falling too rapidly, and had anticipated that eventuality: he had deliberately punched the hole low in the bag so he could easily reach it with the pole-hook. Turning the pole around to its blunt end, he pushed it into the hole and held it fast. The makeshift plug worked, and the hissing stopped. The balloon glided downward at a safe and steady speed. Only now the wind began to blow southward, and the vessel gradually drifted away from the wall.

There was nothing more he could do but wait and see where nature would deliver him. Securing the pole so it wouldn't slip out of position, he sat down on the floor of the basket to rest himself. Picking up the kit, he placed it on his knee and stroked its soft fur, listening to its little engine purr contentedly. It looked up at him and meowed, and he noticed that its tongue had a familiar greenish tint. Strange, he thought. He rubbed his own tongue with his finger and saw it too was slightly green. He laughed.

"Well little fellow, it seems the liquid we drank from the pool in the cavern wasn't just reflecting green from the phosphorescent walls. It was green itself. And I recall tasting its sweetness before—in the Temple of Klell. It's the Imshis' elixir of life. There must be an underground stream that carries it beneath the wall to a secret place known only to the priests. You know what? With that one drink I'll bet we both added ten years to our life. But I guess you have nine lives already."

The kit looked at him with its large doleful eyes and yawned. It began to lick its paws in obvious disinterest in the one-sided conversation.

"Come to think of it, you've probably been drinking from that pool for a while. You could be any age. Tell me your secret. How old are you, little one?"

The kit raised its head and met its questioner's gaze. Jonathan looked deeply into the feline's dark eyes, and the ageless knowledge he thought he saw there made him wonder.

"By kidnapping you I'm afraid I've robbed you of immortality, my friend," he said in an apologetic tone. "But I think you'll find growing up to be an exciting experience."

The sound of human voices reached Jonathan's ears. Looking out over the basket he saw the rooftops of the Klellian village rising up to meet him, and on the road below he saw the captain and Llanya running toward him waving and shouting—a welcome sight indeed.

The balloon came to a bumping halt in a field just outside the village. Llanya was the first to reach him, and she fairly leapt at him in a bear-hug embrace. The captain came up behind, panting from his run, and grasped his friend's hand.

"Welcome back, lad. You sure had us worried. Are you all right?"

"I'm fine, sir. Just a couple of minor bruises."

"And Zyl? Where's Zyl?"

Jonathan lowered his eyes. "Zyl's gone. A Zytox got him at the top of the wall. He…he gave his life to save mine."

The captain sighed deeply. "I didn't know the little guy very well—he was new. But it seems there was a lot to him. Well, you'd best get back to your quarters before the whole island arrives. You need rest and we'll talk later. I'll stay behind and explain matters to the crew and also talk to the priests. Uh, what should I tell them about the black stone?"

"The stone is back in its place."

Walking back to the dormitory, Jonathan took the kit out of his pocket and presented it to Llanya.

"A present for you," he said.

"Oh, Jon, I love her!"

"It's a him."

"But where…"

"I'll tell you later. Right now if I don't lie down, I think I'll drop."

As they reached the dormitory building, a green-robed Bhukar emerged from around the corner. When he saw them he stopped dead in his tracks, and his face contorted in a look of utter horror. With a trembling hand he pointed at the kit.

"You've g-g-got a trocht!" he screeched. And with that he lifted his robe to his knees and ran off down the road as fast as his spindly legs would carry him.

Llanya giggled. "What a strange man. Imagine being afraid of a little kitten."

CHAPTER 9

THE HIGH CATEX

Next morning at breakfast, after a restful night's sleep, Jonathan told Llanya and the captain about his experiences of the previous day, though he softened the story so as not to alarm his bond-mate. From his friend's face, though, he knew the skipper was not fooled. He decided it was probably best not to mention his discovery of the source of the elixir of life: it could serve no good purpose. He doubted the High Catex would want the secret revealed, and he needed the old priest's good will if he was to obtain his help.

"I'd say you had a close call or two," said the captain, wishing he had been able to share the adventure. "But you've made a lot of priests mighty happy, which we'll all benefit from. And you found a pet for Llanya. Cute little fur ball, I must say."

"The kitten frightened a priest yesterday," said Llanya. "The silly man called it a trocht."

The captain frowned. "A trocht you say? I've heard of such a beast—always thought it was mythical. Come to think of it, I once saw a drawing of one, in an old book in the Zuralia central library. If memory serves, it looked like a big toothy tiger. Hmm, maybe I better tell Nynt the cook to stock up on some extra rations of meat."

"He likes milk," said Llanya, pouting. Suddenly her face lit up. "Jon, I don't know if he's a trocht, but we can name him Trok for short anyway. Trok: yes, I like that name."

"Fine with me. But maybe you'd better ask him what he thinks about it."

The conversation was interrupted by a knock on the door. Llanya opened it and the temple Poonwat entered. Espying the kit, the priest stopped short and his eyes widened. He took a step backward. Llanya picked up the kit. Satisfied now that there was no immediate danger, the Poonwat bowed low to Jonathan and spoke in a respectful voice that bordered on the obsequious:

"O Dhak-Llan-To, healer of the sacred wall, I have come to escort you into the presence of the Honorable High Catex himself."

Jonathan was delighted, and he saw the sparkle in Llanya's eye.

"Great! Can my bond-mate come along?"

"My sincere regrets. The Ancient Father has asked that only the Dhak-Llan-To be shown into his presence."

Jonathan looked annoyed. Llanya pouted.

"Don't take it personally, lad," said the captain. "Despite having fathered many offspring, the old boy has probably never seen a woman in the flesh before. The shock might kill him."

The Poonwat grimaced, which required only a slight modification of his normal expression.

Jonathan shrugged. "Very well, I'll go alone. Llanya, I shouldn't be very long."

The Poonwat escorted Jonathan to the temple. Once inside, the priest turned him over to a Bhukar, who was a personal attendant of the High Catex. The Bhukar pressed his palms together and bowed.

"You will forgive me, O Wall Healer, but you must now be blindfolded, though only briefly. The location of the room within the temple wherein dwells the Ancient One is a secret known only to few. I will guide you there. Once within the master's presence the blindfold will be removed."

Jonathan consented and the Bhukar tied a black ribbon about his head, covering his eyes. The green-robed priest then led him by the arm down several long corridors, thence up a long winding staircase, and finally through a door that required a key to open. The door creaked fretfully on its hinges. The Bhukar then removed the blindfold, bowed, and departed, locking the door behind him.

Looking about, Jonathan saw that he was in a large dimly lit hall, circular in shape and windowless, its floor, walls, and domed ceiling all of white stone. A faint odor of mustiness hung in the air and the silence was leaden. At first he thought the room was empty, but as his eyes grew accustomed to the dimness, he saw there were two high-backed wooden chairs at the far end of the hall, one of which appeared to be occupied. He received no sign or summons, and so walked across the room towards the seated figure, the sound of his footsteps echoing like hammer blows against the stone floor. He could feel each step chipping away at his confidence.

The two chairs were set facing each other, placed in such a way that the empty chair was in the light and the occupied one in the shadows. Jonathan stopped beside the empty chair and peered at the seated figure, but all he could make out was the outline of a black hooded robe.

"I am the High Catex of Klell. Welcome, Wall Mender. I beg you to be seated."

The sound of the Catex's voice surprised Jonathan. He expected it to be laden with the weight of the ages, but it was vibrant and unhesitating with no trace of the somber undertone common to the Klellian priests.

"Thank you," said Jonathan as he lowered himself into the chair.

"It is I who thank you. By returning the black stone to its rightful place in the wall, you not only restored tranquility to our humble community, you retied a binding thread in the very fabric of our ancient society. And, indeed, in the fabric of the dimensional plane itself. Your heroism, and that of your lost comrade, has served many more than you know. I am truly sorry about your friend. All Imshis will honor his memory."

The Catex hesitated a moment before continuing.

"I wonder, will you indulge an old man and allow me to ask one or two questions about your adventure yesterday?"

"Yes, certainly." This is a very unpriestly priest as Imshis go, thought Jonathan.

"Since a black stone has never fallen from the wall before, I have been wondering what might have been the cause. Did you happen to notice anything that might help to explain it?"

"Now that you ask, yes. There were some bits of a hard bony substance in the gap, like from the beak or claw of a bird. It could have come from the same bird—a Zytox—that tried to kill me but killed my shipmate instead."

"A Zytox you say. I feared as much. A most troublesome sign. The Zytox are dangerous, and are known to be susceptible to mind direction—they can be mind-trained to carry out deeds for their masters. There was evil intent here, and one can only wonder why the Zytox attacked the wall, and you. Do you have enemies, Wall Climber?"

"No, not to my knowledge."

"We Imshis have many, mostly those who seek control over the sacred elixir. Injuring the High Wall and creating havoc in our community could be a means to that end. But for the moment that must remain an unresolved question. Meanwhile, my advice to you is to stay alert. You may be in mortal danger."

The Catex spoke these last words in almost a whisper, which sent a shiver down Jonathan's spine. The old priest struck him as both honest and wise, and he was inclined to take his words seriously.

"One more question, if I may, Wall Healer. You were observed emerging from the balloon with a young trocht, an animal that could only have come from the north side of the wall. My own ancestral origins are also from beyond the wall. Anything you can tell me about what you saw there would be most gratefully received. Indeed, you would be writing sacred words in our Klellian book of history."

Jonathan deliberated a moment and decided there was no reason not to divulge what he had learned to the High Catex.

"Very well. But then you must answer my question."

"That has always been my intention."

"I discovered the source of your sacred elixir."

At those words the Catex started, and he leaned forward and gripped the arms of his chair. By so doing his face and hands became momentarily exposed.

Jonathan's breath caught. He saw that the high priest's face was that of a young man not much older than himself; though, as might be expected of the father of all, it resembled Tabber's and every other priestly countenance on the island. He now realized what a continual diet of elixir could accomplish, if indeed the Catex was as old as everyone said.

But more than the High Priest's face, it was his hands that drew his attention. The skin, like that of the face, was taut and youthful, but it bore a faint design upon its surface—a diamond pattern identical to the one he had seen the day before on the giant snake skin in the wood. He swallowed and tried not to show his surprise. He continued his story.

"I discovered a large underground pool of the elixir in a cavern. It was dripping from stalactites."

"And you thought that was the source?" asked the Catex, his voice relieved and tinged with amusement.

"Yes. Do you mean it wasn't?"

"It was not. I know what the true source is. It is part of my ancestral memory and is verified by the tablet writings of the ancient Daduks. But have you told anyone of your discovery of the pool?"

"No. I thought it best not to."

"I thank you for that and beg your continued silence. If the secret became known and the northern side of the island were invaded, we on the southern side of the wall would be hard put to use our mental powers to dispel the usurpers."

"Then what is the source?" inquired Jonathan, without considering the magnitude of his question.

The priest paused. "I will tell you, Wall Healer, but only in a transitory voice. By that I mean I will speak in such a way that you will not remember my words once you have left my presence. Only thusly will I reveal to you a secret that not even a single one of my children knows. Is the condition acceptable?"

"Yes." Jonathan shifted in his chair.

"Know, then, that the elixir is the milk of she who is the ancestral mother of all Klellians. We Imshis, one and all, are of reptilian origin on our maternal side. Our ancestral mother is the great serpent, Ish. Ish is immortal and creates within herself her own offspring—all males. It is her curse that she cannot produce females. Though she has tried for eons, she has never birthed a daughter. Thus she is bitter in her hatred of all males, and all her sons she devours.

"But one serpent son escaped his mother's wrath and hid from her. He discovered a trickle of his mother's milk running beneath the ground, which he drank, and he too shed the skin of mortality. In time he learned the tricks necessary to escape his vengeful ever-searching parent, and by his scurrying and squirming down through the ages he developed arms and legs, and eventually he evolved into the semblance of a man.

"In time other quasi humans, male and female, came to the shores of Klell, and so began the race of the Daduks. It was the early Daduks who built the wall to shut out Ish. At that stage of their evolution they were strong and still had suction cups upon their hands, and so they were able to climb and built up the wall to a great height. In later generations all primordial features fell away and the Daduks became fully human. In their golden age they were noble and wise, but they knew not the secret of the magic elixir, and in time they and their memories withered away.

"The pool you discovered, O Wall Healer, lies below the lair of Ish, and her milk, unconsumed by her devoured children, trickles down to the cavern below. Beneath the pool is an underground stream which carries the elixir under the wall to a secret place within this very temple.

"From such beginnings did we Klellians emerge. Thus it is that Ish's curse and her hatred of all males is necessary to the continuous flow of her milk—the elixir that is the very life source of the Klellian priesthood. By devouring her sons, Ish gives life to mine.

"It is fortunate for you, Wall Mender, that when you walked in her garden, Ish did not detect your odor. Surely, after your brave deed among the heavens, the spirit of the wall was with you."

For a moment no one spoke. Jonathan was awestruck by the High Priest's tale. He wondered, could the Catex himself—this youthful-looking man who sat before him—could he be the age-old serpent son of Ish? Could he be the one who escaped the great serpent mother and evolved to found and rule the all-male race of Klellians? Were the short-lived sons of Ish his brothers? Was his fathering of a tribe of priestly sons but a form of retribution, an elaborate vengeance against his mother?

He remembered something Tabber had said about the sacred elixir, that in its purest form, unlike the diluted drink given to guests and workers, it was highly potent and doubtless accounted for the Catex's extreme age. He, himself, had drunk the elixir from the cavern pool, close to its source. Was what he drank undiluted? The Catex would know. But perhaps it would be better if he didn't ask. Such knowledge could be a curse. The thought of Llanya growing old while he remained young made him shudder.

"Now what is it you would have of me?" asked the Catex.

"Is your transitory voice turned off?" inquired Jonathan. "I may need to remember what you tell me."

"You will remember."

"My question is simple. I am seeking a dream reader. Do you know where I can find one?"

"You have not presented your question in context. Additional information would be helpful. Is there anything more you can tell me?"

Jonathan hesitated, recalling the old dream sender's warning to keep his own counsel. Should be make an exception in this case?

"No," he replied.

"Very well. There are a few dream readers on this plane, but I do not know exactly where they are. But if you wish I will try to locate one for you."

"But that will take a long time. I need…"

"I will try to locate one for you now. It will not take long."

"Now? How can you do that? Is there one on Klell?"

"No. But I have certain mental abilities. Dream readers also have highly developed mental faculties and are capable of receiving mind messages. So I will send out a mind search. I only ask for your patience and a moment of silence."

Jonathan sat motionless, only half believing that the high priest would be able to locate a dream reader by telepathy. He watched the Catex intently. Minutes went by, and from time to time he could see the hood of the priest's robe move slightly.

"Wall Mender, I have found a dream reader." Though the high priest's words were softly spoken, his voice broke the silence so suddenly that Jonathan started. "But I am having some difficulty communicating and will need the benefit of your assistance. You see, the dream reader is a… female. I am not experienced in speaking with the human female. Therefore, before initiating a conversation, I need to know if there are any gender-related preliminaries required of me, or any customary courtesies I should be made aware of."

"Uh, well, that depends. Actually, no, not really. It would probably be best if you spoke with her as you would with a man. But would you mind giving voice to your thoughts so I can hear the conversation too?"

"Gladly. I will reestablish contact.

"Greetings once again, O Dream Reader. Yes, your thoughts are clear. Your name is Skekiloreida, but you prefer to be called Lorie. Very well… Lorie. That is correct, I am a priest of Klell. You say you reside on Cruor

Island, in the Decylian chain. Yes, we are practically neighbors. Lorie, I have a young man with me who would like an audience with you. Spenser, Jonathan Spenser. No, he is not a priest. You want to know why he wishes to see you?"

"To ask her about a dream," interjected Jonathan.

"To ask you about a dream," repeated the Catex. "Yes. Well, considering the short distance, he could be there in a few days. A condition? You will see him only if he brings you…what? Blue devils? They are nuts, you say? I see, they are mind-expanding nuts that help you in your work. They are blue and about the size of walnuts, and they grow on Mast Isle, at the southern tip of the Decylian chain. Yes, I have heard of Mast Isle. I understand—a ship coming from Klell would have to pass by the island on the way to Cruor. Mast Isle is uninhabited and it would be a simple matter to gather the nuts. Very well, I will tell him.

"Me? As I said, just a priest. I have a what kind of voice? Mongo sexy? I am not familiar with that phrase. No, I regret that is not possible. Why? Because the priests of Klell are all celibates, and we don't travel. I certainly appreciate that you think priests are trustworthy and will not— what? Spill the beans? I regret I am not familiar with that expression either. No, I am sorry, that kind of activity is strictly forbidden. As I said, we are celibates. No, not even among ourselves. I cannot obtain special permission. It is a rule of the high priest. No, I cannot ask him. I am the high priest. Yes, it may be true that no one else on Klell will know except me, but that is sufficient. I can appreciate your problem, from your point of view. Yes, I'm sure it is difficult living alone, without men. Do I miss women, and doing what? Well, that is not a subject priests dwell upon. I agree that priests are clean and disease-free. That is a tenet of our faith. No, I regret I cannot indulge in a thought exchange with you of that nature. In that respect we are also mental celibates.

"The young man? Yes, he has a bond-mate. Yes, she is traveling with him. His ship is called the Pelagin. You don't trust sailors. You like priests better. No, I am sorry, I cannot come even for a brief visit. No, there will be no priests aboard ship, only a former priest. His name? Tabber. No, I cannot give him such a message. Why not? For many reasons. Propriety, for one. Also, he is my son. No, I have more than one son. Even more than that. Yes, they're mostly all grown. Then how can I be a celibate? I am afraid that is a very complicated question and would take more time to answer than we have at the moment. No, I do not lie. Yes, that is true, I must admit to being quite old. Oh, you say you must go now? I understand. Very well. You may expect to see Master Spenser soon. Good-bye."

"Is she gone?" asked Jonathan.

"Yes. The lady Skekiloreida—she prefers the name Lorie—will be glad to receive you, provided you meet her condition, as you heard. It seems the wall climber must now become a tree climber. The lady insists that the task is a simple one. She is also quite insistent that you keep her identity and whereabouts a secret, and further, that you are to be the only one on your vessel to set foot on Cruor island. It seems she is, to use her own expression, hiding out. She did not say from what or whom. She is also distrustful of mariners for some reason I do not quite understand. Indeed, much of her conversation was puzzling to me.

"But, fortunately, Cruor is not very far from Klell and is close to Mast Isle. She described Cruor island as small and egg-shaped with beaches of blood-red sand. I expect your ship's captain knows its location. According to the lady, passing ships avoid stopping at the island. She says it is considered bad luck, which gives her the privacy she desires. Though at times I gather she gets lonely for company. She says she is the only human resident on the island, and that you will be able to easily reach her dwelling from the south shore.

"As you heard, she was quite forthcoming with information—I gather because I am a priest and she trusts priests. She was clever enough to verify my occupation and location by sending out a thought scan at the beginning of the conversation. I permitted her that insight for your benefit. I was also able to determine that her thoughts were honest and that you need not fear treachery. As to her other character traits, however, I cannot speak.

"I hope the arrangements are to your satisfaction."

Jonathan was flabbergasted. "Yes, very much so."

"Good. Now if you permit me to make one further inquiry. It's about my son, Tabber. As you may know, he left our priesthood some years ago. I was disappointed when he left. He showed much promise, though I am pleased he has found a place among the good men of the Pelagin and is able to make use of his talent. But I am concerned about him, as I am about all my sons. So I want to ask you—is he content and well?"

"Yes, he seems to be. Tabber and I are friends. I haven't known him very long, but I know he has a good soul and a gentle heart, and he's well liked by his shipmates."

"I am pleased. But I have been told his hair is whitening and he is showing signs of age. Has this distressed him?"

"Not that I can tell."

"Will you give him a message for me?"

"Certainly."

"Tell him that he is in his father's thoughts, and that if ever he wishes to return to the Imshi priesthood, he will be welcome."

"I will tell him."

"Thank you. I bid you safe journey, Dhak-Llan-To. You will long be remembered for your brave deed. Our shores will always be open to you. Remain watchful, live long, and bear many sons."

Jonathan bid the Catex farewell. The Bhukar arrived, and he was blindfolded as before and led out of the temple. Llanya was waiting for him in the courtyard.

"Oh, Jon, you took so long. Is everything all right? Was the High Catex able to help you?"

"Yes, everything went fine. He gave me the information I needed. Now all I have to do is convince the captain to make a short sail to Cruor Island in the Decylian chain."

Oh, goody!" Llanya clapped her hands. "We'll visit another island. This place is getting a little boring, anyway."

CHAPTER 10

THE BLUE DEVILS

"What? The Decylian Isles?" The captain was clearly annoyed. "Jon, I can't just up and take the crew to a strange port for no good reason. We've had a successful voyage, and now the men are restless and want to return to Zuralia. They're anxious to spend a little of the bonus they got from Celeucia, and with some extra youth thrown in, they want to do a little candle burning too. Can't blame them for that, can you? When the men are in this mood, they're not much good as sailors anyway. It's my plan to set sail for Zuralia at daybreak tomorrow."

Jonathan and Llanya looked down at the floor of the captain's cabin and said nothing. Their pained expressions softened the captain a bit. The skipper threw up his hands and muttered a sailor's oath.

"Jon, you say going to Cruor Island is important to you, but you won't tell me why. I know you have your little secrets—that's been clear for some time. And it's none of my business. I try to go along with you when I can. But now you're asking me to do something that affects the lives of everyone on board. That's not right. If you don't trust me, that's fine. We'll just leave it at that."

The captain's expression displayed hurt as well as irritation. Llanya reached out and touched her bond-mate's hand. He looked at her and read the meaning in her eyes. He nodded.

"Of course I trust you, Captain. And you're right. It's time I told you more about myself. But I think you had better sit down first.

The captain seated himself on the edge of his bunk and folded his arms.

"You see, sir, I'm not from this plane. Here's the whole story."

Nearly an hour passed before Jonathan stopped talking. The captain leaned back in his chair and put his hands to his brow. His voice was tense.

"A weighty story, lad. Weighty indeed. Wow! There are big stakes in this game, I think. And my guess is you're the gold chip on the table. The question is, who are the other players and what are they after? The High Catex read it right. You're in danger. The Zytox that got Zyl was after you for a reason. And there's something else I have to tell you—Balu also knows. Your fall into the sea wasn't accidental. The tie line was cut."

Llanya's breath caught and she grasped Jonathan's wrist. The captain went on.

"Whoever is out to get you has a minion on board as well as Zytox on the hunt. And you say you have no idea who it might be. Well, if whoever is behind this is powerful enough to control Zytox birds, then the islands could be in danger too. Your enemy obviously knows something about you and about whatever it is that's giving you that mental itch. From what you say the key to all this might well be in your head, maybe in a dream you don't remember. You're right, we need a…what do you call it?"

"Dream reader."

"Right, dream reader." The captain sighed. "Very well, the Decylians it is. The island chain isn't far from here, and I think I know the right two words to say to the crew: Mast Isle. I've sailed by the isle, though I've never weighed anchor there before. It's famous for its nuts, especially its beetle nuts. I've never heard of the blue devil nuts your dream reader wants. But the beetle nuts are much sought after in Zuralia as an aphrodisiac. Very potent. Or so I'm told—never use them myself. They're a good barter item in the Zuralian underground market in exchange for, uh, things that can't readily be bought with currency or jewels. I'm pretty sure the crew will tolerate a brief digression for that kind of purchasing power. And since Cruor Island is practically next door to Mast Isle, a brief stop there shouldn't raise any hackles. I'll talk to the men and have the ship ready to set sail on the morning tide.

"And remember, lad, we have an unknown assailant on board, so I want you to be extra careful. When you're on deck, I want both of you to be sure you're in my or Balu's sight. Keep your eyes peeled. And tell absolutely no one what you've told me."

A crowd of Imshis gathered at the dock at daybreak to see the Pelagin off. The bay wind was moody and the water choppy, but Tabber steered the heeling ship cleanly through the outer reefs into the open sea. Later, when the captain took over the wheel, Jonathan took the opportunity to give Tabber the message from the High Catex. The helmsman slowly shook his head from side to side.

"I do not understand my father or my brothers," he said, sadly. "They lengthen their years that they may more deeply probe the mysteries of life. And yet by so doing they trap themselves within it and so cannot reach the doorway to the greatest mystery of all. It is a door I would open in my time. Until then I would see something of the world beyond the shores of Klell. Am I not also my mother's son?"

The captain had little difficulty convincing the crew that a brief visit to Mast Isle would be worthwhile. Indeed, for the next two days the men talked about nothing but the delectable goods and services they would be able to purchase off-market with a store of Mastian beetle nuts.

At dawn's light on the third day out of Klell, a cry from the crow's-nest rang out: "The Isle of Mast, hard off the port bow."

From on deck Jonathan and Llanya, her pet, Trok, cradled in her arms, watched the island grow like a multi-hued mushroom out of the sea. They saw it was hilly and heavily treed and fringed with wide sandy beaches. The inshore waters were calm and reefless, and the captain had no difficulty gliding the Pelagin into a protected inlet on the western shore. It was a deep water bay, enabling the ship to anchor only a stones throw off a golden shell-strewn beach.

"Oh Jon, it's beautiful!" cried Llanya. "Trok's asleep and doesn't need looking after, so I can go ashore with you. We can swim to the beach."

The captain, approaching, overheard. "No, swimming would be dangerous. These are shark infested waters. And who knows what else is down there? We'll go ashore in rowboats. Each of you take a string sack from that pile by the hatchway there—for collecting the nuts—and tie it around your waists. We'll form two parties. The crew will hunt for the beetle nuts, and the three of us will go looking for the...what did you call them?"

"Blue devils," Jonathan replied.

"Oh no," protested Llanya. "You two can hunt for devils. I want to go with the others and look for beetle nuts. Jon, I want you to try some of them. It might be fun."

Jonathan blushed a deep red and the captain guffawed.

"Very well, if you must," mumbled Jonathan. "But stay close to Balu."

Just then Balu came walking up and handed the captain a spyglass.

"Captain, the island is not uninhabited as we thought. Look there on the beach, at the edge of that large dune."

"Mmm. Yes, I see him. Seems to be alone, though, and looks harmless enough. A runty old graybeard—ragged clothes—no weapon that I can see. Strange. There are other ships that pass this way, so I doubt he's stranded. Probably just an old hermit living high on those mind-stretching devil nuts. He'll probably run for cover when he sees us coming ashore.

"Balu, have the men lower the boats. Give the order that everyone who can be spared is to go ashore to hunt nuts, which means everyone except Nynt the cook. We'll need a decent meal after our day's labor."

Three rowboats slid softly onto the sandy shore side by side. As the crewmen assembled on the beach, the old graybeard emerged from behind a dune and began to jump up and down and wave his arms.

"Welcome! Welcome!" he called out in a high squeaky voice. "Welcome to Nut Island. Nuts everywhere. We're all nutty here. Hee, hee, hee."

"As a fruit cake," whispered the captain to Jonathan.

The graybeard hopped about on one foot in a circle and his squeak became singsong.

"I've got big nuts, small nuts, round nuts, oval nuts, blue nuts, red nuts, sweet nuts, bitter nuts, happy nuts, sad nuts—nuts, nuts, nuts. Just bring along your hat and I'll show you where they're at."

"Ahem!" interrupted the captain. "Tell me, old timer, do you live here on the island alone?"

The graybeard stopped twirling. "Yes, all alone except for all my nutty friends. Hee, hee, hee. You'll be the cap'n. That makes two. I'm a cap'n too."

"Tell me, Captain, seen any big Zytox birds flying around here lately?"

"Zytox? No, them's bad. Nope, none of them."

"And can you tell me what kind of food—besides nuts—there is on this island? And how about fresh water?"

"Fresh water yes. And lots of sea goodies—fish, oysters, clams, crabs, eels. And fruits, many kinds of fruits—blueberries, blackberries, gooseberries, red pears, green pears, star pears...."

"Thanks, I get the picture. Well then, from one captain to another, maybe you can show us around."

"Aye-aye, sir. Glad to. Glad to."

"Good. You can start by showing us where the happy nuts and the blue nuts are that you mentioned?"

"Yes, yes. But they're in different directions. Happy nuts are that way," squeaked the graybeard, pointing to the forest to the east, "and the blue nuts are that way," pointing west.

The captain signaled to the chief mate.

"Balu, you and the men go with the captain here. He'll guide you to the beetle nut trees. Llanya will be going with you, so keep an eye on her. Jon and I will search in the opposite direction and will meet you and the men back here in a few hours."

The groups separated. The captain and Jonathan walked along the treeline that bordered the beach and soon came upon a narrow path that led in a westerly direction into the forest. They followed it. The wood was dense and dreary, though rich in a variety of fruit and nut trees. But there was no sign of the blue nut trees they sought. The path branched off several times, and the captain marked each turn with branches so they wouldn't lose their way. Further along the trees began to thin out and the land became hilly.

The captain suddenly stopped and cocked his head.

"Listen, Jon. Do you hear that?"

"Yes, it sounds like a bunch of squawking birds."

"That's exactly what it is. They're parrots. And from their merry conversation, my guess is they're all feasting on your blue happiness-nuts. Let's follow the sound."

Upon reaching the parrot roost the captain broke out in a broad smile.

"I was right. Trees full of drunken birds eating blue devils. Look at the scurvy lot, like a bunch of tipsy sailors in native getup."

Jonathan couldn't help laughing at the comical sight.

"Well, lad, you wanted the nuts, so you can do the climbing. If you avoid getting bird-spattered, it'll be a miracle. Look at the ground—the critters are even crapping blue."

Jonathan surveyed the area trying to decide which would be the easiest tree to climb.

"Captain, look over there, just beyond the blue-nut grove. From your description, aren't those beetle nut trees?"

"Well I'll be an oyster's uncle! They are, lad. And by the look of them they're loaded with nuts. We've hit it double! Hmm, I wonder why the old hermit took the men in the opposite direction?"

"Maybe the other grove was nearer or had better pickings," speculated Jonathan.

"Maybe. Anyway, you'd best start making like a monkey or we'll be here all day. There's some beetle nuts on the ground over there. I'll gather those."

The graybeard carried on an animated conversation with himself as he led Balu, Llanya, and the contingent of seamen up one forest trail and down another. They walked for some time, and Balu began to wonder if they were going in circles.

"We're almost there," squeaked the hermit. "But I need to stop a moment to catch me breath. This cap'n's getting old, he is. Ah, look! Here be some blackberry bushes. Delicious. Yum, yum. Lunch time! Try some, try some!"

The seamen didn't need prodding and were glad to have something tasty to munch on as they waited for the graybeard to resume the trek.

Suddenly the hermit began to jump up and down and howl with glee.

"You've eaten the berries! Now you be mine!" he squealed. "Listen up, all of you. I'm your cap'n and you're me crew. And you obey only me. Do you hear?"

The crewmen and officers alike, including Balu, looked at one another with blank faces and nodded dumbly in agreement. Llanya could hardly believe what she saw and became terrified. The men were behaving like mindless slaves. What had happened? The blackberries! That had to be it. She and the hermit were the only ones who hadn't eaten any.

Should I make a run for it, she asked herself, and try to find Jon and the captain? Or pretend to have eaten the berries and try to help the men? She doubted she would have the courage to brain the old man with a branch, which made her wonder about the value of her pacifistic upbringing.

She decided to pretend to be drugged like the others, at least for the time being. That way she might learn what the old hermit was up to and find a way to help the crewmen.

"Now listen up," barked the graybeard. "Here's the plan. I've got a treasure hid and we're going to take it aboard my ship, the Pelagin. Took me ten years to find the goods, but find it I did. Pirate treasure. Hee. hee, hee. Now I'll have me a palace on the golden isle of Kros and you'll all be me servants. And you, me lady, a pretty decoration you'll make. Every day I'll have you sing me a tune and dance a sailor's jig. Hee, hee, hee."

With that the graybeard began to hop about in circles on one foot and sing a merry song.

"Oh, fa-la-la-la, fol-der-re-la, here's a riddle for sailors to sing, who want to be free like birds on the wing: Oh, sailor, sailor, beware the night. Out of mind, out of sight. Oh, sailor, sailor, the tide's at flood. Sail away in a sea of blood."

The graybeard's jolly expression suddenly transformed into a scowl as he pointed at Balu and three crewmen.

"There's work to be done. You four men go to the shore and guard the rowboats. If anyone shows up, take them captive. There's two loose ones wandering about, but they're trapped on the island. If they try swimming for the ship they'll be shark bait. The rest of you men come with me to haul the treasure, two chests full. Hee, hee, hee. And you, girl, go to my shack, down that path there, and pack up my shell collection. I couldn't be leaving old Nut Isle without my beautiful shells."

The group broke up as ordered. Llanya followed the path the hermit had indicated, pretending to do his bidding. As soon as she was out of sight, she dashed into the woods and headed in a westerly direction. It seemed pointless now to remain with the old man. She needed to find Jon and the captain.

The woods were dense, but she stumbled upon an animal trail which enabled her to pick up her pace. She prayed she would be able to find the captain and her bond-mate before they were captured or the graybeard got his treasure aboard ship and cast off. Then she remembered the bit of Hhor's skin she carried. She touched it and felt its warmth, and as she traveled in a particular direction, it became warmer. She followed its lead.

Jonathan jumped from a low branch of the blue devil tree to the ground with a grunt.

"Well done, lad," said the captain. "You've got a sackful of blues and I've got one bulging with beetle nuts. And not a bird dropping on either of us. Now that..."

The captain's voice suddenly dropped to a whisper. "There's someone coming this way. Duck down."

A figure came running through the brush, and just as it was about to pass, Jonathan leapt out of his hiding place into full view.

"Llanya!" he cried. "What are you doing here? Why aren't you with the others?"

"Oh, Jon, Captain. I'm so glad I found you. There's been trouble. I..."

"Whoa. Calm down," exhorted the captain. "Catch your breath first."

Jonathan held his bond-mate's hands while she rested a moment. She then told them about the graybeard's treachery.

"We've got to hurry," she urged. "He's going to steal the ship with the help of the crew."

"Hmm. He may not be able to," said the captain. "If the drug or whatever it was in those berries has robbed the men of their memories, then maybe they've also forgotten how to be seamen. It takes a savvy bunch to get a ship like the Pelagin under way. But we can't take any chances and had better go after that old faker right away. But tell me, Llanya, out of curiosity, why didn't you eat the blackberries like everyone else?"

Llanya pouted. "Because they make my teeth black, which looks so ugly."

The captain looked up toward the heavens. "I swear I'll never poke fun of female vanity again."

"Captain, what exactly are we going to do when we find the graybeard and our shipmates?" asked Jonathan. "We're far outnumbered."

There was a long silence. "You've got a point, lad. We need a plan. What we can't do seems clearer. Fighting isn't a good idea because we don't want to hurt our mates—or get ourselves killed. And with the rowboats guarded, we can't get back to the ship to arm ourselves. Even if we were armed, that madman might still order the men to charge us. Since we won't injure them, we'd be taken captive. If we surrendered and then tried to overcome the graybeard, the men would come to his aid. And no doubt we'd be force fed some of the tainted blackberries, or worse."

"If we could find a way to delay the ship's departure, maybe the effect of the berries would weaken or wear off," offered Llanya.

The captain shook his head. "Even if we could do it, that might take forever. Besides, the graybeard could feed more berries to the men anyway."

"Maybe there's a way to counteract the effect of the drug," suggested Jonathan. "Like an antidote of some kind."

"You could be right," mused the captain.

"The Hhor teaches us there is balance in nature," interjected Llanya. "If one fruit is the problem, then perhaps another fruit is the solution."

The captain's eyebrows rose. "Maybe. But there are many kinds of fruit on this island. And where are we going to find a guinea pig to experiment on? Nice idea, but we don't have that much time."

Another long silence followed.

"Llanya, that song-riddle you said the graybeard sang," inquired Jonathan. "You said something about 'out of mind.' Do you remember the words exactly?"

"Yes, I think so. It went: 'Oh, sailor, sailor, beware the night. Out of mind, out of sight. Oh, sailor, sailor, the tide's at flood. Sail away in a sea of blood.' The graybeard also said something like 'here's a riddle for sailors to sing, to fly away free like birds on the wing.' That's all there was."

"I think there may be a clue here," said Jonathan. "The sailor being out of his mind certainly fits the situation. And the night is black, like blackberries."

"Yes, that fits," agreed the captain. "You could be on to something."

"And to be free like a bird might mean to be free of the effect of the blackberries," said Llanya, her excitement growing.

"Yes, that makes sense, too!" blurted the captain. "The riddle may hold the answer."

Jonathan licked his lips. "If the counteraction to the blackberries is to be found in another fruit, then we have to figure out what the words 'tides at flood' or 'sea of blood' tell us about fruit?"

"Well, blood is red," said Llanya. "Maybe the fruit is a redberry."

Jonathan grinned and the captain stared at Llanya in astonishment.

"Yes!" exclaimed Jonathan, planting a kiss on his bond-mate's cheek. "That's got to be it!"

"I think you've got it, lass," added the captain. "It all fits into place. Now we have to find some redberries."

"That's easy," said Llanya. "I passed some redberry bushes not far from here when I was looking for you. I'm sure I can find them again."

"The bigger problem will be how to get close enough to the crew to try out the redberries on them," muttered the captain, rubbing his chin.

Llanya beamed. "Maybe I can do it. The crazy man still thinks I've lost my memory and won't be watching me closely. I'll try to get the men to eat the redberries when he isn't looking."

The captain smiled and winked. "You are one classy lady. And even if you only restore some of the men, that might be enough to take the others by surprise—assuming the berries work. If we have to do a little force feeding, I just hope it's not on big Balu.

"If the fruitcake hermit is still out hunting up his treasure, the four men guarding the rowboats will be alone. We can start with them."

"One of them is Balu," reminded Llanya.

The captain sighed. "Let's go."

Llanya soon located the redberry bushes and filled her sack with the fruit. The captain leading the way, they headed back to the beach. From the cover of a sand dune, they could see Balu and three of the crewmen standing by the rowboats.

"All right, Llanya, do your thing," whispered the captain. "We'll keep an eye out from here. If they won't eat the berries, or if the berries don't work, just wander back this way like nothing has happened."

Llanya approached the men with a wave and a smile, saying she had brought them some fruit to eat while they were waiting. She held out some berries to Balu first. He shook his head in refusal.

"Eat them, you big mackerel," growled the watching captain beneath his breath.

Llanya next offered the berries to the other men, and they took some.

"Three out of four," whispered the captain. "If it works. But without Balu, it will all be for nothing. It would take more than the three of them to hold down the big man."

When Balu saw the other men gobbling up the berries with obvious relish, he had second thoughts and took a bunch for himself.

"Ah, the mackerel's been caught," chirped the captain. "Let's see what happens."

The men soon finished eating the berries, then resumed their watch over the boats. Llanya studied their faces but could discern no change in their demeanor. Nonchalantly, she walked away, and when they weren't looking, she ducked behind the dune and rejoined Jonathan and the captain. She shrugged.

"I can't see any difference."

"Blast!" shouted the captain, loud enough for the crewmen to hear. "I can't take this anymore." Stomping out from behind the dune, he made directly for Balu who was now standing ready and waiting for him. He stopped a foot in front of the giant Zwegian.

"All right, Balu, make your move. I'm ready for you."

"Sir?" inquired Balu, a puzzled look on his face.

"Uh, Balu? Do you know who I am?" asked the captain, his tone now distinctly milder.

"You're the captain," Balu replied, looking bewildered. "Don't... don't you know who you are, sir?" The three crewmen looked at one another with worried expressions.

"And you three," the captain shouted, "do you know me?"

Too stunned to speak, the crewmen simply nodded.

Relieved, the captain wiped the perspiration from his brow with the back of his hand.

"Come on out you two," he called to Jonathan and Llanya. "It's all clear. The berries worked."

The captain hastily explained to his men what had happened and the reason for his strange behavior.

"So you see the mess we're in. What we have to do now is rescue our shipmates from that madman."

"I'll take care of that personally," offered Balu, his voice brimming with anger.

"Hold on, old friend," asserted the captain. "Let's try to avoid violence if we can. Remember, the other men will protect the graybeard—they think he's their captain. But the old nut cake also thinks that Llanya's under the influence. So maybe she can do for our mates what she did for you. Are you willing to try it again, Llanya?"

"Of course, Captain. It was fun."

"Good girl. Since you say the crazy will be returning to his hut, let's head there. Balu, I want you and the men to stay here and guard the boats in case the others take another trail and we miss them. We'll leave some redberries with you, and if worse comes to worse, you may have to do a little force feeding."

Balu put on his widest grin. "If you say so, sir."

The captain, Jonathan, and Llanya carefully made their way through the forest, keeping a sharp eye out on the path ahead. As yet there was no sign of the graybeard and the crewmen. Before long they reached the area of the blackberry bushes.

"I don't think the hermit and crewmen have arrived yet," said Llanya. "The graybeard's hut is down this side trail. I'll go there and pack up his shells as he asked, so he won't get suspicious. I won't be long."

Jonathan and the captain hid themselves behind a row of blackberry bushes next to the path and waited quietly. It wasn't long before they heard the sound of tromping feet, and moments later the graybeard came into view on the trail followed by the men of the Pelagin carrying two wooden chests. Upon reaching a fork in the trail, which was close by the blackberry bushes, the graybeard ordered the men to put down the chests and wait for him while he retrieved some belongings from his hut.

At that moment Llanya returned. She curtsied to the graybeard.

"I've packed your shell collection as you asked, Captain, and put it in your duffle bag. I left it on the floor next to the door." Her voice was melted butter.

"Good, good. There's one more thing I need to take along, heh heh. It's secret! You wait here with the others while I fetch it. And no peeking at my treasure!"

"The men and I will eat some berries while we're waiting," Llanya said, idly.

"Yes, good idea!" cackled the graybeard. "I want my men to eat lots of fruit and be healthy. Especially blackberries. Hee, hee, hee."

"Well just to be sure they eat well, maybe you'd better tell them yourself. A good sailor has to obey his captain's orders," cooed Llanya.

"Yes, yes, you're right. You men eat plenty of berries while I'm gone. They're good for what ails you. Hee, hee, hee. And that's an order."

With that the graybeard disappeared down the path to his hut. Llanya immediately sprang into action, passing out the redberries from her sack to the waiting men.

Jonathan, listening to the conversation from his hiding place, fairly swelled with pride at his bond-mate's cleverness. The captain clamped his hand over his mouth so as not to burst out laughing.

As the men munched contentedly on the redberries, the captain and Jonathan emerged from behind the blackberry bushes. No one noticed that Tabber was not eating the redberries that Llanya had given to him, but instead was eating berries from a blackberry bush.

At that moment the graybeard appeared carrying a duffle bag over his shoulder. Upon spying the captain and Jonathan, he dropped his bundle in alarm.

"Grab them!" he yelled to the men. But no one moved; that is, all except Tabber, who was still under the influence of the blackberries. The helmsman immediately sprang into action, rushing at the captain and wrapping his stick-like arms around him as tight as he could. The captain, at first flabbergasted, began to laugh uncontrollably, lifting poor frail Tabber bodily up and down in his convulsions. A crewman came over and pried Tabber loose from the captain and held him secure.

Regaining his composure, the captain ordered two of his men to hold the graybeard fast. He then approached Tabber, addressing him in an almost brotherly voice.

"I'm sorry old friend, but this is going to hurt me almost as much as it does you. But it has to be done. Llanya, you have the redberries, so will you do the honors? I'll hold his nose until he opens his mouth."

The captain clamped his fingers over Tabber's generous nasal appendage, but the ex-priest defiantly clenched his teeth and refused to open his mouth. The captain waited patiently, watching with surprise as Tabber's face turned from its usual pallor to a light pink and then to red. But still he would not open his mouth. Llanya stood by, holding up a handful of redberries before the helmsman's face, waiting for the moment of surrender.

"It's all that priestly training that's the problem," grumbled the captain as he tightened his grip on Tabber's nose. "They practice mind control over the body and all that kind of nonsense. But, come to think of it, he lost his mind when he ate those blackberries, so I wonder where he's getting the strength to hold out. Just old Imshi stubbornness probably."

The helmsman's eyeballs rolled up into his head, and just as the captain was about to release his hold for fear of killing his friend, Tabber's mouth suddenly snapped open in a desperate gasp for breath. Llanya, ever alert, plunged her hand into the open maw, smearing redberries over the helmsman's face in the process, but managing to push enough of the fruit down his throat so that he had no choice but to swallow. The captain released his hold, and he and Llanya stepped back to observe the outcome of their efforts.

The helmsman sputtered and choked, and his face gradually returned to its natural color. He blinked several times, and a confused expression came over his face, which in turn gave way to a look of utter humiliation. The captain read the transformation in his shipmate's eyes and signaled the crewman holding the helmsman to release him. Looking quite solemn now, and making a heroic effort to uphold his dignity, Tabber simply sniffed and walked away in his usual mincing steps to join the other men. Everyone strained to suppress their mirth.

The captain then explained to the recently restored men what had happened. They were wont to deal with the madcap graybeard then and there, but the captain stopped them.

"I have a better idea, men. What the aspiring captain here needs is a late lunch—of delicious blackberries."

The men howled with glee. Grabbing a handful of blackberries from a bush, the captain went over to the now shaking graybeard.

"The choice is yours," said the captain. "Either the berries or I turn you over to my men. Choose."

"It takes a long time for the effect of the berries to wear off," screamed the graybeard. "Oh me, oh my. What'll I do? What'll I do?"

Balu took a menacing step forward. Without hesitation the little man opened his mouth wide and the captain stuffed it full of blackberries. When he was certain they had all been swallowed, the captain ordered the captive released. A blank expression came over the graybeard's face.

"What's your name?" asked the captain.

The hermit looked around, confused. "Me? My name? I don't know. Does it matter?"

"Well, we'll call you Barry. Barry Black. How's that?"

"Barry Black? Sounds fine. A nice name. I'll be Barry. Barry, Barry, Barry."

The men snickered.

"Barry," continued the captain, "see those two chests over there? Do they belong to you?"

"Chests? Nope, never use 'em. Not mine."

"Well then, since they don't seem to belong to anyone, I'll just go ahead and claim them. Now, I'd like you to do me a small favor, Barry. Will you open the chests for me?"

"Glad to, glad to. Barry'll do it." The hermit hopped over to the chests, deftly unlatched one and then the other, and threw open their lids. The men gasped. Each chest brimmed with shiny gold coins, a treasure to excite a king.

"Equal shares for everyone!" pronounced the captain, and a cheer rang out among the men. Suddenly the graybeard grabbed up a coin from one of the chests and ran off helter-skelter into the forest.

"Shall I catch him, Captain?" asked one of the men.

"No, let him go. But it shows that, memory or no, old habits run deep. Maybe one day old Barry Black will eat some redberries, and that gold coin will be something to remember us by. Or should I say to forget us by."

The men laughed.

"Well, there are some things gold can't buy, and I've got my bagful of beetle nuts to buy them with," teased the captain. "Which is more than I can say for you sea dogs. All those who want to fill their sacks pay heed and I'll tell you where to find beetle nuts aplenty. But first the treasure to the boats."

At the beach Balu and the three crewmen boisterously greeted their shipmates and exchanged stories; that is, except for Tabber, who had not yet recovered from his ordeal. For the moment he chose to nourish his indignation in solitude and so remained aloof from the rest.

The chests were loaded into one of the rowboats. The captain, his sack full, and Tabber, wholly uninterested in the subterranean economics of beetle nuts, elected to ferry the treasure back to the ship. Jonathan and Balu volunteered to go along to help carry the chests aboard. The other crewmen, with the benefit of the captain's directions, opted for beetle nut collecting.

Llanya tugged at Jonathan's sleeve.

"Jon, I'd like to go along with the men to get some beetle nuts. I want you to try one tonight."

"Shh," whispered Jonathan. "Very well. But not so loud."

"You men have two hours to gather your nuts while ye may," announced the captain. "The Pelagin sails at twilight and should make the isle of Cruor by dawn. And by this time tomorrow we'll be Zuralia bound."

Chapter 11

THE DREAM READER

The treasure safely aboard ship, Jonathan headed for his cabin to look in on the trocht. As he passed by the galley, he heard some strange sounds coming from within. The galley's deck-side porthole was partly open and he stopped to listen. It was Nynt's voice, although it wasn't the cook's usual complaining conversation with himself; it was an eerie guttural chant in a strange tongue that rose and fell like a dirge upon the waves.

"Ihng-na-shob-dath, whng-dth, a-brg-hsth-knrr, ek-dri-kla-nkt."

The chanting stopped and Nynt's speech became understandable. His tone was now cowering and adulatory.

"Yes, Mistress. The creator seeks a dream reader. I understand. He will not escape me again. The Zytox failed, but this time I will succeed. Yes, Mistress, I will destroy the earthling and his bond-mate too."

Jonathan's initial shock gave way to blind fury at the mention of his bond-mate being harmed. Without thinking he pushed open the door to the galley and rushed in.

Nynt was kneeling on the floor with upraised arms as if in prayer. Upon spying the intruder, his initial look of surprise gave way to one of pure malice. He quickly made some odd signs in the air with his hands, as though sending a message, then lowered his arms in a sweeping ritualistic motion. Jumping to his feet, lips twitching, he snapped open his forefingers as though they were knives; his eyes became as ghostly orbs, their pale crystalline glow locking onto the young seaman like steel talons.

Jonathan felt his body freeze under the power of Nynt's gaze. Fear overcame him and he now regretted his impetuous behavior. He tried calling for help, but his voice too was frozen. Only his eyes and his brain seemed to be functioning, and he could only watch in helpless fascination as the cook reached for a carving knife from a nearby counter, still holding his hypnotic gaze upon him.

A maniacal grin crept over Nynt's face as he slowly raised the knife, and Jonathan saw the fingers that gripped the knife handle split open like sprouting pods and lengthen into fleshless claws. Terror clutched at his heart, and he strained mightily to move his arms. But he could not. He waited breathlessly for the blow to fall. Suddenly something flashed by him at the edge of his vision and he heard a dull thud. He saw a Zwegian ceremonial dagger buried to the hilt in Nynt's chest.

The cook's jaw went slack as he looked down at the dagger handle in bewilderment. He then fell to the floor like a dropped doll.

His mobility suddenly returned to him, Jonathan swung about and saw the captain standing in the doorway.

"A well balanced blade," said the captain, as though he had just accomplished a routine chore. "It was a gift from chief Zwez. Always thought it would come in handy some day."

"Th…thanks," murmured Jonathan, feeling a bit wobbly in the knees.

The captain saluted in acknowledgment. "You'd better take a seat, lad, until you get your sea legs back. You're not hurt, are you?"

"No, I'm all right."

"Well, at least now we know who the assassin is, or was. Too bad though—he was a good cook. But why would he be after you? I doubt killing you was his idea, and he was too brainless to plot out a strategy without outside help. He had to be working for someone else. Did he let anything slip that might give us a clue?"

"Not much. He was in mental communication with someone—someone who was giving him orders. He called her Mistress, so it must be a woman."

The captain's eyes widened. "A woman? Hmm."

"Nynt said he would kill me and knew that a Zytox had tried. He also knew I was on my way to see a dream reader. When I heard him say he was going to destroy Llanya, that's when I barged in. But his eyes froze my movements and I was helpless."

"It sounds like some mysterious bitch is pulling more than one string. It's scary. She may not even be human. Nynt's not, that's for sure." The captain pointed to the dead cook's mutated eyes and hands. "We'd better throw the body overboard before the men return, otherwise there will be more questions asked than we want to answer—or will be able to answer. We'll say that Nynt mysteriously disappeared, and since there's no place around here to go but down, everyone will think he fell overboard and the sharks got him. At least the last part will be true."

"Don't think so, sir," exclaimed Jonathan. "Look at Nynt's body. It's melting!"

Jonathan and the captain watched in amazement as the cook's distorted remains gradually dissolved before their eyes into a pool of dark liquid, and in moments that too evaporated, leaving no trace.

"At least the little viper won't be making a liar out of me," the captain mused as he bent down to pick up the Zwegian dagger. "He disappeared all right. Brr! Supernatural comings and goings give me the shivers."

"Captain, please don't mention what happened here to Llanya. I'll tell her myself at the right moment."

"Very well. But stay alert. Whoever we're dealing with is powerful and well informed. Let's hope the dream reader can tell us something more. And I hope the old priest was right when he said she can be trusted."

The captain returned the dagger to a sheath hidden beneath his belt. "What say we retreat to my cabin, lad. I have a bottle of Cyrilian Brandy. We could both do with a few drops. We can also look over the charts for the next leg of our voyage. We'll get under way as soon as the men return, and sometime about midnight we should be entering the warm currents of the Hanybulan Stream. The Stream runs north and should carry us to Cruor Island."

When, two hours later, the rowboats came alongside, Jonathan went to the after deck to greet the returning crewmen and to help Llanya aboard. All smiles, she swung her bulging sack of nuts to and fro in front of her bond-mate's face.

"Beetle nuts!" she pronounced, triumphantly, a coy glint in her eyes.

Jonathan mumbled his congratulations and swallowed the sigh he felt rising from his midsection.

"How's Trok?" Llanya asked.

"Still sleeping, the last time I looked."

"He might be awake now. Let's go see. The poor baby must be hungry. I'll ask Nynt for some milk on the way."

"Uh, Nynt's left us—disappeared.

"Disappeared? But where could he disappear to?"

Jonathan broke eye contact. "I can't say. He just…evaporated."

"Strange. But then he was a strange one anyway, grumpy and always complaining. I don't really think he liked his work, or people for that matter. He probably stole ashore and decided to become a hermit, like Barry. Now there's a likely couple."

A thoughtful look came over Llanya's face. "Jon, with Nynt gone, what's the captain going to do for a cook?"

"Good question. I suppose we'll all have to make do eating fruit and raw vegetables until we make port in Zuralia."

"No need for that. Cooking was a hobby of mine in Celeucia. I can be the cook! Then I'll be a crewman—crew-woman?—too."

Jonathan's eyebrows rose. "Wonderful! I'm sure the captain will be delighted."

Jonathan accompanied Llanya to the galley where she poured some canned milk into a saucer; then they headed for their quarters. Jonathan pushed open the cabin door for his bond-mate since she was holding the saucer with two hands. She entered, and as he was about to follow her in, he heard a crash. Suspecting danger, he leapt into the cabin, poised for action, only to see Llanya standing motionless in the center of the room, a look of confoundment on her face. The milk saucer was in pieces on the floor.

"Jon! Look!" cried Llanya, pointing to the bed.

Jonathan's head jerked sideways and his eyes widened in amazement. There, lying peacefully on the bed, looking dolefully at its master and mistress as might a pet kitten, was the trocht. Only it was ten times larger than it had been just hours before. It had suddenly grown to the size of two large men. Its fur was longer and thicker and had lightened to a pale cinnamon, and its eyes had darkened to coal-black circles. But its most outstanding feature was completely new—two long backward-curving fangs that protruded from its upper jaw, twin weapons to give pause to the bravest man or beast.

The trocht yawned and began to idly lick its huge padded paws, revealing two rows of fearsome teeth and claws like curved spikes.

Jonathan slowly reached out for Llanya's arm, his voice a whisper.

"Step back quietly. We'll edge out the door and I'll close it."

"Oh Jon, don't be silly," proclaimed Llanya, brushing off the suggestion. She pulled her arm free of her bond-mate's grasp and went over to the bed. "He's grown, that's all. But it's our old lovable Trok just the same."

Before Jonathan could act, Llanya reached out and stroked the creature's head.

"See, he's purring, you silly goat. He's as gentle as a kitten. Come over here and see for yourself."

Jonathan hesitated, then approached gingerly. He imitated Llanya and saw there was no change in his pet's usual tranquil behavior.

"Well, he seems tame enough. But look at the size of him. We had better inform the captain before someone else discovers him and has a heart attack. I'll go get the skipper. You be careful."

A few minutes later Jonathan returned with the captain in tow.

"Blazing sunfish!" blurted the captain. "You said he was big, but you didn't say how big. He's a monster. Are you sure he's completely tame?"

"Yes, quite sure," replied Llanya confidently as she continued to pet the purring feline.

"How in Hadrian's Hell do you suppose he grew so fast?" asked the captain.

Jonathan shrugged, though he felt sure it was caused by the trocht no longer having access to the Klellian elixir of life. He had promised the Catex to keep the existence of the hidden pool a secret, so he said nothing.

"And who knows," the captain continued, "he may not be fully grown yet. How big will he be tomorrow?"

Llanya frowned. The captain softened his voice.

"Llanya, I know how you feel about Trok, he being a pet and all that. But a ship's no place for an animal that size. Besides, he'll scare the barnacles off the men. We really should put him ashore—at the right kind of island, of course."

A look of anger flashed over Llanya's face, but it quickly yielded to a sly smile and a glint in her eyes.

"I'll strike a bargain with you, Captain." Her tone was even, with a deliberation that bespoke her former station, and which didn't fail to impress the skipper. "I'm willing to be the Pelegin's new cook. Cooking is my hobby and I know how to please the male palate. In exchange you let Trok stay aboard until we reach Zuralia. Meanwhile, I'll keep him confined to the cabin except for a brief walk on deck in the early morning and late afternoon, with a leash."

The captain pondered the offer, doing his best to look serious, though he was smiling inside at the boldness of the proposition. He knew it would have only taken the flat refusal of a determined princess or a few feminine tears to weaken his resolve, but this way the outcome was better. Now he had a cook.

"Very well. A fair bargain. I'll forewarn the men about Trok here so that nobody jumps overboard. Oh, and some of that wonderful Celeucian stew would make a hearty meal tonight after a hard day ashore. And don't feed all the best meat to that…to Trok."

"You can have my share, Captain," countered Llanya, affronted. "I'm a vegetarian."

The captain cleared his throat and his face reddened slightly, and he excused himself.

Later, while Llanya prepared dinner in the galley, Jonathan walked about on deck, enjoying the wind in his face and thinking about all that had happened to him since he last sat in the old shopkeeper's chair by the fire. Zuralia lay heavy on his mind, and even now he seemed to hear its voice calling to him on the wind. Whatever the dream reader might say, wherever she might direct him, he vowed that after Cruor his next port would be Zuralia. He could no longer deny its call.

Llanya labored to prepare an elaborate meal for the men. She wanted it to be special if only to forestall any objections to her keeping the trocht.

And, indeed, later at mess the men praised her cooking to the heavens, even joking that she could bring an elephant on board if only she would continue to provide them with such sumptuous fare.

The captain, seated at a dining table next to Jonathan, leaned over and whispered in his friend's ear. "Let's see how brave they are when they see your little pet strolling around on deck."

That night Jonathan and Llanya had a difficult time trying to evict the trocht from their bed. Pushing, pulling, and pleading proved useless, and Llanya only finally succeeded by bringing a piece of raw meat from the galley and tossing it to the floor. Instantly the trocht hopped from the bed and downed the tidbit in one gulp. The bed vacated, Llanya seized the opportunity and took a commanding position at its center, from which location she shook an admonishing finger at her pet. The trocht seemed to understand, and settled down on the floor for the night.

"Jon, come to bed now," pleaded Llanya. "Trok made it nice and warm for us. I have a special after-dinner dessert to give you—a fine plump beetle nut. Let's see if it will do what the captain said it's supposed to do."

Jonathan got into bed wearing a worried look, though less because of the beetle nut than the trocht.

"Llanya, try not to make any noise tonight. Trok is protective, and we don't want him to think I'm hurting you."

In their lovemaking Llanya, cooperative as always, did her best to suppress her moans of pleasure, though at one point she could not help herself and sighed audibly. Jonathan froze and jerked his head toward the trocht, only to see it eyeing him suspiciously.

Llanya giggled. "Hmm. Maybe we don't need the beetle nuts after all. I think I've found another way to make you last longer, my love."

At morning's first light Jonathan stirred groggily, then came to with a start when he remembered the trocht. Nervously, he peered over the edge of the bed, not knowing what to expect. A whistling sigh of relief escaped his lips—the still sleeping pet had not grown more in the night.

Llanya awoke, kissed her bond-mate hurriedly on the cheek and scrambled out of bed, explaining that it was time for her to feed the trocht and prepare breakfast for the men. In minutes she was out the door.

Jonathan did a little tidying up around the cabin, then went on deck where he found the captain at the helm.

"Morning, lad. You're just in time. There she is coming into view, dead ahead. Cruor Island." A cry from the crow's-nest corroborated the skipper's eagle eye. At almost the same time a bell rang out from the galley signaling breakfast was ready. "Well, I guess I don't have to tell you which call the crew's going to jump to first," said the captain. "You go chow down. I'll stay by the wheel. By the time you've finished stuffing yourself with Llanya's good cooking, we'll be close enough to get a clear look at the island."

After breakfast Jonathan returned on deck with some fresh-baked rolls for the skipper.

"Thanks, lad. Best deal I ever made was letting your bond-mate be cook."

The captain noted the pensive look on his young friend's face as he studied the shoreline of the fast-approaching island.

"Aye, lad, it's a weird looking place all right. Those blood-red beaches give me the creeps. I sure hope we're doing the right thing. But I guess it's the only card we've got to play.

"We're coming round to the south shore. We'll drop anchor close in and you can take the small skiff. I don't know why the dream reader insists you go ashore alone. I don't like it. If anything goes wrong you hightail it out of there fast."

"I'll be all right. The Catex was able to sense that the reader is alone and not dangerous."

"You're putting a lot of trust in that old faker. He had better be right."

Jonathan heard his name being called and turned to see Llanya coming on deck with the trocht in tow, walking him on a leash as casually as if he were a pet poodle.

The captain guffawed at the incongruous sight of the beauty and the beast. "Now there's one overgrown pussy cat for you. I only hope that rope she's using for a leash is strong."

Although the captain had forewarned the crew about the trocht, upon seeing the monstrous creature in the flesh, the men on deck either froze in their tracks or began backing into the rail. In an effort to reassure them, Llanya put on a small demonstration for their benefit.

Kneeling, she first petted the trocht, slowly running her fingers through its soft affluent fur, then she scratched it under the chin and behind the ears. But that only induced the giant feline to yawn and stretch lazily, thereby revealing its fearsome teeth and stiletto-like claws, a sight which unnerved the men even more. She then straddled her pet's back and gently pulled on its ears, and in a final gesture of playfulness she hugged it and put her hand into its mouth.

The captain shook his head. "You've got some bond-mate there, Jon. If that doesn't embarrass the men into showing a little courage, nothing will."

Llanya and the trocht resumed their walk about the deck, and the crewmen returned uncertainly to their tasks. Though the men put on a brave front, they somehow managed to find work a healthy distance from wherever the two strollers happened to be.

The Pelagin came to anchor and a skiff was lowered for Jonathan to go ashore. The crew lined the rail to see him off.

"Hurry back, Jon," called out Llanya, waving, "I'm making Celeucian curry for dinner."

A rippling carpet of wavelets carried the skiff gently to the beach. Once on shore Jonathan saw that his feet became quickly stained a bright blood red from the sand. Though he wasn't superstitious, it was a discomforting sign.

Recalling the directions the Catex had given him, he made his way along a narrow trail above the beach, which led into a hilly wood beyond. He hadn't walked very far through the trees when the sound of splashing water reached his ears, and he came upon a waterfall pouring down a cliff side into a ravine. A thin mist from the falls gathered beneath the leafy canopy overhead, penetrated by scattered rays of sunlight, which created a lovely sparkling inner sky pierced by rainbow-colored spears. Stopping a moment to admire the colorful display, he saw through a gap in the mist the outline of a small house standing alone upon the summit of a nearby hill. Doubtless this was the dwelling of the dream reader, Skekiloreida.

The hill was steep, and by the time he reached the cottage he was out of breath. He saw it was a somewhat dilapidated house of rough-hewn logs, and as he stood surveying it, the front door swung open and a woman appeared at the threshold. She was stocky and somewhat disheveled, in her middle years, with stringy hair and wearing a wrinkled blue housecoat. Her morose expression was hardly inviting, and he wondered if he had found the right place.

"So you're the one, huh?" The woman's voice was gravelly and gruff, though it carried a note of respect. "Been expecting you. Did you bring the blue devils?"

Jonathan untied a pouch from his belt. "Yes, I have them here."

"Let me have them."

Jonathan held out the pouch, which the woman snatched from his grasp. She sniffed the bag suspiciously, then untied it and peered inside. A broad grin sliced across her face, revealing a random pattern of blue-stained teeth.

"Good! Come in." Her voice was distinctly friendlier now. "You can call me Lorie. I'm your local dream reader hereabouts. Also seer and mystic. You name it, I do it. Let's see, the sexy priest said you're called…"

"Jonathan—Jon."

"Yeah, Jon. Well, come into the parlor. But wipe your feet first. I hate that red sand all over the place."

He entered a small dismal room sparsely furnished with two stuffed well-worn chairs and a sprung sofa. A crudely executed painting of ghostly figures embracing colliding planets hung on the wall. Several books lay scattered about the floor.

"Well, Don, have a seat," said the reader as she planted herself in the middle of the sofa. "It's always helps to relax a little before getting into the dream thing."

Jonathan sat down. "It's Jon."

"Right, Jon. So if you're not in any hurry we can get to know one another a little better first. You know what they say—pleasure before business."

Jonathan remembered the reader's thought conversation with the High Catex and decided it would be best to nip the flower she was trying to water in the bud. But he didn't want to offend her since he needed her help.

"Uh, unfortunately I don't have much time. My bond-mate and the men of the Pelagin are waiting for me, and the captain wants to set sail before twilight."

The reader's arm swept the air. "All my life sailors have been a pain. Bah! And you say your bond-mate's waiting? Too bad, too bad. Well, can't win 'em all. In fact, not any, lately. Tell me, was that priest on Klell really as old as he said?"

"I'm not sure. I think so."

"Oh well. So, Don, tell me about your dream. Oh, never mind, that'll take too long. Now that I have some blue devils, I can do it quicker. Hold on."

The reader extracted a nut from the pouch, placed it on the floor, and stomped on it. Picking up the blue kernel of meat from the broken shell, she popped it into her mouth.

"Ah, that should do it," she mewed with satisfaction. "That devil's got a good kick. Now come over here and sit next to me so I can touch your head. Heh, heh, your forehead."

Jonathan moved over to the sofa, avoiding the broken spring. The reader placed the fingers of her right hand to his brow, then shut her eyes. A long silence ensued. Jonathan watched her face intently and could see her eyes twitching beneath her closed lids. Her breathing grew rapid and a disturbed expression came over her face. Suddenly she pulled her hand away and opened her eyes, pushing herself a few inches away as though in awe or fear. When she spoke, her tone was deadly serious.

"I'm reading more than your dreams, earthling. You're a powerful creator, as your aura warned. But your enemy is also powerful. I can't tell who it is, though I sense a female presence. And even now your island creation is being threatened."

Jonathan's breath caught. "I don't understand. Do you mean Zuralia? What threat? What aura? How do you know I'm a creator?"

The reader shook her head. "My, you're really ignorant, aren't you? All dream creators emit an unmistakable aura—it surrounds you. But only certain people, like readers and other creators, can see it. Creators can't see their own aura, but yours is strong and bright. Because of it, I was able to see you coming from afar. As to the threat, yes, it's your dream creation, Zuralia. Your dream gave Zuralia life, and now it's in danger and needs your help. It's been calling to you for some time. But what the danger is isn't clear."

Jonathan jumped to his feet. "Oh, how stupid I've been. Zuralia was calling me, but instead of staying where I was needed, I abandoned her and went looking for answers elsewhere. Now Zuralia's in trouble and I'm far from her shores."

"Don't be hasty in your conclusions. True, your island creation needs you now, but it may or may not have been what summoned you to this plane. It might have been an enemy trying to lure you here, perhaps to kill you. Perhaps you were beyond reach on your earthly plane, but a potential threat nevertheless."

"A threat? Why? I can't do anything."

"You have as yet undiscovered powers."

Jonathan shook his head in confusion. "I can only act on what I know and feel. I know now that Zuralia needs me, and I must return there as fast as possible."

"And then what?"

"I…I don't know."

"Perhaps you simply need to do what creators do—create. Why else would Zuralia need you? What else are creators good for? Well, there may be one other thing."

Jonathan began pacing. "Create what? I don't know how to create anything. If I did create Zuralia, it was my unconscious dream that did it."

"You have to learn how to create consciously, by the force of your will."

"But how? Create what?"

"I can't help you there, boy. Hmm. Tell you what—let me try another blue devil. Sometimes a double dose squeezes out a little more information."

The reader rooted around in the nut pouch and withdrew a dark blue nut, larger than the rest.

"Here's a big ripe one. That might do it. Sometimes two makes me a little drunk, so you'll have to make allowances."

The reader broke the shell and gulped down the kernel in a single swallow. Jonathan resumed his seat, and she placed her fingers to his head as before. This time her expression didn't change, though one corner of her mouth twitched spasmodically. A full minute passed before she lowered her hand. Her brow knitted; she hiccuped and licked her lips before speaking.

"Uh-oh. I sense a threat to your island creation emanating from two planes, from this one and a higher plane. On this plane follow your instincts and look to Zuralia, and also the twin isles of Zis and Zat. What the nature of the danger is I can't tell, but it's powerful. There is also a threat from a higher plane, but it's unclear—the message is too weak.

"I also sense a disturbance between this plane and another, as if the fabric between planes has been torn. That could only happen if there's an interplane imbalance. Hmm. Then it would be possible for someone or something from another plane to enter our own. It could be the source of the danger. In which case the threat would not be to Zuralia alone, but to the whole island plane itself. Wow! This is big time stuff, no doubt about it." The reader hiccuped again and smiled blankly. "Sorry about that—it's the effect of the blue devil."

"An interplane imbalance?" asked Jonathan, more confused than ever. "What's that?"

"Good question, but I'm no scientist. Let me think. It's what happens if the worlds on one plane get out of whack with those in a neighboring plane. The relative masses get out of kilter, or something like that, and you get interplane instability. It's like when a man and woman make love. If the man's penis shrinks, there's an imbalance. Uh, no that's not exactly right. Urp! Sorry. It's the nut.

"Anyway, imbalance is a mischief that could be caused by careless creators, even unconsciously, or deliberately by a creator with big ideas, like dimensional conquest. There are bad guys everywhere, you know. Especially sailors. Hic."

The reader's revelations made Jonathan's head spin. He felt queasy. What should he believe? It seemed too dangerous not to believe any of it. He couldn't deal with problems of other islands and planes right now—that was too big. But he must try to help Zuralia.

"I can't thank you enough for your help, Lorie. Now I must return to Zuralia as fast as possible. And I think I know the best way."

The dream reader grimaced and shrugged. "The good looking ones always leave the fastest. Well give us a hug, love, before you go." The reader lurched toward Jonathan, arms outstretched, and he complied out of gratitude. The smell of devil nuts on her breath had a depressing odor.

"Umm, you feel good, Don. How about a little kiss?" Jonathan tried to squirm free of her embrace, but she held on and backed him against the wall. "Ouch!" he cried as he bumped his head against a log. "Lorie, I really have to go."

The reader released him and sighed. "Oh well. The next time you visit me, bring along that priest. What's his name? I mean the son, not the old man. Maybe we can have a little threesome party. That is, if the planes don't collapse and we're not all dead. Go on now and save the world. And be careful. Urp!"

Jonathan ran all the way back to the beach. Once aboard ship, the captain suggested they go to his cabin to talk about what had transpired with the dream reader.

"Not now, Captain, if you don't mind. Please. I'm in a terrible hurry." Jonathan's voice was tense, and the captain, somewhat taken aback, nodded.

Jonathan asked Llanya to come with him to their quarters. There he sat down on the bed and asked her to sit beside him. The trocht slept quietly on the floor. In the background they could hear the captain's voice calling out to make sail for Zuralia.

"Llanya, I learned from the dream reader that Zuralia is in danger at this very moment and needs my help. I feel it too. I must go there at once."

"But we're going there now. In a week we'll..."

"No, I must go now. Immediately. Waiting could mean disaster. I sense it."

"But even if Zuralia is in trouble, how can you help? You can't get there any faster than by ship anyway."

"I don't know how I can help, but I know I must try. And I do have a way to get there faster than by ship. Remember me telling you about the return pill the dream sender gave me? I still have it. I can use it to go back to Earth in a flash, right to my old friend's house. He can then give me another pill to send me directly back to Zuralia. It can all be done in minutes."

Llanya's eyes grew moist. "Oh Jon, I don't want you to go without me."

"I must. I only have one return pill. But I'll be waiting for you on Zuralia. It won't be long. Please try to understand."

Llanya feigned courage and smiled, though her heart ached. "Of course I understand, silly. But shouldn't we tell the captain first?"

"No. I'm afraid he might not understand and try to prevent me from using the return pill. You tell him everything after I'm gone. And tell him the reader said there was danger to this plane on the isles of Zis and Zat. Maybe he knows something about it or can find out."

"Very well. Please be careful, my darling. Trok and I will see you soon. And take your half of the Hhor's piece of skin with you. It could be of help."

"Yes, I have it here in my pocket."

"This will be our first separation," she said softly. "A kiss before you go." They clasped urgently, and time seemed to oblige their youthful love and hold its breath a moment.

Jonathan took a step backward. "This will be our first and last time apart. That I swear."

Llanya couldn't bear to see him disappear before her eyes, so she ran out of the room and back to the galley. There she wept. But when she heard some crewmen approaching, she dried her eyes and continued with her cooking.

As soon as Llanya was gone, Jonathan took the pill from his pocket, popped it into his mouth, and swallowed it without a further thought.

The trocht, lying on the floor, dreamily opened its eyes and looked up at its master. Jonathan could see his own reflection in his pet's dark gleaming pupils. The trocht's ears twitched, and somewhere in the distance Jonathan could hear the faint squeaking of the sail rigging. Suddenly the trocht jumped to its feet and looked about the room, puzzled. Its master was nowhere to be seen.

CHAPTER 12

THE INNER SPHERE

The dream sender, Hecuticar Lemselecus, was seated in his favorite chair sipping tea. He pursed his lips and tapped his fingers as he studied the manuscript resting on his lap. A mouse sat on the old man's shoulder leisurely washing its face, looking up whenever the smoldering wood in the fireplace crackled.

"Ah, I tell you, Lemanuel," said the old man, nostalgically, "science in the old days was straightforward and plain spoken. Nowadays its all Greek letters and obscure terms. Listen to the title of this paper: 'On the Multi-refractive Nature of Unconsciously Created Spheroids.' Why don't they just call it what it is—dream world reflection? And nothing seems to be done by one person any more. Now it's whole groups. Whatever happened to individual discovery? This paper's got six authors, and in a footnote they thank seven assistants. Hmm. Wonder which one's got two assistants? It's always the assistants that do the work anyway. Probably government funded. Let's see. Yup, sure enough. Pity the poor taxpayer."

The mouse stopped washing its face and looked at the empty chair opposite the old man. Its nose twitched and its eyes took on a reddish glow. The chair creaked as though a weight had been put upon it. The old man looked up.

"Well bless my bunions!" he exclaimed. "If it isn't Jonathan Spenser returned to us."

Jonathan, slightly dizzy, waited a moment for his head to clear. Then seeing his old friend, he smiled. The mouse, unaccustomed to abrupt appearances, decided it was time to depart: it ran down the chair and disappeared behind a stack of books on the floor.

"Hello," said Jonathan. "I seem to have scared your little friend away."

"Oh, don't concern yourself about Lemanuel. He's a paper lion. Or is it tiger? But how are you, my boy? All right? I've been worried about you."

"Yes, I'm fine. Tell me, how long have I been gone in Earth time?"

"Nearly two weeks. You should have returned sooner. But knowing you, I'm not surprised. Anyway, here you are, safe and sound.

"Now, you must tell me everything that happened to you. But first I'll get us some hot tea."

Jonathan pushed to the edge of his chair. "I'm sorry, but there's no time for tea or a long discussion. This is an emergency. I have to return to Zuralia at once."

The old man's brow knitted. "What kind of emergency? And haven't you just come from Zuralia?"

"I've come from an island on the second plane where a dream reader told me that Zuralia is in serious danger. I sense it myself. What the danger is I don't know. But I've got to go back immediately to try to help. The fastest way for me to do that was to return here first and get a sending pill from you."

"Mmm. What you say is consistent with the signs we read earlier. But if there's risk, perhaps you should reconsider whether it's wise to go back. Hmm, I can see by your expression that's out of the question. But must you really leave so soon? I want to hear more about the second plane and your experiences there."

"If all goes well I'll return soon and tell you all about it. But it's urgent that I go now."

The old man sighed. "Why are young people in so much of a hurry to rush in where widows fear to tread? Or is it devils? Angels? Whatever. Very well, I'll get you a sending pill. And, of course, another return pill."

"Two return pills. I'm married now, and I'd like to take my bond-mate with me on my next visit."

The old man clapped his hands to his chest. "Married? My, my, you have been busy. Well if you're happy, so am I. I'm a firm believer in that institution, walls and all. Like the poet said, a wife in life is rife with strife.... No, that's not right. Let's see, it's a wife in heat.... No, that's not right either. Oh well, you know what I mean. Wives, companionship, and all that other good stuff.

"Hmm. Companionship. That gives me an idea. My boy, I wonder if I could ask a small favor of you—for our mutual benefit really. When you return to Zuralia this time, would you take someone along with you?"

"What? Who?"

"Lemanuel. That is, a reasonable facsimile of Lemanuel."

"A mouse? You want me to take a mouse?"

"Calm down, my boy, and let me explain. You may be going into danger. It's in my power to create a kind of duplicate of my friend, Lemanuel—a kind of shadow image. He will be no bother and will tuck nicely in a pocket or behind your collar, just about anywhere. I'll transfer a bit of my own consciousness into his brain—not much, since a mouse brain isn't much to speak of. Which doesn't mean, of course, that mice aren't smart. They are. But that way I'll be able to see a little of what's going on, long distance so to speak, and maybe even help you. It's a technique that will let us hear one anothers thoughts.

"The only thing is, I haven't completely perfected the technique, so the duplicate will be temporary and is apt to disappear anytime. I can't say when. But when it goes, there will be no harm done to anyone. So, what do you say?"

"Well, I guess it's all right."

"Good, good. I'll get your pills, and a special chocolate flavored one for Lemanuel to nibble on."

The old man shuffled into his shop—Jonathan could hear some bottles and tins being moved about—and in a few moments he returned, seated himself, and peered around the room.

"Lemanuel? Come on out. I've got a treat for you, which you've probably got a whiff of already. Come and get it."

As if on cue, the mouse dashed out from behind a stack of books and scampered up the old man's armchair. Darting to his friend's open palm, the mouse sniffed the tidbit nestled therein and began munching it without further ado. Jonathan waited expectantly. Suddenly, in a flash, there was another mouse sitting on the old man's hand next to the first, whose sudden appearance caused the original to leap into the air in alarm and land four square on the old man's knee. Squeaking in protest at the scandalous turn of events, the irate rodent scurried to the floor and vanished into a hole in the wall.

The old man pursed his lips. "I might have known. Lemanuel's madder than a wet wren. Hen? I'll have to apologize to him later. Now, let's take a look at his twin brother here. Mmm. You're a fine specimen, I see. I hope you don't mind me crowding your brain a little. There, that does it—I'm all moved in. Now we need a name for you. Let's see. I have it. Since you're a twin, we'll call you Deucer.

"Jonathan, meet Deucer. Deucer, Jonathan. Looks like the real decoy, don't you think? Or is it McCoy? Anyway, here you are, my boy, he's all yours. Got an empty pocket?"

Jonathan carefully lifted the mouse, which sniffed his fingers curiously, its eyes burning bright red. It was solid enough and felt real. He slipped the small creature into his trouser pocket where he kept the Hhor's skin. He felt sure the two would find each other's company compatible.

"And here's your sending pill and two return pills. That should do it." The old man sank back in his chair, a sad look on his face.

Jonathan smiled gratefully and touched the old man's hand. "I'm sorry to leave you so soon, but time is important. Farewell, dear friend. You have given me a new life."

Jonathan swallowed the sending pill. Almost immediately his head grew light and the room began to blurr and recede. A swirling vortex grew at the periphery of his vision, churning ever faster until it swept him up into a vast darkening space. The darkness enclosed his thoughts and embraced him in a silent stillness.

The old man stared at the empty chair before him. He felt proud of his young friend. Not long ago he had sent a boy to another world in search of a dream. Now he had sent a man with a dream to save a world.

When next he opened his eyes, Jonathan saw that he was sprawled in the grass atop a familiar hill overlooking the city of Zuralia. He blinked at the sky, waiting for his eyes to fully regain their focus, vaguely thinking that something about the sky wasn't right. He shut his eyes, then re-opened them. Something was wrong: though it was midday, the heavens were dim and the twin suns were nowhere to be seen.

He leapt to his feet, his heart pounding. A dense shadowy layer pervaded the atmosphere, its great mass blocking out the Zuralian suns. The dark ceiling seemed to have solidity. And it was moving! Moving lower, towards the land! It seemed to pulsate, as though alive.

A terrible realization struck him. The thing in the sky *was* alive. It was some awful alien monster of titanic proportions, and it was slowly descending upon the island. Surely this was the danger the reader had warned him about.

He watched in helpless silence as the titanic creature descended further. Bits of mist and cloud hovering below it churned wildly about, only to be sucked into its great mass. A flock of terrified seagulls flew in whirling circles, and they too were drawn upward and torn apart as though by a cyclone. The thing was acting like a gigantic destroyer-vacuum, pulling up and annihilating everything in its path. Such would be the fate of Zuralia, Jonathan realized, once it reached the land.

He strove to dispel his panic. He had to concentrate, to try to think of something, anything, to stop this terrible cosmic destroyer. But what could he, one insignificant person, do? Nothing! In his fury he raised his fists and screamed at the aerial leviathan, demanding that it go back where it came from, tears of anguish streaming down his face. But he could only watch helplessly as the vast pulsing underbelly of the gigantean mass descended upon his beloved island. First it reached the high twin peaks that guarded the island harbor, and before his eyes the mountain tops melted away as though ice consumed by flame.

He knew that soon the throbbing mass would reach the next highest elevation on the island—the very hill on which he stood. Closer it came. He could see clearly now its dark palpitating flesh, pocked and slimy, covered with vibrating horn-like extremities and writhing suction discs. The vast undermass was pitted with large crater-like openings lined with wriggling pulpish antennae. One of the great depressions was directly above him.

If his island dream-child, as he now believed it to be, was about to perish, then let him perish with it. He regretted that he had failed his offspring, and he wondered why it had called to him, a feeble mortal, for help. Perhaps, after all, it was but a child crying for its father in its hour of need. But his deepest sorrow was that he would never see his beloved Llanya again, at least in this life.

He touched the bit of Hhor's skin in his pocket and felt its pulsing warmth, sensing that Llanya too was touching it at that very moment. Something tickled the tip of his finger, and he remembered the little mouse, Deucer. Tragic as circumstances were, he knew his old friend, the dream sender, would want to see what was happening. So he placed the mouse inside his shirt collar where it could peek out and have an unobstructed view of land and sky. The old man's thoughts reached out to him, and he sensed their alarm.

The descending creature's charnel odor reached him and the awful fetor made him gag. A gaping crater was just above him now. He could feel its powerful suction and hear the lapping sounds made by its squirming feelers. He picked up a rock and fruitlessly hurled it at the noisome bulk, but it was swallowed up in the blackness. The grass about him fluttered wildly, and he suddenly felt himself rising—he was being pulled into the belly of the mammoth creature.

As he passed into the darkness of its body, its great bulk shuddered as though it had been painfully stung. Its motion ceased, though only momentarily. Looking down, Jonathan could see through the crater opening that the land was now retreating from him. The creature was rising, leaving the island!

Despite his plight, a wave of relief swept over him. Zuralia was saved! But how? Could it be he whom the creature wanted, not the island? Or did it find his taste unpalatable? Deucer squeaked from behind his collar, and he could sense its maker's feelings of relief. In his mind he could hear the old man's thoughts: "I don't think the monster is out to destroy you. Take courage and stay alert."

As he floated deeper into the crater, he wondered what was holding him aloft and if he was being directed or summoned by some intelligent force. The blackness around him gradually fell away, and he entered into a vast open space, as though an inner universe. Yet it seemed impossible that a seemingly boundless inner space could exist within the creature, a space that looked infinitely greater in size than the creature itself. Deucer relayed a thought: "You may have entered another plane."

As he gazed about he saw it was indeed a cosmos of its own, replete with a multitude of planetary worlds spinning in their separate orbits. The surrounding space was mysteriously illuminated by a pale white light, though from no discernible source, for he could see no glowing suns, moons, or stars. The existence of such a universe defied the laws of earthly science. But that was no longer shocking. Perhaps the dream sender was right: perhaps he had passed through a gateway into another plane. Perhaps a separate dimension-space did exist within the roving macrocosmic creature itself. Or maybe when he passed through the gateway, he had been instantly transported somewhere else.

As he drifted through the ether, he saw that centermost among the myriad spinning planets was a small whirling brown sphere with oddly striated markings. The planet seemed to be moving closer to him, but then he realized that it was he who was moving closer to it. It seemed to be drawing him. His speed rapidly accelerated until the passing constellations were but flashing blurs on the periphery of his vision.

The path he traveled arced through time-compressed space, and epochs seemed to fall away in seconds. He blinked as though in slow motion, his eyelids falling and rising like the movement of the planets. And in an eye-wink it seemed as though he had traversed half the continuum of the vast inner universe.

His speed slowed as he neared the now looming brown planet, and an eerie spheral music reached his ears. It was softly melodic, despite its strange micro tonic harmonies. But gradually it increased in volume and tempo until it became a maddening cacophony, a multi-chordal fugue of earsplitting dissonance. He clapped his hands to his ears to keep out the daemonic pandemonium, only to feel something brush against his face. At first he thought it might be Deucer, but the mouse was hidden beneath his collar. Something touched him again. Whatever it was was invisible, though it felt soft, like a feather, and beneath the harshness of the celestial music he thought he heard the muffled fluttering of wings beating against the darkness.

Yet another noise rose up around him, at first only a low humming sound, but it soon rose in pitch like a siren call shearing through the ether. As though in reply, it was joined by a medley of unseen voices that mewled and twittered in a rising crescendo, finally escalating into a shrill chorus that might be the primordial wailings of dead souls wandering in the nightmare reaches of space. He closed his eyes and screamed to drown out the noise, and the sound of his own voice was as a balm to his tormented brain. He could feel Deucer trembling beneath his collar.

As the warm soothing air of the approaching planet embraced him, he opened his eyes and stilled his voice, relieved to find that the awful alien sounds had died away. Slowly he glided down toward the brown sealess world, and as he approached its surface his flight path gradually became horizontal. He felt certain now that his journey was being directed. The thoughts of the dream sender concurred.

A dense forest passed below him, and he saw that the vegetation was of a somber hue, devoid of chlorophyllous life. The trees were curiously hybridic, their branches covered with yawning cephalitic pods and cilial creeper vines that whipped at him as he passed. Beyond the forest he passed over steaming effluvial fens, bubbling sulphidic pools, bizarre fungal mires, and dead prairies overwhelmed by a white plague-like growth. Beneath the glazed quiescent surface of a vast misamic swamp he saw images that looked like the withered pleading faces of uncounted tormented souls; and beyond, in the slime of foetid bogs, he shuddered to see hosts of eyeless reptiloids devouring the decayed remains of their own kind.

Yet further, rising above the mephitic lowlands, he came to a great mountainous wasteland, and amidst its supine ridges and barren valleys jutted forth a lofty green plateau, as though an oasis in a desert wilderness. Giant umbral ferns, spiraling stalks, and burgeoning scarlet pedicels abounded in arboreal splendor, and at the center of the sylvan garden stood a megalithian edifice, a palace of black chalcedony resplendent with tall adamentine towers and knifelike porphyritic pinnacles.

He drifted down to the roof of the palace and came to rest upon a high parapet beside a scalloped dome. The air was dense and fog-like, and he could see no sign of life about. In the dimness a narrow band of light shone through a recessed opening in one side of the dome. Peering through the aperture, he saw that he was looking down into a great hall.

Strange yet magnificent, the chamber was of polished obsidian, its walls hung from floor to ceiling with lavish tapestries depicting preternatural semi-human figures in erotic embrace, its furnishings of heavy ebon wood extravagantly carven with serpentine ornature. The center of the hall was dominated by a long rectangular table at which sat three figures in the midst of dining.

At the table's head, smiling demurely and nibbling at sweetmeats, languished a tall exotic lady of indeterminate years. Dark and sultry, she was garbed in a shimmering black gown, her affluent sable tresses cascading over a lithe seductive form, her half-closed eyes staring absently into space. Jonathan could not help but admire her pale raven beauty.

Seated to the lady's right was a man-sized reptilian, vaguely humanoid, with an elongated tapering head, gaping holes for ears, lidless erubescent eyes, a black forked tongue, serrated teeth, clawed arms and legs, a stubby tail, and a narrow low-slung body covered with a hygric scaly skin that was moulting in patches.

The third figure, seated to the lady's left, was quasi-batrachian, short, squat, and neckless, with a broad flat head, bulging ochreous eyes and a pulpy slug-like body, sickly greenish-brown in color, from which sprouted six rubbery arm-like appendages and two stubby webbed feet.

Lying on an open platter before the saurian was a large trussed-up mantis-like insect, alive, with a horned beak protruding from a triangular head, waving antennae, and sentient multi-faceted eyes that followed every movement of the reptilian claw that made teasing threatening motions in front of its face. Whenever the claw came close, the pincer-like beak of the insect snapped viciously at its tormentor, though to no avail. Seemingly bored with the game, the saurian in a quick motion reached out and broke off one of the insect's jointed legs and proceeded to devour it, oblivious to the creature's still watching eyes. Next the reptile broke off the insect's head and neatly snapped it into two pieces, one of which was replaced on the platter and the other stuffed into hungry waiting jaws.

The batrachian provided its own food. Reaching around with two of its groping hose-like appendages that protruded from the left side of its body, it pushed them into a hidden aperture in its right side and proceeded to rapidly raise and lower itself in a pumping motion as though injecting itself with fluid. Withdrawing the appendages, the creature squatted, waited a moment, then exuded a brown pulsating soft-shelled egg the size of a large grapefruit from a cavity low in its body. Gently lifting the egg to the table, it peeled away the viscid outer shell, exposing the white quivering mass within. Sniffing the agglutination with apparent pleasure, the batrachian forced it whole into its cavernous mouth and swallowed it in a single gulp.

Jonathan stepped back from his watching place, sickened by the grisly repast, and he wondered at the incongruity of the beautiful lady dining in such repulsive company. Deucer had no thoughts on the subject, having refused to gaze upon the outlandish feast.

Curiosity nibbled at Jonathan, and he resumed his spying. He saw now that the dark-clad lady's two dinner guests had departed and she was alone. She had moved to the far end of the room and was reclining on a low pavonine divan. Her eyes were closed, though the outstretched fingers of one hand gently caressed her brow.

Suddenly he heard a voice. Somehow he knew it was hers. She was speaking to him, not in words but in thoughts. She beckoned to him, ever so sweetly, as though she had known of his presence all along. Her voice was soft and alluring, and strangely compelling. He drifted slowly down to the garden below. Whether his body was obeying his will or was being directed by the lady, he wasn't sure. A windowed door opened before him and he entered into the great hall.

The lady nodded to him and gestured for him to approach. When he stood before her she bowed her head and her full sensual lips parted in a smile.

"Welcome, Creator." Her voice, no longer silent, was a trilling half-purr, and her large dark eyes, russet flecked, fairly glowed as though in approval of her visitor. "I'm delighted you accepted my invitation. I so rarely have the pleasure of human company—you saw my dinner companions. I hope you found your journey to the third plane interesting, and not too uncomfortable.

CHAPTER 13

THE EGGS

The captain listened in grim silence as Llanya told him about Jonathan's experience with the dream reader and his sudden disappearance from the ship. He shook his head.

"Whew! That's heavy stuff. Dream sending, dream reading, dream creating—it's all a bit much for me. But if this what's-her-name reader is right, and you say Jon thinks she is, then Zuralia and maybe the whole plane is in big trouble."

"Captain, Jon also said there was some kind of danger to the island plane on the isles of Zis and Zat, but he didn't know what it was. He wondered if you might have heard something about it."

"Zis and Zat. I know them. They're twin islands not very far from our present position. They're not much as islands go, just two small hunks of rock a few miles apart, uninhabited except by singing seals. The seals are the only dangerous things there that I know about."

"Seals?" asked Llanya. "How can seals be dangerous? We have many on Celeucia, and everyone loves them."

"Not ordinary seals—singing seals, which are a breed apart, and peculiar to Zis and Zat. It's their music that's deadly. They croon night and day, a ghastly piercing sound. At least that's how it was described to me by a half-crazy old salt deep in his beer. He was the only survivor from his ship, and that was because he was half deaf in the first place.

"The seals' cries reach out more than a mile offshore, and pity any poor sailor within earshot. Many are the tales of ships in the night that sailed too close to Zis or Zat. They ended broken on the island rocks with all hands lost. The old salt called the seals' song a seamen's dirge—it drives you stark-raving mad."

Llanya wrinkled up her nose and shivered. "Ugh, that's horrible. But I don't think that was the danger Jon meant."

"Neither do I. And I don't think it's right that Jon should be taking all the risks while we sail on our merry way. We'll take a look at Zis and Zat and see what's there. If we discover any danger, maybe we'll be able to do something about it. With a fair wind we should make the islands before midday tomorrow."

"But Captain, what about the singing seals?"

"My dear, haven't you ever heard of earplugs?"

Llanya grinned.

"Well, Princess, I'd better go now and have a talk with the men. I'll have to share a little bit of the story with them to explain Jon's absence and to get them to go along with the diversion to Zis and Zat. I'll talk to Balu privately and fill him in on more of the details. If I know the big galoot, he'll insist on going ashore with me—I hope. It may be more than a one-man job."

"It will be. I'm coming too."

The captain jumped to his feet. "What? Oh, no you're not! It could be dangerous—you heard Jon say so."

"I'm coming just the same. Jon's in trouble and I want to help. I have to. I love him."

The captain saw the moisture gathering in Llanya's eyes and dreaded the thought of her weeping. He threw up his hands. "Oh, all right. You women find a man's weak spot and probe it for all its worth. But you'll follow my orders. Is that understood?"

Llanya smiled gratefully. "Yes, Captain. Thank you."

Once back in her cabin, Llanya stretched out on the floor with the trocht, using his shoulder as a pillow. She withdrew the Hhor's bit of skin and gently rubbed it. Touching it brought her closer to her bond-mate; she knew he too would feel its warmth.

The trocht exhaled deeply, and she saw that it was sleeping, perhaps dreaming. What do trochts dream of? she wondered as she nestled closer to her pet. She yawned and soon drifted off and so did not hear the captain's voice on deck cry out: "Altering course twenty degrees to leeward. Destination—the isle of Zis."

When Llanya awoke it was nearly daybreak. She saw that her pet had grown larger during the night, though it did not greatly concern her. As her mother often said, love is big enough for all sizes.

There was work to be done. She washed and dressed, fed the trocht, then took him for a stroll around deck before the crewmen appeared. Tabber, at the wheel, greeted her with a nod, though he kept a wary eye on her furry companion. Next she set to making breakfast for the men—cereal, fruit, rolls, and Celeucian pancakes—tasting each dish as she prepared it to be sure it was to her satisfaction. She also made sandwiches for the men so they would have something to eat while she was ashore with the captain.

After breakfast, as she was washing plates in the galley, she heard the captain on deck give the order to lower the mainsail and drop anchor. She hurried out to investigate and joined the captain and Balu at the rail. The captain had a spyglass trained on the horizon. Her eyes followed the direction the captain was looking, and she could make out the hazy outline of a small rocky island in the distance. The captain muttered a seamen's oath as he passed the glass to Balu.

"Do you see what I see?" the captain asked.

Balu peered through the glass. "It's Zytox birds all right. Two big ones perched on a high pinnacle of rock. They're facing away from us though, and may not have seen us. They're just sitting there and don't seem to be affected by the seals' song. And the seals are there too, on the rocks above the shoreline."

The captain turned to Llanya. "This complicates matters. Those birds are deadly and have sharp eyesight. From what we already know, they could be spies, or worse."

"Captain, do you think the Zytox are the danger that Jon spoke about?" asked Balu.

"I doubt it. Not just two of them. More likely they're guarding something on the island. The question now is, what's our next move?"

"Well," said Llanya, "I understand that Zytox don't see well at night. So we could wait till dark, then sail in close to the island, take a rowboat ashore, and investigate as best we can without exposing ourselves to the birds. There should be plenty of time for us to look around, return to the ship, and sail out of sight before dawn."

The captain feigned a cough. "Good thinking. That's just what I was about to suggest. We'll go ashore at the southern tip of the island where the Zytox are least likely to spot us. It looks rocky there, but it'll be the safest spot. Balu, see that everyone gets a wad of cotton to stuff in their ears, and come dark, check every ear on board to be sure it's stuffed tight. And that includes the trocht, too. If he goes berserk, we're all in for it."

Balu gulped and nodded. Llanya giggled. "I'll do Trok's ears." Balu breathed easier. "Thank you, Princess."

Shortly after dark the captain gave the signal to make sail, and Tabber steered the Pelagin in close to the south shore of the island. A rowboat was lowered. Balu manned the oars, with Llanya seated behind him and the captain at the bow. Llanya thought they looked like Zwegian squirrels, with the tufts of cotton sticking out of their ears.

As they neared the shoreline, the captain pointed to a large opening on the side of a high cliff. Balu nodded and steered toward it. The captain was relieved that the cliff blocked out the view of the Zytox. If they couldn't see the birds, the birds couldn't see them. Llanya pointed to a group of mottled seals lounging on some nearby rocks, some with their heads raised and mouths open as though crying out. She shivered; a shudder ran through the captain and Balu as well.

Approaching the cliff opening, they saw it was a gigantic deep-water sea cave. The captain motioned for Balu to row into it. Inside the cavern the high walls gave off a dim greenish glow, and in the distance toward the back of the cave they could make out a sandy beach rising up out of the water. As they neared the beach, the captain suddenly began to wave his hands in the air in a signal for Balu to stop rowing. Balu complied, though the boat continued to drift forward, pushed along by the incoming tide. The captain's eyes rolled and he butted his head with his hand in apparent frustration, then began gesturing wildly at Balu again, this time raising and lowering his hands in a grabbing-swooping motion. Balu's brow wrinkled in puzzlement. The captain then jumped to the back of the boat, nearly knocking his shipmates overboard, grabbed at the anchor and tossed it over the side. The anchor rope grew taut and the rowboat ceased its forward drift, to the apparent relief of the captain, who mopped a perspiring brow with the back of his hand.

He pointed toward the shore, and his companions now saw what the skipper's eyes had first spotted. The beach was covered with crabs, hundreds of them, each about the size of one's palm, their shells decorated in pretty red dots. And above the beach, on rising shelves of rock, were row upon row of giant black eggs.

The captain began gesturing again and mouthing words at the same time, but with their ears stuffed neither Balu nor Llanya could make out his meaning. Having anticipated the possible need, Llanya reached into her blouse and pulled out a small pad and pencil which she handed to the captain. The skipper looked at her in amazement, then began scribbling down a message. It read: "Poisonous spitting crabs—they can spit deadly poison up to twenty feet. Kills upon contact. But they're land crabs and won't enter the water. The eggs are Zytox eggs. Looks like someone is preparing for an invasion. This is a hatchery. See the smoke coming up through a vent in the rocks—there's heat to incubate the eggs. Look at the slope of the walls. This is an old volcano. The Zytox we saw are guarding the eggs. This must be the danger Jon spoke of. We must destroy the eggs."

Llanya took the pad and pencil. "How?" she wrote. "We can't get near the beach, let alone the higher rocks where the eggs are. The cavern wall behind is sheer." Balu, looking over her shoulder, nodded as if to underline her question.

The captain pursed his lips. "Think," he wrote.

There was a long silence. Then Balu's eyes widened, sparkling with the glimmer of an idea. He rummaged around on the bottom of the boat and came up with a length of wound rope. He thought if the boat got in as close as possible to the beach—about twenty feet offshore to keep out of range of the spitting crabs—then the remaining length of rope could be thrown onto the shore from the boat. Something heavy tied to the end of the rope could be used to break the eggs. He measured the rope in arm lengths and it came to forty feet—not long enough even to reach the first row of eggs.

The captain and Llanya, watching Balu measure the rope, caught onto his idea. Balu took the pad and wrote: "If we tie the anchor rope onto this other piece and get in a little closer, it might be long enough to reach the eggs. Using the anchor at one end of the rope as a hammer, I'll try to swing it in circles, letting it out a little at a time, until it's out far enough to smash the eggs."

Llanya took the pad. "But without the anchor, how will be keep the boat from drifting into shore with the tide, into the spitting range of the crabs?"

Balu wrote: "You can see from here that the water's not very deep twenty feet offshore. You and the captain can push the oars down into the sand below the boat, and hold the boat in place while I make the throw."

Llanya looked at the captain with a questioning eye. The skipper shrugged and wrote: "Let's try it."

Balu hauled in the anchor and let the boat drift shoreward. At twenty feet out, the captain on one side of the boat and Balu on the other each drove an oar into the sand. The boat held fast, with only the handles of the oars above water to grasp onto. Llanya took the oar from Balu as he prepared his weapon of destruction. The crabs on shore, aware now of an alien presence, shifted from side to side nervously. One of the foremost shot a stream of poison toward the boat. The purplish liquid arced over the water and landed with a hiss a foot in front of the bow.

Balu, his weapon now ready, signaled his companions to keep their heads down. Then, standing at his full height, he began swinging the anchor in ever-widening circles above his head. Ten feet, twenty, thirty, forty. Muscles bulging, his massive body strained mightily under the effort. Fifty, fifty-five. The rope was almost played out. Sixty, and the swinging anchor smashed through the first row of eggs like a breakfast knife through hen's eggs. Blood and gore splattered over the surrounding rocks, revealing that the Zytox chicks within the eggs were close to hatching.

Balu kept the engine of destruction in motion, but the rope wasn't long enough to reach the second row of eggs. Balu had no choice but to pull it back to the boat.

"Good work," wrote the captain, slapping his mate on the back.

"But I missed most of them," replied Balu, forgetting to write down his response and speaking out loud instead. Immediately the crabs on the beach began to scuttle forward, moving toward the sound of Balu's voice.

The captain had seen Balu's lips move. He grabbed the pad: "Did you see that? Sound moves them. Maybe we can lure them away from the area of beach between us and the eggs so we can get in closer. Let's move the boat to the left twenty feet, then I'll call out and see if I can draw them aside."

The boat in its new position, the captain called out to the crabs. They didn't move. He tried again with the same result. Then Llanya tried, also with no luck. The captain signaled to Balu to try again. Balu called out, and immediately the crabs in a single mass scurried ten feet to the side. But after a moment of silence, they quickly moved back to their original ground. "As an experiment, try calling out longer and in a high voice," wrote the captain to Balu. "They may respond to special vibrations." Balu cleared his throat and sang out in a high falsetto: "Come ov-er here, you crab-by bas-tards." At that the mass of crabs scuttled a full twenty feet down the beach towards the caller. But when Balu's call ceased, the crabs again returned to their original places.

The captain wrote: "Balu, there's only one solution. You'll have to get out of the boat, right here. The water is about six feet deep, and you're taller than that. So you'll be able to stand up with your mouth and nose above water. I'll take the boat back to where we were. Llanya will hold the boat in place with the oar to be safe. Then you sound off and draw the crabs over to one side. I'll jump out of the boat, run in, and break the rest of the eggs with the anchor."

Balu passed the note to Llanya, and everyone just stared at one another for a moment.

"What'll I say to keep the crabs interested for that long?" wrote Balu.

"Whatever it is, make it high pitch. Sing them some Zwegian ditties. That should do it."

Balu grimaced, then hopped over the side. The water was warm and came up to his ears. He had to tilt his head back to avoid getting a salty mouthful, though an occasional swell was more than he could protect against. The water he spewed out made an arc that would have impressed the meanest of spitting crabs. He kept his body steady by the deft movement of his hands below water.

The captain rowed the boat back to its previous position, pushed an oar through the water into the sand, and gave it over to Llanya to hold secure. It took all her strength to keep the boat steady. The captain waited to see if she was up to the task, and she smiled and nodded that all was well. The captain then signaled to Balu to begin.

Balu spewed out a mouthful of water and commenced to sing in a high falsetto voice:

> *"A maiden of Zweg at a tribal dance*
> *Said to a warrior, 'show me your lance.'*
> *His courage fled,*
> *And the warrior said,*
> *'I left it in my other pants.'"*

The crabs, clearly impressed, scurried across the beach to a position directly in front of their aquatic serenader. At that, the captain jumped out of the boat, rope and anchor in hand, and made for the beach. Once there, he stopped to look about to be sure all the crabs had vacated the area.

Balu was forced from time to time to hesitate in his song in order to spew out sea water, and in that brief moment the crabs became agitated, quivering on their spindly legs. But he quickly resumed his crooning, which immediately settled his audience down.

> *"A Zwegian warrior named Dong*
> *Had a lance seven feet long.*
> *When the ladies complained,*
> *He asked why. They explained:*
> *'It's too short, that's what's wrong.'"*

The captain scampered up the beach toward the eggs. The sand was warm from the volcanic heat and so loose he found it hard to walk. The incline steepened, and he was able to make better progress by crawling on all fours. Upon reaching the first level of rocks he saw he would have to wade through the fleshy mess that Balu had wrought with the anchor in order to reach the eggs above. He could also now see, between the second and third tier of eggs, just below a rocky ridge, the smoking volcanic vent that was providing the warmth for the eggs to incubate.

Llanya, from her vantage point in the boat, had a better view of the rocky area above the beach than did the captain. It was just as he reached the row of broken eggs that she noticed some movement behind an egg on the second row, not far above the captain. Crabs! She could make out at least two of them. And the ten foot distance between them and the captain was well within the creatures' spitting range. Doing her best to hold the oar steady with one hand, she frantically waved her other hand to try to get the captain's attention. But he was facing the other way and couldn't see her. Desperately, she grabbed the writing pad, wrapped her arms tightly around the handle of the oar and, despite her awkward position, managed to scribble a few words down on paper. She folded the small rectangular sheet into the shape of a miniature glider, took careful aim, and sailed it off in the direction of the captain, making a silent prayer to Hhor the while.

Balu, in the midst of a song, saw Llanya waving desperately at the captain and guessed something was wrong, though he didn't know what. But he knew he couldn't help, that he had to stay where he was and continue singing, which was becoming increasingly difficult. The tide was getting rougher and regularly filling his mouth and nose with water. He didn't know how much longer he could keep up an unbroken stream of song.

> *"A Zwegian warrior named Mope*
> *Tied his lance with a rope.*
> *But a virgin untied it.*
> *She said, 'Please don't hide it,'*
> *And so he gave it great scope."*

The paper glider, well aimed, struck the captain behind the neck, causing him to leap into the air in a fright. He whirled around, and then he saw Llanya wildly gesturing at him from the boat. He picked up the paper and read its message: "Crabs behind egg on second row." He looked up toward the rocks just as a crab was crawling out of its hiding place into full view. The crab quivered and released its deadly stream. The captain leapt sideways just in time. The poison spray struck the paper he had dropped, and it sizzled and crumpled into ashes. In great strides the captain bounded down the sandy slope, slipping and sliding, and so did not see the second stream of poison as it struck the ground only inches from his leg. He stopped at the water's edge and turned to see if the crab was coming after him. It wasn't: it hadn't moved from the second row of eggs. He was well out of its range now. Relieved, he dropped the anchor and plopped down on the sand to think.

Llanya began waving at him again, pointing toward Balu. The captain saw she was having great difficulty holding the boat in place. His eyes turned toward his crooning shipmate. Balu, sputtering and coughing, was struggling mightily to hold his head above water. Judging from his mouth movements, he was apparently able to sing out only spasmodically.

"Said a Zwegian wife in disgust,
'My husband is terribly unjust (sputter).
His lance is at least
Six feet and well greased (cough),
Yet he won't ever give me a thrust.' "

Time was running out, the captain knew. But there was no way he could get around the crabs on the rocks and get to the eggs. Even if he swung the anchor from a safe spot part way up the beach and was able to break a few more eggs, he would still never be able to reach the greater numbers on the higher rows.

An idea struck him. Standing on the ledge just above the volcanic vent was a boulder about the same size as the opening of the vent. If he could grab the top of the boulder with the anchor, maybe he could topple it onto the vent. The boulder would act as a plug. By closing off the source of heat that was incubating the eggs, the unhatched chicks would die in their shells. He should be able to make the throw from a position well up the beach and still be out of the range of the crabs.

Both Llanya and Balu watched in puzzlement as the captain crawled through the sand to a spot some twenty feet below the second row of eggs. Then he began to swing the anchor as Balu had done, only now, when the rope was ten feet out, he released it and the anchor hurtled through the air toward the rocky ledge above. It clanged off the edge of a large boulder and fell to the ground. Almost instantly, a crab skittered out from behind the boulder onto the ledge.

The captain muttered a curse. He reeled in the anchor as fast as he could, keeping an eye on the jittery crab. His second attempt hit the mark. The anchor caught the top edge of the boulder and held. He pulled in the slack and tugged on the rope gently. When he was sure that the grip was secure, he gave the rope a mighty pull. The boulder toppled forward, even as the crab released its poison, which struck and instantly melted through the rope. The anchor, free of its tether, went tumbling over the rocks. The boulder, as though guided by an invisible hand, fell straight toward the vent. But to the captain's horror, it failed to wedge itself in the opening, and instead fell through it into the volcanic depths below. The stone had been too small.

The ground began to rumble and shake. The captain ran helter-skelter toward the boat, hoping the while that Balu wouldn't stop his singing until he was aboard lest the crabs move back within range. The half-drowned chief mate bravely kept up his song, which by now had re-gressed to a broken atonalism, until the skipper was safely aboard. Then he quickly swam the short distance back to the boat. On the beach the crabs scurried about in confusion.

The tremors worsened as Balu rowed hard toward the cavern entrance. Stone stalactites broke loose from the ceiling and stabbed through the water around them. The tide was turning and helped pull them out to open water. As they cleared the cave and headed toward the Pelagin, Llanya pointed to the great numbers of singing seals swimming away from the island. The captain nodded and pointed toward the neighboring isle of Zat. The seals were heading there en masse.

Suddenly a subterranean explosion shook the island and a stream of molten rocks spewed out of open crevices atop the highest peak. Balu hunkered down and rowed for all he was worth as the captain covered Llanya with his body to protect her from falling fragments. A flaming cinder fell into the boat, which Balu quickly stamped out. A thin coat of ash settled over the surrounding water.

Balu pointed seaward and the captain and Llanya saw that the Pelagin was on its way to retrieve them. "Well I'll be a skirla-rat's relative," the captain muttered, quite pleased. "Them's my lads." Fortunately Llanya, her ears still plugged, did not hear the appellation, otherwise he would have received a wilting look.

As the threesome boarded ship, a deep rumbling shook the ocean floor.

"Tabber, go with the wind," yelled the captain. "Men, prepare for rough water."

When the Pelagin was well out of danger, another explosion shook the island and its great cliffs shuddered and fell crashing into the sea.

"Not enough of a bang to create a tidal wave," said the skipper to Llanya, noting her worried look. "But it's sure big enough to demolish those devil eggs." Llanya's face brightened.

A white flash appeared on the horizon, momentarily lighting up the night sky.

"That's Zat," said the skipper. "Looks like it went up too. Likely there was an underground volcanic link between the sister isles, probably from the time of their formation. So when Zit went, Zat went. That means any Zytox eggs on Zat have also been destroyed, which sure simplifies matters for us."

The captain saw the questioning look in Llanya's eyes. "But just to be sure," he added, "we'll sail by what's left of Zat and have a look. Things seem to be calming down now, and in a while we'll come about. Meanwhile, Llanya, maybe you'd better look in on your pet. We don't want him getting agitated by all the ruckus and go blaming it on the captain. But before you go, I want to say that you were a very brave lady tonight. Both Jon and your father would be proud of you, as I am."

Llanya broad smile expressed her appreciation, though she thought the captain was being a bit of a chauvinist. As she walked to her cabin she touched the bit of Hhor's skin that she carried and hoped that the destruction of the Zytox eggs would somehow aid her bond-mate's quest.

The captain noticed that Tabber had given over the wheel to Balu and was leaning over the port rail with a pole-net. He joined the helmsman, who was in the process of hauling an object out of the water.

"Tabber, the water's rough and we need your night vision at the wheel right now," said the skipper.

"Excuse me, sir," Tabber replied, "but I saw something unusual floating beside the ship, and I thought it might be of value." With that the helmsman dumped the contents of the net onto the deck.

"The devil's drawers!" exclaimed the skipper. "It's a Zytox head. Must be what's left of one of the critters we saw perched atop the island. The explosion must have blasted it apart and blown its remains out to sea. But what possible use could it be?"

"As you know, Captain, I was once a priest of Klell and studied many strange things. I learned of the Zytox bird's magical vision and where its secret lies. The creature has an extra lens over its eyes, for which men of knowledge will pay much. If you will lend me your pocket knife, Captain."

The captain complied. Tabber bent down and with the tip of the blade he deftly removed the bird's outer eye lenses, then tossed the rest of the grisly head overboard.

"You see, sir, they are hard and clear, almost invisible. Some believe they have powers yet to be discovered. In any event, it was not a thing I thought wise to let drift out of our grasp."

"You did right, my friend. My pardon for speaking too hastily."

Tabber bowed respectfully. "Please take one of the lenses, Captain. It could prove useful. I will take the other and experiment with it, and possibly learn something more."

Chapter 14

ZILMARA

"Forgive me, Creator, for not introducing myself," said the dark-clad lady, her voice smooth as her satiny gown. My name is Zilmara, mistress of this dream plane. Welcome to my palace. And you are?"

"Jonathan Spenser. I came from Zuralia on the second plane. But I'm not exactly sure how I got here."

"You entered a dimension portal through the Qog—the cosmic dweller within whom this plane exists. I detected your presence and took the liberty of directing you to the safety of this planet. It seems your creator's aura singed the Qog a bit and drove him off just as he was about to consume your island world."

"Consume? You mean destroy?" Jonathan asked, his tone betraying his alarm.

"Consume, absorb, destroy—whatever you like. It seems the Qog has begun a rampage. Oh, but you mustn't be overly concerned. I doubt he'll destroy everything on the second plane. Any nightmare isles he happens upon he will simply inhale and relocate into this dimension. This is a nightmare plane, after all, and they will fit in nicely here. But as for the rest of the islands, yes, he'll probably eat them. If not today, then another time. In the end the second plane will be no more."

Jonathan was appalled and amazed at the lady's words, so calmly stated.

"But...but this Qog can't just go around destroying islands and planes, just like that."

The lady's brows rose and her eyes sparkled. "Oh? Why not?"

"Because...it's not right."

"Not right? I see." The lady smiled, obviously amused.

"And because the balance between planes could be disturbed," he added.

"Ah, you know about interplane balance. Well, I should tell you, there is already a dimensional disturbance between the second and third planes. Otherwise the Qog would not have been able to penetrate the second plane."

Jonathan shifted about nervously.

"How did that happen?" he asked.

Deucer, hidden beneath his collar, peeked out from time to time, being careful not to be seen. Jonathan felt the mouse scratching at his neck to try to get him to open his mind and give the dream sender's thoughts room to enter. Having forgotten momentarily about the mouse, he instinctively rubbed the offending area with his hand, only to hear a cry of "Ouch!" ring out in his head. His heart nearly stopped when he realized what he had done. "It's all right," came the message from the dream sender. "Deucer's not hurt."

"Is there something wrong?" asked the lady.

"Uh, no—just a hitch—I mean, itch."

"The answer to your question is quite simple. The nightmare plane also has its creators. Additional dream worlds were created on this plane until the weight of their numbers overbalanced that on the second plane. Consequently, the interplane fabric was stretched until it eventually tore, enabling the Qog to enter the adjacent dimension. The tear occurred in the space above your island, so the Qog naturally started there, until your nimbus stung him and drove him off. For the moment."

The glint in the lady's eyes belied her friendly, almost sympathetic, tone. And, as though in empathy, the ruby-red eyes of the spider pin she wore on her right shoulder brightened, a nuance which did not escape Deucer's attention.

Fragmentary thoughts from the dream reader forced themselves into Jonathan's mind: "Learn more…ask questions."

"But why is the Qog doing this?" pressed Jonathan. "Where did it come from?"

The lady mused a moment. "Why? Well, I suppose because Qog's a destroyer by nature, and that's simply what destroyers do when the opportunity arises. My, what strange questions you ask. All living entities seek pleasure. There can be as much pleasure in destruction as in creation, you know. Perhaps more."

The lady's eyes narrowed slightly, as though reassessing her visitor. "Perhaps the Qog also has a hunger for unity and power—to contain all nightmare worlds within a single plane, within himself. The desire for power and domination is universal, and are common traits in other dimensions as well. Besides, with so many creators running around these days recklessly raising up worlds everywhere, a little destruction is necessary to make more room—to avoid overcrowding. Obviously, creation, for its own survival, needs destruction. And vice versa.

"As to the Qog's origins, I'm not entirely sure. He may have come out of the limitless void between planes where he often likes to travel, though I suspect he emerged out of the boundless space within himself."

At each reply the lady made, a dozen more questions flashed into Jonathan's mind. "If the Qog is a destroyer of dream worlds, does he also create them too?"

The lady looked aghast. "Heavens, no. He doesn't have that power, thankfully."

"But someone is responsible for creating the additional dream worlds on this plane that caused the interdimensional imbalance. Perhaps that creator is in league with the Qog."

The lady's eyes momentarily hardened, but quickly returned to a gaze of amiable tranquility.

"What a lively imagination you have, Creator."

"But it's possible, isn't it?"

The lady raised her hand in a gesture of dismissal. "Perhaps. But quite unlikely. After all, I am mistress of this plane."

Jonathan pondered the reply, and again felt the mouse nibbling and trying to gain entry into his mind. He relented, and like a torrent the dream sender's thoughts flooded into his head: "Beware, Deucer smells evil. Trick her with questions…sound innocent."

"A thought occurs to me," he said as matter-of-factly as he could. "A hypothetical question, actually. If a creator were to add dream worlds to the second plane, wouldn't that bring it back into balance with the third? And wouldn't that prevent the Qog from returning to the second dimension?"

No sooner had he spoken than he realized from his host's expression that he had revealed too much by his question. A flame leapt into the lady's dark eyes, and the watchful Deucer again saw the pulsing brightness in the eyes of the spider decorating her shoulder. The mouse's observation was picked up by the dream sender who quickly sent his thoughts to Jonathan: "The spider is not a piece of ornamental jewelry, but a living creature, and probably serves the lady in some magical way. Careful."

Her reply was cloaked in caution.

"I'm not sure. But would it matter? Another imbalance could easily be created and the process resumed."

A period of silence followed; it lay heavy on the air, laden with the unspoken doubts and questions of two competing minds. When the lady next spoke, her voice was warm and inviting.

"Oh, but I'm being a neglectful hostess. You must be weary from your journey and in need of refreshment. Come, sit down beside me and we'll have a soothing drink together. Then we'll talk about how I might help you."

There being no chair nearby, Jonathan sat on the divan, though at a respectful distance from his hostess. He tried not to be distracted by her beauty. The lady reached over to a small table which held a golden urn shaped in the head of a dragon and two jewel-encrusted goblets. From the urn she poured a sparkling auramine liquid into the cups; one she handed to her guest, the other she took for herself.

"A toast, young Creator," she said in velvet tones. "May dreamers dream and sleepers wake, and dreaming not, dream worlds unmake."

She lifted her cup to her lips and drank. Jonathan took a sip of the dew-like beverage absently as he contemplated the meaning of the toast. Deucer was tickling his back again and nudging at his thoughts, which in his deliberation he ignored.

He found the drink's honeyed flavor exquisite. Its effect was wonderfully refreshing and relaxing, and he soon forgot about the lady's enigmatic rhyme.

"A delightful potion," she said as she slowly turned the goblet in her hand, though her eyes never left her guest. "It's called the Nectar of Lethe. I hope you like it."

"Yes," replied Jonathan, feeling slightly lightheaded. "Quite delicious."

"Let's not be so formal. Please call me Zilmara, and I will call you Jonathan. Now, Jonathan, what was it you were asking me a moment ago?"

"Asking? I'm not sure. Was I asking you something? I...I can't seem to remember." His will and concentration seemed like feathered birds taking flight. He no longer noticed the tickling at his neck.

The lady smiled. "It probably wasn't important. Let's change the subject. Oh, I should mention that I've taken back your ability to fly about on the third plane. So do be careful. I wouldn't want you to fall or hurt yourself."

"Can't fly.... Very well. It doesn't matter." He felt quite giddy.

The lady almost envied what her guest was experiencing. Her own senses had long ago become immune to the carefree pleasures of the drug—the unhappy price of overindulgence.

She reached out and took his hand in hers. "Come a little closer," she coaxed. "That's it."

She gently caressed his hand, and he could smell the intoxicating fragrance of her jet-black hair.

"Tell me, Jonathan, do you find me attractive?"

"Yes...you are very beautiful."

"If I may return the compliment, you're quite a handsome young man. I haven't had the pleasure of a young mortal's company for a very long time. So come, let's not be coy. Let's embellish our mutual admiration with the gift of pleasure. Are we not alike? Are we not both dream creators—you, a prince of the second plane, and I, mistress of the inner sphere? So come, my prince, cling to me that our souls may be bathed in the mysteries of creation, that our auras may also embrace and our powers commingle with the joys of the flesh."

Her scented touch was as a gossamer veil encircling him, enwrapping him in a sensual oblivion that banished any remnants of hesitation or doubt. An irresistible sea of passion swept over him—he could only yield—and together they drifted on the pleasure tides of unrestrained desire, were lifted up on wave upon wave of ecstasy. And finally, their bodies exhausted, they were cast upon the soft sands of contented sleep.

When the enchantress awoke, Jonathan yet slumbered, still heavy with the drug of Lethe. She gently kissed the closed eyelids of her young lover that he might be blinded to her greater purpose, kissed his brow that his thoughts might sleep and not probe the malefic maze of her intentions, brushed her lips against his ears that he might be deafened to the whisperings of her dark soul.

How well she remembered the blazing announcement of his birth as it streaked through the ether, how the emanations of his power had buffeted her thoughts in the dark of night. Patiently she had waited, and in fear, until she had found a way to lure him to the second plane where he would be within her reach. It had been a simple matter to plant the suggestion in the mind of the innocent old dream sender. The call of the creator's island offspring, which she easily enhanced, had made the task all the simpler. True, she had been fortunate that the creator had reached manhood still in ignorance of his powers. But who on that backward planet, Earth, could have enlightened him?

She had been unable to do him harm on the distant earthly plane. And now she was glad that her minions on the second plane had failed to kill him. He had posed a threat and she had sought his death. But fate had been kind and delivered her enemy into her hands. Now he was under her control. To destroy him had been her original purpose. But now she realized that letting him live, at least a while longer, could bring her the lifelong victory she hungered for.

She smiled at the slumbering creator, her eyes abrim with vision and eager hope. Now was the time. To his sleepless inner self she now spoke, to that hidden psyche whence springs the essence of imaginings, that secret spirit-place wherein the creator's dreams are given birth.

"Sleep and dream O Creator," she whispered. "Dream for Zilmara, mistress of nightmare. Dream for your lover a nightmare world to wonder at and behold. Search in the eternal darkness that haunts your mortal spirit, reach deep within the primeval abyss of your soul, find within the chaos of your inmost self that which is the stuff of nightmare dreams. Bring it to life, O Creator, build and bring forth a dream world for Zilmara, and set it among the demon-ridden firmament of the inner sphere. Let it be a world inspired by your deepest fears, a world peopled with the unspeakable chimaeras that haunt the nethermost regions of your mortal soul. Bathe your dream in the nimbus of your secret power. Deliver me your dream child that it may add power and strength to my universe and give nourishment to him, the mighty Qog, that my destiny may be fulfilled."

And Jonathan dreamed, and by the power of the dark enchantress his dream was darkest nightmare. He dreamt a planet world of bewildering chaos wherein dwelt all the nameless terrors of his long-forgotten childhood, creature-things that hovered at the edge of human sanity, forever tearing at its fragile veil, and he gave them life and form. Deucer trembled beneath his collar.

Eyes ablaze, her pulse quickening, Zilmara saw that he was in the throes of dream, and she rushed to the window of her chamber and gazed anxiously into the sky, searching the vast canopy of the inner sphere that was her universe. And lo! she saw materialize in the heavens before her eyes a planet newly born. Dark it was, a world of blackest dream turning slowly in the dim starless void. Uttering a shrill cry of joy, she flung her arms wide as to embrace the dark orb.

"A black planet!" she cried. "A planet of power—the first of my dimension. Spin, O child of nightmare, spin on O rarest jewel in my crown. Welcome to the bosom of the great Qog. Impart to him your malefic might, strengthen him with your terror-born puissance that he may conquer all for my pleasure."

Turning, she looked upon the sleeping figure of the creator, her face now distorted with jealousy and hate.

"Never have I been able to create a black world of power, though I have tried many times," she muttered to herself. "The mortal is more powerful than I, curse him. Perhaps he is too dangerous to let live. I may not be able to keep control of him. Should I risk letting him live to create other worlds for me? Or should he die? I must decide soon. But until I do, he needs to be tamed with a potion stronger that the Nectar of Lethe."

The lady went over to the long table in the center of the chamber. At that moment Jonathan, reclining on the divan, stirred from his sleep and opened his eyes. The fog slowly drifted from his mind and his wits fell into place. He didn't move, but pretended to still be asleep. Suddenly he felt Deucer move and in his mind he heard a voice call to him: "Wake up, Jonathan, wake up!" It was the dream sender. Then yet a second voice popped into his head, but from where he didn't know.

"Jon, it's me, the captain. If you can hear me, blink an eye. Good. I can see everything that's going on at your end, and you can receive my thoughts. I hope. But it's a one-way transmission, so I can't receive from you. I'm in my cabin with Tabber. He says I should explain what's happening so I don't scare you. I'm holding the eye lens of a Zytox over my eye to see you, and I have one of your shoelaces in my mouth to make contact with you. And in my other hand I'm holding the Hhor's piece of skin, which I stole, er, borrowed from Llanya, which is making this whole thing work. Tabber figured it out. I'm here to help you. Hey! There's someone else in here with me—I mean in your head. Blink once is it's a friend, twice if a foe. Oh, good, a friend. Well, can you tell him to shut up? If you can't, move him over. This is no time for idle chatter. Jon, listen, about this new girl friend of yours. I know she's one hell of a romancer—I couldn't help noticing. I wasn't eavesdropping, mind you. I was only trying to make contact and just happened to get through at that moment. But then I lost you. No doubt about it, she's good looking and all that, but from the way the Hhor's skin heated up when I focused in on her, she has to be bad news. The Hhor knows about these things. I'd get out of there fast if I were you.

"Holy herring! Don't move, Jon! There's something moving under your collar. Hey—it's a damned mouse. What in blazes? Jon, blink once for yes if you know about it. Uh, you do. I've been hearing some kind of squeaking sound in your head, like the thing is trying to talk to you. Jon, did you just blink accidentally? Or are you telling me it talks to you? It does. Oh-my-gosh. Have you lost your marbles, boy? Don't answer that. Oh crap, you're beginning to fade again. It's this lens. The damn Zytox must have had bad eyes or something. I'm losing you. I'll keep trying...."

Jonathan could no longer hear the captain's voice. But what he had said didn't make sense. What romancing was he talking about? The dream sender's voice chimed in: "I don't know who your rude friend was, but I'm glad he's gone. Despite his good intentions, he just doesn't understand the complexities of the situation."

From his reclining position Jonathan could see Zilmara at a table across the room pouring a liquid from a dark urn into a chalice. She then removed a serpentine opal ring from her finger and touched it to the liquid in the vessel; a thin wisp of smoke rose up. The spider at her right shoulder, as if in response to a silent command, suddenly scampered over to her left shoulder, and she bent her head down to whisper some-thing to it. Smiling, she then made her way back to the divan, chalice in hand. Jonathan closed his eyes, then felt his arm being gently shaken.

"Wake up." The lady's voice was sweet and soothing. "The night is ever young for the young at heart."

Jonathan sat up and feigned a yawn.

"How are you feeling after your sleep?" she asked as she touched her hand to his cheek.

"Rested, thank you," he replied, a little taken aback at her familiarity. "Though I don't seem to remember falling asleep." His clothing was askew, which he straightened out as he rose to his feet.

"I brought you a drink to revive your spirits," she said sweetly. With a smile she handed him the chalice containing a pale yellow liquid. He accepted it.

"My thanks, lady. If I may say so, you have a lovely palace." He be-gan to leisurely walk about the room. "The tapestries particularly interest me."

"Oh, I'm glad you like them. They are cleverly woven, one might think by demon hands."

He casually made his way over to a windowed door that opened into the garden, the same by which he had entered, and idly gazed up at the dim night sky. Turning, his eyes settled on a large tapestry directly across the room.

"That tapestry with the three satyrs is intriguing, but I'm not sure what type of creature it is they're chasing."

Zilmara turned toward the hanging, and as she did so, he pushed open the door, tossed the contents of the chalice into the garden, and quickly closed the door again.

"The creature is an Oralik, a native of a red planet on this plane," she explained. "It's both male and female and is self-reproducing. Though some might think it ugly, it emits an erotic chemical that irresistibly at-tracts other species, both male and female. When pursued, it usually lets itself be caught, though what transpires then is always a surprise to its pursuers."

"Fascinating," said Jonathan.

The lady approached him and saw that his chalice was empty.

"Would you like another drink?" she asked as she gently touched her fingers to his hair.

He stepped back, as nonchalantly as he dared. "No, but thank you." He yawned. "It seems I'm still a little tired. Would you mind if I take a nap on the divan?"

"Certainly not. Meanwhile there are one or two matters I must attend to. But I will return shortly. Then perhaps we can...entertain one another again."

Jonathan wondered what she meant by "again," since he had no recollection of any prior entertainment.

She took the empty chalice from his hand, and he went to the divan and lay on his side as though to sleep. He felt Duecer under his collar scrambling to the other side to avoid being crushed. He had forgotten about the mouse again.

Out of half closed eyes, he watched the lady take the spider from her shoulder and set it down on the far end of the divan. He guessed she had set it there to spy on him, and a thought message from the dream sender by way of Deucer confirmed his suspicion. The old man warned that the lady would be able to see his every movement through the spider's eyes, and admonished him not to stir as yet. The old man had a plan.

Jonathan surreptitiously watched the lady's silken step as she went to the large tapestry in the corner of the room, pulled it aside, and disappeared behind it. A sudden tickling sensation running across the back of his neck told him Deucer was on the move, and out of the corner of his eye he saw the mouse dart down the leg of the divan and disappear from sight. He waited motionless, his half closed eyes glued to the tarantula-like spider perched on the far end of the sofa. Then he spotted Deucer again: the mouse had climbed the far leg of the divan and was now coming up behind the spider. He guessed what Deucer was up to, and worried that the spider might be poisonous or possess some kind of magic that would harm or even kill his little friend.

Having reached its prey, Deucer, without hesitation, leapt on the spider's back and clamped its jaws on its hairy neck. The spider instantly sprang to life, straining to turn its head around to bite its attacker. But Deucer held it fast, tightening his grip, and soon the spider went limp beneath him. He had been clever enough to grasp the spider on the back of the neck so it couldn't turn its eyes in another direction. That way the spider's view would not change in case its mistress was watching through its eyes. Indeed, the dream sender thought that the lady might still be able to see through her pet's eyes even though it was dead, so he instructed Deucer to slowly turn its body around from behind until it was facing the back of the divan. Hopefully, the lady would think her pet had simply gotten lazy or was misbehaving and wouldn't become suspicious.

Jonathan jumped to his feet and put his hand out for Deucer to climb aboard. But no sooner did his little friend's front paws touch his finger tips than pooft—the mouse disappeared. It happened unpredictably, in an instant, just as the dream sender had warned. Jonathan said a silent thank you to his departed friend and hoped its abrupt disappearance was as harmless as the old man had said.

"What next?" he asked himself. He had a chance now to escape. But to where? He couldn't fly anymore and had no idea of how to return to the second plane. All he could think to do was to keep a close watch on the lady Zilmara in the hope that he might discover a way to return to Zuralia.

He stole to the tapestry behind which the lady had disappeared and, peering behind it, he saw that it concealed an arched doorway and a stone staircase leading down into the semi-darkness. Treading on tiptoe, he made his way down the stairs into what he guessed must be an underground cellar beneath the palace. The air was stale and heavy. A downward sloping passageway ran off to his right; he followed it. Clusters of phosphorescent fungi growing out of the stone ceiling cast an eerie glow to help light the way. As the downward slanting corridor became steeper, the mushrooms thinned out so he could hardly see. He held his hand out, touching the wall as a guide, but he quickly withdrew it when he felt something slimy and palpitant clinging to the damp stone.

The passage finally leveled off and widened into a small open court. A flickering wall torch gave added light, and he saw that he was in an ancient crumbling catacomb, its broken galleries laden with the decayed bones of long-dead creatures of alien cast. He wondered if these might be the offspring of some demented dream-creator out of nightmare antiquity. Why would they be here in the lady's palace? he wondered.

Beyond the subterranean cemetery the passageway resumed, only now it was regularly illuminated by girandoles. After many twists and turns the corridor quite suddenly debouched into a large cavern. As he was about to enter it, his mind fairly exploded with sound: "Jon! It's the captain. Don't go in. There's danger." He could feel the Hhor's skin in his pocket pulsing with warmth as though in corroboration.

He jumped aside and hugged the outer wall of the cavern. The captain was still trying to communicate with him, but the connection was going bad and he wasn't able to understand the occasional garbled words that came through. The last thing he heard was: "Don't go listening to any mice."

Cautiously, he peeked inside the cavern entrance and saw that the underground room was part of an old crater. High above, the slanting roof of the cavern opened up to the outside world. He gasped at what next met his eyes.

In the center of the great hall, he saw perched on a row of massive stone columns protruding from the cavern floor six giant Zytox birds, their crystal-white eyes fixed on the demure figure of Zilmara standing before them. Their powerful black wings twitched nervously as though awaiting their mistress's command. One of the great birds turned its head toward the cavern entrance and emitted a soul-searing screech. He jumped back into the passageway and waited with pounding heart. Nothing happened. Apparently he hadn't been seen.

The next sound he heard was the lady's voice. Peering carefully into the cavern again, he saw that she was speaking to the Zytox birds in some strange avian language, her voice uttering low piping notes interspersed with harsh guttural throat sounds. When her converse was done, she turned toward a dimly lit corner of the cave and cried out in an angry impatient voice.

"Dak! My pets are hungry! Bring them food!"

A crouching coarsely-furred figure shuffled out of the shadows dragging a large basket behind him. Jonathan saw that the stunted figure was dog-headed and thumbless and wore a terrified expression.

"Move faster, you incompetent," screamed Zilmara, "or I'll add you to the dinner—though I doubt you'd even be fit carrion."

The cowering demi-canine winced and struggled to move faster with the heavy load. It pulled the basket over to its waiting mistress and groveled before her; she dismissed the servant with a wave of her hand. It shuffled quickly back into the darkness at the back of the cave, whimpering and whining the while.

Zilmara, now all smiles, turned to her pets and spoke to them in a voice overflowing with warmth and motherly affection, this time in words Jonathan could understand.

"Here you are, my loves, freshly gathered morsels, nice and bite-sized the way you like them. For you, only the choicest bits of nightmare spawn. And of my own creation. Who knows, perhaps there will soon be younger, more tender meat to please my babies. A creator, no less. The very one you naughty girls let twice escape on the second plane. He is my guest now, and I would be distressed if he were to leave unexpectedly and upset my plans of conquest. So you must remain alert and see that he doesn't escape through the dimension portal. I depend on you, my babies—you know how unreliable that Dak is."

Reaching into the basket, Zilmara pulled out ichor-drenched chunks of crudely dissected body parts, only remotely anthropoidal, some of which still twitched spasmodically. She tossed the pieces one by one to her impatient pets, who deftly caught the dripping chunks in their beaks and, throwing their heads back, swallowed them in a single gulp.

Revolted by the ghastly feeding and the thought that he might end up the same way, Jonathan held his stomach and turned away. The lady's evil was now revealed to him in all its ugliness. He now knew it was she who planned the attacks on his life on the second plane. And it was none other than she who was the mother-creator of the nightmare worlds that caused the interplane imbalance and consequent rip in the dimensional fabric.

Feelings of impotence and frustration overwhelmed him. How could he, or any mortal, combat one so powerful? Yet he must try. He knew it would be fruitless to try to attack Zilmara in her own domain. Nor could he in fact think of anything useful he might accomplish by remaining here. He must try to escape. She had spoken of a dimension gate which the Zytox guarded and which she feared he might find. That meant the way out was probably somewhere here, in the creatures' roost. But where?

He peered once more about the great hall but could see no sign of a portal. The lady was speaking again, though now her tone carried the weight of command.

"My raven beauties, you have eaten of the flesh of my flesh, and now you must help provide nourishment for the great Qog. For is he not our protector, the caretaker of the nightmare spawn of my domain, the mover of worlds, the cosmic destroyer of dream planes? And am I not his mistress? Go, my daughters, be my eyes as mine are the eyes of the Eater of Worlds. Fly! Fly to the second plane and ease the way for his coming, for he will soon descend again and avenge the loss of your children. Go, my pets, go! Seek out all creators and destroy them!"

Unfolding their mammoth wings, the giant Zytox rose up, beating the air with a thunderous clapping, circling ever higher, their soul-shattering screeches reverberating through the chamber, finally disappearing through the open roof of the cavern.

Jonathan shuddered. It was Zilmara who was the driving force, the motivator, behind the monster Qog. She was using the creature to serve her own grandiose schemes—her evil ambition to destroy the second plane and increase the power of her own nightmare dimension.

The birds departed, he now had an unobstructed view of the opposite side of the cavern. An erubescent glow caught his eye, coming from a recess in the far wall directly across from him. Could it be the dimension portal? Even if it were, and he were able to reach it, he didn't know where it would take him. No matter, he must take the risk.

A soul-searing cry suddenly pierced the vast chamber. It was Zilmara! Once again the lady's voice rose up, this time in a high daemonic wail that echoed through the distant corridors, and the plaint transposed into a strange alien song, an unhallowed canticle conjured out of the primordial depths of her being. From within the churning currents of the unworldly strains, from the depths of the passionate paean, emerged a single word that rose and fell in tenebrous tones: "Qog! Qog! Qog!" She was calling to the terrible world eater!

Though his wits were alert, Jonathan could feel his body trembling and he quieted it only by force of will. The lady was deeply immersed now in her alien communings, oblivious to her surroundings. Now was his chance to steal around the chamber and get a closer look at the strange glow in the far wall.

Slowly he crept along the rim of the cavern in a half crouch, the lady's tortured chanting flailing at his mind. As he approached the shadowy outcropping behind which her dog-faced servant had retreated, he heard a low growl and knew it had seen him or smelled his presence. But nothing more happened, and he guessed, correctly so, that the poor mistreated creature was repaying its mistress for her cruelty in the only way it could: by its silence.

As he neared the luminant recess, he saw that it was in a state of constant flux and had no solidity. It must be the dimension portal.

Suddenly the lady's chanting ceased, and the chamber became deadly quiet. He ducked down close to the floor, partly hidden by a rocky protrusion. When, after a moment, he looked up, his heart leapt as he saw the dark figure of Zilmara standing over him. Her look was unexpectedly serene, and she wore a disarming smile.

"You seemed to have lost your way, Creator." She spoke in dulcet tones. "Perhaps you took a wrong turn. Tell me, how long have you been here?"

He said nothing and hoped the knowledge in his eyes would not betray him.

"Well never mind. Come along, let's return to more pleasant surroundings. This way."

He didn't move.

The lady's eyebrows rose. "So, I see you are no longer open to suggestion. Recovered your wits, have you? Perhaps you didn't drink as much of the potion as I thought." Her tone took on a sharper edge. "Is it yonder portal you seek, then? So near yet so far. Oh, am I blocking your way?"

He made no reply.

"Ah. Harken! I think I hear another of my beautiful daughters approaching. I can tell by the sound of her flapping—so musical—that it is Zena, my youngest. And if I'm not mistaken, she is bringing us a guest."

The lady made a ritualistic motion in the air with her hand, and Jonathan's vision momentarily blurred.

A loud flapping and a rush of wind announced the arrival of the Zytox. The giant bird glided down through the open dome, and Jonathan saw that it clutched a limp body in its claws. The creature came to rest on the cavern floor nearby its mistress. She motioned for it to release its burden. The body slid onto the stones and, to Jonathan's utter horror, he saw that it was none other than his bond-mate, Llanya.

The lady Zilmara laughed merrily. "A disobedient servant sometimes needs to be shown a whip. And here's one made to order."

Jonathan started toward Llanya, but the Zytox nimbly hopped in front of him, blocking the way.

"Be calm, Creator," crooned the lady. "Your mate is unharmed. She simply fainted. And she will remain unharmed as long as you are an obedient guest. Do we understand one another?"

He nodded.

"Good."

"And if I should ask you to consciously create a special world for me to set within my sphere, will you comply?"

"But...I don't know how."

"Oh yes, of course. You're unschooled. But there's another way. Will you dream for me then, Creator, if I ask? It is best if it be voluntary. The unconscious mind of a creator soon learns to reject the effect of suggestion or drugs."

"I'm not sure I can even do that. But if I try, you must promise not to harm my bond-mate in any way."

A thought message suddenly popped into his head: "Jon, it's me, the captain. Be careful. The bitch is trying to trick you. Hold on while I pass on this finicky lens before it blanks out again."

In a moment another voice came through: "Jon, my love, it's Llanya. I'm here with the captain. That's not me lying on the floor. Don't..." The connection broke. Slipping his hand into his pocket, he felt for the bit of Hhor's skin. He felt a warm tingling in the tips of his fingers, and he sensed the presence of his beloved from afar.

In a single quick motion he withdrew the skin from his pocket and flipped it past the Zytox at Llanya's, or what looked like Llanya's, reclining body. The skin fell against her leg, and no sooner did it touch her than her body disappeared. It had been an illusion, a hoax perpetrated by the enchantress to gain his obedience.

The lady's face contorted with anger. She hastily spun a mystical figure in the air with her hand and seemed to fling it toward the cave entrance.

"Enough of this nonsense," she screamed. "Either you will agree to obey me now, Creator, or die. Choose!"

Jonathan glanced toward the portal: so near and yet so far. The Zytox's crystal-white eyes were fixed on him, and he knew it would be useless to try to get around the hulking creature. The hard unswerving look in Zilmara's eyes was hardly less daunting.

A hollow clacking sound reached his ears, like the rattling of bones against stone. And out of the dimness of the passageway beyond the cavern marched a grotesque skeletal army of the undead: the necrophagous remains of the nightmare creatures he had earlier encountered in their crypt, now fouly resurrected by their mistress. Some of them stopped and blocked the entrance of the cavern. Others in the charnel legion entered the great hall, broken swords in hand, and took up positions along the outer wall, their empty eye sockets fixed upon him.

"Will you or will you not obey me?" she repeated.

Jonathan's lips parted as though he were about to speak, but no words emerged. A long silence ensued during which an expression of cold fury crept over the lady's face.

"Zena, kill!" she cried as she stepped aside out of the Zytox's path.

Jonathan stumbled backward as the great bird hopped across the cavern floor toward him in long awkward strides, its curling claws scraping the stone at each step. As it neared it partly unfolded its wings and leapt into the air at its prey, claws outstretched. Jonathan instinctively dropped down, ducking behind a large rock protruding from the floor. The claws of the Zytox swept past within inches of his head, striking against the rock and breaking off its tip.

The creature was now behind him, and the way ahead was momentarily clear. Jumping to his feet, he dashed toward the glowing niche in the wall. He could hear, mixed with the lady's strident cries, the scratching of claws against stone coming up fast behind him and the clattering of boned feet approaching from all sides. As he ran by the Hhor's skin where it had fallen, he swept it up, and in the same stride he leapt headfirst into the scintillant maze, scattering shimmering droplets of polychromatic light all about.

The dark lady shook her clenched fists and cursed in an alien tongue. Her eyes narrowed as she watched the disturbed surface of the dimension portal gradually coalesce to a calm glow. She dared not pass through the gate herself, for well she knew its egress. Turning on her heels, she stalked to the center of the chamber and gazed out of its open roof at the starless heavens beyond. Her eyes settled on the spinning black planet, newly created. A sly smile came to her lips. Raising her arms, she once again began to sing, and the words of her unsacred song lifted up to the ether, a clarion call to bestir a cosmic giant from its torpor.

Chapter 15

THE DREAM LORDS

Jonathan tumbled weightlessly through the plane-dividing vestibule, enveloped in a chromosphere of blinding light. The radiant shower pelted him like falling rain and his body churned helplessly, as though caught in a cosmic maelstrom.

Amidst a burst of luminescence, he pitched through the space curtain and had the momentary sensation of falling, only to land with a sudden bump, rump first, on a firm surface. Slightly dizzy, he held his head down until his vertigo dissipated. Then, looking about, he saw that he had landed on a broad empty plain. There was no sign of the dimension portal, and he guessed it must have been a one-way gate. The air was windless and pleasantly warm, and above him, in the clear blue sky, floated three small full moons and four gently glaring miniature suns. Whatever plane he had landed on, it wasn't one he was familiar with.

Not knowing which direction to travel, he decided to consult the Hhor's bit of skin. It had once made a fire for him; perhaps it would serve as a compass as well. Getting to his feet, he held the skin out before him and slowly turned in a circle. The skin was cool to the touch, but when he faced in the direction of the lowest moon, it grew warm. His direction thus determined, he set out with an open mind and expectant but fearful heart.

The space between the suns and moons gradually widened, and as the lowest moon kissed the far horizon, he saw in the distance where it touched the land a hazy blue-white luminescence. As he continued on, the glow sharpened and brightened, and he saw it was the suns' reflection on a lofty pinnacle rising out of the smooth carpet of land. Its sparkle he used as a beacon light to guide his way. Yet closer, he saw that the spire was but one among several atop a palatial building shrouded in silvery mist, its glistening wings stretching out on either side like some great celestial bird.

As he neared the majestic structure, he passed over an arched bridge of compressed light, as though a candied rainbow, beneath which poured a tinkling cataract of polychromatic light beams into a deep cloud-like rift. The bridge led him to a broad concourse paved with translucent stone that flickered as though covered with uncountable spectral fireflies, and in the air he could hear a soft echoing music, strange but not displeasing.

As he climbed the wide-spanned stairway leading to the palace, be-gowned figures, men and women of mortal demeanor, their garb glisten-ing iridescently like the necks of doves, appeared between the pillars of the high colonnade to greet him. They bowed to him at his approach, and heralds cried out his name, calling him Creator and Maker of Worlds. He halted at the top of the stairway in bewilderment, and a tall elderly man of regal bearing stepped forward and extended his hand.

"Welcome and well met, Jonathan," he said, his voice strong yet friendly. "I am Secunon, dream lord and overseer of the lower planes. And this place is Cimorium, also known as Azar-Lal, home of the dream lords."

Jonathan was momentarily speechless.

"You…you know my name. And somehow I feel I know you, though we've never met."

"We have met, in a dream you have long forgotten. But we will talk of that anon. For the moment let us be glad of your safe arrival after a dif-ficult journey. My brothers and I have been greatly concerned about you. Come into our house and rest yourself. Then you will meet my brother dream lords and some of our guests. As you can see, you are somewhat of a celebrity. Although dream creators often visit Cimorium, it is sel-dom that we are treated to the presence of an arch creator like yourself."

Jonathan looked puzzled. "An arch creator…?"

"Forgive me, I'm getting ahead of myself. I beg your patience and all will be made clear. Now come, this way."

The dream lord led him past the great pillars of the colonnade, through graceful arched entrance ways and porticos, down tapestried corridors, and thence into a spacious apartment, its rooms decorated with furnish-ings of xanthic gold and saffron jade, simple of design yet tastefully elegant. The dream lord opened his hands.

"These will be your rooms while you are among us. I hope you will find them comfortable. Please sit down and I will pour us some liquid refreshment."

Jonathan sat in a virent armchair that might have been cut from solid emerald, while the dream lord went to a cabinet and withdrew a crystal-like carafe. Its contents he poured into two argentine goblets, one of which he handed to Jonathan. The old gentleman smiled at his guest's uncertain expression.

"I can understand your wariness, but be assured that this is quite un-like the Nectar of Lethe the lady Zilmara gave you. This is but a quaff from the incarnadine springs of the Valley of Shrrn—invigorating and delicious, and by no means harmful."

"Oh, you know about the lady? Than perhaps you can helpl me. I..."

"Drink."

The dream lord drained his cup, and Jonathan, feeling a little foolish, did the same. He found the draught quite delicious, and could feel the tiredness falling from his limbs. Somehow his worries and fears seemed less urgent.

"Is that better?" asked the dream lord.

"Yes, much. Thank you."

"Now, as to your question: yes, I know about the lady Zilmara. I have been observing her for some time, and you also. I regret that I was not able to intervene on your behalf in your moment of need, but, alas, even the powers of dream lords are limited. Fortunately, you had friends that were of some help to you. I should mention that while you are on Cimorium, your friends on the second plane will not be able to contact you. We are quite insulated here. But I see from your face that you have another question."

"Yes, many. To begin with, just what is a dream lord?"

"We are the overseers—managers, you might say—of dream world creations. We keep track of creators from the time of their birth, and when they create dream worlds we sort them out and try to direct them to a plane and location where they fit in best. Of course, we are not always successful. Some powerful creators are able to place their creations where they choose. But, all in all, we have been able to distribute new worlds in such a way that balance has been maintained both within and among planes. At least most of the time."

The dream lord saw that Jonathan looked puzzled. "Well, for example," he continued, "I would not place a tropical dream world that required warmth in a cold dimension, nor would it be a good idea to locate a pacifistic world too close to a warrior world on the same plane. That's one kind of balance. Nor would I place too great a number of worlds on one plane lest it strain the interdimensional fabric between planes. That's another kind of balance."

Jonathan, greatly impressed, nodded, though he was still not sure he fully understood.

"What about me? My creation?" he asked.

"Thus far, placing your creations has been a simple matter since you are unable to create consciously. Unconsciously created dream worlds are the most easily manipulated, and I for one much prefer dealing with them. The placement configuration of several of your island creations on the second plane I designed myself because of your lack of conscious control. I take some pride in the result."

Jonathan gripped the arms of his chair. "You...you mean I created more than one island, not just Zuralia?"

"Oh, yes. There are several others you are not aware of, one in particular that is quite attractive, called Hanybula. As I recall, you accomplished most of these creations in your late childhood years, under unusual circumstances, illness I think. I hope you will have the opportunity to visit them one day."

The dream lord stopped short of revealing Jonathan's unconscious creation of the black dream world while under the influence of the evil enchantress, Zilmara. He saw no point in needlessly distressing his young guest.

"But, unfortunately, not all dream world creations are as pleasant as yours. As you know, there is a pressing matter facing us at the moment, namely the threat of the creature, Qog, to the second plane. His nefarious mistress and controller, Zilmara, you already know. Regrettably, we have little influence over either her or the Qog, or indeed, over the third plane itself because of its bizarre location within the creature. Thus, Zilmara has been recklessly creating nightmare creations on her plane, which brought about the present interplane imbalance. If the imbalance is not corrected and the tear in the interdimensional fabric closed, I fear the monster Qog will completely destroy the second plane and invade others as well."

"How many planes are there?"

"There are eight known planes, or layered dimensions. We lords on the fourth plane oversee the lower planes—the first three; although, as I said, we have little control over Zilmara's inner plane. And our brother lords on the eighth plane are caretakers of the upper planes—the fifth, sixth, and seventh. The lady's Zilmara's ambition, I fear, may be nothing less than the destruction of the positive worlds on all planes, and a concomitant expansion of the third plane by the transfer and creation of nightmare worlds."

Jonathan shifted about in his chair. "Couldn't the interplane imbalance be corrected by the offsetting creation of other worlds?" he asked.

"Yes, it is possible. But it would require a very special talent."

"Special? How?"

"Answering that question requires that I more fully explain the concept of interplane balance: dream worlds are ultimately made up of energy, and it is the relative magnitude of the energy among planes that must be kept in balance within an acceptable range of error in order for the interplane fabric to remain secure. At the moment there is an imbalance that exceeds the safe margin of error, owing to the negative world-creating excesses of the lady Zilmara. But correcting that imbalance it is not simply a matter of creating more positive worlds on the second plane. It is total quantum energy that is important, and different worlds carry different amounts of energy depending on their size, density, location, the power of the creator, and several other factors. To create the necessary amount of energy to reestablish balance requires taking all these factors into account. Otherwise too much positive energy could be created and another, and perhaps more serious, imbalance could result. Is what I have said clear to you so far?"

"I think so. But if you know how to correct the imbalance, why don't you just do it?"

"I cannot. Nor can most creators. The imbalance has become too great. Its correction can only be accomplished by one with rare powers—by an arch creator like yourself."

"Me? But I can't create consciously at all."

"Nevertheless, I am afraid you are the only arch creator available at present. Given the limited time we have to act, you are the only chance we have. That is why I have been so closely monitoring you of late, hoping you would make your way here.

"As a dream lord, I can teach you how to make fuller use of your powers—how to create at will. And, more important, I can teach you what only an arch creator can master—how to measure and control the precise energy content of your creations at the very moment of creation. Also, how to create multiple worlds simultaneously and direct them to a place of your own choosing. Without such knowledge, it would not be possible to return to equilibrium between planes. So if you are willing to try, and are able to learn quickly, then there is still a chance to save the second plane, and its inhabitants."

Jonathan's heart skipped a beat. Llanya—her life was at risk. And the captain's, and his shipmates'. Indeed, his beloved island itself. And perhaps the Earth.

"Tell me, Lord Secunon, why is a particular person born a creator? Why me? And why an arch creator?"

"Those are difficult questions which we on Cimorium have long pondered and researched. To a limited extent genetic and prenatal influences probably play a role. The ancestral genetic influence is believed to be primordial, often skipping many generations, even centuries, before expressing itself. Certain confluences in the concurrent dreams of a mother and her unborn child are also thought to be a factor, particularly in encouraging the growth of a latent nimbus. My brothers believe that environment plays a role, though I do not fully subscribe to that theory.

Well, perhaps, in cases like on Earth today, where there is spreading corruption of mind and soul. In such a world, on purely probabilistic grounds, there is a greater chance that a newborn creator will be diseased and hence become a generator of nightmare worlds. In time that could become a serious management problem for us.

"There is even disagreement among researchers on the basic question of whether the wellspring of creative power resides in the mind or the soul. So you see, your question cannot be answered with any degree of certainty.

"What gives an arch creator his special powers is even more of a mystery. But there is no question that you possess that rare gift. Auras do not lie. If I were to speculate I would guess that your imagination and creative proclivities during your childhood helped to nurture your talent, even though your unconscious mind suppressed it for many years. It was in fact during one of the suppressed dreams of your youth that our minds first touched. But whatever the origins of your gift, it is a weight you must carry all of your life, though it can have its recompenses. As you say on Earth, it is a double-edged sword."

Jonathan sighed. "I should have tried to kill Zilmara when I had the chance. It would have made matters so much simpler."

A sad expression came over the dream lord's face. "That is foolish talk. The lady Zilmara has magical powers. She would have easily destroyed you. You would have had little chance against her in her own domain, and I doubt she will ever leave it. Besides, killing is not your way. If worlds are to be saved, if the interplane balance is to be restored, it will be through creation, not destruction."

Jonathan rose to his feet. "But even if balance is restored, Zilmara will only unbalance it again and send the Qog out to ravage."

"Not necessarily. Once balance is restored, the lady's creations can be matched by those of an ever-vigilant arch creator. She will then be effectively neutralized. If she sees there is no point in continuing, she may relent, and the Qog will no longer be a threat.

"Now, are you ready to begin your instruction, Creator?"

Jonathan did not hesitate. "I'm ready. I only hope I don't fail you... and others."

"I felt sure you would reply thus. I personally will be your teacher. Your first lesson will begin when the Cimorium moon, Hyla, passes beyond the sun, Llen—a time equivalent to four of your earth hours. Meanwhile, I invite you to a gathering to meet my two brother dream lords and some of our guests. I have told my brothers much about you and they will be delighted to make your acquaintance. And if you will consent to try our Cimorium garb, you will find several choices in the corner cabinet of the adjoining room."

While the dream lord waited, Jonathan picked out some new clothing, glad for a fresh change. He chose a long iridescent robe not unlike the dream lord's. Secunon then took him to a covered pavilion at the rear of the palace where he was introduced to the other dream lords, Fflayn and Zabryn. They were kind and grandfatherly and made a bit of a fuss over him because of his status as an arch creator. He graciously withstood the praise, though not without feelings of doubt and inadequacy.

He listened quietly as the two brothers discussed a problem that had arisen earlier that day. It seems a hybrid world had just been created by a being called a Hormaph on the planet Yassus. Yassus had characteristics that qualified it to be allocated to two different dimensional sectors. One of the qualifying sectors fell into the territorial jurisdiction of Fflayn, while the competing sector was the responsibility of Zabryn. A trans-spectral locational analysis had been performed to assist in making the final determination of where to place the planet, the results and interpretation of which were the subject of the debate between the two brother lords. Though he listened with interest, Jonathan was unable to understand most of what was being said.

He noticed that the three dream lords bore a striking resemblance to one another, so much so that he wondered if they might be triplets. He inquired of Secunon, who explained that the brothers were indeed trines, as were their three brother lords of the upper planes. By tradition, dream world governance was an inherited occupation, and Secunon's family was renown for its multi-natal propensities.

Secunon introduced Jonathan to some of the other guests, and as he sipped the liquor of Shrrn, he listened with interest to a green-skinned wizard tell of the terrific galactic winds that ever buffeted the planet Iroes; and he in turn explained the phenomena of earthly tides and earthquakes, which greatly fascinated his other-worldly acquaintance. They were joined by a creator from Thayl-Ra on the fifth plane, and Jonathan was aghast to learn that the life span of worlds on that plane was no longer in years than that of a mortal life on Earth. It was only after the creator had departed that the wizard explained to him that the shortest orbital year of planets on the fifth plane was equivalent to a million Earth years.

Three dwarfish magicians of indeterminate sex introduced themselves and began a discussion about the preferred method of measuring the angle of consciousness tangential to the physical reality of a hyper thought passing through polydimensional space. Jonathan smiled politely, though his eyes glazed over.

His fingers idly sought out the Hhor's skin in his robe pocket, and his thoughts turned to his bond-mate. He closed his eyes and could almost feel her presence in the room. She would still be aboard the Pelagin, he knew, though the ship would be arriving at Zuralia soon. He pictured her in the galley preparing a meal for the crewmen and in her cabin playing with the trocht.

Excusing himself, feeling momentarily sick at heart, he went to his quarters where he plopped down on the bed to think about his beloved in private. One by one, he pictured her every feature in his mind's eye. How he longed for her sweet kisses and warm embrace.

His reverie was interrupted by a knock at the door. It was the dream lord, Secunon, come to give him his first lesson. They sat down at a small round table.

"I will start by outlining what your instruction will cover. Today you will learn the art of concentration. Your mind is the voice that summons the creative life force, but it is concentration that gives the mind focus and enables it to carry the mind's message to the seat of power. Tomorrow you will learn how to create a waking dream at will. Next you will learn how to animate and project that waking dream beyond yourself. Next you will learn how to tap into your spirit-double and create two dreams simultaneously. Then you will learn how to dream within a dream to again double your output. You will learn the techniques of dream division and multiplication. When you have mastered multiple-world creation and projection, you will learn the art of intuitive dream-measurement. Next you will learn how to mentally enumerate the energy units contained in dream world mass. Finally, you will be given an examination in which you will demonstrate your dream world creation abilities."

Jonathan's heart sank at what seemed an impossible task. The dream lord read his pupil's thoughts and nodded understandingly.

"You will see that it is not as difficult as it sounds. You must begin with a positive attitude. You have the talent and need only learn how to control and release it. I have every confidence in you. We will proceed one step at a time, and soon you will be using your talent with skill and pleasure."

Jonathan still looked doubtful.

"Now," the dream lord went on, "before we begin the first lesson, do you have any questions?"

Jonathan thought a moment. "Yes. In your outline you mentioned a spirit-double and dreaming within dreams. Could you clarify their meaning for me?"

"Only briefly. The concepts will become clearer to you after you have completed your first few lessons. All mortals have a spirit-double.

It is your living shadow self and resides within. Once you learn how to contact and direct your spirit-double, it can be used to create dream worlds independent of your primary consciousness. Thus, when you call upon your double, there will, in effect, be two Jonathans available to create dream worlds instead of one. The technique of dreaming within a dream is in some ways similar. It is simply the conscious act of dreaming yourself into one of your own dreams. By so doing you will be creating a second creator, a duplicate of yourself, thereby doubling your dream-creating capacity. Third and higher iterations—that is, dreaming within a dream within a dream and so on—are possible, but not recommended since the process can become unstable."

"Is it possible, then, for a spirit-double as well as the primary self to dream within a dream and thereby quadruple the individual creator's dream potential?" asked Jonathan.

The dream lord beamed. "An excellent question. You have not only grasped the dual concepts but you have integrated them as well. The answer is yes. Now let us start at the beginning with the first lesson—the art of concentration."

Jonathan quickly became engrossed in the dream lord's lecture, and before he realized it the session was over. For his homework he was given Cimorium mental drills to practice and one of Secunon's early papers on thought control to read.

Later he dined with the three dream lords and was introduced to several exotic dishes from the sixth plane, two of which he found quite palatable: Sakjin, a yellow meaty vegetable from the planet Org, which was shaped liked an eggplant but tasted like lobster, and Uquala, a nutty paste-like pudding exuded by the leaves of the Temel-Sut, a common arboreal plant, which is scooped up and eaten with wafers much like a fondue.

That evening, mentally exhausted, no sooner did his head touch his pillow than he fell sound asleep. At Secunon's request he wore a silver training headband to bed to relax his subconscious mind and prevent the possibility of accidental dreaming.

The days that followed flowed into one another like waves upon the tide. He kept to a strict regimen of lectures and study from early morning to late night, a span on Cimorium that amounted to two-thirds of a solar rotation cycle. More than once he fell asleep in a chair while studying in the palace library.

The day of the examination finally arrived. He felt both glad and frightened: glad because he knew he would soon be leaving the celestial plane and returning to his beloved Llanya, and frightened that he might fail the test and be unable to help his island creation. He couldn't help but feel that his teacher had overestimated his abilities. The weight of responsibility that had been placed upon him seemed more than he could carry.

Secunon placed his hand on his pupil's shoulder as he esorted him into a large room on the second level of the palace.

"This is the Hall of Maps," he explained, "which contains atlases of all the known planes. The large wall maps around the room are cartographic reality charts. Whenever a dream world is created on any of the eight planes, it instantly appears here on one of the maps. You will no doubt recognize that corner map depicting the third sector of the first plane. It shows your solar system and the planet Earth.

"Planetary details are contained in the smaller maps filed on the lower shelves. You might be interested to know that some of the cartographic data on Earth's western hemisphere were supplied to us by one of your fellow creators, a contemporary of yours. A tall quiet gentleman. As I recall, he created a home world for himself on the second plane, some distance south of Zuralia. His name was Friendship."

Jonathan brightened. "Yes, I know him," he said excitedly. "I mean I know his writings. We have a mutual friend. I would very much like to meet him. Can you show me on the map exactly where he lives?"

"I think so. Let me see. Yes, here it is—Celeshir."

At that moment the two dream lords, Zabryn and Fflayn, appeared and seated themselves at the back of the hall. Jonathan gave Secunon a questioning look.

"They are here to observe your examination," he explained. "All things considered, I am sure you can appreciate their interest."

"But something's wrong," said Jonathan. "I sense it in Zabryn's mind. It's got something to do with the Qog."

Secunon nodded. "You are right, of course. I am pleased to see that you are able to extrapolate the use of you newly acquired skills. Zabryn was not on guard. Fflayn and I have blocked our minds to you, but only to spare you certain knowledge that could upset you. I did not want to disturb you prior to your examination. Any upset could affect your performance. I planned to tell you the news immediately afterwards."

Jonathan tensed. "I must know, now. Please tell me."

"Very well. The Qog is active and is moving toward the break in the interplane fabric, toward Zuralia. There is another development as well. Due to the creation of a powerful black planet on the third plane, the interplane imbalance has worsened and now extends to the perimeter of the first plane. The protecting fabric between the first and second planes is loosening, and we fear the Qog will attack not only the island plane, but Earth as well."

Jonathan tensed. "I must do something. My aura frightened off the Qog once before. I'll do it again."

"I'm afraid not," replied Secunon. "The black planet has strengthened the creature so that the sting of your nimbus is no longer strong enough to drive it away. To stop him by using that technique would now require an aural jolt many times more powerful than the combined nimbi of an army of creators."

Jonathan's heart pounded as horrible images of the space monster gobbling up whole worlds flooded through his mind. "I must return to the second plane at once," he cried.

Secunon put his hand on his pupil's shoulder to calm him.

"You will. But first we must be sure you are ready."

Fflayn waved his arm. "Are we ready to begin, brother Secunon?"

"We are ready," answered Secunon. "Jonathan, sit here by me and face the wall map directly in front of you. It depicts a region partially familiar to you—the first sector of the second plane containing three hundred islands, including your island of Zuralia. I am going to mentally point to a vacant area on the map and I want you to create an island world—just one to begin with—in that spot. Take a moment to determine the characteristics you want, then let me know when you are ready."

Jonathan took a deep breath and closed his eyes. He found it difficult to concentrate. He could only think of the monster Qog moving ever closer to Zuralia. Llanya would be there, waiting for him.

"Arch Creator, you are not concentrating." Secunon's voice was stern and tinged with impatience.

Jonathan stared at the map and tried to bring his mind into focus. Concentrate, he told himself. Concentrate. Drawing upon his newly learned skills, he entered deep within himself, striving to blot out all external distractions. Then, touching his thoughts to the palette of his imagination, he painted a small mountain island upon the canvas of his mind, replete with tropical rain forests, exotic birds, cascading waterfalls, and broad white beaches. When he was satisfied with the waking dream image, he opened his eyes.

"I'm ready," he said.

"Proceed," said Secunon.

He fixed upon the spot on the map that his teacher had chosen. It was a lonely place in the southern ocean a goodly distance from any other isle. As he reached deep within himself to the center of creative power at his soul's heart, a current flashed between his soul and mind, igniting the image in his thoughts. Unfettered now from its mortal casing, the image sped outward from his body, and in but an instant a dot appeared on the island map in the very place of his choosing. He relaxed his mind, and he knew that in that distant place on the second plane an island had been born, his island, the first child of his waking dream. He had succeeded! A wave of relief swept over him.

Suddenly the dot on the map began to flicker; then it disappeared. Bewildered and alarmed, he turned toward Secunon.

"What happened?" he asked.

"Alas. Your creation did not hold. It was not strong enough. But it was not your fault. I rushed your lessons. Tomorrow we will review…"

Jonathan jumped to his feet. "No! I know I can do it. I just had trouble concentrating, that's all. We've run out of time. The Qog will not wait for my lessons. I must return to the second plane at once." His expression hardened and his voice became grim. "Tell me how to get back to Zuralia. I refuse to listen to any more lectures or take any more examinations. I want to go. Now!"

Secunon looked down at the floor pensively, then glanced toward his brother dream lords. They nodded somberly.

"Very well, Creator, you may depart, but against my better judgment. When you arrive on Zuralia, try to mend the interplane fabric as best you can before the Qog arrives at the breach. Remember your lessons. Even if you are only partially successful, you may be able to tighten the fabric enough to keep the monster temporarily at bay.

"I want you to take this ring with you." The dream lord withdrew one of two rings from his left hand and gave it to Jonathan. "The stone in the ring is an indicator of the Qog's proximity. When it is gray the Qog is at a safe distance. When pink, the creature is approaching. When red, he is near upon you. When black, though I have never seen it so, it means the Qog has departed to the far outer reaches of the interplane void.

"Now, follow me and I will show you the portal that will take you to your island world on the second plane. If you find you are unable to restrain the Qog, make use of the pill you carry and escape to Earth. There you may be able to strengthen the cosmic fabric between the first and second planes and protect your home planet."

Jonathan made his farewell to Fflayn and Zabryn, who sighed and wished him well. Secunon then led him out of the palace to the arched bridge of petrified light beneath which tumbled a cataract of variegated light beams through a cloud-like rift. The dream lord pointed to the fissure, through which poured the dazzling stream.

"The gate is there," he said.

Jonathan swallowed. "You mean I have to jump? Into that?"

The dream lord nodded. He could have reassured the young creator, told him there was no danger, that the leap was painless and had been used by many others before him. But Secunon knew that his pupil would soon be facing real dangers and thought it unwise to spare him what was but the illusion of risk. If he lacked the courage to make the leap, there was little hope for the future.

Jonathan turned to his teacher and held out his hand. "Thank you for all you have taught me. I will try to live up to your expectations, and I hope we will meet again."

Secunon clasped his pupil's hand and smiled warmly. "Farewell, Arch Creator. And fare thee well."

Jonathan looked down into the rift and for a brief moment watched the silent cascading torrent of colors disappear into nothingness far below. Then, holding his breath, he stepped from the bridge and dropped into the rushing waterfall. As he fell, his body was bathed in countless points of light, and his nimbus merged with the flowing stream, creating a dazzling double rainbow that arched into the sky as though in celestial farewell.

CHAPTER 16

ARCH CREATOR

Jonathan felt himself becoming lighter as he fell deeper into the prismal chasm, his body shattering the chromatic stream into glistening fragments that spun about him like butterflies in a whirlwind. His descent slowed, and he floated into a twinkling cocoon-space whose fleecy contours trembled at his presence, as though he were an alien threat to its ethereal perfection, a poison to be expelled. The light-studded envelope suddenly burst open into nebulae of streaking stars that flared up and consumed themselves in their own brightness, hurling him into a vast abyss of outer darkness. The emptiness engulfed him, its vastness an exile to time itself.

He seemed not to be drifting aimlessly and could see coming toward him in the distance an opening of light in the dark curtain. As he neared it the light brightened, and he felt himself being pulled into its blinding radiance. His eyes complained and he shielded them with his hands.

Suddenly all motion ceased and he felt firmness beneath his feet. Blinking away the remnants of brightness, he saw that he was standing on a high palisade overlooking a blue-green sea. Although the spot was not familiar to him, the twirling twin suns in the heavens told him it was Zuralia, and his heart gladdened at the sight. Walking to the cliff's edge to get his bearings, he saw in the distance the peakless mountain sentinels that guarded the city's harbor, and he knew he had emerged on the coastal outskirts of the city. There was no sign of the portal he had passed through.

Something struck him from above, and the next thing he knew he was sprawled out on the rocks with blood trickling down his face. Quickly rolling over, he scanned the sky and saw the outspread wings of a giant Zytox gliding upward in a slow arc. His scalp had been raked by the bird's claws, and he pressed his hair into the raw furrows in an effort to stem the flow of blood.

He saw that the Zytox was turning for another pass. Jumping to his feet, he dashed toward a large boulder not far away trying to outrun the great bird, which was now hurtling toward him. As the Zytox's outstretched talons swept down, he flattened his body and leapt behind the boulder. The wind from its huge wings whipped at his face as it passed overhead. Heart racing, he peered around the rock and watched the dark creature as it rose again into the sky. But this time, instead of turning for another dive, it began to circle slowly above, like a vulture watching its prey. It screeched. The piercing cry cut through the air and was answered by a like cry in the distance. Another Zytox!

Unsure where the answering call had come from, his eyes searched the sky for signs of his attacker's sibling. He could see nothing, until his eyes came to rest on the lip of the nearest mountain that guarded the harbor. Its smooth plateau was marred by five protruding objects, which from a distance looked like large lumps of coal. Except that the objects were moving. Zytox! Five of them were perched atop the headless mountain.

Once more the circling bird called to its sisters, and this time they heeded the summons. One by one they spread their great wings, and in what seemed like slow motion they lifted from their lofty perch and rose into the Zuralian sky, marring its perfect blueness with their great black bulks. Effortlessly they climbed the sky on invisible currents and began to slowly circle, each revolution taking them closer to the lonely palisade and their helpless quarry.

Jonathan watched the silent aerial ballad in fascination and horror, knowing he would have no chance against so many of the fearsome creatures. Looking about, he saw there was no place he could run: he was trapped. The dark aeronauts circled lower, and he could see their unblinking candent eyes and unfolded spike-like talons. The Hhor's bit of skin in his pocket pulsed against his thigh as though trying to tell him something.

He closed his eyes and sent his thoughts reeling through his imagination. Within that wondrous vault he searched desperately about for an idea; and instantly, as if by magic, it revealed itself to his mind's eye. Grasping it, shaping and smoothing its rough edges, he gave it life and scope and sent it spinning through the dark tunnels of his mind and to the hidden corners of his soul where it merged with the bridled power of his creative force.

Opening his eyes, he gazed out upon the broad sea, focusing upon a gentle swell in the tide not far offshore, and lo! a mountain isle appeared amidst the waters in that very spot. And from an aerie high upon the newborn island's tallest peak, six giant eagles rose screaming into the sky. Swiftly they flew, toward the very promontory that was the destination of the titan devil birds.

Jonathan saw what he had accomplished and a bolt of excitement shot through him. He gazed with pride upon his island creation, and in that moment all feelings of self doubt melted away.

Espying their solitary victim now just below them, the Zytox broke formation and descended as one upon the rocky cliff, their crystal-white eyes ablaze, their shadows a chill upon the land. Intent upon their mission of death, they did not see the formation of great eagles sweeping down upon them from above, beaks agape and claws unsheathed. In a blur of speed the eagles smashed mid air into the dark squadron, exploding it into a chaotic mass of mangled flesh and feathers, and as the sleek birds of prey swooped up, Jonathan saw that each clutched the limp remains of a Zytox in its talons. Singing a shrill medley, the eagles climbed into the sky and crossed the expanse of sea to their lofty aeries on an island newly born.

A cloud of broken Zytox feathers darkened the twin suns as they see-sawed downward through the air, spreading a black carpet over the rocky bluff as though a shroud upon the land. But even as the last pinion settled upon the cliff's edge, still the bright Zuralian sunlight did not return: the sky was yet cloaked in dimness.

Jonathan's heart sank within his breast. Another, more terrible, blight had visited his world, one only too familiar to him—the monster Qog!

He cursed himself. He had forgotten to look at the ring the dream lord had given him. It would have warned him of the Qog's closeness, and perhaps he would have had time to close the dimension curtain before the creature had passed through. Too late now—the stone in the ring was shining bright red, and the destroyer was here. If it had been the lady Zilmara's plan to distract him while the monster Qog got through, it had worked. Now if the cosmic fabric was mended, the Qog would be trapped on the wrong side of the curtain—within the island plane.

His head reeled as he watched the leviathan world eater once again descend toward his beloved Zuralia. Bitterness and frustration seized at him and he cried out in anguish, his plaint swallowed up in the demon wind that seared the land and the pounding waves that assaulted the shore. The pull from the creature was even stronger than before. The stones about him rattled and shot up into the monster's craterous maw. Lizards rushed about helter-skelter among the rocks and they too were flicked into space like bits of flotsam.

The large boulder that had been his refuge from the Zytox shuddered and toppled over as a roaring whirlwind swept across the cliff top, and he leapt aside to avoid being crushed. The ground began to crack around him, and the air filled with terrified birds driven from shaken trees. In their panic they rose higher into the sky, only to hasten their doom.

White currents of lightning shot from the underbelly of the descending creature and exploded into the land, leaving smoldering craters where they struck. A sudden quake shook the precipice, knocking Jonathan to the ground. He saw that the monster would soon reach the shaven peaks of the twin mountain sentinels.

Lying on his back, his hair and clothing aflutter, he looked up into the creature's gaping venter, into the universe that was to be his grave. In his mind's eye he saw its spinning worlds of nightmare birth, its terrible black sphere of power, and, not least, the planet home of its dark mistress.

A calm deadly fury gripped him, and its steely edge sharpened his thoughts. He delved deep within himself searching for an idea, an answer, and this time his mind effortlessly penetrated the boundless storehouse of his sleeping thoughts and sped a message to his consciousness.

He remembered that the inner universe of the third dimension was bereft of brightness. It had neither glowing suns, moons, nor stars, nor any luminant world. And perhaps with good reason. Perhaps because a radiant world would be intolerable to the Qog. If so, perhaps he could create one.

But how? His aura! It had stung the monster and driven it from Zuralia once before. Maybe he could draw upon it again. Maybe it would lend its power to a world of his own creation. No, that would be too dangerous. The creation of another world within the third plane would only worsen the interplane imbalance and widen the tear in the dimensional fabric. Unless...

The wind shifted, and the putrid odor of the Qog's vast underbelly reached him. He covered his nose with his hand and closed his eyes, striving to purge his mind of the creature and focus his concentration upon a single thought.

Gradually in his mind's eye he formed an image. With utmost care he planted seed upon seed of its nature in every detail, nurturing it, giving it substance, and when he was satisfied that it was complete, he reached deep within himself, drew upon the force of his creative powers, and gave it life. Like a blazing comet, his waking dream sprung from its soul's keeping and burst forth upon his will. He thrust his arms upward as his mind gave release, and projected the child of his creation to the very center of the Qog's inner universe.

Zilmara, mistress of the nightmare plane, gazed out the window of her palace at the black planet of power whirling in the dark spaces of her universe, a smile upon her lips and her heart full to overflowing with pride at the stepchild she had coaxed into being. Had it not been for her black beauty the Qog would not have achieved its new gift of power, and she would not have been able to send her monstrous minion forth so soon. Even now her creature was descending upon the pitiful islands of the third plane. Soon the curtain protecting the earthly plane would be rent, and the Qog would enter and destroy that realm too. And in time the upper planes would fall to her, one by one, including Cimorium. Yes, finally she would be rid of her old enemies, the dream lords. Then there would remain only one cosmic dimension—hers! Then she, Zilmara, would be all powerful, the mistress of all creation.

Suddenly, a blazing light filled the sky before her eyes and cast its searing brightness far across the dim reaches of the inner universe. The lady raised her hands to her face in disbelief and watched in stark terror as a great haloed sun took shape in the firmament. No sooner was it formed than it began to spin and set out upon a fiery orbit through the heavens.

Many were the nightmare planets in its sweeping path, and one by one she, Zilmara, the proud mother of worlds, watched her nightmare children burst into flame and explode into star-like fragments. Utter horror engulfed her. Ever larger grew the sun's reflection in her palace window as it wheeled in its orbit; and the lady gasped in pain, her face aglow, as she watched her beloved black planet ignite and shatter in a shower of cosmic brightness. Closer came the haloed sun, and as its outspreading aura touched her world she recognized its brilliance and knew well its origin. Her awareness was but brief as her planet-world shuddered, became incandescent, and disintegrated.

Seared by the sun's radiance within and weakened by the loss of nightmare worlds destroyed, the Qog's great mass trembled violently, sending fierce winds through the Zuralian sky. Jonathan watched breathlessly as the monster began to rise upward, twitching and convulsing like a wounded animal. Free now of its mistress' control, it sped toward the break in the dimensional fabric, seeking to escape into the vast interdimensional void from which it came.

When the creature had disappeared from sight, Jonathan looked at his ring. The stone had faded to a pale pink. The Qog had departed from the second plane. But his task was not done. As he had planned, the orbiting sun's destruction of nightmare worlds had subtracted enough planetary mass to offset its own, thereby preventing the tear in the interplane fabric from worsening. But now the fabric had to be repaired; it had to be closed off from the Qog and from possible invasion from other planes. Now he would find out if he was worthy of the title, Arch Creator.

Once more he called upon his powers, this time with the ease of a master creator. And many were the island worlds born that day upon the second plane. First he created a tranquil isle of a thousand lakes where proudly swam great black swans and leaping fish of many hues, in whose blue mirrored waters were reflected lush meadows and rolling hills, and above whose high escarpments, filling the sky, flew endless flocks of green herons, roseate flamingoes, and egrets white as snow. Next he created a rocky isle of smoldering lava-brimmed volcanoes, gushing geysers, and steaming lizard flats hissing forth their hot breath from the bowels of the land. And he created an eyot of lush rain forests, its flamboyant trees of leafy green and gold laden with succulent fruit and harboring purpled-winged moths, beneath whose sweeping branches grew fantastic ferns and giant blooms with pollen-laden hearts aflutter with silver-winged bees and emerald hummingbirds. Too, he created an isle of dazzling snowcapped mountains, raging rivers, green velvet valleys, and windswept plains where dwelled great-horned elkons and singing horla-beasts. And he made a desert land of rolling golden sands and towering star-tipped cacti, dotted with oases of quim and fig where nested scarlet-crested doves and orange-frilled pigeons. And a lovely isle of broad white beaches and hidden coves he brought to life, where at suns' set the yellow-striped andelains made tryst with the wooley caddifs and together galloped to the water's edge to listen to the plaintive mating cries of the hoary siren-whales offshore.

But he saw that the islands he had created were not enough, that the energy needed to complete his task was great indeed. And so he drew upon his spirit-double and created waking dreams within a dream, and so multiplied his worldly offspring. He remembered from the dream lords' map of the second plane that its northernmost reaches were but a vast frozen sea. Mentally calculating the remaining energy mass he required, he called upon his powers and brought forth a continent and set it in the northern wastes. No sooner had he done so than the great breadth of sky beyond the twin suns shivered, then brightened, and he knew the dimension curtain had been made whole again.

The three dream lords stood side by side in their hall of maps and observed with wonder the inspired creation of a haloed sun within the third plane and witnessed the magnificent havoc it wrought. And they rejoiced as dot after dot appeared on the wall chart of the second plane, glad at heart to see so many new island worlds spring to life. Fflayn and Zabryn clasped their brother's hands in congratulations, and Secunon was proud indeed at the brilliance and originality of his pupil.

Then on the map before their eyes, lo! a great continent appeared, and the second dimension was an island plane no more. A cosmic vibration touched the dream lords' minds, and they knew that the interplane balance had been restored and the dimensional fabric made whole. Elated and relieved, they could now resume their duties without fear: the universe had regained its equilibrium.

The dream sender, Hecuticar Lemselecus, stood at the window of his shop looking up at the sky. A gray mouse sat quietly on his shoulder.

"The storm is over, Lemanuel, thank heavens for that," said the old man. "Strange occurrence, though. Lightning but no thunder or rain, and lasting for days. And worldwide. Mmm. It must have been caused by a weakening in the interdimensional curtain between the first and second planes. But there's not a scientist on Earth who would agree with me about that, let alone know what I was talking about. Ah, well, no surprise there.

"And I suspect it's not the heavens we should be thanking for the return of our good weather. I expect it should be someone else, someone we both know. But we helped a little ourselves too, didn't we?

"Come along, little friend. Now that the world is safe again I can go back to my reading. How does a chocolate cookie sound to you? Too bad young Jonathan isn't here to enjoy one with us. But maybe he'll come to visit soon. He promised to bring along his new bride, so I'll need to buy a fresh can of tea. When they come, we won't mention that little indiscretion of his we happened to witness, will we? After all, he was drugged at the time and didn't know what he was doing. I'm sure a sensible fellow like you stays clear of such problems, hmm? Which reminds me, why don't you bring along your little spouse to meet the newlyweds when they arrive? Now don't go looking at me that way. Where are you going, Lemanuel? Leaving already?"

Jonathan whistled a sailor's tune as he made his way across the Zuralian countryside, his heart as light as the puffs of clouds that drifted lazily through the sun-drenched heavens. The city soon came into view, and he was glad to see it had not been badly damaged by the Qog. A young couple picking up fallen branches in front of their cottage smiled and waved to him as he passed. Returning their greeting, he noticed that the stone in his ring was now black—Qog had returned to the far reaches of the interplane void. For that he was grateful, and he hoped the creature would remain harmless without the direction of its evil mistress.

His path took him to a familiar hill, the same one where he had first landed on his journey from Earth. Upon reaching its broad summit he saw in the distance two figures sitting amongst the windblown grass looking out over the city and harbor beyond. He watched them a moment. Could it be? he wondered. He quickened his step. Yes! It was Llanya and the trocht!

Shouting and waving his arms, he ran toward them, tripping over clumps of turf in his haste. He saw Llanya jump to her feet and wave as the trocht set out over the grassy hills toward him. He opened his arms to his galloping pet, who was even more enormous than he remembered. But as it got closer it showed no sign of slowing down. Much to his dismay he saw that it wore a savage look on its face, its eyes ablaze with fury. It must not recognize him, he thought, and there was no mistaking its intentions.

The great cat leapt into the air, and Jonathan threw his body flat to the ground. The trocht passed cleanly over him, and he heard a dull thud. Quickly rolling over, he was amazed at what he saw.

The trocht was sitting quietly in the grass, as calm as a kitten, with a limp Zytox hanging from its jaws. The bird's neck was broken. The giant feline shook its head from side to side, and when it was satisfied that its prey was lifeless, it let the carcass fall to the ground.

Jonathan called his pet to him. The trocht promptly trotted up to its master and planted a large wet lick on his face. He hugged his furry friend and it began to purr.

Llanya arrived, panting from her run. No words were spoken as the bond-mates embraced and kissed, and kissed again, their hearts over-spilling with happiness. And not until the twin suns overhead had moved perceptively toward the horizon did their arms finally unfold, and only then did the gentle hilltop breeze find a space to pass between their beating hearts.

Llanya wiped a tear of joy from her eye. "Are you all right, my love? That awful bird didn't hurt you, did it?"

"I'm fine, thanks to Trok."

"But your head has been cut."

"That happened earlier. It stopped bleeding, nothing serious."

Llanya grasped his hand. "I hope there are no more of those evil birds around."

"I think Trok killed the last of them."

"And did you see that awful dark thing hovering in the sky, and the terrible windstorm? I thought the land was going to blow away."

"It's gone now, and I don't think it'll be back."

The trocht nuzzled up to him. "I see our little pet has grown more. And, if I'm not mistaken, his mistress has grown too—more beautiful than ever."

Llanya blushed. "You wonderful liar. You probably say that to all the ladies." She glanced at him sideways. "Like the beautiful one I saw you with through the Zytox lens."

"Her? No, she was old and nasty. She wanted to kill me."

Llanya looked reassured. "And what's that silly gown you're wearing? I almost didn't recognize you in that dress."

"Oh, it's a present from an old gentleman I visited while I was away. I'll tell you all about it tonight, in bed. And some other things as well."

Llanya pouted. "I have things to tell you too. But it won't be tonight. Tonight, after a special dinner of beetle nut stew, beetle nut bread, and beetle nut pudding, you'll be occupied a long time."

They both laughed. Llanya suddenly became serious. "Is Zuralia safe now, Jon? And the second plane?"

"Yes."

"Then you won't be going away any more, will you?"

"Yes, but only on vacations, and certainly not without my bond-mate. That I promise. The search that led me to you and took me from you is over. Now, as the poet said, all's well with the world—to which I add the plural and include both thee and me."

Llanya's eyes widened and fairly glowed with delight.

"Vacations are fun. I love to travel."

Jonathan nodded. "Talking about travel, where's the captain and the Pelagin?"

Llanya pointed to the harbor. "There, you can see the ship anchored just offshore. The crew's been released, and only the captain and Balu are left on board. I've been staying on the Pelagin too, waiting for your return. It's a lot easier cooking for only three, but I'd like it to be only two from now on."

Jonathan raised her hands to his lips. "Two it will be, plus Trok of course. Maybe we can build a house right here on this hill overlooking the city. It's where I first arrived on Zuralia."

Llanya beamed. "Oh yes, that would be perfect!"

"Meanwhile, we can take a cottage near the water, one of those pretty ones covered with ivy. And we can do some of that traveling you enjoy so much."

"Oh, where shall we go?" Llanya spun round in a circle in her excitement.

"Well, not far offshore there's a pretty mountain isle—Eagle Isle— which might be fun to see. And there's a lovely island to the west I've heard tell of, known for its rainbowed waterfalls, called Hanybula. And to the south is an island called Celeshir. A famous writer of dream tales lives there, Friendship by name, whom I would like very much to meet. But it's your vacation too, so what island would you like to visit?"

Llanya pursed her lips in thought. "There are many islands with so many different attractions. But I can't think of one that has all the things I like best."

"Tell me, what things are those?"

"Well, a small island, one that has all the different kinds of natural beauty of all the places I've seen—like Zuralia and Celeucia and Klell, all put together."

Jonathan smiled and closed his eyes. "A tall order. But let me see if I can imagine—er, remember—such an island and where it might be." In a few moments he opened his eyes again, inwardly pleased with his newest creation, which he calculated was well within the margin of error required for planal balance. "Yes, an island such as you described does exist, though it's not one of the older ones. And as it happens, it's not too distant from here so we can visit it whenever you like."

Llanya clapped her hands with glee. "What's the island called?" she asked.

"It doesn't have a name that I know of. So why don't we call it Llanya's Island."

"Oh Jon, how wonderful! Thank you!"

"But before we visit your namesake, I would like to take you on a very special vacation trip. I want you to meet the person who sent me to Zuralia, and to you. He's my dearest friend on Earth—Hecuticar Lemselecus. I told him about you, and he gave me two of his very special pills that will take us to him in a flash."

"Oh yes, let's do that first. I've never visited another plane. We'll take your friend a gift. Do you think he might like some of the beetle nuts we collected on Mast Island?"

Jonathan laughed. "Probably not. Although he's a man of many remedies, it's not one that would particularly suit him. I don't think. But he does have a small friend who lives with him, who has a mate."